THE IMMORTAL RIDER

SPARKS TRILOGY BOOK III

KERRY LAW

Copyright © 2023 Kerry Law

All rights reserved

ISBN-13: 979-8-8653-2161-3

For Colin
Your dragon would be all the colours

TO LORSOKE
GRIYDAK SEA
NORWEN PEAK
LAKE TOIG
TUNNEL
SHINE
EAST BARTER
ANTELL
WEST BARTER
QUORELLE SQUARE
HARBOUR
THE PALACE
CITY OF KIERELL
JASTAK PEAK
GRIYDAK SEA

CHAPTER 1

DREAMS AND STARS

Aimee was trapped in a horrible dream. She wanted to wake up so badly but the dream had chained her mind and wouldn't let go. Everything was frighteningly vivid as she flew over the Empty Warriors' army again only this time Jess's belly skimmed the top of their heads. Hundreds of flaming eyes stared up at her. Even in her sleep her whole body was tense, waiting for one of them to grab Jess and pull them both down.

She couldn't look up but she knew Pelathina and Aranati were in the sky high above her. She longed to fly up into the safety of the open sky, but she couldn't get the command along her connection to Jess. The door between them had closed.

'Let me in,' Aimee mumbled in her sleep.

Below her the silent rows of Empty Warriors stretched in every direction, disappearing off into the four points of the compass. Were the Ring Mountains still behind her? Aimee couldn't turn her head to look back. There was a dragon ahead, pearlescent scales shimmering. It was Glaris and her Rider, Lwena, gliding above the army. Aimee tried to scream at the older Rider to fly away but her lips were locked shut.

She could only watch in silent horror as the bolt shot from the army, piercing Glaris and her Rider. Blood splattered Aimee's face but still she couldn't scream. Glaris was pulled down into the rows of warriors, just as she had been, but this time Lwena fell with her. Aimee desperately pushed on Jess's horns, wanting to fly over to them, to snatch their bodies away before they were butchered. But Jess's horns disappeared from her grasp and she fell, tumbling over Jess's head and down into the Empty Warriors.

'Aimee!'

The spike of fear made her bolt upright, gasping awake. She blinked away her dream, confused for a moment. Then she saw Pelathina's dark face, the edges highlighted by moonlight and remembered she was out on the tundra.

'You were shouting,' Pelathina told her.

The other girl reached forwards and squeezed Aimee's knees, just at the sensitive part which made her twitch and laugh involuntarily.

'What are you doing?' Aimee asked.

'Tickling you,' Pelathina replied as if it was the most normal thing in the world.

'But...'

'You look like you've had a rough night so that means you should start the day with something fun to wash the badness out of your mind.'

Pelathina reached forward to tickle her some more but Aimee scrambled backwards on her bum. 'Careful, you shouldn't touch me.' It hurt her to say those words but she was terrified of sucking the life from anyone, the way she'd done with Jara.

'Hey, it's okay, the bracelet's in neutral, isn't it?' Pelathina's voice was gentle.

Aimee shoved back her sleeve and checked Kyelli's bracelet, the wide gold cuff that was stuck on her arm. The little needle was pointing to the circle, the closed loop that meant the bracelet would neither steal someone's spark, nor transfer to someone else the energy in her own spark. She could see her spark as a glowing white-green light in her chest and Pelathina's was where it should be in her own chest, pulsing in time with her heartbeat. Still, Aimee didn't trust the bracelet.

'See, it's safe,' Pelathina said, reaching out to take Aimee's hand.

Aimee pulled back, shoving both hands in her coat pockets. 'What if the dial had gotten knocked while I was sleeping.'

The words felt like they were tearing Aimee's throat on the way up. All her life she'd been a freak that no one wanted to touch, scared her weird skin would infect them too, and now they were right. A hug from her could mean death.

Pelathina's face crumpled at the edges. She was still smiling, like always, but now it was a sad smile and her dimples were gone. Aimee felt bad. Pelathina had pulled her from her horrible dream. She'd also saved her yesterday when she fell from the cliff above the caravan compound, and she'd been the one to call their little gang Team Aimee. She wanted to be her friend but Aimee felt she had no choice but to push her away.

Taking her sad smile with her, Pelathina walked back across to Skydance and sat beside him, her back and head a black outline against the deep blue sky. Aimee looked around for Nathine and saw her and Malgerus were huddled together in the darkness over to her left. Surprisingly Aimee's shouting hadn't woken them. Nathine had complained, a lot, about having to sleep outside with nothing but wiry heather for a bed. Apparently it was all Aimee's fault. But she'd curled up with Malgerus around her and been asleep within moments. Now she was snoring. A tiny smile touched Aimee's lips as she imagined informing Nathine that she snored.

She felt a weight in her lap and looked down to see Jess, her long neck curled across Aimee's legs, her head in Aimee's lap. She placed a hand on Jess's cool scales and took several long, deep breaths. Her heart, which was still hammering from her nightmare, began to slow. The cold wind tugged at her short curls and she focused on that, and the springy heather beneath her, and Jess's calming presence in her mind. She was out on the tundra, not trapped inside the Empty Warriors' army. Lwena was still dead, though. That part of her dream had been taken from her memories and was as real and sharp as dragon's teeth.

Aimee stroked Jess's feathers and felt them quiver

with pleasure at the attention.

'Do you have nightmares?' she asked softly. 'I don't think you do. Maybe I can sleep inside your mind until this is over.'

Jess snorted a small cloud of smoke that was quickly blown away by the wind. Aimee's legs were going numb with Jess's weight on them but she was grateful for her dragon's warmth. It was the middle of summer but when the sun had sank into the Griydak Sea it had taken all the warmth with it. Aimee shivered and snuggled her chin down into her scarf.

There was no shelter on the tundra and the wind whistled across it constantly, rustling the heather and pushing ripples across all the small streams. The Ardnanlich Forest was not far north-west of them. The three Riders could have made it there before stopping to rest, but prowlers skulked through its shadows.

The tundra felt so open around them, its emptiness tugging at Aimee as if it wanted to swallow her. When she'd travelled with the caravan the landscape hadn't felt so vast but she'd been with all the councillors and city guards, and more Riders. Out here with only Nathine and Pelathina, she felt very small.

Needing a distraction from her thoughts, Aimee gently shoved Jess's head off her lap and walked over to Pelathina. Skydance was curled up on the grass beside her, his wings partially unfurled, the tips dancing with the wind. He twisted his neck around, watching her approach, his head bobbing side to side. Skydance could never sit still.

Before Aimee sat down she checked, again, that Kyelli's bracelet was in neutral, and even then she made sure to leave a gap between her hips and Pelathina's. She knew Pelathina might be upset with her, and she should probably apologise, but she wasn't sure what words to say. So instead she stuck to practical matters.

'I can sit watch now, if you'd like to get some rest,' Aimee said, her voice small in the darkness. 'I don't think I'll be able to get back to sleep.'

Pelathina cocked her head like a dragon and regarded Aimee with a smile.

'I hate sleeping out here too,' Pelathina admitted, as Aimee crossed her legs and wrapped an arm around Jess who'd followed her.

'But you're always out here, aren't you?' Aimee asked. She remembered Lyrria telling her that Pelathina always volunteered to travel with the caravans. It was why Aimee hadn't seen much of her during her first few months up in the mountains.

Pelathina smiled and the moonlight caught on her dimples. 'I love the sky and the feeling of freedom out here. I sometimes think Skydance and I could fly forever and never come down.' She turned to look at Aimee, her dark eyes sparkling. 'But sleeping in a soggy bog,' she shivered dramatically, 'it sucks.'

Aimee laughed. 'It does suck,' she agreed.

'But you have to look for the upsides.'

'There are upsides to sleeping in a bog?'

'Well, the view's pretty good.'

'It's just grass and heather,' Aimee pointed out.

Pelathina laughed again. 'Look up, *bevikoop*.'

Aimee wanted to ask what *bevikoop* meant but she was a little intimidated by the fact that Pelathina spoke four languages. So instead she tilted her head back and stared at the stars. The darkest part of the night, which only lasted a few hours at this time of year, had come and gone and now blue was seeping back into the sky. It was deep blue above their heads but was fading in the east already. The moon was a curved dragon's claw, sinking towards the horizon but the stars still sparkled like thousands of tiny dragon's scales.

Pelathina was right, it was a good view. Aimee shrugged, feigning nonchalance in an attempt to tease the other girl. 'It's alright, I suppose,' she said.

'It's beautiful,' Pelathina whispered and with a fizz of excitement Aimee realised she was looking right at her as she said it. For a wonderful, dizzying moment Aimee looked into her dark eyes.

'The patterns of the stars are different here from what they were at home, but you can see them better. It's one of the good things about being so far south.'

Pelathina was looking back up at the sky and Aimee studied her face. Her spark's soft glow gave enough light for her to see the way Pelathina's long dark eyelashes rested on her cheeks, and the way the little hairs on the back of her neck stood up where her coat collar had ruffled them. She had a small face, with delicate features, but she didn't look fragile; she looked strong, resolute.

When Pelathina turned from the sky back to Aimee

she was wearing her sister's frown.

'Are you angry with her?' Pelathina asked.

'Who? Nathine?' Aimee was confused.

'Not Nathine,' Pelathina shook her head. 'I meant are you angry at Kyelli? She was your city's saviour, or at least that's what you all thought for three hundred years.'

Aimee had been trying not to think too much about Kyelli or the revelation that she was the Master of Sparks and had created the Empty Warriors. But now that she did, she realised she was furious with her. She was angrier than she'd ever been with Nathine, or Jara, or even with any of the bullies from her childhood. Jess growled and Aimee realised she'd been squeezing her feathers.

'I used to imagine that Kyelli would come back to the city one day and fight off the bullies for me,' Aimee admitted. She'd never have said this to Nathine but in the dark with Pelathina it somehow didn't seem such an embarrassing confession. 'I thought that if she'd saved a whole bunch of our ancestors from the Empty Warriors then surely she'd be the sort of person who'd protect me. But somewhere along the way it all got muddled.' Aimee twisted her hands together in a vague gesture.

'What got muddled?' Pelathina asked softly.

'The stories, our history, what we thought we knew about Kyelli. It got all jumbled like…' Aimee faltered as she tried to explain what she meant.

'Like a dragon who flew into a cloud, got turned around and flew out in the wrong direction?' Pelathina offered.

Aimee nodded, glad she'd understood. 'Yeah, like that. And no one in the city knows that we went in the wrong direction. Or at least they didn't. I suppose they will by now. Jara will have told the council.'

'Do you think that's a bad thing?'

'No, I think people should know. I don't know if Kyelli lied to everyone, or if the stories got lost, but it's wrong that we've been thinking of her as some great hero when in fact she's a monster.' An image popped into Aimee's head of the statue of Kyelli pointing the way up the cliffs. 'I wish it wasn't her who'd created the Sky Riders. I wish we had nothing to do with her.'

'If we're tainted by association with Kyelli then I think the whole of Kierell is too,' Pelathina said. She had one arm around Skydance and her face turned towards Aimee.

'But we're tainted more because we're *her* Riders.' Aimee thought of Jara carrying the weight of this secret for years and was amazed it hadn't crushed her sooner. 'If we were still in the city I'd get Jess to pick up that statue of Kyelli by the cliffs, and then we'd fly really high before letting it go.'

'You'd smash her statue?'

'And the one in Quorelle Square, and all of them.' Aimee swept her arms wide as if encompassing the city they couldn't see. 'She's everywhere in the city smiling down at us all like some amazing saviour woman but she isn't. She's a liar and she's evil.' Aimee held up her wrist, letting her coat cuff slide back, revealing the bracelet.

'She had the power in this bracelet, power no one should have and she used it not to help people but to create thousands of monsters.'

Jess was growling again, this time because she was sharing Aimee's anger. Aimee knew she should be careful not to let her feelings spill over into Jess but right then she felt like she had too much anger to contain it all in her own mind. She knew it was important to keep control of Jess but if Kyelli suddenly magically appeared in front of them Aimee would let Jess blast her with dragon's breath, then bite her head off.

'Do you not feel angry at Kyelli?' Aimee asked.

Pelathina thought for a moment. 'I'm angry that someone with power would use it to hurt ordinary folk, but I don't feel as betrayed as you do. I came to your city when I was sixteen, so four years ago. Obviously I heard all about Kyelli after Aranati and I made the climb but I didn't grow up with the stories about her being a saviour.'

Aimee opened her mouth to ask another question but there was a rustle and a squelch behind them. Jess and Skydance were instantly alert, heads up, wings unfurled. Aimee and Pelathina spun around at the same time, both reaching for their scimitars. Then they relaxed when they saw Nathine.

'Sparks!' Nathine swore as she lifted her boot from a puddle, trailing bog slime. She stomped over and seated herself on the other side of Aimee. 'How's a girl supposed to sleep when you two are nattering all night.'

'I'm surprised you didn't wake yourself with your

own snoring,' Aimee threw back at her.

'I do not snore,' Nathine objected.

Aimee looked to Pelathina for confirmation. She nodded. 'Like a trumpeting elephant.'

'What's an elephant?' Aimee asked.

'It's a rubbish insult if no one knows what you're talking about,' Nathine pointed out.

'And Nathine would know, she's the expert on good insults,' Aimee added.

'I am,' Nathine agreed.

Pelathina stared at them both for a moment then burst out laughing. 'I feel like I'm being ganged up on. And I always forget how isolated Kierell is and how little you know.'

'I know plenty,' Nathine said, picking bits of heather from her ponytail.

'Really? *App kaya u janneti*?'

'Yeah, I know you said something stupid.'

Pelathina kept throwing phrases across Aimee's head at Nathine, varying the language each time, and Nathine kept batting them back with sarky comments. Aimee wanted to join in the banter but Pelathina's comment about Kierell being isolated had reminded her with a sickening jolt why they were sitting out on the tundra. Kierell was alone, with enemies literally at the gate and thousands of lives resting on the success of Aimee's mission. Her self-appointed task to assassinate the Master of Sparks.

Fear churned in her belly and for a horrible moment she thought she was going to be sick. Nathine would never let her forget it, and Pelathina would never like a girl who'd thrown up over her.

'Sparks, Aimee are you alright? Is it the bracelet?' Concern poured into Pelathina's face.

Aimee shook her head and was about to answer when a low growl rumbled through the tufts of long grass. All three dragons were up instantly, their feathers all standing on end. Aimee jumped to her feet too, staring around wildly. Then she saw it: a long mane of black hair slinking through the grass. There was movement to her right and she saw another. A growl from behind tightened her fear and told her there were more.

'Prowlers,' Pelathina whispered.

They were being surrounded.

CHAPTER 2

DISTANCE

'GO!' PELATHINA YELLED.

The first of the prowlers leapt at them and Aimee screamed. It sprang from the grass, powerful back legs propelling it over a wide stream. It had the head of a wolf, but so much larger, and its teeth were as big as a dragon's. The beast roared as it landed in front of Skydance. The dragon's ruff of feathers stuck straight out in anger as he blasted the prowler with a full burst of dragon's breath. The prowler leapt aside and the grass crackled with flames.

Aimee had grabbed her saddle as Jess stood and she was pulled upwards, scrambling awkwardly to get her leg swung over. Jess's primordial fear exploded into Aimee's mind and she screamed again, trying to release some of it.

'Fly, Jess!' Aimee cried.

Jess began flapping but she was panicked and uncoordinated. Her wings slapped Malgerus, and Nathine yelled at her. Another prowler ran through the heather towards them. Jess roared out her flames. She was still a juvenile though, and her burst was much smaller than Skydance's. The prowler easily dodged the dragon's breath and sprang at them.

Jess kicked out with one back leg, the movement nearly knocking Aimee from her saddle. She felt the impact as Jess's clawed foot collided with the prowler's head. It roared in pain as Jess raked its face with her talons. Then they were airborne. The prowler leapt, snapping at Jess but she was lifting them up through the air and its teeth closed on nothing.

Aimee desperately looked around for the others. Pelathina and Skydance were already in the sky above them. But she couldn't see orange wings.

'Where's Nathine?' Aimee yelled.

A glance down answered her question. Malgerus had pinned a prowler to the ground and both he and it were roaring. Nathine was in her saddle adding her own voice to the cacophony. As Aimee watched, Malgerus, fierce and angry, tore out the prowler's throat. Blood sprayed across the heather. The beast kicked weakly a few times before its life left it.

'Distract them!' Pelathina yelled across the sky at Aimee.

'Who?' Aimee didn't understand.

Skydance swooped past them, Pelathina pointed, and then Aimee saw. Three more prowlers were advancing on Nathine. They were moving cautiously, wary of Malgerus, but they were closing in. The black manes running down their spines rippled like the grass.

From above they were almost invisible. Nathine hadn't seen them and that was typical of her. Her fear had made her, and Malgerus, angry and they'd attacked the prowler closest to them, forgetting about the others.

The scene reminded Aimee of their trip to the nesting site when Nathine had been injured, clinging to her unconscious dragon as the other hatchlings turned on her. Back then Aimee had hesitated, wondering if maybe her life would be better without Nathine to bully her. Now, leaving Nathine behind never crossed her mind.

'We need to distract the others so she can take off!' Pelathina shouted again and this time Aimee understood and acted immediately. She didn't think about the danger, only about helping Nathine.

Pelathina swept left, guiding Skydance to skim over two of the prowlers. His claws missed the first but raked the second. A roar split the air. Copying her, Aimee urged Jess into a dive and they flew at the prowler closing in on Malgerus from behind. It sensed them coming and crouched. Jess's talons caught nothing but grass.

'Get into the sky, Nathine!' Aimee yelled as she swept past.

Malgerus was flapping, his huge wingbeats stirring the air and swirling up the stench of the prowlers. Jess growled as she caught their wet fur and rotting meat odour. Aimee could feel her tugging at their connection as instinct told her dragon to fly back down and fight the prowlers. Aimee kept a tight hold of Jess in her mind and squeezed her spiralled horns.

Malgerus was airborne. A prowler launched itself at the dragon but Malgerus was already too high and its jaws snapped closed on empty air. Aimee saw its full body for the first time and swallowed a fresh wave of fear. Dark stripes marbled its fur, except for its paws, tail and head which were as black as the sky in winter. Its eyes shimmered iridescent in its huge wolf-like head. It could have torn Aimee's arm off without even trying.

Aimee pulled her eyes from the beasts and into the sky as Jess took them higher. Skydance was soaring above them, Malegus on his tail and Aimee pulled Jess's horns, steering her upwards, and squeezed her ribs for more speed.

'Is everyone alright?' Pelathina called as they all levelled off in the sky.

Aimee nodded and glanced at Nathine. The other girl was grinning, her eyes wide with awe.

'We killed a prowler!' she yelled across the sky.

Aimee guided Jess over so she was flying wingtip to wingtip with Malgerus. 'Why do you look so happy about that?'

Nathine threw her a *you're an idiot* look. 'Because, mushroom head, every time I was out here with my father's caravans, prowlers were the thing everyone was most afraid of. Even with Riders to protect us I was terrified of being eaten in my bed.' She reached forward and stroked the top of Malgerus's head. 'But tonight I wasn't a scared little girl, because I am a woman with a dragon and we can fight back!' She yelled her words into the sky.

Aimee could see how happy this revelation made Nathine and she was glad for her. Aimee looked down, trying to see the prowlers but they were already invisible in the long grass. All she'd felt when they attacked was fear. All she wanted was to get Jess and fly away. Escaping was what she'd thought about, not attacking.

Pelathina swooped over to Aimee and Nathine, Skydance's wings fluttering softly in the sky. 'I think since we're up and flying we should continue on.'

Aimee nodded in agreement. They'd only had a few hours' sleep but it would need to be enough. The Empty Warrior army had broken through the outer gate in the Ring Mountains in less than a day, and they'd have been hammering at the inner one all night. Unless the councillors collapsed the tunnel, the army would break through into the city sometime today.

'How are your dragons' wounds?' Pelathina aimed her question at both Aimee and Nathine.

The hole in Malgerus's wing, where a bolt had pierced him, whistled as he flew. 'Mal's fine, he can fly all day,' Nathine assured them.

Aimee knew that wasn't true. Jess was tired, and she and Malgerus were the same age. It would be next spring before either dragon was a year old and fully grown with an adult's strength. Aimee worried they were pushing them too hard, but they had no choice. An entire city of people was relying on her to save them.

She'd checked Jess's wounds last night before they curled up to sleep. She had a tear in her wing membrane and a cut on her neck from her fight with Faradair, but both were clean and had stopped bleeding. Dragon saliva had healing properties and Jess had been licking her wounds like a cat grooming itself.

Skydance rose into the space between Jess and Malgerus and the three dragons flew in a row. 'And what about your wounds?' Pelathina asked them both. 'We were going to change your dressings this morning before setting off.'

Almost as if the mention had awoken it, the burned handprint on Aimee's arm began to throb. Nathine had a deeper one on her leg. Both Riders had been grabbed by Empty Warriors, their hands burning through clothes and skin. Aimee watched as Nathine put on her brave face.

'It's fine, I can hardly feel it anymore.' Nathine shrugged off Pelathina's concern.

Pelathina turned her dark eyes to Aimee and she too shrugged. 'We don't have time to stop and we can't go back.'

'Though if you have some breakfast hidden away in your saddlebags I'll take some of that.' Nathine raised a hopeful eyebrow.

Pelathina laughed. 'You ate everything I had with me last night and I'm sure you had twice as much as Aimee and I.'

'Yeah and I was still hungry,' Nathine grumbled.

Aimee didn't mind skipping breakfast—her stomach felt like it was full to bursting with fears and worries. Though a hungry Nathine would be a grumpy Nathine, and she wasn't looking forward to that. They'd let their dragons hunt last night and all three had had their fill of hares. Skydance had also eaten several frogs, apparently they were his favourite.

'Okay, shall we just press on to Vorthens then?' Pelathina looked over to Aimee for confirmation.

Aimee nodded. 'Let's get this over with.'

'Will there be hot buttered toast when we get there?' Nathine called over.

'There'll be an immortal who we have to kill to save the world,' Aimee called back.

Nathine shrugged. 'I suppose that'll do instead.'

Carefully letting go one of Jess's horns, Aimee tugged her goggles from her coat pocket and awkwardly pulled them on. She got some of her hair stuck inside the left lens and couldn't flick it out with one hand but there was no way she was letting go of the other horn. She watched in terrified awe as Pelathina took both hands off Skydance's horns and quickly slipped on her own goggles. Aimee couldn't remember which pocket she'd shoved her woollen hat in, so she'd fly without it and hope the day warmed up quickly.

The sky was already lightening around them, and over to the east streaks of orange and rose gold lit the way for the rising sun. Daylight danced over the rolling hills of heather, kissing the purple flowers as it went, bringing them to life. There were rocky tors poking up from the grass and the quartz in their stone sparkled as the sun caressed them. It was the most beautiful sunrise Aimee had ever seen.

She glanced to her right, seeing Pelathina and

Nathine. They were looking eastward too and the lenses of their goggles shimmered with the reflected sunrise. In the early light Pelathina's bronze skin seemed to glow from within and Nathine's high ponytail floated behind her in the wind, looking more copper than brown this morning. Their dark clothes and long black coats seemed to suck in the lingering shadows and beneath them their dragons were vibrant sapphire blue and blazing orange. In each of their chests their sparks glowed like mini suns. They looked incredible.

She wished they were all off on a mission of peace, not war. She wished they were all flying out here, three friends, for the joy of it.

The cuff on Aimee's coat had slid back and the gold of Kyelli's bracelet gleamed dully. Aimee knew she couldn't fob this responsibility off on another Rider. She couldn't remove the bracelet, so she had to be the one to use it to assassinate Kyelli. It was her mission and she would do it. But, and she wouldn't admit this to the others, she was scared of the bracelet and the power it gave her.

Aimee could feel the pressure of how little time they had squeezing her chest, making her feel panicky. She took a deep breath of fresh, cold air, then tried to exhale her dread. If they could find Kyelli today and if Aimee could use the bracelet to steal her sparks, then it would all be over by dinnertime.

As if sensing her thoughts Pelathina called over, asking if she was alright. Aimee guided Jess a little closer to Skydance and their dragons flapped in synchrony.

'I will be when this is all done,' Aimee replied.

'I'm not doubting you in any way, because I've seen how determined you are to see this through, but are you sure you can use the bracelet to take someone's life?' Pelathina asked.

Aimee wondered if she was asking if the plan would physically work or if Aimee was mentally capable of doing what needed to be done. She searched around inside herself for a moment and realised the answer to both was yes. She'd felt the power of the bracelet when she'd sucked out Jara's spark and it was relentless. And as far as killing Kyelli went, while her mind still baulked at the idea of hurting the woman she'd always admired, she'd do it to save everyone in Kierell.

'Though I'll feel bad about it forever,' she said, quietly so only Jess would hear.

She was trying not to think about what it would feel like to use the bracelet deliberately. All morning, any time she'd thought about the bracelet, she could sense its power hovering around her mind, occasionally pushing against her, looking for a way into her thoughts.

Nathine swooped Malgerus underneath them and popped up on Aimee's other side. 'Are you sure that when Kyelli's gone the Empty Warriors will all die?' she called across.

Aimee was less sure about this part of the plan but she didn't want to admit that.

'They're not human,' she replied, 'they don't have sparks and the engraving on the breastplate said they are fuelled by their purpose. The Master of Sparks gave them their purpose so I think if that person's gone then the fire in their eyes will go out.'

Nathine looked at her for a moment, absorbing her words. 'And if we can't find Kyelli, do you think that instead you could use the bracelet somehow to stop the Empty Warriors?'

Aimee immediately shook her head. That was something she wouldn't do. She wasn't sure how, but she knew that the more she used the bracelet the easier it would be to keep using it. She didn't want to be able to suck out people's sparks, killing them and stealing their life energy for herself. She would use the bracelet once, to kill Kyelli, then she'd find a way to get it off.

Without meaning her too, Jess had slowed, sharing Aimee's worries, and the feathers of her ruff were all twitching.

'Aimee,' Pelathina called over, 'it's okay to feel scared.'

'Hang on, what are you giving her comfort for?' Nathine called from Aimee's other side. 'With that bracelet on she's got power no human has ever had before. She should be the least scared of all of us.'

Aimee shook her head but didn't say anything. Nathine couldn't understand—she hadn't felt the sickening wrongness of having someone else's spark in her chest. The power of the bracelet didn't make Aimee feel strong, it made her terrified of what she could do, of how easily she could hurt people.

'Aimee?' Pelathina's voice was full of concern but

Aimee didn't want to share her fears. She was supposed to be leading this mission. So she forced a wobbly smile on her face.

'I'm fine. Hungry, and I think there's a hole in my boot because my right foot's wet, but otherwise I'm fine.'

It was hard to read Pelathina's eyes through her goggles but Aimee was pretty sure her lie hadn't been convincing. Thankfully Pelathina didn't push it and they all fell into silence.

Aimee watched the world opening up around them and its vastness amazed her. She had always known there was a world beyond the Ring Mountains but she'd never stopped to think about how big it was. And all she could see at the moment was the tundra. It was hard to wrap her head around the notion that beyond the rolling hills of grass and heather there were cities. And beyond them there were mountains hiding yet more world, including the country Pelathina was from. She began to appreciate why Pelathina thought Kierell was so isolated.

They flew on past the Ardnanlich Forest, the tops of the pines rippling like a giant rug in the wind. From this height Aimee could see the crescents of pale sand all along the coast, their outer curves edged with the dark green trees and their inner ones lapped by the cold waves of the Griydak Sea.

After a couple of hours of flying, a long thin lake appeared to their left, ripples glinting with sunlight. Pelathina told them it was Lake Ceil and the land to the west of it belonged firmly to the Helvethi, especially the tribes least inclined towards a peace with Kierell. Aimee strained her eyes, hoping for a glimpse of the Helvethi galloping across the landscape, but the world below looked empty. Though the openness of the tundra made her feel vulnerable there was a wild beauty to the landscape that she liked.

Jess was tired, Aimee could feel it. She was tired too, but still they kept flying, watching the rolling hills grow steeper, shedding their blankets of purple heather in favour of long grass and wildflowers. As their distance from Kierell grew greater, so did Aimee's desire to reach Vorthens. Just a few more hours and they'd be there. She could use the bracelet, kill the Master of Sparks, then find a way to get it off her wrist.

CHAPTER 3

RACES AND PLANS

'THAT'S IT? HE was "just someone you knew before you made the climb". I don't believe you.' Aimee shook her head at Nathine who in turn glared back.

The hours had been passing too slowly and so Aimee had sought a distraction in asking Nathine about Halfen, the young guard they'd met behind the waterfall. They'd known each other, that much had been clear, but there was an awkward dynamic in the way Halfen couldn't stop looking at Nathine and the way she guiltily avoided his gaze. But Nathine was refusing to be drawn into a conversation and Malgerus snorted a large puff of smoke that wafted right into Aimee's face.

'Maybe if she doesn't tell us we could invent a story about how they met?' Pelathina suggested with a cheeky smile.

They were flying lower now, and a range of rounded hills to the west gave them some shelter from the endless wind. It meant they could talk while they flew rather than yelling at each other across the sky.

'What kind of story?' Aimee jumped on Pelathina's idea, keen for a way to tease Nathine.

'I'm thinking a tale of misadventure where Nathine and Halfen are master thieves. Perhaps there could be stolen jewels and a heist gone wrong.'

Nathine snorted. 'Halfen couldn't commit a crime if his life depended on it. He's got too many morals.'

Aimee motioned for Pelathina to keep quiet. She knew Nathine well enough now to understand that if she didn't say anything then Nathine would convince herself to speak. It took a few minutes but finally Nathine sighed dramatically.

'Fine, I'll tell you about Halfen if you stop staring at me with your stupid determined face. But first, Pelathina, do you have an Irankish insult for someone who's really annoying?'

Pelathina gave a casual shrug. 'Nope, I don't know any.' She gave Aimee a conspiratorial smile which Nathine caught. She sighed again. Aimee squeezed her lips together to stop herself from grinning like a complete idiot. Did it even mean anything that Pelathina had sided with her in a silly argument?

Nathine turned from them both and fixed her eyes on the horizon. Sometimes it was easier to admit things if you weren't looking at anyone. Aimee understood that, but she also cursed herself for pushing Nathine for this story at a time when she couldn't give her a hug. She had a feeling this was going to be another sad tale from Nathine's childhood.

'Halfen and I grew up together,' Nathine began. 'His father is a tanner and had an exclusive contract with my father. The tailors that cater to those with money, mainly from Shine, all buy reindeer hides from my father, and the top-end ones are all tanned by Halfen's father. Anyway, it meant Halfen was always hanging around our warehouses when we were younger, following me like a lost puppy.' Nathine had filled her voice with scorn but Aimee saw through it. She and Halfen had been friends.

'Did you fall out?' Aimee asked, knowing there was more to the story than that.

Nathine was silent for a long while.

'He liked you, didn't he?' Aimee asked gently.

Nathine's face twisted with guilt, then denial, and finally hurt.

'Well of course he fancied Nathine,' Pelathina said, her tone light. 'How could he not?'

Nathine shot Pelathina a grateful look, so quick Aimee nearly missed it. She was pleased to see the guilt vanish from Nathine's face, replaced with her usual smugness.

'Yeah, well, I was way too good for him, obviously,' Nathine continued. 'I could beat him in a race from the floor to the warehouse roof, up the shelves, every time. And the idiot wished he could make the climb.'

'He wanted to be a Sky Rider?' Aimee interrupted.

Nathine nodded, smiling now, lost in joyful memories.

'There has never been any male Riders, has there?'

Pelathina asked.

Aimee thought of the ledger she'd found in the box in the armoury. She hadn't looked through every page but from what she'd seen it had only listed female names.

'Only girls are allowed to make the climb. It's one of Kyelli's rules but since we're off to kill her, maybe what she decreed doesn't matter any more.' Nathine shrugged.

Aimee winced at the casual way Nathine spoke about assassinating Kyelli. It was easy for her; she wasn't the one who was going to have to actually do it.

'Would you have wanted Halfen to make the climb with you if he could?' Pelathina asked.

'You climbed with your sister, didn't you?' Nathine answered the question with one of her own.

'Don't change the subject, Nathine,' Aimee ordered. As much as she was eager to know Pelathina's story too, she wanted Nathine to finish hers first.

'Ugh, you're so annoying.' Nathine shook her head but kept talking. 'I was fifteen the first time my father took me with his caravan. It was a simple trip to Lorsoke, only a few days. He was trading reindeer hides for silk from Taumerg. The merchant didn't speak our tongue and my father only had a few phrases of Glavic. It felt like they haggled forever, mostly waving their hands at each other.

'Anyway, that's not important, I just remember it really well because I've blocked out so much else of that trip. It was the first time my father touched me.' She looked at Pelathina. 'My father abused me. On that trip and every other one for two years until I made the climb.'

'*Gari chingreth*,' Pelathina swore. Aimee had learned to recognise that one, even if she didn't know what it meant. And she realised that Pelathina didn't know why Nathine had made the climb.

'I'm sorry for making you talk about him,' Aimee said.

'Don't be,' Nathine told her. 'It happened, but the shame belongs to him, not me.'

'If we weren't flying I'd give you a really big hug right now,' Pelathina said.

'Not you too.' Nathine shook her head in mock despair. Then she looked at Aimee. 'It went on for a year before I said anything to Halfen about it. When I did tell him he went really quiet, didn't say a single word then walked off. I thought he didn't want to be my friend any more. I hid in the warehouse, up in the rafters and I didn't know anything had happened till I heard the commotion as the healer arrived.'

Nathine's words dried up again and Malgerus snorted a small puff of smoke. 'I know, Mal,' Nathine said softly. Then she tipped up the bottom of her goggles, letting her tears run out.

'Halfen confronted your father, didn't he?' Pelathina picked up the story.

Nathine nodded. 'The idiot thought he was defending me, said he was going to report my father to the city guards. You know those spears they use to hunt reindeer? Well my father beat Halfen with the butt of one. No one ever found out why. As Head of a Guild my father has so much power that no one questioned why he'd beaten the son of one of his employees. Halfen's father walked away from his contract, though. I visited him a couple of times until my father found out. Then I didn't see Halfen again till yesterday.'

'Oh Nathine, I'm so sorry. Was Halfen alright?' Aimee asked.

'No, and that's the worst part. I can handle what my father did to me because now he can't touch me, and if I ever see him again I'll get Mal to bite his head off. But he beat Halfen so hard that he broke something inside his head. It's why he's deaf in one ear. I'm to blame for that.'

'You are not.' Pelathina's words were so firm, and tinged with anger, that Aimee almost didn't believe they'd come from the smiley Rider.

Nathine looked like she was going to argue but Pelathina cut her off. 'Your father hurt Halfen, and you, so all the blame, all the guilt, it belongs to him. And I hope that one day it weighs him down and drowns him.'

'Huh, I wish it would,' Nathine said.

'Well, till then, don't you dare carry his guilt for him,' Pelathina ordered.

'And from what I saw yesterday, Halfen doesn't blame you,' Aimee added. 'I think he's missed you.'

Nathine angrily wiped more tears from her face. Aimee liked that Pelathina seemed to understand.

Nathine's anger could rub people the wrong way but like Aimee, Pelathina saw through it.

'Alright, enough of this, I need to fly,' Nathine announced, shaking herself.

'Do you see that bend in the river?' Pelathina asking pointing ahead of them.

To their right the hills had become steeper, their slopes clustered with pine trees, but below them the land was flat, a valley of neat green fields. Ahead a wide river sparkled in the sun, meandering towards them in a big loop.

Nathine had nodded so Pelathina grinned at her. 'Race you!' she called, then immediately pushed Skydance for more speed. His long blue wings beat the air and they shot ahead. The colourful ribbons tied to Pelathina's saddle streamed out behind her.

'Cheat!' Nathine called as she urged Malgerus after them, her dragon hardly needing any encouragement.

The two dragons shot across the sky, bright blue and blazing orange scales shimmering. Aimee could feel Jess tugging in her mind, eager to join the race and Aimee relented. She pushed Jess's spiralled horns for more speed and felt her dragon's strong muscles working beneath her. Aimee understood Nathine's need to feel the rush of adrenaline from flying fast. Nothing else could dispel uncomfortable thoughts in such a fun way.

Skydance was still ahead and widening the gap with every beat of his wings. Malgerus was big but he still wasn't fully grown, and he was injured. There was no way he'd catch Skydance. Jess was smaller than both of them and didn't stand a chance in a race against two male dragons, but Aimee savoured the rush of adrenaline anyway.

Skydance reached the bend in the sparkling river and Pelathina pushed him into a dive. They skimmed across the surface, his tail trailing in the water, sending ripples towards either bank. Then Rider and dragon swooped back into the sky, water droplets flying from Skydance's scales, and they sped back towards Nathine and Aimee. In Pelathina's chest her spark shone brightly and the pure joy on her face made Aimee grin so wide that the wind chilled her teeth. Jess shared her delight and Aimee felt like her mind might explode with happiness. This was what she'd wanted—a dragon to love her and friends to fly with. The appearance of the Empty Warriors had stolen her chance to enjoy being a Rider before the weight of responsibility settled on her.

'Show off!' Nathine called as Skydance skimmed the water again, this time snatching a fish in his claws. 'And I would have won if Mal wasn't injured.'

'I'll take that challenge,' Pelathina called as she and Skydance landed on the riverbank. 'As soon as he's healed we'll have another race.'

'Deal,' Nathine agreed, somehow managing to look smug even though she'd lost.

Jess landed on the riverbank beside Skydance, her talons sinking into the muddy grass. Now their adrenaline from the race was ebbing Aimee could feel how tired Jess was. She was looking around, her long neck swinging side to side and Aimee knew she was searching for somewhere safe to curl up and sleep.

'Sorry girl, not yet,' Aimee whispered. They had to keep moving. The sun was high above them and it had been about sixteen hours since they'd left Kierell. The Empty Warriors could have broken through into the city by now. That thought twisted Aimee's guts.

'Do you think the council will collapse the tunnel?' Aimee asked.

Pelathina and Nathine both faltered for a moment, taken unawares by her question. Nathine shrugged so Aimee turned to Pelathina, but she too looked uncertain.

'I don't know. It'll trap everyone inside the mountains, and anyone who is left out on the tundra, or at Lorsoke, will never get home again. Or Jara might have decided that with our Riders and the city guards we can hold the tunnel entrance against them, even if they do break through.'

Aimee didn't like the sound of that. She couldn't see how anyone could stand against that tide of monsters if they broke through the gate. She hated the thought of Jara and Dyrenna, or Aranati and Lyrria, fighting against that. She knew they would—they'd give their lives to protect the people of Kierell.

'We're taking too long. How far to Vorthens now?' Aimee asked Pelathina.

'Did you see the spire on the hillside?' Pelathina pointed along the river to the north-east. Aimee nodded. It was hidden from view now but from the sky she'd seen a square white tower with a pointed brown roof.

'That's Vorthens. The town stretches up the hillside and it's surrounded by vineyards.'

'Okay, let's go.'

'Wait, Aimee, what's the plan?' Nathine demanded.

'I don't know yet,' Aimee replied feeling flustered.

Jess had begun to flap and Nathine shouted over the snap of her wings. 'We can't just barge into a town and demand they bring out Kyelli so we can kill her. Even with your stubborn face on you can't make that work.'

'Nathine has a point.' Pelathina's voice was softer but she still had to raise it over Jess who was now growling.

'I know but let's just get there first. Then I'll work out what we need to do,' Aimee said.

'But you don't—' Nathine began but Aimee cut her off.

'We just need to go, we're running out of time!' She had to shout down at Nathine because Jess had taken off. Aimee was feeling so anxious she couldn't keep her dragon on the ground.

She knew they needed a plan but they didn't have time to sit around thinking up the best way forward. Aimee needed the others to follow her, now. Thankfully they did and a few minutes later all three dragons were flying along the side of a steep hill, the tower straight ahead of them.

Neat rows of vines passed beneath them and Aimee saw faces turn upwards as they swept overhead. There were a few cries of alarm and she felt bad for that, but she didn't have the time to explain to these workers that

Jess wouldn't hurt them.

Everything was new and different around Aimee and she wished they had the time to stop so she could admire the view. The slopes of vineyards rose up both sides of the valley and at the bottom the wide river meandered peacefully northwards. The grass, the trees, the vines: they were all a more verdant green than what they'd been looking at for hours across the tundra.

Straight paths divided up the vineyards and people walked them carrying baskets or pushing carts. Some paths were wider and Aimee caught a glimpse of a sort of round, metal wagon. It had big spoked wheels and a small chimney at the back puffing out smoke like a dragon. They flew over so fast she barely had time to register what she'd seen and how strange it was.

There were barges on the river, laden with goods that Aimee could only guess at. A mile downriver, jetties jutted out into the water, their legs a crisscross of metal beams. Aimee gawked. There were no metal structures like that in Kierell. The jetties were bustling with barges and people, and to Aimee's amazement they had cog machines. They looked like big metal insects which puffed out jets of steam and lifted crates.

Nathine was pointing and Aimee realised they'd reached the end of the vineyards and the edge of the town. She checked there was no one nearby then waved for them all to land. The moment her claws touched the dirt Jess tried to take off again and Aimee had to pull on their connection to get her to settle. Jess could feel her Rider worrying and that was making her uneasy.

Nathine and Pelathina had landed beside her and the two Riders, plus their dragons, looked at her expectantly. For about the hundredth time that morning, Aimee wished she'd never put on Kyelli's bracelet.

'Now would be a good time to think up that plan,' Nathine suggested.

CHAPTER 4

FOUND

Just beyond where they stood, a cobbled road led into the town. A low wall ran along one side of it, topped with bushes of bright pink flowers. Aimee's eyes followed the road between two tall buildings where it curved to the left. It was odd, seeing a town so open to the world, no mountains or even a high wall encircling it.

Aimee heard voices behind them in a language she didn't understand and froze for a moment, until she realised they were heading away, further into the vineyards.

'I don't think we can leave our dragons here,' Aimee said. She was struggling to keep Jess calm and knew that if she left her alone in this strange place, and Jess could still feel her worries, then her dragon might attack any person who happened past.

Pelathina looked critically at Jess who was kneading the dirt with her talons. She also hadn't folded in her wings, staying ready to fly off at any moment.

'It's easier for me to keep her under control if I'm right beside her,' Aimee admitted.

'I know,' Pelathina switched to a smile. 'It took me about a year before I could get Skydance to do what I wanted without me standing right next to him. I'm amazed you have such control already, actually. Both of you.' She looked to Nathine as well. 'So, we'll take the dragons but we walk.'

'Won't that make us kinda conspicuous?' Nathine pointed out. 'I thought we were going to "sneak in and get her". Wasn't that what Aimee said?'

'But we've got no idea where Kyelli lives,' Pelathina said.

It was then that Aimee realised something: Kyelli didn't know why they were here. If three of her Riders showed up at her door then surely she'd invite them in. Then, when she wasn't looking, all Aimee had to do was switch the bracelet to *ura* and touch her. It felt like a cowardly way to do it but Aimee couldn't face a confrontation. Not with Kyelli, a woman she'd always admired and who'd let her down.

She explained her plan to the others. Pelathina nodded solemnly and Nathine shrugged.

'It's not one of your better plans, but you've had worse,' Nathine said.

'I sometimes think trying to be your friend was my worst plan.'

'Kyelli's sparks, are you mad? That's your best one.'

It was comfortable banter and should have made them both smile, but it didn't. Fear was clawing at

Aimee's insides, making her hands shake and her legs feel all wobbly. And Nathine's face was pale, her freckles standing out like copper dots. Everything was riding on the success of this mission. Everything. And it was hard to joke or smile around that horrible weight of responsibility.

Pelathina grabbed her hand and Aimee flinched, trying to pull back but the other girl held on tight.

'You need to stop touching me,' Aimee warned her again.

'I trust you, Aimee.' Pelathina turned her around so Aimee was looking right into her dark eyes. They were so close that the glow from their sparks mingled between their chests. 'Yesterday morning did you ever think you and Jess would be here, hundreds of miles from Kierell? And that you'd have tracked down Kyelli, someone who's been missing for a century?'

Aimee shook her head, curls bouncing around her face. It was almost impossible to believe how much had happened in a little over a day. If she stopped and thought about it though, it would be overwhelming. It was easier to just keep going. Maybe only another hour or so and her part in this would be done.

'I can do this.' She looked around at the others. '*We* can do this,' she corrected.

'We can.' Pelathina gave her hand a squeeze.

Before they moved, Aimee took a moment and pressed her forehead to Jess's snout. Her scales were smooth and cool. She could feel Jess's pleasure at the attention and she smiled a small, sad smile. Hopefully very soon they'd get a chance to be just a Rider and a dragon, and fly together for fun.

'Until then I need you to follow me and stay calm, okay girl?'

Jess nuzzled her, and her spiralled horns caught in Aimee's hair. Aimee wrapped her arms around Jess's long neck in a quick hug, then she pulled back. In the still moment before she moved Aimee felt the power of the bracelet again, pressing against her mind. She pushed back, keeping it out. After a deep breath, she headed into the town.

Jess followed, walking so close she kept bumping into Aimee. Pelathina walked beside her, Skydance hopping along as if he was struggling to keep his feet on the ground. Nathine was last, one hand on Malgerus's shoulder as they walked. The dirt track turned into cobbles and their boots, and the dragons' talons, clacked loudly on the stone. This road into town was quiet and Aimee had a chance to marvel at the buildings before worrying about seeing people.

They were all four or five storeys high and very different from Kierell's red brick and peaked grey slate roofs. Here, each building was painted a different colour—yellow, orange, teal, or red. And they all had doors and shutters of a wood so dark it was almost black. The biggest difference was the pipes that ran up the sides of all the buildings—there were fat ones and skinny ones, and all the way up, blooming from them like flowers, were big round valves. And up above, it was steam that puffed from the houses' chimneys, not smoke.

The road narrowed and they followed it over a humpbacked bridge of riveted metal painted red. The river below rushed down the hillside, tumbling over boulders and churned milky-white with froth.

'Is this what the city states look like too?' Nathine asked Pelathina.

'I've only been to Taumerg and it had tall buildings like these but more canals, and factories,' Pelathina replied.

Aimee looked around for more of the metal machines she'd glimpsed down at the jetties but all she could see were houses. And then the street opened out into a square and she could see people too. Her legs felt jittery with suppressed energy as if they wanted to run, and her eyes automatically flicked to the edges of the square, looking for the shadows and alleys where she could hide. It took a lot of willpower to keep herself walking forward, right into the middle of the square, heading for a fountain.

It was only as she reached it that Aimee realised the fountain was made of copper cogs gone green with age and the water gurgling from the central spout trickled down through the cogs, setting them to spinning. The whirring of the cogs and the splash of the water made a strangely relaxing melody.

There were people all across the square, sitting at tables in the shade of trees Aimee didn't recognise, or passing through, shopping baskets on their arms. The air smelled like warm bread and burnt sugar. The chatter in the square died down as if Aimee and the others had pushed a bow wave of silence before them. Everyone stared and Aimee instinctively hunched her shoulders. At least they were probably staring at the dragons and not her odd face. They might have heard tales of the city far to the south with its dragon riders, but they'd likely never have seen one before. Aimee heard a cup smash on the cobbles, dropped from shocked fingers.

She hadn't been in a crowd since she'd put on Kyelli's bracelet and she wasn't prepared for what it was like. She could see everyone's sparks. She'd quickly gotten used to the glow in her own chest, along with Pelathina and Nathine's, but now there were balls of greenish-white light everywhere.

They pulsed faintly in time with people's heartbeats and bobbed around as they walked or stood up. A little boy ran past them, calling for his father, and his spark was the brightest Aimee had seen yet. But three older women were sitting around a little table outside a cafe and their sparks were dull, their life force almost used up. The worst one, though, was the young man striding towards them. He could only have been ten years older than Aimee but his spark was duller than those of the old women and it flickered erratically in his chest. What was wrong with him? Why was his spark running out? Did he know he'd only live for another few months? Should Aimee tell him?

'This is horrible,' she moaned.

'What's wrong?' Nathine demanded.

'I can see all their sparks. I know how much life each of these people has left. I shouldn't know this. No one should.'

'Oh, Aimee.' Pelathina's voice was sympathetic and she gave her hand a quick squeeze.

The young man with the weak spark approached and said something Aimee didn't understand.

Nathine leaned forward and whispered to Pelathina. 'Time for you to earn your place on this mission.'

Pelathina raised one dark eyebrow. 'And what do you bring to the group?'

'I keep up Aimee's morale so she doesn't freak out on us,' Nathine replied.

The young man repeated whatever he'd said. '*Wassind du nutried-gurd?*'

Pelathina replied, her words slower and she hesitated a couple of times. Clearly she wasn't as fluent in Glavic as she was in their tongue. Aimee was still impressed that she knew any of the words the man was saying. Then she saw him point at her and wave a hand over his own face. Aimee knew that gesture, and the look in his eyes.

'He said something about my face, didn't he?' she asked Pelathina.

Aimee knew if Lyrria had been here she'd have brushed away Aimee's question, or made something up, but Pelathina understood that Aimee wanted honesty. 'He thinks we've come looking for help from their healer. He thinks that's why we've made such a journey from our home.'

'He thinks we're looking for someone to fix Aimee's face?' Nathine asked, giving the man her best scornful look.

'Well, we know that Aimee's pretty face doesn't need fixing,' Pelathina replied before switching to Glavic again. The man nodded and talked for a while, finally pointing to a steep cobbled street heading up through the town towards the hillside.

'*Da, hurtgard*,' Pelathina replied, then surprised Aimee by reaching out and placing her hand on his shoulder. He did the same to her and they both nodded once, foreheads nearly touching. Clearly Pelathina knew common gestures here as well as their language. When all this was over Aimee resolved to be more like Pelathina and learn about other communities.

Pelathina turned to her and smiled. 'And now we know what you contribute to the mission, aside from all the plans.'

'What?' Aimee was confused.

'Your face.' Pelathina looked delighted and behind her Skydance was fluttering his feathers, but Aimee still didn't understand. 'We wouldn't have gotten the information we need nearly as quickly if he hadn't mistakenly assumed we were looking for their famed healer.'

The man had taken a few steps back but he was still watching them warily. His eyes kept flickering to their dragons.

'He says people regularly travel here to visit the healer,' Pelathina continued. 'Apparently she can cure anyone and she's become a bit of a folklore figure. He remembers stories about her from when he was a boy.'

'And you think this healer is Kyelli?' Nathine didn't bother to hide her scepticism.

'Well, the rumours say she's as old as the hills and she's been living just outside the town for as long as anyone can remember. He says her knowledge of healing is better even than the healers who train at the university in Nallein.'

Aimee thought about it and decided Pelathina was right. This healer did sound like she could be an immortal who arrived in the town a century ago. And who else would have superior knowledge of healing? Only someone with hundreds of lifetimes in their blood allowing them to spend centuries learning.

'Did the man tell you where she lives?' Aimee asked.

'We go up Innstrab,' she pointed towards the cobbled street heading up the hill, 'then turn left onto Highstrab and follow it to the edge of the town. Apparently we'll see her house.'

Aimee nodded and turned resolutely in that direction, but before she could take a step Nathine grabbed her arm.

'Doesn't it seem odd that the Master of Sparks, someone who has sent an army to destroy our city, is a famous healer who helps people?' Nathine asked.

'Nathine, we don't—' Aimee began but she cut her off.

'I'm not trying to be awkward, but think about it. It's weird.'

Aimee opened her mouth to argue but nothing came out. Nathine was right: it didn't make sense. But then neither did it make sense that Kyelli had sent thousands of Empty Warriors to destroy them, but that's what was happening. And if Aimee didn't stop her, everyone in Kierell would die.

'I don't know why Kyelli's doing it or why she might also be a healer,' Aimee admitted. 'All I know is that we have to stop her. We don't have time to figure out her reasons. Oh sparks! Those monsters might be in the city already. I can't, I…' her words trailed off as tears blurred her eyes.

'Hey.' She felt Pelathina take her hand and she tried to pull back but the other girl held on tight.

'The bracelet,' Aimee whimpered.

'It's fine, see.' Pelathina pointed down at her chest. She couldn't see her own spark but she knew Aimee could. 'And you're right, it doesn't make sense, none of this does. And Nathine's point is valid—'

'Yeah, it is,' Nathine interrupted.

Pelathina sensibly ignored her and kept going. 'But we can't start questioning ourselves now. I was so surprised when I came to Kierell and learned that you all know so little of your past. To me, that didn't make sense. You all know Kyelli and her father rescued you from your old home, which was destroyed by Empty Warriors but none of you even know where that home was. And Kyelli vanished from the city and no one knew where she went. You all seemed so ignorant but it didn't matter, you had your city, your world, and you were all safe there.'

'Is there a point to this?' Nathine butted in.

Nathine was angry because she was afraid, and Aimee wanted to apologise for her. But thankfully Pelathina didn't let Nathine get to her. She seemed to have figured out already how Nathine worked and when to ignore her tone.

'My point is,' Pelathina continued calmly, 'that the only thing that makes sense is saving the city and saving our friends. So let's do that.'

Aimee looked around the square. People were still watching them, including the young man, who despite talking to Pelathina seemed not to trust them. Aimee's tears turned everyone's sparks into blurry blobs and her anguish grew when she looked back to the young man with his dull spark. He'd been nice to them and he was dying but didn't know it.

She wanted the bracelet off. She didn't want to know these things. She didn't want this power—one simple flick of the dial on her wrist and Aimee could kill everyone in the square just by touching them.

Jess head-butted her gently and Aimee reached a hand around to stroke her cool scales. With her other hand she wiped away her tears. She was so grateful that Jess didn't have a spark, that she could touch her dragon without thinking, without needing to panic and check the bracelet.

'Come on, let's get this over with,' Aimee announced, turning her back on the square and facing up the street Pelathina had called Innstrab.

Nathine still looked doubtful but she followed when Aimee started walking. Pelathina did too and their dragons' talons clacked loudly on the cobbles. Aimee glanced over at Pelathina. The light caressed her bronze face and in the sun Aimee could see there were hints of copper in her black hair. For every one of the horribly important decisions that Aimee had made over the last day, Pelathina had supported her. Aimee didn't understand. She'd had to fight to make Nathine her friend, and with Lyrria she'd felt she needed to impress her the whole time to keep her attention. But Pelathina just seemed to like her, simple as that.

Aimee shoved these thoughts aside. It was something to think about later when this was all over.

Once they left the square the street quickly steepened. The houses rose up on either side, all four or five storeys high, each one painted a different colour and with a collection of pipes running up the outside. Some of their wooden shutters had carvings on them and a few had wooden balconies with flowerpots. It was a pretty town, though the openness of it made Aimee feel uneasy. Her eyes kept flicking up between the buildings looking for the Ring Mountains, checking to know they were safe.

Linden trees lined the street, their roots wriggling beneath the cobbles and making them buckle like waves frozen in stone. Nathine stumbled on one and cursed this stupid town with its stupid trees. Pelathina giggled at her and Aimee would have done too, but as she walked further up the hill it felt like she was leaving all other emotions behind—all she carried now was anger and fear.

At the top of the street, beside a teal-coloured building with a pointed roof and a shop on the ground floor, they turned left. They passed other people who all stared but none approached. Aimee forced herself to hold her head high, showing her face to everyone who looked. Hopefully one glance at her and people would think these strangers with their dragons were here to see the healer and that they meant no harm to anyone.

Half way along Highstrab they saw it—Kyelli's house.

CHAPTER 5

TAKE A LIFE

THEY KNEW IT was Kyelli's house because of the dragons. The colourful buildings on either side of the street grew smaller, like steps going down, turning into cottages at the edge of town. There the cobbled road turned back into a dirt track and at the end of the track was a lone cottage. The garden gate was painted sunshine yellow and two carved wooden dragons stood proudly on either side of it.

'She doesn't deserve to have dragons guarding her house, even if they're only wooden ones,' Aimee said.

'I could get Mal to set them on fire,' Nathine suggested with a shrug.

'You're really quite violent, aren't you?' Pelathina asked, shaking her head. 'Let's not start a fire that could burn down the town. Most of these buildings are wood, not like the brick in Kierell.'

Nathine shrugged again. 'Fine. Aimee always dismisses my great ideas too.'

As they headed along the dirt track Jess tucked her

wings and pulled in her neck, feathers all lying flat. Malgerus was the opposite with his neck stretched out, snapping at flies as they buzzed past. Skydance looked almost as if he was skipping, like there was barely anything keeping him on the ground and the sky was pulling him upwards.

They reached the yellow garden gate. It was quiet up here. The town was behind them and ahead stretched row upon row of neat green vineyards. Dirt paths wiggled between the vines, following the curve of the hillside. To their left, and below, the river sparkled blue in the sunshine. They were too far up now to hear the sounds of the docks but they could see the hubbub and the barges heading up and down the river, the waterway as busy as any of the main streets in Kierell.

'In stories people always carry out secret, dangerous missions at night, in a storm. Not on the sunniest day of summer. I'm too hot,' Nathine complained.

Aimee was staring at Kyelli's cottage, fear seeping through her. 'Take your coat off,' she snapped, in a tone very like her aunt Naura's had been when she was annoyed.

'That's what I'm doing,' Nathine threw back as she bundled her coat into one of Malgerus's saddlebags. 'So, what's the plan, Aimee?'

'Why do I always have to come up with the plans?'

'Because you're the self-appointed plan maker.'

'But it's not just me who—'

'Stop, both of you,' Pelathina interrupted, in a tone sharper than Aimee had ever heard her use.

Aimee instantly felt ashamed. She was bickering with Nathine because she was scared and now she was here she just wanted it all to be over without her having to actually do anything. And definitely not anything like assassinating an immortal.

'Aimee started it,' Nathine said. Pelathina threw her a look and she shut up.

Without realising she'd done it Aimee had put one hand on the garden gate, gripping it tightly, her fingernails scraping the wood. Jess rested her head on her shoulder, peering at the cottage too. It was a nice cottage with whitewashed walls, wooden shutters and flower boxes at the windows.

'Aimee,' Pelathina began softly but Aimee shook her head and held up a hand to stop the other girl saying anything else.

She didn't need a pep talk right now. She didn't need comforting words or Nathine's sarcasm to cut through her messy thoughts. She just needed this to be over.

She pushed open the gate and resolutely walked through, Jess following behind her. She heard Nathine hiss something but she ignored her and kept on up the path. The garden was full of herbs and wildflowers, their scents mingling in the air. She could feel Jess enjoying the smells of new things and wished she could share in her dragon's delight.

The cottage looked so still and quiet—Aimee couldn't hear anything from inside. As they neared the front door she felt the anger squeezing her mind again and was grateful for it because it left less space for fear. The front door was wooden and carved onto it was a tree—the same tree that marked the Kyelli statues on the map Aimee had found, that had been embossed on the front of Kyelli's diary, and that was engraved on the breastplates of all the Empty Warriors.

Aimee crouched down, pulling Jess's saddle to make her crouch too and gestured for the others to do the same. Pelathina looked at her questioningly and Nathine rolled her eyes, but both girls crouched and shuffled forwards. With her fingertips on the windowsill, Aimee very slowly raised her head to look inside the cottage.

'Is she in there?' Nathine demanded before Aimee had even had a chance to take in what she was seeing.

The ground floor of the cottage was one room with a kitchen at the far end. Copper pipes ran along the ceiling and bent down to a stove, linked to it by a series of complicated-looking valves and levers. Summer light streamed in from windows on all the walls, coating the inside with a soft yellow glow. Aimee gasped at what she saw.

There were paintings, everywhere. The walls were covered in them, more were stacked against a bookcase, and an unfinished one sat on an easel in the middle of the room. And every painting was of a dragon. Some were flying through the sky, colourful scales bright on the canvas. Others were perched on ledges in the Ring Mountains, the grey rock rendered in such detail that it looked razor sharp even in paint. On the far wall was a close-up of a dragon's head, his ruff of feathers all standing on end and his scales the same emerald green as Jess's.

'Great big sparkly sparks,' Pelathina whispered beside her. She'd lifted her head up to peer through the window too.

'Wow, they're amazing,' Nathine said from Aimee's other side and there was not a hint of sarcasm in her voice. 'Do you think Kyelli painted them?'

Aimee thought of the wonderfully detailed map and the little sketches in Kyelli's diary. How dare she sit here creating beautiful things while she sent monsters to destroy Kierell. How could someone do that, be that duplicitous? Be that callous?

Then someone appeared, walking down the wooden staircase from the upstairs of the cottage. Aimee's heart skipped a beat then rushed to catch up, pounding in her chest. Her fingertips buzzed with adrenaline and her palms sweated against the windowsill.

Carrying a book, the woman walked across the room and seated herself at large battered table pushed against one wall. She had her back to them. Aimee had been too shocked by the sight of her that she hadn't fully taken her in, but it was Kyelli. She looked mid-thirties, even though she was hundreds of years old, but her face had the same regal look as all the statues in Kierell. Her long blonde hair cascaded in a waterfall of loveliness down her back and was exactly as Aimee had always imagined it.

Aimee had thought she'd be able to see all Kyelli's

sparks. She'd pictured them sparkling in the immortal's body, like fireflies trapped beneath her skin. But when Kyelli had walked across the room Aimee had only seen one really bright spark in her chest.

'That's her, isn't it?' Nathine asked, her words rushed and breathless.

'It has to be,' Aimee replied. She couldn't stop staring at Kyelli's back. She was right there. Anger fizzed in Aimee, mixing with the adrenaline and making her feel jittery. Jess was clawing the grass beneath them and had her lips pulled back in a silent snarl.

Kyelli was sitting so peacefully at her table, book open beside her, doing something with jars and herbs. Aimee thought of the confused and scared people in Kierell, of the councillors trying desperately to think of a way to protect them, and of Jara, terrified for the lives of her Riders. How could Kyelli do this to them?

'This is a big window,' Nathine said, leaning back to look up. 'I think our dragons would all fit though. We could just smash it and send them in to kill Kyelli. If they all blast her with dragon's breath and Mal bites her head off, surely even an immortal with thousands of sparks wouldn't survive that.'

That was tempting. Aimee could hide out here and let Jess do what needed to be done.

'We can't,' Pelathina said firmly, quashing Aimee's hope.

'Why not? That's a great plan,' Nathine argued.

'I keep forgetting you're both such new Riders. There's so much you should have had the time to learn.'

'Well that's not our fault.' Nathine was instantly defensive.

'Why can't we use our dragons?' Aimee asked before an argument rose.

'Because before you bonded with them, your dragons were wild creatures. If you hadn't taken them as hatchlings and formed your connection with them, they'd see you as prey. It's why we have to kill the unbonded hatchlings.'

'Yeah but we are bonded,' Nathine pointed out.

'I know, and your bond overwrites their natural instincts but if you start sending your dragon off to kill people those instincts will resurface. You'd probably be able to get Malgerus back under control this time but it'd be hard, and would cause a weakness in your bond.'

Aimee knew Pelathina was right, not just because what she said made sense but because she could feel it. Her bond had changed Jess and Aimee wanted to keep that. She didn't want to see Jess revert to being wild, and become a danger to anyone. Aimee didn't want to risk losing the love she had with Jess and she knew Jess wouldn't want that either—her dragon liked being part of a clutch with the other dragons and Riders.

'I'm sorry, Aimee, but you're the only one who can do this,' Pelathina said softly, and there was a sadness in her eyes that Aimee didn't like seeing.

Aimee took a deep breath. 'I know.'

Fear, doubts and a strong desire to run away were making her shake and she clenched her fists so the others wouldn't see.

'Move away,' Aimee ordered. 'Please.' And she gestured to the bracelet.

Pelathina and Nathine stepped back and Aimee turned the dial to *ura*, the setting that allowed her to suck the spark from someone else.

'You can't touch me now, okay?' She stared intently at both of them, making sure they definitely understood.

'We won't, I promise.' Pelathina tucked both hands behind her back and gave Aimee a quick smile.

'At least I won't need to suffer your hugs now,' Nathine said.

Aimee put a hand on Jess's cool scales, grateful she could still touch her, and borrowed a bit of Jess's strength along with her dragon's unwavering belief in her own abilities.

'Alright, can you two kick down the door and I'll run in and grab Kyelli. As soon as I touch her the bracelet will begin sucking out her sparks. I don't know how long that'll take, so you might need to hold her down,' Aimee laid out her plan.

'That's it? Simple as that?' Nathine asked, adjusting her ponytail, pulling it higher onto the crown of her head.

Aimee wanted to point out that there was nothing simple about using unnatural powers to suck the life from someone but she didn't want to argue. She just wanted to get this over with.

'Ready?' Aimee asked.

The two girls nodded. Part of Aimee had been hoping they'd say no, that they'd tell her it was a terrible plan and there was another way, but there wasn't. She had to do this to save her city, and she would. Kyelli deserved to pay for the fear and death she'd already caused.

Aimee touched her forehead to Jess's. 'You have to stay here, girl. And very soon this will be over and we'll go flying for fun, okay?'

Making sure to keep a lot of space between her and them, Aimee motioned for Pelathina and Nathine to go. They headed for the door and Pelathina took Skydance with her. Aimee was confused for a moment until she saw what Pelathina was doing. Directing his head, she got Skydance to breath heat—no flames—over the hinges of the door. The metal glowed red and weakened. A man might have had the strength to kick open the door in one go but they couldn't, and Pelathina had given them an advantage to keep their element of surprise. Aimee wouldn't have thought of that.

'Do it?' Pelathina asked, twisting round to look at Aimee.

'Do it,' Aimee confirmed.

'One, two, three.' Pelathina counted them down, then together she and Nathine slammed a kick right into the middle of the door. On the weakened hinges it burst inwards with a crash. Squeezing her arms tight to her body so she didn't accidentally touch them, Aimee dashed between the others and into the cottage. Outside, Jess roared.

Aimee sprinted across the room, knocking the canvas off the easel which clattered to the floor. Kyelli spun upwards from her chair, eyes open wide with shock. Before she could speak, Aimee flew at her. Her momentum knocked them both to the floor. Kyelli landed with a gasp and a thump, Aimee on top of her.

All the anger and disappointment that had been building inside Aimee burst out in a scream. It helped her do what she needed to. She grabbed Kyelli's wrist with her left hand and instantly felt the woman's spark. The bracelet sucked at her life force and it began to pour into Aimee. She felt the sickening wrongness of having someone else's spark inside her but ignored it and gripped tighter.

Kyelli gasped and began panting. Aimee could see the shine of a second spark growing in her own chest. She couldn't look at Kyelli. She knew she had to do this, that Kyelli deserved it, but she didn't want to look into the woman's eyes as she killed her. Instead she focused on the bracelet, on what she could feel.

But something wasn't right.

She could feel the energy of only a single spark. Where were the thousands of others? Why couldn't Aimee sense them?

She looked down into Kyelli's face. Her blue eyes were open so wide Aimee could see the whites all around and she was gasping like a fish out of water. She looked utterly terrified. Outside, Jess roared again, and this time Skydance and Malgerus joined her. The rumbles of sound seemed to vibrate through the cottage walls. Aimee realised she was crying, her tears dripping off her chin and onto Kyelli's face.

Then Aimee became aware that someone was shouting. The energy from Kyelli's spark was almost all in her chest now. Aimee could feel it running out, like pouring water from a jug and knowing by the weight that it was almost empty. She just had to hold on a little longer and it would be done.

But why did Kyelli only have one spark?

'Sparks! Aimee, stop!'

Pelathina's voice finally made it through the hubbub in her head and the absolute panic in it made Aimee push her will against the power of the bracelet and let go of Kyelli's wrist. She scrambled off Kyelli and stared around. Pelathina was crouched on the floor beside her, arms out as if she'd been about to grab Aimee. Nathine was standing in the middle of the room, hands clenched to fists and staring open-mouthed at another woman.

Aimee wiped tears from her eyes with her sleeve and stared as well. An old woman was standing in the doorway. Outside, behind her, all three dragons were crouched, bellies to the ground and wings tucked, as if they'd been cowed by something.

'Oh sparks, Aimee, what have you done?' Nathine's voice was a coarse whisper.

The old woman had silver hair and a dull spark. She stepped over the fallen canvas and glared down at Aimee.

'I told you to only use the map to find me if absolutely, unavoidably necessary,' she said. 'And why have you attacked Petra?'

CHAPTER 6

MAKING A WARRIOR

THE OLD WOMAN marched across the room and grabbed Aimee's arm, being careful not to touch her skin. When she saw the bracelet a wave of sadness swept across her lined face.

'You found my bracelet and you put it on.' The old woman shook her head, wisps of silver hair brushing her cheeks. 'Why?' she sighed.

Aimee stared up at her. Her face was all wrinkles but it was symmetrical and regal-looking. Her hair was silver and bundled into a bun on top of her head but Aimee could tell it was long and straight. Her eyes were the pale grey of a winter sky and slightly almond-shaped. There was a depth to them that hinted at all she'd seen.

'You...' Aimee's words stuttered out and she tried again. 'You're Kyelli?'

The old woman sighed again. 'I go by Eylla now but yes, I am Kyelli of the Quorelle.'

'Sparks!' Nathine swore.

'*Gari chingreth*,' Pelathina agreed.

'But...' Aimee stuttered again. How could this old woman with a faint spark be Kyelli?

'Questions and swearing can wait till later, right now you need to give my assistant her spark back.' Kyelli's voice was firm and before Aimee could stop her she'd grabbed the bracelet and flicked the dial to *zurl*.

In her shock at seeing the real Kyelli, Aimee had forgotten the woman, Petra, on the floor. The sudden realisation of what she'd done hit her like a punch to the chest.

'Oh sparks,' she moaned, crouching down and grabbing Petra's arm again. She'd attacked and nearly murdered this innocent woman. The wrongness of Petra's spark swirled through her body.

The moment she felt the last of Petra's energy pass through the bracelet and back into her chest, Aimee slammed the connection shut in her mind.

'I'm so sorry,' Aimee said, scrambling to her feet and away from the woman.

'She doesn't speak your language,' Kyelli said as she helped Petra to her feet. '*Vassin du ornung?*'

Petra's eyes were still too wide and her teeth were chattering as if she were cold. Kyelli kept speaking to her softly in Glavic, trying to keep Petra's attention on her but the woman's blue eyes kept slipping to Aimee. And they were full of fear and accusation.

Aimee felt sick. She couldn't breathe. The edges of her vision went all blurry. She staggered across the room, not seeing the others, or the painting on the floor that she stood on, leaving a muddy bootprint on the canvas. She needed outside. She needed Jess.

'Put the bracelet in neutral before you hurt someone else.' Kyelli's command followed her and Aimee leaned on the splintered doorframe and tried to flick the dial to the closed circle. Her fingers were shaking so much it took her three goes.

Then she staggered outside and collapsed to the ground. Jess was instantly there, wrapping her body around Aimee's, cocooning her in cool scales and the comforting smell of woodsmoke. She knew she should get up, go back inside and suck the spark from Kyelli's chest. That was her mission. But she couldn't do it. Pulling the spark from Petra had been sickening and wrong.

'I can't do this, Jess.'

Jess nudged her gently, spiralled horns tangling with Aimee's short curls. Aimee wrapped her arms around Jess's neck and pressed her face against her scales. She wished she could slip inside Jess, become part of her and they could fly away together.

She heard footsteps and looked up in time to see Petra emerge from the back of the cottage, slip out of the garden through a side gate and sprint for the town. Though it twisted Aimee's heart to see someone running from her in fear, she couldn't blame the young woman.

Wilfully using the bracelet had awoken the power in it and she could feel its desire to be used again. It pressed against her mind. She closed her eyes and focused on her connection with Jess. She sat there for a long time until Jess growled low and Aimee opened her eyes to see Nathine staring down at her, hands on hips.

'What are you doing? You have to go back in there and kill Kyelli,' Nathine said. Malgerus was standing right behind her, his ruff of feathers up and his head sweeping side to side.

'Nathine, give her a moment.' Pelathina appeared and crouched down beside Aimee and Jess.

Tears welled in Aimee's eyes and she let them fall down her cheeks, dripping off onto Jess's head. 'I nearly murdered an innocent woman. I can't go back inside and risk doing the same to someone else. What if that old woman isn't really Kyelli?' Aimee thought about the one dull spark she'd seen in the woman's chest.

'She admitted to being Kyelli,' Nathine pointed out.

'And there's something about her eyes,' Pelathina mused.

'Yeah, I noticed that too,' Nathine agreed.

'They look... *ithancsis*. Ah, I'm not sure how to say it in your language, but like really old and knowing.'

'Are you saying she is definitely Kyelli and I should take her spark?' Aimee asked.

Both girls stared at her but neither spoke. She could see the answer in their eyes though, in the fear that they, like her, were trying to mask. Fear for their city, their families and their friends. Aimee didn't have a choice. She pulled free of Jess and got to her feet.

'I have to stop the Master of Sparks,' she said, partly to the others, but mostly to herself. 'It's my mission. Jara approved it.'

She stepped away from Nathine and Pelathina, then

flicked the dial on the bracelet back to *ura*. The moment she did the power pressed more eagerly against her mind. She hastily built a mental wall to keep it out.

'Last time,' she promised herself, and stepped back through the door of Kyelli's cottage.

Kyelli was fussing with something in the small kitchen at the far end of the room. She had her back to the door. All Aimee had to do was run over, grab her and steal her spark.

'Come on, do it,' she whispered, trying to make her feet move. But her body was still reeling from the wrongness of having taken Petra's spark and it refused to obey her.

Kyelli turned, a tray of food in her hands. Her face was calm but she wore a sad smile. 'I never again thought I'd meet any of my Riders.'

Then Kyelli looked at her and seemed to really see her for the first time. Her old eyes roved over Aimee's face, down to the gold cuff stuck on her wrist and she sighed.

'But if you're here for the reason I fear you are, then this is not a happy meeting.' Kyelli placed the tray of food on the large wooden table.

'What do you have to fear?' Aimee snapped, and her words came out sharp as blades. Kyelli wasn't the one surrounded by Empty Warriors. The memory of fiery eyes and hands that burned was enough to rekindle Aimee's anger. It was the boost she needed.

She dashed into the cottage and grabbed for Kyelli. The old woman jumped back with surprising speed, knocking over a chair which clattered to the floor. Kyelli's calm composure was gone as she backed away across the room.

Aimee felt the eagerness in the bracelet swelling.

'Wait!' Kyelli yelled. 'I can think of only one reason why my Riders would have used the map to find me, and why you are wearing my bracelet. You found some Empty Warriors, didn't you?'

'Found?' Aimee spluttered in disbelief. 'They weren't lost. The Empty Warriors were gone and we were safe. Until you created new ones and sent them to kill us!'

Kyelli began to speak but Aimee didn't want to hear her excuses. She closed the distance between them just as Kyelli drew a dagger from her belt and swiped at Aimee. Aimee's training saved her and she swerved back, the blade cutting through the air where her chest had been.

'Stop!' Kyelli shouted, both hands held up, one gripping the hilt of her dagger. 'I understand now why you're here, but killing me won't save you. The Empty Warriors you're speaking of all look the same, don't they?'

Aimee had been about to attack but Kyelli's words stayed her feet. Nathine and Pelathina had joined her in the cottage and stood on either side of her, ready. She could reach Kyelli in three steps but Aimee hesitated. It had been bothering her that the Empty Warriors all had the exact same face.

'Empty Warriors are created using the energy from

their master's sparks, so they all look identical. And they look like their creator,' Kyelli explained. 'Are the ones you've fought male or female?'

'They're all male,' Aimee found herself replying.

'Then they can't be mine,' Kyelli said simply.

Silence fell in the cottage and no one moved. Outside their dragons were all on their feet, stretching out their wings, snapping at the air, all keen to do something because they could feel their Riders' anxiety.

Kyelli's words were like a jigsaw piece clicking into place. It explained why the Empty Warriors all had the same face—they were replicas of their master, created using sparks from his blood.

And it wasn't Kyelli's face they wore. She wasn't the Master of Sparks.

'Do we believe her?' Nathine asked.

Aimee was still on the balls of her feet, left arm twitching, ready to lunge at Kyelli, but she didn't. They were wrong, Aimee realised it now. The clues had brought them here but they'd misinterpreted them.

Their mission had failed.

'Yes,' Aimee answered Nathine's question.

She did believe Kyelli, because although there were still questions in her mind, it made sense now. But with that realisation came fresh dread. If it wasn't Kyelli she needed to kill to save Kierell, then who?

'If the Empty Warriors are not yours then who do they belong to?' Aimee asked.

The panic had gone from Kyelli's face, but the fear was still there, gathered in the lines on her forehead, the crinkles around her eyes. It wasn't fear of Aimee and the bracelet though, because her eyes were looking beyond Aimee, seeing something in the past only she could remember.

Aimee was still on edge. It felt like her mission was unraveling at the seams and she had no idea how to stitch it back together.

'If you didn't create the Empty Warriors then who did? And why can I only see one spark in your chest? Where are all your thousands of others?' The questions tumbled from her and she couldn't stop them. 'And why did you leave your bracelet in Kierell when you left? Why did you leave the city at all?'

She needed answers desperately, needed to know everything so she could plan what to do next. She was supposed to be saving Kierell, but if Kyelli wasn't the Master of Sparks then who was? And by now, unless the council had collapsed the tunnel, the Empty Warriors would have broken through into the city. What if the Riders were right now fighting for their lives, hoping with every breath that Aimee would succeed in her mission? She was letting them down. Their deaths would be her fault as much as if she'd sucked out their sparks.

Kyelli was watching them keenly. 'I'll explain everything but we all need some tea first, and food,' she said.

'You aren't angry that I just tried to steal your spark?' Aimee asked as Kyelli moved towards her. This time it was Aimee who backed away.

Kyelli's smiled ruefully. 'I always hoped my Riders

would be women who were bold and decisive.' She took a seat at the table and gestured to the tray of food she'd laid out. 'Sit down and eat.' She waved a hand towards Nathine. 'Your friend there looks like if I don't feed her she'll slip out back and start eating my chickens.'

Nathine nodded. 'I was considering it. Mal could roast them for me.'

Aimee felt a hand on her elbow and jerked away. She turned just in time to see Pelathina hide the hurt on her face and give her a reassuring smile.

'Come on, Aimee, let's take a seat.' Pelathina nodded towards the big wooden table.

Aimee's legs felt like they'd seized up but she forced herself to walk over and sit down. She sat facing the door so she could see Jess outside. And she turned the dial on the bracelet back to neutral. The others joined her and Kyelli dished out tea, bread and herb butter, and some sort of little fruit tarts. She put a silver pot down in front of Pelathina.

'*Mattca kofee ante ju,*' Kyelli said.

'Really? *Kofee?*' Pelathina's face lit up. She poured a stream of dark liquid into a small cup, brought it to her nose and inhaled, a look of pure bliss on her face. 'Oh I wish Aranati were here.'

'What's she got?' Nathine demanded as she took a huge bite of bread.

'This is life in a cup.' She grinned at Nathine. 'It's coffee.'

Nathine eyed it suspiciously then poured herself a mug of tea. She didn't bother pouring for anyone else.

Kyelli filled a cup for herself and also pushed one across the table to Aimee. But Aimee couldn't face touching her tea or the food. She still felt sick at what she'd done to Petra, and nearly done to Kyelli.

'Before I answer your questions, tell me about the Empty Warriors you've fought,' Kyelli said.

Nathine and Pelathina looked to Aimee, and she supposed they were right, this was her story to tell. So she started with the caravan of councillors heading out to Lorsoke to meet with the Helvethi, and told Kyelli everything from then until yesterday evening when they had found her bracelet in the cave behind the waterfall. Kyelli watched her intently as she spoke, taking occasional sips of her tea. Aimee's own tea had gone cold by the time she finished.

'It was wrapped in a yellow scarf, wasn't it? My bracelet,' Kyelli said and Aimee nodded. 'That was my favourite scarf.'

'But if you didn't create the Empty Warriors then who did?' Aimee asked. 'Because you said in your diary that only a Quorelle could make and undo them.'

'Did you bring it?' Kyelli answered with a question of her own.

Aimee tugged Kyelli's diary from her coat pocket and pulled out the pages that had been missing, the ones Jara had hidden. A wistful pang flickered across Kyelli's face when she saw her diary but she didn't reach for it.

'And you're the only Quorelle left,' Aimee pointed out. 'None of the others survived and escaped from Kierellatta, only you and your father, and he's dead because we've seen his tomb.'

'When you live for hundreds of years it's incredible the number of regrets you collect,' Kyelli said, her eyes still on the pages of her diary. 'But I think one of my biggest was not giving you your full history. My father and I thought we were protecting you.'

'What don't we know that we need to know now?' Pelathina asked.

'You've already pieced a lot of it together. The Quorelle did create the Empty Warriors back on Kierellatta, though they were not meant as warriors, not at first. They were workers,' Kyelli explained and as she talked her words conjured images in Aimee's head of a world long destroyed. 'There were four kingdoms on Kierellatta, each ruled by Quorelle. It was the northern-most kingdom, ruled by Doralleni and Guison, who created the first Empty Warriors, though we didn't call them that to begin with. They were simply an expendable workforce, created to toil in the deepest mines, the ones where the risk to human life was too great.'

Kyelli's wintery-grey eyes had taken on a far-off look as she shared her memories. 'Mornvello, their capital, was built into the mountains and rose in tiers. Down low, streets led off the back into the mines and production areas. They were so proud of their steam-powered machines that carried raw materials along the valley floor to where the factories were. Doralleni especially, she liked that their home was a display of their wealth and progress. They did have a beautiful bridge that spanned the city, leading to the gold and silver striped tower at the city's peak where she and Guison lived. I liked their statues that stood all along the bridge, encrusted with the precious stones they mined.'

Kyelli looked down, swirling the tea in her mug. 'They were my friends but they were too ambitious and it wasn't long before creating a workforce morphed into creating an army. The first Empty Warriors. And yes, they eventually destroyed everything on that island, despite all my father and I did to try and stop them.'

'Wait, hang on, are you saying they can't be stopped?' There was a flash of fear in Nathine's eyes which Aimee felt too. She held her breath as she waited for Kyelli to answer.

CHAPTER 7

RUNNING OUT

KYELLI TOOK HER time before replying. She poured herself more tea and added a spoonful of honey. Aimee didn't care if these were painful memories for Kyelli; they needed answers and a plan, now.

'Our city doesn't—' Aimee began but Kyelli spoke over her.

'Empty Warriors can only be created by a Quorelle, using a bracelet,' she gestured at Aimee's wrist, 'and each one you create requires the sacrifice of one of your sparks. They aren't human. They can't think and act like people, they don't have emotions or compassion, they can't feel love or hate. A person is created from two sparks, from the energy of their parents' sparks merging to create a new one. The Empty Warriors are a sole creation, meaning they're made from the sparks of one Quorelle combined with an element.'

'Like fire,' Pelathina whispered.

'Yes fire, or earth. Metals work too. And they have to be imbued with a purpose. They can't make decisions themselves so you have to give them a reason to be, and they'll follow that command, continuing to do it until they are stopped.'

Aimee thought of the Empty Warriors' breastplates, engraved with the words "We are fuelled by our purpose" and "We will not stop until Kyelli's city is destroyed". The Uneven Council couldn't negotiate with the Empty Warriors or bargain with them. They'd just keep coming until everything inside the Ring Mountains was ash.

'Right, thanks for the history lesson. So, how do we stop them?' Nathine asked.

Kyelli didn't seem bothered by Nathine's brusque manner, but then she'd probably met plenty of people like Nathine over the centuries.

'You give an Empty Warrior one of your sparks to create it, but that doesn't give it life, not like we have,' Kyelli explained. 'So they will always be linked to the Quorelle who created them. Kill the Quorelle and their Empty Warriors will die too.' Kyelli had to take a deep breath before continuing. 'My father and I killed the other Quorelle after the war had engulfed the entire of Kierellatta. We realised it was the only way to destroy the Empty Warriors. But, by then my father and I had also contributed. We'd made Empty Warriors too, giving them the purpose of defending our kingdom.'

'But if all the Quorelle are dead apart from you, then who made the warriors attacking Kierell?' Pelathina asked the question they kept circling back to.

Kyelli shook her head. 'I don't know. What do they

look like?'

'Dark hair, tall, fire in their eyes,' Aimee replied.

'Hang on.' Nathine slipped out the door and rummaged in her saddlebags, pulling out the small blue journal Aimee had seen her with yesterday. 'You've still got my pencil,' Nathine reminded Aimee as she re-entered the cottage. 'Here.' Nathine flipped open her journal and passed it to Kyelli.

Aimee caught a glimpse of sketches in the open pages. She didn't know Nathine could draw.

'Are you sure this is what they look like?' Kyelli's fingers hovered over the open journal as if it was too hot to touch. Then she flipped it around, holding it up for everyone to see.

Nathine's sketch of the Empty Warriors was eerily accurate. She'd captured the terrifying way the flames swirled in their eyes. They all nodded in response to Kyelli's question.

'Sparks,' Kyelli swore.

'What? Who is it?' Aimee asked.

Kyelli was hundreds of years old. She'd lived through a war that destroyed an entire island. So seeing the mix of fear and anguish on her face was really scaring Aimee.

'It's my brother, Pagrin,' Kyelli replied, her grief-stricken eyes fixed on the sketch.

'Pagrin? I've heard that name. Why have I heard that name?' Nathine asked the room.

It had clicked in Aimee's mind the moment Kyelli said it. 'Because the letters we collected from the statues spelled out two clues. *Palest grain* which led us to the trapdoor in the library ceiling, and *Pagrin's Tale.*'

'I thought he was dead,' Kyelli said the words so softly Aimee almost didn't hear her. 'Oh sparks, we left him.'

'Why was his name part of the clues?' Aimee asked.

Kyelli pulled her eyes from Nathine's sketch. 'It wasn't, not really. I just wanted to include him, to weave him into the city. Escaping with as many survivors as we could and establishing a new home had been his idea. But he didn't make it, he never came with us.'

'Why not?' Aimee asked.

'He disappeared. My father and I were gathering as many people as we could, taking them to the harbour where we'd scavenged a fleet. You must understand, war had been raging across Kierellatta for decades by this point. The kingdoms had all crumbled, everything was chaos.' Kyelli clasped her hands to her chest, muffling the glow from her spark. 'Pagrin had gone out beyond Vienthon, our capital city, to kill Doralleni. She was the last of the Quorelle apart from my family. Her Empty Warriors from the north were approaching and we only had a limited time to get off the island. Pagrin didn't make it back to Vienthon before the Empty Warriors broke through the city walls. We had to go.'

Kyelli stood, backing away from Nathine's sketch which she left lying on the table. Then she collapsed to the floor like her legs had turned to water. Pelathina rushed to her side and grabbed her before she toppled over. Tears were running down her face, gathering in the wrinkles around her mouth.

'Oh sparks, we left him. When he didn't come back we assumed he'd been overrun by the army or killed by Doralleni. So, we left him.'

Aimee had been feeling intimidated by Kyelli, and angry that she'd kept so much of their history from them. But right then she wasn't an immortal with all the answers, she was just a woman crying for a brother she thought she'd lost. Aimee plucked Kyelli's tea from the table.

'Here,' she said sitting on the floor beside her and offering Kyelli the cup.

'Thank you.' She took the cup and drained it in one long swallow. 'You would think after more than six hundred years that it would get easier to deal with your emotions. Let me tell you, it doesn't. Love still breaks your heart and grief still rubs you raw.'

'Well at least now you know Pagrin's not dead, if he's sitting on Ternallo Island turning his sparks into monsters,' Nathine said with her usual lack of tact.

Aimee winced but Kyelli only turned to Nathine, confused. 'Ternallo Island. Why did you say that?'

'It's engraved on the Empty Warriors' breastplates,' Aimee answered. 'Though none of us know where it is. Do you?'

'It's an uninhabited volcanic island, directly south from Kierellatta.' Kyelli shook her head. 'It's just bare rock and volcanoes.'

Aimee thought of the lava that had poured out of the Empty Warriors when she fought them. Remembered the fire in their eyes, and the blackened skin of their hands that was all cracked, showing lava swirling beneath.

'You said that Empty Warriors were made of elements,' Aimee began, voicing her thoughts, 'so could Pagrin have made them from fire and lava on Ternallo Island?'

'Yes, that would be possible.' She looked towards Nathine's sketch lying on the table and shook her head. 'I haven't seen his face for over three hundred years. But I can't understand why he would create more Empty Warriors. He saw how each kingdom turned on the others, how the Empty Warriors destroyed Kierellatta.'

Kyelli looked up at them and her pale eyes were wells of sorrow and regret.

'The first ones we created were peaceful. They worked the mines, or farmed blush pearls from the river at Deltance where a human would have been swept away by the currents. But the Empty Warriors were creatures made from greed and anger, and could not be controlled,' Kyelli told them, and Aimee began to understand why she'd kept this history from them. Not that she agreed, but she understood.

'Once given a purpose and set on a course, they cannot be stopped,' Kyelli continued. 'So, if you tell them to destroy a town, they will attack until they have completely razed it to the ground and killed everyone. They will not stop for mercy or bribes, or even conscience because they have none. So on Kierellatta thousands upon thousands were slaughtered. Our standing armies of humans were wiped out. And setting Empty Warriors to kill other Empty Warriors meant they would do this and keep doing it until they were all dead, but also kill or destroy anyone or anything that was in their way. Why would Pagrin risk that again?'

Aimee watched as Pelathina put a hand over Kyelli's, her fingers a rich bronze against Kyelli's pale ones.

'This is why you left Kierell, isn't it?' Pelathina said softly. 'On the map that you drew, that Aimee found, you wrote that it wasn't safe for people if you stayed.'

Kyelli nodded slowly as if her head was too heavy to carry. 'After my father ran out of sparks and died, I was the only Quorelle left. I wanted to stay and watch the city grow, to see brave girls take up my challenge and become Riders, but I knew that the power of the bracelet would always tempt me.

'What if a threat appeared that my Riders couldn't deal with? Would I create just a few Empty Warriors to help protect the city? Or what if we wanted to build and we needed a greater workforce. Would I create a few to be workers, like the original ones we made on Kierellatta? It could have started all over again and I might have ended up destroying the city.'

'And that's why you left the bracelet behind too?' Aimee asked.

'Without it, I can't create anything that could become a monster. But if Pagrin's still alive and he's created Empty Warriors then I have to stop him. *Gari fu ithu chingreth*!'

'Indeed,' Pelathina agreed.

'Your language is so much better for cursing in. It's much more expressive.'

'Come on, let's get you up off the floor,' Pelathina said, wrapping an arm around Kyelli's waist.

Kyelli shook her off. 'I can get up fine. I know I look old but my body hasn't aged as yours will. There's still a lot of strength in these bones.'

And as if to demonstrate, Kyelli stood quickly and easily. She walked across the room to a recessed window seat and sat there. 'Tiredness though, that I get. Or perhaps it's more weariness.'

Pelathina sat herself on the cushions beside Kyelli as if not quite trusting that she was as strong as she claimed. Nathine leaned on the wall beside them and folded her arms.

'So why are you old?' Nathine asked. 'Aimee says you only have one spark in your chest. Aren't you meant to have thousands so you can be immortal?'

'I used to have so many that my blood sparkled with them. But that's a story for another time. Right now we need to figure out how to find Pagrin.'

'So Aimee can kill him? That's our new plan?' Nathine asked.

Grief flickered on Kyelli's face again. 'I still can't believe he would do this, but yes, if Pagrin has created these monsters then I need to stop him.' Her expression was stern and Aimee caught a flinty glint in her eyes.

'How do we go about finding him?' Pelathina asked. 'We searched the army for the Master of Sparks but it's made up entirely of Empty Warriors. And Lwena died because of that search.'

Pelathina's voice was full of pain, a pain that Aimee shared. She didn't want to see any other Riders killed by those monsters.

'Pagrin will likely be with his army somewhere but he could be right in the middle of it and you wouldn't see him.' Kyelli pointed to Nathine's sketch. 'The Empty Warriors are exact replicas of him.'

Aimee thought of the thousands of identical faces staring up at her as she'd flown over the army. Had the Master of Sparks been watching them all along? She shuddered at the thought.

'I have an idea though, about how we can use the bracelet to locate Pagrin.'

Kyelli had wiped her face and her tears were gone. She looked once again like the commanding woman who'd strode into her cottage and stopped Aimee from killing Petra. She looked like a woman with a plan. A strong wave of relief washed over Aimee.

All through the quest yesterday, as they hunted down the clues across the city, Aimee had been longing for the moment when she could hand the problem of saving the city over to Kyelli. Then those hopes had been crushed when they found the bracelet and Aimee had hated Kyelli for betraying them. But she hadn't betrayed anyone, and here she was making plans to find the Master of Sparks and stop him. Aimee didn't need to carry the responsibility of saving the city any more, she could give it to someone who wasn't scared and who wouldn't screw up.

'Here,' Aimee held out her arm, pulling back her sleeve cuff to display the bracelet. 'You can have it back now but I need you to show me how to take it off. I tried before but pain shot up my arm. There's a spike that's gone into my vein.'

Kyelli stared at her, pale eyes as unreadable as a dragon's.

'Please,' Aimee begged.

'Oh child,' Kyelli said with a sigh. 'You can't take it off without killing yourself.'

'But...' Aimee didn't understand. She looked around at Pelathina and Nathine who both looked concerned. 'You used to wear it and now you don't, so it does come off,' Aimee insisted.

'Come here.' Kyelli held out her hands, beckoning Aimee.

She stepped over to the window, stopping in front of Kyelli. The older woman gently took Aimee's arm, being careful to only touch the bracelet, not her skin, until she'd checked the dial was in neutral. Then she took both of Aimee's hands in her own. Her fingers were rough with callouses.

'The bracelets were made by the Quorelle and were only meant for us. We never intended, nor expected, a human to put one on.'

Kyelli ran one finger across the engraved gold cuff that was starting to feel more and more like a shackle on Aimee's wrist.

'The bracelets are powered by sparks,' Kyelli continued. 'That spike which has gone into your vein? It's linked to your spark now. To uncouple it and remove the bracelet requires a large amount of energy. It would pull out most of the life in your spark if you took it off. You're young though, so it might leave you with a little energy left.'

'How much?' Aimee asked, her voice a whisper.

Kyelli shrugged. 'Perhaps a few weeks. When I removed the bracelet I still had spare sparks. I used one of them to remove it.'

'I'm stuck with it, forever?'

Aimee couldn't quite take it in. She didn't want to spend the rest of her life seeing people's sparks, knowing who was going to die soon and who'd live for years. She'd finally found people who hugged her, and touched her, and didn't care about her skin. But now she'd always be terrified that she'd accidentally steal their sparks. The thought of spending the rest of her life that way made her choke on a sob.

There was a growl from the doorway and Aimee turned to see Jess. She couldn't fit her shoulders or wings through but she'd stuck her long neck into the room. Her yellow eyes were boring into Aimee and the tips of her feathers were quivering.

'Oh, Aimee.' Pelathina's face was so full of sympathy that Aimee had to look away in case she burst into tears.

Kyelli squeezed her hands. 'I wish I could tell you that you'd be stuck wearing the bracelet forever. That would be better.'

'Better? What the blazing sparks is that supposed to mean?' Nathine was wearing her angry face and the fact that she was mad on Aimee's behalf almost made the tears come. She bit her lip to keep them in.

'I said the bracelets are powered by sparks,' Kyelli continued. 'Not just when you take them off, or use them to create Empty Warriors, but continually.' She reached up to cup Aimee's face. 'I'm sorry, child, but the bracelet is drawing on your spark. It's slowly draining your life energy.'

'Oh, *yithansasis*, Aimee.' Pelathina clasped her hands to her mouth and there were tears in her eyes.

Nathine punched Aimee on the arm, hard enough that it hurt. 'Why did you have to go and put it on, idiot.'

'I…' Aimee felt like she couldn't breathe. 'How long?'

'I don't know for certain. A human has never worn one of our bracelets before, but I'd guess maybe a few months.'

She was dying. She couldn't feel it but in a few months her spark would be empty. Everyone was staring at her, waiting for her to say something. Their faces were full of pity, tinged with fear, and Aimee couldn't stand to look at them. All her life people had looked at her with pity or been afraid of what they saw. Now they were right to do so, and she hated them for it.

CHAPTER 8

SCREAMS AND DRAGONS

Pulling her hands from Kyelli's, she turned and ran. Jess moved as she did, backing out of the doorway. Aimee leapt into her saddle, and without needing any command Jess took off.

'Aimee!'

Someone yelled from below but Aimee ignored them. She needed space. She needed the openness of the sky and the wind in her face. She had no plan other than to get away. Jess soared above the town, catching a thermal and riding it higher and higher, until the buildings were tiny coloured blocks far below. The vineyards ran in green lines round the hills, and way off to the north Aimee could see the shimmer of a much larger river.

She screamed into the sky, letting everything from the last two days—all her worries, her fears, her hopes—pour out of her. Jess joined her, letting out a huge roar. She was probably scaring the people in the town below but she didn't care. When her scream petered out she took a deep breath and did it again. Then she swore. Every curse word she'd ever heard, even the ones Pelathina used that she didn't understand, she yelled them out into the sky.

They'd been drifting higher but now Aimee took control, pulling on Jess's spiralled horns and steering them downwards. She spotted a wildflower meadow on the slopes above the vineyards and guided Jess towards it. They landed but Aimee didn't dismount, instead she sat in her saddle looking out across the unfamiliar landscape. The scent of wildflowers was heavy in the air and bees buzzed everywhere, ignoring the dragon who'd landed amongst them.

'It's not fair, Jess,' she whispered. Jess snorted her agreement.

She spotted Malgerus and Skydance enter the sky and she tensed, but they didn't come after her. They must have seen her because they flew closer but circled in the air, not landing, giving her time but letting her know they were there if she needed them. That must have been Pelathina's suggestion because Nathine would never have the tact to give her space.

Aimee stroked the ruff of feathers around Jess's neck, their softness a wonderful contrast to the cool hardness of her scales. She could feel Jess's pleasure in her mind, almost like a purr along their connection.

'Jess, when the time comes you have to promise me you'll leave,' Aimee told her, trying to make her voice firm though she could feel it cracking at the edges.

Jess snorted a small puff of smoke that drifted up

into the sky.

'I mean it, Jess. When the energy in my spark runs out you have to fly far away. Do you understand?'

Aimee felt a pulse of love along their connection and didn't know what that meant. When Kyelli told her that the bracelet was killing her, Aimee's first thought had not been for herself and the life she wouldn't get to live. It had been for Jess. Without a Rider a dragon would once again become a wild creature. And a wild dragon was a danger and would be killed, the way Jara and Dyrenna had killed Ellana after she and Hayetta crashed on their first flight. Aimee didn't want Jess to suffer because her Rider had been an idiot and put on a bracelet she never should have touched.

This high on the slopes the wind was strong, and it buffeted Jess's wings. Aimee could feel her desire to take off again, to soar through the sky bursting apart clouds and swooping down to skim the river so the spray tickled her belly. Jess was still so young, so full of life.

Aimee looked down at the spark glowing brightly in her chest. It didn't look any dimmer than yesterday but if Kyelli was right, and she only had a few months left, then soon she'd start to see it fading. That thought squeezed her throat and for a moment she couldn't breathe. It took all her willpower to shove the panic back down. Maybe, when she could see that her spark was really dull, she and Jess could fly away, go somewhere very remote where no one would find them. Then when she was gone, Jess could live there.

'That's what we'll do, girl. You'll be alright.' Aimee

gave her a reassuring stroke on the top of her head.

Now that she had a plan for Jess she felt better. The enormity of losing her own life, all the things she'd never experience, kept nudging her brain but she shoved it firmly away. If she let those thoughts in, they'd break her. And right now she had to keep herself together because Kyelli needed her. She had to use the bracelet to find Pagrin, and though it scared her, Aimee would help. There was no way she could leave all the people in Kierell to die.

'Come on, Jess.'

Aimee squeezed gently with her knees and pushed on Jess's horns. They sprang from the meadow and into the sky. Nathine and Pelathina met her and together the three of them descended back to Kyelli's cottage. She was waiting for them in her garden and despite everything, she smiled as she watched the dragons land, even though Malgerus squashed her potato plants.

'I honestly never thought I'd see dragons again,' she said as Aimee dismounted. 'I thought I'd remembered how glorious their colours are but now I see how they had faded in my memory.'

'You did all those lovely paintings, didn't you?' Pelathina gestured at her cottage.

Kyelli nodded. 'I hated leaving my Riders and I wanted a way to still have dragons around me.'

While Aimee had been away Kyelli had changed from the long, striped skirt she'd been wearing into brown trousers and a pale blue shirt. She'd pulled her door closed but it was splintered at the hinges where

Pelathina and Nathine had kicked it in, and it wouldn't lock.

'I'm sorry about your door,' Pelathina apologised just as Aimee was about to. 'Will your cottage be alright left open?'

Kyelli waved away her concern. 'I doubt I shall be returning so if anyone from the town wants to help themselves then they are welcome too.'

'That's a bit pessimistic. I'm sure you'll be back,' Pelathina said with a smile.

When Kyelli threw her a look Aimee realised that she'd told the others that Kyelli only had one spark in her chest but not how little life remained in that spark. Kyelli didn't say anything so neither did Aimee, and Kyelli gave her the tiniest of nods. Kyelli had a backpack resting against her legs and she pulled a long black coat from it, slipping her arms inside and turning up the collar against her neck.

'That's a Rider's coat,' Nathine said.

It was a different cut to the one she wore but Aimee too had noticed the long slits up to Kyelli's hips that would allow her to climb into a saddle, and the deep pockets to hold goggles and a hat.

'What was your dragon called?' Pelathina asked.

'I never had a dragon, child,' Kyelli replied.

'What? But you founded the Riders so I always assumed you'd had a dragon.' Pelathina looked around at Aimee and Nathine. 'Did I misunderstand something when I was learning about the Riders?'

'No, I always assumed you'd had a dragon too,'

Nathine said.

Aimee nodded in agreement, though she realised not a single one of the statues or paintings of Kyelli in the city showed her with a dragon.

'Oh I wanted a dragon, I really did, but I couldn't bring myself to bond so deeply with a creature I knew I'd outlive. Especially because my heart was still hurting from losing so many of our people on Kierellatta.'

'So did you steal someone's coat?' Nathine asked.

'Nathine!' Aimee scolded her for being rude but Nathine just shrugged.

'This,' Kyelli said as she did up the buttons, 'belonged to Efysta. She was the first Sky Rider and a very good friend.'

Aimee remembered she was mentioned in Kyelli's diary.

'And she used to take me for rides on her dragon, Dream. His scales were the lightest blue, almost white and they glittered like snowflakes.'

'So you have flown before, that's good. I bet you've missed it?' Pelathina's eyes were glittering with excitement and Skydance was hopping from foot to foot. Both were keen to get back into the sky.

'I have.' Kyelli picked up her backpack, slung it on and stepped towards Aimee. 'It's a big thing, letting someone else ride your dragon with you, and I'd be honoured if you would let me.'

Aimee fumbled for a moment, not sure what to say. Of course Kyelli would need to come with them back to Kierell and obviously that meant flying, but Aimee hadn't considered what it would be like to offer her a lift. What if Jess hated it and Aimee couldn't keep her under control? What if she dumped Kyelli off into the sky?

Aimee turned to look at Jess but her dragon was staring intently at Kyelli, then slowly Jess lowered her head.

'May I?' Kyelli asked but she was already moving, reaching out a hand to place it gently on Jess's forehead. Aimee was sure she was about to get her arm bitten off but Jess didn't move. Back in her first days of training Jara had told her that you could never touch another Rider's dragon but Aimee heard a low rumble of pleasure as Kyelli stroked Jess's head.

'The dragons sense something in me, perhaps the weight of centuries, I don't know, but they've always been calm around me,' Kyelli said and she stepped back, giving Jess a small nod.

'Okay,' Aimee said but she was nervous about this and felt she had to explain now in case something went wrong. 'Jess is still young and we've only been bonded for a few months.'

Kyelli looked surprised. 'I can tell she's young but you both act like you've been bonded for far longer. You must have an extremely strong connection.'

'I...' Aimee floundered. She'd just been given a compliment by Kyelli. She'd always dreamed of a moment like this and it had sneaked up on her and happened without her even realising. She felt a blush warm her cheeks and quickly busied herself rearranging her saddlebags so Kyelli wouldn't see.

It was going to be a squeeze with both of them on the one saddle, but dragon saddles were larger than those for horses and with the saddlebags mostly out of the way they'd both fit. Kyelli stepped up beside her.

'I know she's the only female dragon here, and it might make more sense for one of the larger males to carry two people, but between you and me, I've always thought the females were actually stronger.' Kyelli gave her a quick smile and a wink.

Aimee felt she had to explain something else before they were pressed together on Jess's back. 'You won't catch anything from my skin, it just looks a bit odd. I'm not infectious or anything.'

To Aimee's surprise Kyelli cupped the colourless half of her face. 'Oh child, I never for a moment thought you were. Living as long as I have, I've seen all sorts of faces and yours is far from the strangest.' Kyelli looked down at the bracelet on Aimee's wrist then back up at her face. 'If you had more sparks...' She let her words trail off and shook her head.

Aimee wanted to ask what she'd been going to say but Kyelli grabbed the cantle and pommel of Jess's saddle.

'Do you need a boost up?' Aimee asked quickly.

'Stronger than I look, remember.'

And Kyelli pulled herself up, slung a leg over and was seated on the saddle a moment later. Aimee was impressed—it had taken her weeks to master that. She carefully jumped up too and seated herself in front of

Kyelli. She could feel Kyelli pressed right up against her back, her thighs around Aimee's hips and her breath on the back of Aimee's neck. For a moment she couldn't quite believe this was happening. Kyelli, *the* Kyelli, was sitting on her dragon with her arms wrapped around her waist. She wished she could travel back in time to her childhood and show little Aimee this image.

She pulled her flying goggles from her pocket, and as she slipped them on she felt bad that she didn't have a spare pair to offer Kyelli. She could hide behind her if the wind got too strong.

'Okay Jess, let's go home, girl,' Aimee said softly.

She heard Kyelli's sharp intake of breath as they took off. Skydance and Malgerus pulled away from them, the extra weight meaning it took Jess longer to find her rhythm and reach the higher sky.

'I'll miss being here,' Kyelli said as they swept over the tall colourful buildings of Vorthens.

Aimee would miss it too, not because she knew the place but because now she never would. She wouldn't get the chance to come back here and explore, to see those machines at the docks close up, or learn to speak Glavic. She shoved that thought aside and focused on flying.

Aimee and Jess had developed a balance when they were flying but that was all thrown off with Kyelli on board too. The older woman hadn't learned to shift her weight as Jess rode the sky, using the thermals, skimming through currents of air, and it made them slower. Still, Jess hadn't freaked out and tipped her off, so

Aimee counted that as a win.

Malgerus had shot ahead, his large orange wings easily eating up the distance. Skydance stuck closer to Jess but he didn't fly straight, he swooped back and forth, cutting circles in the air. He looked so playful, and Aimee wished she and Jess could join in.

Now that they were together just the two of them, Aimee felt like she had five hundred questions she wanted to ask Kyelli and was trying to decide which one to start with. She glanced over her shoulder. Kyelli was beaming, eyes open wide drinking in the view from the sky. Aimee decided to let her enjoy it. Her questions could wait.

CHAPTER 9

BEGIN TO LEARN

THEY FLEW STEADILY for hours, the landscape of hills turning back into the wide open tundra. Malgerus led the whole time, Jess trailing behind and Skydance swooping back and forth between the two. When they'd set off Jess had been eager to get back into the sky but now Aimee could feel her exhaustion. She worried she was pushing her dragon too hard.

When the sky turned pink and gold, Pelathina headed downwards. Aimee and Nathine followed, landing beside Skydance on the tussocky grass.

'Great, bogs again,' Nathine complained as she dismounted and landed with a squelch.

'If anything can bring me down from the high after Kyelli's coffee, I think it's bogs.' Pelathina wrinkled her nose as she looked around.

Aimee, careful not to kick Kyelli, dismounted too. 'I thought you were always happy. Isn't that your mantra?' Aimee said.

'I definitely try but ugh, bogs.' But despite complaining Pelathina still threw Aimee a smile and laughed.

Aimee felt her mouth twitch in response but a full smile wouldn't come.

'I hope you haven't stopped because of me,' Kyelli said. Aimee noticed she dismounted a lot more stiffly than she'd mounted.

'We need to let the dragons rest for a few hours or they're going to drop from the sky. I can feel how tired Skydance is so Jess and Malgerus must be exhausted,' Pelathina said.

Aimee glanced at Nathine, waiting for some bravado about never feeling weary, but instead she stroked Malgerus's neck and nodded. Aimee knew they needed to rest but she could feel the panic rising in her at the delay.

'What if the army has broken through into the city already?' she asked, looking around at the others.

Pelathina was quick to shake her head. 'We've been gone too long. They'll have collapsed the tunnel by now.'

'How can you be sure?' Aimee asked.

The other girl stepped over and placed her hands gently on Aimee's shoulders. 'I can't, but thinking the worst won't help us. Have faith in Jara and our friends. They'll have done what they could to buy us more time and to protect the city. And by now, that means collapsing the tunnel.'

Pelathina was right and Aimee realised that if she'd stopped to think about it, she would have known that.

But she'd never had friends to rely on before. It was a strange, but welcome realisation. So she encouraged Jess to lie down in the long grass. To her surprise Malgerus and Skydance curled up right beside her. Malgerus snapped at her playfully and Skydance flicked her with his tail. It seemed Aimee wasn't the only one needing some comfort tonight.

'I can take first watch,' Pelathina offered.

'No, you two should sleep,' Kyelli disagreed, pointing at Pelathina and Nathine. 'Aimee and I will keep watch.' She turned to Aimee. 'I would like months to teach you properly but we don't have the time, so I'll teach you what I can about the bracelet as quickly as I can. I hope you're a fast learner.'

Nathine shrugged and pulled out her blankets. Pelathina looked like she might argue but instead she too settled down. Aimee could see both girls' eyes though, open and shining in the last light of the sunset. She felt an unexpected surge of love for them both, for staying awake and watching out for her.

Kyelli pulled a patchwork blanket from her backpack, spread it on the grass and invited Aimee to sit beside her. About a minute after sitting down Aimee could feel damp seeping through, making her bum wet.

'So—' Kyelli began but Aimee spoke at the same time cutting her off.

'I'm scared,' she blurted out.

Kyelli took one of her hands in both of hers. 'I had this idea when I created the Sky Riders that they'd be the bravest girls. That people would look up to them and feel safe because they knew these amazing women were there to protect them.' Kyelli ran a finger across Aimee's patchy knuckles. 'I'm glad I stayed in the city long enough to see it happen but I couldn't help wondering what had become of my Riders after I left. News doesn't really make it from Kierell to the north. Then I met you today and in a few short hours you've demonstrated every quality I hoped my Riders would have.'

Aimee blinked. This praise, from Kyelli herself, was the most amazing thing she could ever have imagined happening. Why did it have to come on the same day that she discovered the stupid bracelet stuck on her wrist was killing her?

'I didn't put on the bracelet because I was brave,' Aimee admitted. 'I put it on because I was upset that we'd found it and not you. I wanted to somehow feel closer to you, and less like I'd failed.'

The Aimee of a few months ago would have been appalled at the idea of admitting weakness to the amazing Kyelli but to the Aimee of now it didn't seem such a big deal. Not even with Nathine and Pelathina feigning sleep and listening in.

'Do you have someone back in the city who's proud of you?' Kyelli asked. 'Your parents? Or a lover?'

Aimee shook her head. 'My parents died when I was a baby. I was raised by my aunt and uncle until they were taken by a sickness. And…'

Her words trailed off as her thoughts turned to Lyrria. She'd never acted like she'd been proud of

Aimee. Any time she'd done well when they were training, Lyrria had always told her that it was because she was such a great teacher. In the darkness her eyes slid over to Pelathina. Could she be someone who was proud of her?

'I have friends,' Aimee finally said, and the joy of saying that eclipsed the sorrow that her family weren't around to see her.

'Good. And from what I can see you haven't failed,' Kyelli said.

'When I first put on the bracelet I didn't know what it could do and I almost accidentally killed Jara. She's our leader,' Aimee told her. 'And then I thought you were the Master of Sparks and I had to kill you to save Kierell. But then when I tried to deliberately use the bracelet I nearly killed Petra.'

What she didn't say was that since Petra she could feel the power of the bracelet constantly tugging at her mind, demanding to be used again. It was less insistent when the dial was set to neutral but Aimee worried what would happen if she gave in to that power. They were sitting side by side but Kyelli was taller and Aimee had to tilt her head to look into her face.

'I've no idea what I'm doing,' she admitted.

'That's life, child. No one knows what they're doing. You make mistakes and you figure it out as you go. There isn't someone out there who's better than you at everything you're trying to do. They might be more skilled at pretending they know what they're doing, but I like your honesty.'

Aimee wasn't convinced. 'You seem to know what you're doing.'

'Well, I am six hundred and twenty-four. I've gotten very good at shrugging off my mistakes and moving on.'

Aimee took a deep breath. She couldn't pass this responsibility to anyone else, so it was time to own it.

'What do I need to learn?' Aimee pulled back the cuff of her coat. She held the bracelet close to her chest, so the glow of her spark lit its engraved surface. 'Do I need to learn to read what's written on it?'

'No. Quorentin is quite a complicated language to learn, it's got almost twenty different tenses, and what's engraved there is mostly just a reminder to use the bracelet responsibly. I think you've understood that already. What you need to learn is something completely new, something even I can't do. It's a theory I have but I'm fairly certain it'll work.'

'What do you mean?' A knot of worry tied itself in Aimee's stomach. She thought Kyelli was going to give her lessons, like Lyrria showing them flying techniques they could copy.

'You are unique, though I'm sure you've been told that before, but I don't mean your face.'

'Freaky was more the word people used rather than unique,' Aimee said wryly.

'Trust me, six hundred years teaches you that most people are fools. I mean you're unique because of your bond with Jess.'

'But all—' Aimee began till she caught the look from Kyelli, the one that told her to stop interrupting with questions.

'The Quorelle who wore these bracelets didn't have the connection you have with your dragon,' Kyelli explained. 'With the bracelet on you can see people's sparks, yes?'

Aimee nodded and couldn't help looking across the shadow-draped heather to where Nathine and Pelathina were curled up, still eavesdropping. Even through the thick wool of their blankets Aimee could see the white-green glow of their sparks.

'As you know, a spark is a person's life force, it's their energy. But when you formed a connection with Jess you used your energy to do that.' Kyelli must have felt Aimee flinch at this because her next words came quickly. 'I don't mean your connection is using up your energy, not like the bracelet is. Jess isn't draining your spark. But you used a tiny chip of your life force to open that door in your mind, to let Jess inside. And as long as the connection exists between you, that tiny chip of energy will be there.'

Aimee thought about that for a moment. It made sense. She touched her connection with Jess and imagined the door in her mind glowing with the light of a tiny spark. The image made her smile. Looking over she saw Jess was watching her. Then she realised both Nathine and Pelathina had silently sat up, blankets around their shoulders, listening.

Kyelli hadn't said anything else and Aimee wondered if she was supposed to understand what this meant. She was very aware that she wasn't as clever as a scholar like Callant, or Pelathina with her four languages.

'I don't understand,' she admitted.

'If you can see sparks, then I think you should be able to also see the connections between Riders and their dragons. And then, if you can see that, it proves my theory and we can use it to find Pagrin.'

'How?' asked the dark huddle that was Pelathina.

'Because a master and his or her Empty Warriors are linked by the sparks used to create them. If Aimee can see the connection flowing between Riders and dragons, then she should be able to see the same flowing from the Empty Warriors to Pagrin.'

'Then if we can find him, we can stop him,' Nathine said fiercely.

Aimee thought of Kyelli crying on her cottage floor when she discovered her brother was still alive. Now they were discussing a way to kill him.

'Once we find Pagrin the only way to stop his Empty Warriors is for me to drain his sparks, isn't it?' Aimee asked.

'Yes,' Kyelli answered quickly and firmly.

'But he's your brother.'

'He was and it broke my heart when I thought we'd lost him. But he's created monsters and I can't let what happened on Kierellatta happen here too.'

Kyelli must have caught the look of concern on Aimee's face because she nodded in acknowledgement of it.

'I know that must seem cold to you, and it will crack

my heart all over again to kill Pagrin,' Kyelli admitted. 'I said earlier that even at six hundred years old I still feel every emotion as strong as I always did, but one advantage of time is that you learn not to dwell on decisions. It was a very long time ago but I remember my first century when I would feel the swirl of a dozen emotions at once, especially when I had to make a decision.'

Aimee was envious of that, thinking it must be nice to always be sure of yourself.

'And, when we find Pagrin, we can also save Aimee,' Kyelli added.

Aimee stared at her but it was Pelathina who asked, 'How?'

'If Aimee has another spark inside her she can sacrifice that energy to take off the bracelet,' Kyelli explained. 'But the only other person in the whole world with sparks to spare is Pagrin. Aimee can use the bracelet to steal a spark from him.'

Even in the dark Aimee could see how Pelathina's eyes lit up at this. 'Now we have two reasons to find him.'

'Double determination, Aimee,' Nathine said with a wry smile.

At Kyelli's words a tiny flame of hope sprang to life inside her. Aimee imagined cupping her hands over it, keeping it small but also sheltering it. They had to find Pagrin to save the city, that was her first mission. But if she could also save herself…

She had to learn how to do this. She looked down at

the spark in her own chest then over to Jess. There was nothing between them but heather, bog and darkness. She could feel their bond in her mind but there was nothing visible showing they were linked.

'I can't see it,' she said, trying to keep the edge of panic out of her voice.

'It's not going to happen just like that, you're going to have to work at it,' Kyelli told her.

'But how long will it take me to learn?'

'I don't know, no one's ever done this before. But I'd suggest you work hard to learn pretty damn quick.'

Aimee spent the next few hours trying to see her bond with Jess. She stared at her spark intently then flicked her eyes over to Jess. Nothing. She closed her eyes and visualised what she thought it might look like—a wiggly line between them, emerald green like Jess's scales—then snapped open her eyes and stared at Jess. Still nothing. She waved the bracelet around in the air, trying to see the energy it was using. Nothing.

Then she did spot something but it wasn't in the air between her and Jess, it was hovering to the west of them. Aimee squinted at the four lights moving through the darkness, bouncing rhythmically, until she realised what she was seeing. They were sparks, and they were too high off the ground to be human.

'Helvethi,' Aimee whispered as a prickle of fear ran down her spine. In the darkness there was no way to tell which tribe the centaurs were from. And this far from Kierell, they could easily be from one of the tribes who still saw the city's people as interlopers on their land.

The others stirred. Her whisper hadn't woken them but their dragons had—Skydance and Malgerus were both on high alert, snouts reaching upwards, scenting the air. Pelathina threw her a silent questioning look, and Nathine opened her mouth to demand to know what was going on. Aimee quickly waved her to silence and pointed.

She watched the bobbing sparks, willing them away. She clutched the tussocky grass, sinking her fingers into its dampness as the four sparks moved closer. But they turned to the north and a few minutes later they'd vanished back into the night.

As the dragons settled down again, Aimee noticed Kyelli staring off across the tundra after the Helvethi.

'I always hoped that, after I left, Kierell would find peace with the Helvethi,' she said softly, more to herself than anyone. 'But I only ever saw a few caravans make it as far as Vorthens so I knew it hadn't happened.'

Aimee felt bad. Jara and the council had been on the verge of forging a peace with three of the tribes until she'd found the Empty Warriors and forced them back to the city, abandoning the peace meeting. Even though they'd all have been killed if they'd stayed out on the tundra, Aimee still felt she had to somehow make up for her part in forcing them to turn back.

They settled back down, though this time Pelathina did keep watch. Aimee went back to trying, unsuccessfully, to see her bond with Jess, growing more and more frustrated when nothing happened. Jess fell asleep which meant at least she was rested when, in the middle of the night, Pelathina said they should get moving again.

CHAPTER 10

TEMPTATION

As THEY WERE packing up Pelathina appeared beside her. It was the darkest point of the night but the soft glow of Pelathina's spark lit her face, and Aimee could clearly see the concern in her dark eyes.

'How are you doing with all this?' Her fingertips brushed Aimee's. With an effort Aimee stopped herself from jerking away.

'I'm fine,' Aimee lied.

There was a flash of white teeth as Pelathina smiled. 'We'll find a way to get that bracelet off you.'

Aimee didn't share her optimism but she was grateful to Pelathina for trying. Slowly, Pelathina intwined her fingers with Aimee's. The warmth of her hand sent tingles up Aimee's arm and down into her stomach.

'Don't keep all the anger and sadness inside you,' Pelathina said. 'It'll twist you up, hurting you, and Jess.'

'Easy for you, you don't feel any anger do you? You're super happy all the time.' Aimee didn't mean to snap and the moment the words were out of her mouth she regretted them. But Pelathina didn't storm off and she didn't throw back an insult of her own like Nathine would have done.

'I do feel anger, and all the other upsetting emotions,' she said softly. 'Yesterday I was furious at the Quorolle for their arrogance. I hated them for making those bracelets that granted them even more power above us normal people. And I was angry at Kyelli for leaving hers behind where some unknowing girl with too big a heart could find it and put it on.'

She took a step closer and Aimee didn't stop her when she gently brushed a curl of hair off her forehead.

'But I don't hold on to my anger. When I'm in the sky I let it flow out of me. I always think if I could see it, it would look like a dirty grey raincloud, and I always avoid those.' She gave a pretend shiver. 'All the bad emotions, they come, you can't stop that but don't let them take up the space in your heart. If you do there will be no room for the good ones.' Pelathina leaned back and smiled at Aimee. 'And those are the ones that make it all worthwhile.'

Looking at Pelathina, all the what-ifs of a life she'd never have suddenly flooded Aimee's mind. She might just have time to learn Pelathina's story, and maybe go to that bakery together and share cheese rolls warm from the oven. But she didn't have enough time left to find out if Pelathina wanted to be her friend or something more. The bracelet would kill her first.

She gasped as the unfairness of it hit her like a punch to the heart. She felt like the sudden grief might pick her up and wash her away. Jess had appeared beside her and she pressed her palm hard against her dragon's cool scales. With her other hand she grabbed Pelathina's and squeezed. Pelathina didn't say anything and Aimee didn't need her to, she just needed her to be there. The three of them, Aimee, Jess and Pelathina stood like that for a long moment, until Aimee had shoved all the pain into a box at the back of her mind and firmly closed the lid. It wasn't quite what Pelathina had advised her to try but it would have to do for now.

'I'm alright,' Aimee said and this time it was slightly less of a lie.

Pelathina nodded. 'Okay, but when it gets too much, I'm here.' She gave Aimee's hand a squeeze in return. 'And I'm sorry but we need to get going. I know it's still dark but it'll be light in an hour or so. It's midsummer.'

'It is? Oh.'

In the chaos of the last few days Aimee hadn't realised it was midsummer already. It was the longest, lightest day of the year, but it was also her birthday. It was her first one as a Rider and her first without her aunt and uncle. Gyron had made her a carved wooden card every year and Aimee had kept them all in a little box in her room. Another thing she lost when she was kicked out of her home. She felt tears sting her eyes and tilted her head back to stop them from falling.

'What's up?'

'I'm eighteen today,' she told Pelathina.

The other girl's face lit up. 'Really? Oh, okay hang

on.'

Aimee watched confused as Pelathina glanced around for a moment, then skipped over the tussocky grass to a patch of heather. When she bounded back she had a sprig of purple flowers which she carefully stuck through the buttonhole on the lapel of Aimee's coat.

'Now, you have to imagine that we're back in the city and these are actually the biggest bunch of flowers you've ever seen. And that I bought you a humongous cake for breakfast, with strawberries.' She pulled back and smiled at Aimee, the glow from her spark catching on her cute dimples.

For a moment Aimee thought she would lose the fight against her tears but she held it together. Then Nathine appeared and interrupted in typical Nathine style.

'I know you're having some sort of moment but Kierell still needs saving so get your bums back in your saddles.' She followed this with a sharp whistle.

'Who put her in charge?' Pelathina asked, deliberately loud enough for Nathine to hear.

Nathine stuck her tongue out as she mounted up. Aimee let Kyelli get into their shared saddle first then she wriggled herself in too. A few minutes later and they were all back in the sky. The thick blanket of night still lay over the tundra, rumpled by the low hills. The wind was light, and the rhythmic flap of the dragons' wings carried across the sky. Clouds drifted above them, their puffy edges highlighted in silver moonlight.

Surreptitiously, Aimee bent her head to inhale the

sweet, mossy scent of the sprig of heather Pelathina had given her. She'd grown bored of seeing miles and miles of heather but now the little purple flowers made her think of Pelathina's smile, and the warm feel of her dark fingers wrapped around her own.

It was a dream, her and Pelathina, because time was running out and Aimee could only save herself if she got the bracelet to work. But for now, she let herself enjoy that dream like it was the last biscuit in the jar.

As they flew through the night Aimee loosened her hold over Jess, just a little, leaving her to follow Malgerus while she tried and tried to see their connection. She couldn't make it work. She could feel their connection easily—it was always there, a part of her insides that she could feel but not see, like her heart or her lungs. And she knew Nathine and Pelathina had similar bonds, but when she looked across the sky at them all she could see was the soft glow of their sparks.

'What's it supposed to look like?' Aimee asked, struggling to keep the exasperation from her voice.

Kyelli didn't need to ask what she meant. 'I don't know, and I'm sorry that I don't have the answers for you. No one has ever seen these connections before. All I ever saw when I wore the bracelet was people's sparks. I never thought to look for the other types of energies we have and share.'

Aimee squeezed her eyelids shut, concentrated hard on her bond with Jess, then snapped her eyes open. Nothing. She sighed.

'I am sorry this has fallen on you, child,' Kyelli continued. 'I wish I'd left myself more sparks, and then I could have given you one of mine and you could have taken off that bracelet.'

'Why do you only have one spark left?'

Aimee wished that she'd found Kyelli at a time when Kierell wasn't in imminent danger of being destroyed. They could have sat in the dining cavern in Anteill, clusters of dragon's breath orbs glowing above them, and Riders gathered on the benches all around. Kyelli could have told her story to everyone, and all those women who'd been inspired by her would have had the chance to meet her properly.

'I don't know how many sparks I had left when I finally decided to leave Kierell,' Kyelli began. 'I'd been watching the city grow and I was proud by how much our survivors and their descendants had built in only two hundred years. My father and I disagreed on one major thing, however. He wanted to keep everyone inside the mountains where he knew they'd always be safe. There was a natural tunnel through the mountains under Norwen Peak and we'd widened and strengthened it to allow caravans though and out into the world. But my father was overprotective and he always wanted to close the tunnel, keep everyone inside and safe.'

Kyelli's voice had taken on a nostalgic tone as she remembered the beginnings of Aimee's city. She wished Callant was here. This was much better than any of his stuffy history books.

'Back in Kierellatta our city, Vienthon, had links to all three of the other kingdoms,' Kyelli continued.

'Merchants came to trade; scholars came to our university; people with different foods, and ideas, and languages all came and mingled in our city. And our citizens travelled elsewhere and could live a different life if they chose. And I wanted that for Kierell. I didn't want ours to be an isolated city forever limited by our own ideas, never with the injection of something new.

'After my father died, I encouraged more caravans to venture across the tundra. I knew there were prowlers and the Helvethi had always resented our incursions across their land, but I was confident my Riders could protect our merchants. And of course they did, but even my Riders couldn't save everyone and we lost caravans. We lost Riders too and that always broke my heart. Then…'

Kyelli's words broke off but Aimee knew better than to interrupt. The sky was lightening in the east to a pale blue streaked with soft pink. In the burgeoning light Aimee looked down at Kyelli's hands clasped around her waist. Her knuckles were white as she squeezed her fingers together and Aimee didn't think it was fear of falling off Jess that was making her hold on so tight.

'I could feel the desire rising in me,' Kyelli finally continued. 'I began thinking that I could maybe create a few Empty Warriors just as extra guards for the caravans. I could imbue them with the purpose to protect. The first few times I caught my mind thinking along those lines I was disgusted with myself. But then another caravan would be attacked by Helvethi and the idea grew more tempting. So that's when I knew it wasn't safe for the city if I stayed in Kierell.'

Aimee understood the words Kyelli was saying but she didn't understand the feeling behind them. The moment she'd realised what the bracelet could do she'd wanted it off her wrist. She hated the power and knowledge it gave her over other people's lives. She hated the way she could feel it, just outside her conscious thought, full of the desire to be used. She didn't think she'd ever be tempted to use it to create monsters, or mindless slaves, even if she had enough sparks to do so.

Then a horrible thought occurred to her. 'What did you do with all your sparks?' she asked, half dreading the answer in case Kyelli told her there were hundreds of Empty Warriors sitting dormant, hidden somewhere inside the city.

'I disguised myself and left with a caravan heading north. It was only going to Lorsoke so from there I continued alone. I'd travelled a little during Kierell's first century and I remembered the tiny village of Vorthens surrounded by a few small vineyards. Perched on the slopes of those green hills I knew I could make a peaceful life there.'

'And your sparks?' Aimee prompted.

'I bled them out of me. Not all at once, but slowly. Over the course of a year I would cut myself and bleed out some of my sparks into the rich soil of the hillsides.'

That sounded a bit gruesome but was something Aimee could understand. She'd have wanted rid of the power of sparks too.

'But then, what happened to the energy from your sparks?' she asked.

Kyelli had her face resting on Aimee's shoulder and Aimee felt her smile. 'I gave my energy to the land. And it flourished. Why do you think Vorthens is the towns of vines, so famous for its vineyards and wines that even isolated Kierell has heard of it?'

Aimee screwed up her face. 'Eww! The wine is so good because it's made from your blood?'

Kyelli laughed, the sound muffled by Aimee's coat. 'I suppose indirectly. But no, I meant that my energy enriched the land.'

Aimee understood, but she still filed away the thought to wind up Nathine with. She'd love to get disgusted over the idea of immortal blood wine.

'How many sparks did you leave yourself with?' Aimee asked.

She felt Kyelli shrug. 'I'm not sure. I didn't have my bracelet any more so I couldn't see them, but it's been over one hundred years since I left Kierell so I must have had maybe three left if what you've said is true.'

'What did I say?'

'That you can only see one spark in me now.'

Aimee was horrified. 'You didn't know you're down to your last one?'

'Not until today.'

'Oh sparks, I'm so sorry.'

Aimee had done what she'd feared doing—told someone how much life they had left.

'Don't be, at least now I know.'

Aimee thought Kyelli had taken the news and hidden the shock very well, but not everyone would. She dreaded someone with a weak spark asking her what she could see. Kyelli had had over six hundred years of life so maybe it wasn't so scary for her to know she was burning through her final spark. But someone who'd had maybe only thirty or forty years? Would they want to know they wouldn't have the same again? Aimee wondered if she could erase the knowledge that the bracelet was killing her, would she want to? She didn't know and her head hurt thinking about it.

Kyelli had fallen silent, perhaps lost in memories. The sky had settled to pale blue all around them though it was still very early. The dark mass of the Ardnanlich Forest appeared on the horizon to their left, and below them hundreds of tiny streams wiggled and glittered across the landscape. It was beautiful in a wild, unknowable way.

They continued their flight in silence. As the hours wore on Jess gradually slowed until Malgerus became an orange dot way ahead of them. Skydance had been flying between the two and Pelathina went ahead to tell Nathine to wait. By the time Jess caught up to them, Malgerus and Skydance were both flying steady circles in the air. Aimee expected a sarcastic comment from Nathine about her tardiness but instead Nathine pulled something from her pocket. Then without warning she tossed it across the sky to Aimee.

'Argh!' Aimee got a hand off Jess's horns just in time for the object to bounce off her fingers and tumble down to land somewhere in the grass below.

'I can't believe you dropped it!' Nathine exclaimed.

'You could have warned me you were going to throw it,' Aimee spluttered. 'What was it?'

'It was the last of the fruit tarts I bought from the cottage. I'd been saving it, but your stupid face looked so tired I thought I'd be nice and give it to you.'

'I've been robbed by a grumpy child?' Kyelli asked, but not seriously, there was a playful note in her voice.

'Well, they'd have gone all mouldy if we'd left them,' Nathine pointed out.

'Sorry. Thank you.'

Nathine waved off Aimee's apology with a 'Pff' and pointed Malgerus south again. Pelathina looked like she could barely keep her laughter from bursting out, and shook her head at Nathine's back. They continued flying but together this time. Aimee could see how often Nathine had to pull on Malgerus's horns, slowing his speed. After another hour the dark jagged line of the Ring Mountains appeared on the horizon.

Aimee wished she could magic away the remainder of the distance and be back already. By the time they reached Kierell they'd have been gone two days. A hundred terrible things could have happened in two days. She really hoped Pelathina was right and that the council had collapsed the tunnel. It wouldn't get rid of the army but it would buy them some time.

That thought made Aimee have another go at trying to see her connection with Jess. After ten minutes she had to bite the inside of her cheek to stop herself from screaming with frustration. Maybe focusing on herself was too hard. She was looking for a physical sign of her link to Jess but she couldn't help looking internally at their connection. So instead she looked at Nathine and Malgerus flying just ahead and to the left of them. Nathine had put her hat on for flying through the cold of night but as Aimee watched she tugged it off and stuffed it in her coat pocket. She seemed so much more at ease with flying than Aimee did.

Aimee let her eyes unfocus, and Nathine and Malgerus become a black and orange blur. Trying not to think about it too hard she looked for something linking Rider and dragon, something flowing between them. She stared until her eyes hurt and she was forced to blink. There was nothing, just Nathine's spark glowing in her chest, pulsing faintly with her heartbeat.

'What are you staring at, mushroom head?' Nathine called over.

'I was just admiring what an amazing Rider you are,' she shouted back.

'Damn right I am.' Nathine grinned, her eyes looking slightly bulgy behind the lens of her goggles.

'Mushroom head?' Kyelli asked.

'Apparently my short hair makes my head look like a mushroom,' Aimee explained.

'I think it makes you look cute,' Pelathina added.

Aimee was glad Kyelli was behind her and couldn't see the blush spreading up her cheeks. But all she had to do was think of the bracelet draining her spark and the heat disappeared from her face.

They fell into silence again as the peaks of the Ring Mountains grew out of the horizon. Aimee felt Kyelli tense the closer they got and that wasn't helping calm her own fears. What would they find? She really, really hoped they weren't too late.

CHAPTER 11

FIRE AND IRON

FINALLY THEY REACHED the isthmus at the edge of the tundra, the familiar sight of the Ring Mountains welcoming them back. Aimee was too nervous to enjoy being home.

'Sparks,' Kyelli swore as they flew high over the army of Empty Warriors. 'There are thousands of them. Oh Pagrin, why did you do this?'

Aimee wanted to push Jess for more speed but she could feel her dragon's exhaustion. Over the last hour her wingbeats had slowed and she soared any chance she could get, using every thermal she could find.

'We're almost home, girl. You're doing so well,' Aimee encouraged her.

The Ring Mountains rose above them, their peaks looking even higher than they had when Aimee made the climb. She tried to send Jess what strength she could through their connection and pushed her for just a little more speed, a little more height, enough to get them over the mountains.

'Go on, don't let Mal beat you,' Aimee whispered.

They rose above Lookout Ledge where Lwena had died and finally Aimee could see the steep-sided gully beside the bulk of Norwen Peak.

Then Jess's wings stuttered. They flapped down and it was like she didn't have the strength to bring them up again. For a terrifying moment they hung motionless in the air above the army.

'Jess, come on, you can do it, just a little bit further.' Aimee's voice was rushed and panicky. Kyelli squeezed her so tightly it felt like she might crack a rib.

Jess's wings rose, slowly, the tips fluttering.

'That's it, girl.'

She managed three more wingbeats. They were still above the army when she stuttered again, simply too tired to keep flying. Jess growled, a low rumble, almost like an apology. Then her head drooped. A few more seconds and they'd tumble from the sky into the Empty Warriors.

'Aimee!' Pelathina yelled.

Skydance swooped underneath them in a flash of sapphire blue. Aimee and Kyelli bounced in their saddle as Skydance nudged Jess from below. Then he swept up and round them and did it again.

'Nathine!' Pelathina yelled.

'I'm on it!'

She guided Malgerus underneath Jess right behind Skydance. This time there were two bumps as both dragons nudged Jess up, keeping her in the sky, keeping her gliding. Jess seemed to realise the other dragons were helping her and she managed a few slow flaps of her wings. It was enough. To Aimee's huge relief they passed over the outer slopes of the mountains and slipped between the peaks.

Jess had brought her head back up and Aimee saw her nostrils flare, and when they did she put what little power she had left into her wingbeats. She could smell the city, she knew they were almost home. Aimee sent a pulse of affection through their bond.

It had taken them all day to fly back across the tundra and evening was pulling in around them, making shadows of the peaks on either side. High above Aimee could see the top of Norwen Peak, still thick with snow. Her heart raced and her stomach churned at the thought of what she might see when they emerged above the city. Her mind conjured horrible images of buildings on fire, bodies in the streets, and dragons slain. Kyelli had fallen silent and Aimee couldn't tell what she thought about seeing her city again.

The end of the gully appeared and Aimee half closed her eyes, wanting to see but also not. The sounds hit her first—shouts, the clang of weapons and a dragon's roar. The noise increased as someone spotted the three dragons emerging from amongst the peaks. Aimee scanned the caravan compound and was hugely relieved to see no dead bodies and no Empty Warriors, but it was full of people, both city guards in their colourful patchwork cloaks and Riders in their black coats.

She guided Jess over to the back of the compound, Malgerus and Skydance following. The moment Jess's talons clacked down on the flagstones, she collapsed. Aimee and Kyelli jumped from the saddle and Aimee dropped to the ground beside her dragon. She lifted Jess's head onto her lap and stroked her long snout.

'You did it, girl. We're home.' She leaned her head down towards Jess's. 'You are the best dragon in the whole world.'

'Aimee!'

Jara's voice rang out over the noise and a moment later she was there, elbowing through a troop of city guards. She skidded, lost her footing and ended up crouched in front of Aimee.

Aimee was shocked to see the difference in Jara. Her flyaway blonde hair was limp and greasy, pulled back into a hasty ponytail. The bags under her eyes looked like bruises and as she grabbed her arm, Aimee couldn't help noticing that Jara smelled like she hadn't washed since Aimee left.

'What happened? They're not dead, they're still coming.'

Aimee knew who she meant and then she realised she could hear the battering ram, still. She jumped to her feet, dragging Jara up with her. She had to clamber onto an abandoned crate to see over the lines of guards in the compound. The gate to the tunnel was still there and even as she watched it shook with the force of the battering ram.

'You didn't collapse the tunnel?' Aimee asked, horrified. She could hardly believe the gate had held this long.

'We're just about to do it,' Jara responded and there was no anger in her voice. The fact that she was resigned to this now told Aimee how desperate Jara was.

'Aimee!' Jara grabbed her sleeve, pulling her back down off the crate. 'What happened? Who's this?' She noticed Kyelli and jabbed a long finger at her.

'She's Kyelli.' Jara's eyebrows shot up. 'It's a long story, but she's not the Master of Sparks, we were wrong about that,' Aimee told her.

Jara thought for a moment, tried to run her fingers through her hair, realised it was tied back and grunted in annoyance. 'Okay, it can wait. Since you're here you can help, all of you.' She spun around to take in Nathine and Pelathina too.

Aimee was as exhausted as Jess. All she wanted to do was curl up in a corner and sleep, but she nodded to Jara. 'What do you need us to do?'

'We waited as long as we could but they're going to break through that gate any moment so we're collapsing the tunnel on them,' Jara explained.

Aimee looked around and properly took in what she was seeing for the first time. The buildings that had housed the caravan wagons had been dismantled and their timbers used to create a curved barricade around the tunnel gate. It looked a lot more formidable than the hastily erected barrier of boxes and crates that had been thrown up before. The space in front of the barricade had been cleared and beyond it the gate shuddered with the force of the battering ram.

Gathered behind the barricade, swords bared and

crossbows loaded, was every guard the city had. They filled the caravan compound, but when compared to the thousands of Empty Warriors outside the mountains they seemed a pitiful force.

The Riders were ready too. Aimee could see Faradair, Black, Burnish and a pale green dragon she didn't know, perched on top of the barricade. Only Faradair's saddle was empty.

'What is your plan?' Kyelli asked. She was scanning the compound with a critical eye.

Jara glared at her for a moment, clearly not liking some stranger appearing at the last minute and questioning her. Then with an exasperated sigh she explained.

'The tunnel's braced along its length with metal supports and beams. We need to break those and then the roof will cave in. But we can't get to them without opening the gate.' Jara pointed across the guards to where the dragons were perched. 'We get the dragons to blast the upper hinges of the gate with dragon's breath. The metal will heat and weaken, and with the force of the flames the gate should start to topple inwards. It'll shear through the lower hinges and slam down into the tunnel. Any Empty Warriors directly behind it will be crushed.'

It felt like there were untested theories in Jara's plan but she outlined it with confidence and Aimee admired her for that.

'Once the gate has fallen we can focus our dragons' breath on the beams and supports inside the tunnel. When the metal in them warps and weakens, the whole entrance will collapse.'

'But the gate will be open,' Pelathina pointed out what Aimee too had been thinking. 'How long will it take for the dragons to weaken the supports?'

'Dragon's breath is far hotter than ordinary flames but while we do it, some Empty Warriors will get through.'

There was a horrible moment of silence as Jara's words sank in and fear swirled in the air like snowflakes. Aimee realised that was why all the guards were here, and why she could see more Riders in the sky, waiting to swoop down on any Empty Warriors.

'Pelathina, get into the sky with Lyrria and the others,' Jara ordered. 'When the gate falls in we'll need fresh dragons to blast the supports, so that's your cue to switch with us. We'll take to the air and we'll continue to switch dragons for as long as it takes to weaken the supports. When you're in the air, you attack. The Empty Warriors are impervious to dragon's breath so we're going to need diving attacks in a line formation. Got it?'

Pelathina nodded and leapt back into Skydance's saddle. She gave Aimee the briefest of smiles before lifting off into the sky. Jara eyed Malgerus who, while not collapsed like Jess, had his head resting on Nathine's shoulder and his wings trailing on the ground.

'Nathine, you and Aimee will join the guards. They're here as a precaution. We will not let the Empty Warriors break though that barricade. Understand?'

Both young women nodded. Aimee looked down at

Jess who raised her head, then sensing something was going on began to struggle back to her feet.

'No, stay there, girl,' Aimee said quickly, gently pushing Jess back down. She took her scimitars from underneath her saddlebags and slipped the straps of the harness that held them over her shoulders.

'I'll watch your dragons,' Kyelli offered.

Aimee remembered the way Jess had let Kyelli stroke her and nodded. Nathine looked hesitant for a moment but then motioned for Malgerus to sit beside Jess. He was so tired he didn't even snap at her. Jara watched, gave Kyelli an unreadable look then turned and began to elbow her way back through the guards.

'Come on.' Aimee quickly checked the bracelet was still in neutral, grabbed Nathine's hand and pulled her through the crowd, following in Jara's wake. When they reached the barricade Jara nimbly climbed up and into Faradair's saddle. He roared, the sound for a moment drowning out the thumping at the gate. The barricade was chest-high on the guards which meant it was too tall for Aimee to see over, but it was roughly made and there was plenty of jutting wood for her to stand on. A guard, his crossbow balanced on the top of the barricade and aimed at the gate, stared at her as she stepped up onto a plank and looked over beside him. Nathine squeezed herself onto the same jutting piece of wood.

'You're standing on my toes,' Aimee said in a whisper, elbowing Nathine.

'I am not.'

All along the barricade guards were waiting with

their crossbows but Aimee wasn't sure what good they'd be. How many arrows would they need to pierce an Empty Warrior with so that enough lava poured out and he collapsed?

Aimee sensed the gaze of the guard beside her and turned to look at him. His face was older, grizzled, his stubbly hair a silvery-grey, and he wore the look of disgust she'd grown up seeing. She was about to turn away when she recognised him. He'd been with the councillors' caravan on the tundra. When she'd spoken to him then he'd been mean to her because of her face.

Aimee dismissed him, though his spark caught her attention. It was almost as bright as her own but he had to be easily thirty years older than she was. Maybe she was seeing it wrong. She glanced behind at the rows of guards and all their sparks shone back at her like fireflies, bobbing in the air as the guards shuffled.

With a faint rasp she pulled both her scimitars free and held them down by her sides, running her thumbs over the smooth dome of dragon's tooth embedded in both pommels. On top of the barricade Faradair and Black were to Aimee's left, Burnish and the green dragon to her right. Jara's voice carried over the thumping of the gate.

'Ready? On my mark.'

She held her arm high and when it dropped all four dragons blasted the gate with fire. The whole barricade vibrated with the dragons' power. Aimee had never seen an adult dragon give a full, sustained blast of dragon's breath before and the heat of it was intense. Even standing behind them Aimee could feel it on her face, drying out her eyes. She licked her lips and the moisture was gone almost instantly. Faradair and Black had aimed at the hinges on one side, Burnish and the green dragon concentrating on the other. Within moments the whole top third of the gate was glowing red.

'What's her name?' Aimee called over the roaring of flames, nudging Nathine and pointing to the pale green dragon.

'Really? Now?' Nathine gave her an incredulous look. 'She's Ryka and her dragon's Smaja.'

Aimee felt better, knowing the names of all the women she was fighting alongside, even if she'd never actually spoken to them.

The screech of tortured metal pulled Aimee's attention back to the gate. The top had become soft, the metal curving inwards. Smaja ran out of flames first, then Burnish. Faradair and Black managed another few seconds then they too gasped, wisps of smoke curling out from between their teeth. The caravan compound held its collective breath. There was no sound from the tunnel—the battering ram had stopped and the Empty Warriors were utterly silent.

Then, the weight of the top of the gate tipped inwards, sheering through the bottom hinges. It crashed into the tunnel, crushing Empty Warriors who died without screaming. Aimee saw rivers of lava pour out from under the gate.

'Switch!' Jara yelled as Faradair launched himself into the air. Black, Burnish and Smaja followed, their wings swirling the hot air.

Aimee squeezed the hilts of her scimitars as she watched Pelathina, Aranati, Lyrria and Sal dive from the sky on wings of blue, gold, purple and green. They swooped down as the other dragons rose up, the air whistling between them as their wings almost touched.

'Empty Warriors!' a guard along the barricade yelled.

They came cautiously, perhaps wary of a trap. Aimee watched in horror as they walked across the still glowing gate, the soles of their boots sticking and melting. It must have burned through to their feet but they just kept walking, not making a sound. The tunnel was dark behind them and all Aimee could see were hundreds of pairs of fiery eyes, glowing as they waited their turn to march into the city and kill.

'Sparks, I hate these guys.' Aimee felt Nathine shiver beside her.

On top of the barricade Lyrria screamed a war cry as Midnight began blasting the metal supports holding up the tunnel entrance. The other dragons joined in and the tunnel entrance, and Empty Warriors, were lost behind flames. The stench of rotten eggs assaulted Aimee's nostrils and she realised it was the lava from the crushed warriors.

Then they reappeared, emerging through the dragon's breath as if it was nothing more than a curtain.

'Marhorn's sparks!' a young guard beside Nathine swore. She looked at him and his hands were shaking as he held his crossbow. He lined it up to fire but Nathine jostled him with her shoulder.

'Wait,' she told him.

Just then Faradair and Black dived from the sky, sweeping across the compound. They skimmed below the jets of dragon's breath, so close to the ground that Aimee knew if she'd tried such a move with Jess they'd definitely have crashed. Both dragons snatched an Empty Warrior in their claws and climbed back into the sky, curving in towards the lower slopes of Norwen Peak. With a roar, Faradair tore his Empty Warrior in two, the fire inside him falling through the sky to land hissing on the cliffs.

When Aimee looked back down, Burnish and Smaja had already swept through the compound and grabbed warriors of their own. Jara and Dyrenna were guiding their dragons round for another pass but seeing no resistance the Empty Warriors had started to emerge more quickly from the tunnel now.

'Shoot them!' someone along the barricade yelled.

'Watch the dragons!' Aimee yelled.

Crossbows twanged all along the curved barricade and shot towards the tunnel. Some bounced off the warriors' breastplates, many more stuck into their bodies, but they just kept coming.

'Hold!' the guard beside Aimee ordered as Faradair and Black swept underneath the flames. Faradair grabbed another Empty Warrior who dropped his sword as they rose into the sky. Aimee gasped as Dyrenna swerved to avoid being skewered by the falling blade, Black's huge wings brushing the cliffs above the tunnel.

Without even slowing down, dragon and Rider swept back across the compound and Black grabbed two warriors in his talons.

'Now!'

The guards had reloaded and fired again. A few of the Empty Warriors were hit, lava pouring down them from the combined wounds caused by dozens of arrows. Those ones stumbled, some dropped to their knees. Three collapsed completely, their bodies so covered in fiery streams that Aimee could hardly see their black armour underneath. A shiver passed through her as she watched their bodies shrivel till they were nothing but blackened bones wrapped in skin. The young guard beside Nathine swore colourfully.

The whole entrance to the tunnel was glowing with fire and heat but just then the dragons on the barricade ran out of breath. Whisper managed another few blasts but then his flames were gone too.

'Jara!' Lyrria cried as she and Midnight swept off the barricade.

Midnight raked her talons across warriors' faces before grabbing one and pumping her wings, nose pointed towards the sky. But an Empty Warrior grabbed Midnight's thrashing tail. One of the barbs went straight through his hand but he didn't yell or let go. Lyrria screamed and Midnight roared. Images of Lwena and Glaris being pulled down into the army flashed through Aimee's mind.

Without thinking about it she boosted herself up onto the top of the barricade, eyes scanning the compound, looking for a way through to Lyrria.

'Aimee, what the blazing sparks are you doing? You're the one person who can't get killed here.' Nathine clanged a scimitar against the gold cuff on Aimee's wrist.

'So come help me and watch my back.'

Nathine glared at her for a moment then boosted herself up too.

'I hate you,' she told Aimee.

Aimee wanted to give her a hug but there was no time. She leapt off the barricade, scimitars in both hands, and landed in the killing zone.

CHAPTER 12

SAFE FOR NOW

AIMEE SPRINTED TOWARDS Midnight, Nathine right behind her. An Empty Warrior moved to intercept her, blade raised high. He brought it down in a huge two-handed stroke and Aimee jumped back, crashing into Nathine. The other Rider stopped her from falling, spitting curses in her ear. The warrior was already attacking again and Aimee only just got her scimitars up in time to block him.

He pulled his sword free of hers and thrust and stabbed, again and again. Aimee sliced and danced around him, letting her scimitars be extensions of her arms. After days of fumbling, not knowing what she was doing, it felt good to slip into doing something she knew. The hours of training with heavy wooden swords had made her nimble and quick. She ducked under a thrust aimed at her neck and sliced her right blade along the outside of the warrior's thigh. Molten fire gushed out and Aimee gagged on the stench of sulphur.

In the moment that he stumbled Nathine attacked

him from behind. The tip of one scimitar burst out his lower belly, just below his breastplate, while the other sliced open his throat. Lava poured down his chest and Aimee jumped backwards. The warrior took two staggering steps towards her. A crossbow bolt pinged off his breastplate, ricocheted off one of Aimee's blades and skittered to the ground.

Then the Empty Warrior collapsed and Aimee leapt over him, grabbing Nathine as she passed.

'Come on!'

Midnight was roaring in anger and pain, still trying to take off while the warrior pulled on her tail. The molten fire from his speared hand hissed on her scales. Lyrria had twisted around in her saddle and she stabbed at the warrior. He ducked her blade and raised his own high. The Empty Warriors were freakishly strong and with one blow he could sever Midnight's tail.

'No!' Aimee cried and sprinted across the remaining distance. The thin blade of her scimitar sank into his armpit with no resistance of muscle or flesh. He turned to stare at her, flames swirling in his eyes, just as Nathine's blade pieced his neck.

'Die you freakish monster!' Nathine yelled, pulling out her blade and letting the lava pour from him.

Midnight thrashed and managed to free her tail, then she smashed it into the warrior's head, splitting open his face. Aimee caught sight of a blackened skull as his skin slid off. Terrifyingly he still swung his blade. It clashed with Lyrria's before he finally dropped to the ground and shrivelled.

'Sparks! Aimee, get out of here!' Lyrria yelled.

There was genuine concern on her face and the sight of it tugged at Aimee's still bruised heart.

'Go!' Lyrria yelled as Midnight took off, an Empty Warrior clutched in her talons.

'Watch out!' Nathine cried, and shoved Aimee aside.

She stumbled, off balance, using one scimitar like a walking stick to stop herself from toppling over. Nathine's blades clashed with another warrior. Aimee hadn't heard his silent approach. Nathine was strong, her broad shoulders powerful, and she lunged far more than Aimee did when she was fighting. Her style forced the warrior back a few paces. Then Aimee saw a flash of blue and heard a shout above them.

'Get back, Nathine!'

Nathine caught the warrior's blade between both of hers, twisted her wrists, making him drop his weapon, then she ducked. Skydance swept overhead and his talons gouged the warrior's breastplate with an ear-splitting screech till they hooked under his shoulders and he dragged the warrior into the sky.

Aimee grabbed Nathine's arm. 'Are you alright?'

'Yeah, no thanks to you and your stupid ideas.' She shook her head. 'Next time—'

The rest of her words were lost underneath a roar of dragon's breath. It shot across the compound above their heads, engulfing the tunnel entrance once again. How long till the beams weakened enough that they collapsed?

Aimee heard a harsh scream and her eyes flicked

towards the sound. At the furthest curve of the barricade, a group of Empty Warriors had reached the wooden structure and grabbed one of the guards. He screamed again as several hands closed around his limbs and dragged him over the barricade. As Aimee sprinted towards him she could smell his burning flesh.

By the time she reached him he was on the ground whimpering. She leapt over him, slicing to either side with both scimitars, feeling them cut through skin and slide through fire. Her right blade had almost severed the warrior's neck and his head lolled back. Drips of molten fire flew from the wound, splattering the guard on the ground. He screamed as it sizzled through his skin. Aimee swore and kicked away the warrior who toppled to the ground.

She spun around to check on the other one. Her left blade had only scored his face, slicing across his nose, but Nathine was attacking him. He pressed her back toward the barricade, his one sword easily matching the strikes from both of hers.

'Aimee!' a voice she recognised yelled from the barricade. 'Down!'

Aimee crouched and dozens of crossbow bolts cut through the air above her hair. The force of them knocked back the Empty Warrior who'd been about to attack her. He struggled to rise and though the lava was pouring out of him he made it to his knees before Aimee kicked him back down. Standing, one foot on his breastplate, her boot muddying the engraved tree, she sliced through his neck. The tip of her scimitar glowed red with the heat from the fire inside him.

She whirled back around, ready to help Nathine but she had the warrior on his knees. She swung both scimitars at once, crossing them inside his neck and severing his head. The stench of sulphur made both girls gag.

Aimee knelt beside the fallen guard. He had silver stubble on his cheeks and fear in his moss-green eyes. She didn't need to look at his wounds to know how bad it was—she could see it in his spark. It was pulsing erratically as his body desperately tried to use its energy to heal him, but with every pulse the light grew fainter. Aimee grabbed his hand and breathed through her mouth, trying not to smell his singed flesh. Watching Lwena die had been awful but this was worse. Now she could literally see his life running out.

'Pass him up,' said the voice she recognised.

Aimee looked at the barricade above them and saw Halfen's anxious round face staring down at her. Then he caught Nathine's eye and held it. Aimee saw the awe in his face for the girl he'd liked and lost.

It was Nathine who broke the awkward moment. 'Come on, Aimee, let's get him safe.'

Above them Halfen and another guard had clambered on top of the barricade and were reaching down, asking the Riders to pass up their friend.

'There's no point, he's going,' Aimee said quietly.

The guard was staring at her, blood frothing on his lips as the last of his energy flared bright in his eyes and the spark disappeared from his chest.

'Sparks!' Nathine swore and kicked the Empty Warrior's shrivelled body beside them. Aimee heard the snap of brittle bones like twigs breaking.

She looked across the compound. Empty Warriors had made it past the dragons on the far side but the guards there were holding them off. In the middle, a dead warrior was lying with his hand stuck deep in between the planks of the barricade and the wood was beginning to smoulder. Aimee heard cries for water to be brought. Above, Faradair and Black were blasting the tunnel entrance with dragon's breath and the heat was intense. Aimee pushed sweaty curls off her damp forehead.

The screech of tortured metal pierced Aimee's ears. It was followed a second later by the thudding crash of rock as the supports finally gave way and the tunnel entrance collapsed. The sound was like a hundred dragons all roaring at once.

Hot dust and embers were blasted across the compound and Aimee threw an arm over her eyes. When the rumbles had faded they left a long moment of silence. The air in the compound was thick with rock dust and Aimee coughed as it coated her throat. Dragons' wingbeats swirled the dust and through it Aimee gaped at what had been the tunnel entrance—it was gone and a large section of the cliff above had sheared off, smashing into the caravan compound. Lava sizzled on the ground as it seeped out from under dragon-sized chunks of rock. Aimee hoped dozens of Empty Warriors had been crushed.

She turned her stinging eyes back to the compound. They'd stopped thousands of monsters from getting through the tunnel, but they'd also trapped about fifty inside with them. Fear was churning in Aimee's stomach as fiery eyes turned towards her, and if she'd had any dinner she'd likely have thrown it back up. But she refused to watch another guard's spark go out.

Behind her Nathine and Halfen, both of them dust-coated, were arguing. Halfen was still on top of the barricade, balanced precariously, his drawn sword in one hand, his good ear tilted towards Nathine.

'I'll help,' he was insisting.

'You don't have a dragon. You'll get your stupid face burnt off.'

'You're fighting without your dragon right now.'

'I'm a Rider,' Nathine threw back at him.

Aimee turned in time to see the hurt on Halfen's face. Then movement flickered at the edge of her vision. Two warriors fixed her with their swirling flame eyes. Silently they ran towards her, swords bared and chainmail clinking.

'Nathine!' Aimee cried.

'Stay!' Nathine yelled at Halfen, and Aimee noticed the word came out as more of a plea than a command.

Aimee grabbed the other girl, spinning her around and pressed her back to Nathine's.

'If you die I'm not putting on that cursed bracelet,' Nathine said as she took a stance, protecting Aimee's back.

'Just shut up and fight.'

'Can I have your room, though?'

'What?'

'Your bedroom. I like the purple crystals in the ceiling above your bed.'

Despite everything Aimee let out a short laugh. 'You can have my room and everything in it.'

'Ugh, I don't want your sweaty vests.'

Then the Empty Warriors were upon them. Aimee and Nathine had never practiced fighting back to back, but she'd watched Lyrria and Sal do it once, sparring with two other Riders. They'd been graceful and mesmerising. She and Nathine weren't. Nathine's warrior attacked first and as she lunged to parry his blow, then swept herself backward, she elbowed Aimee right in the spine. Aimee grunted, stumbled and only righted herself just in time to block the warrior's first thrust.

Their blades clanged together above Aimee's head, both of her scimitars pushing against his one longsword. She couldn't tell where his terrifying eyes were looking, and she could feel the searing heat from his hands. But, before the fear could get its claws into her, she moved.

She swept her blades free of his, letting his blow continue downwards as she slipped inside his reach. Her right blade screeched along his breastplate, scoring the black metal, but her left missed its mark and she had to twist away. He'd tucked his elbow and pulled his sword back in. It almost sliced through Aimee's side, cutting her coat but not her skin. His left hand grabbed for her, but she ducked and danced away.

Bouncing lightly on the balls of her feet she attacked again. The handprint burn on her arm throbbed with every movement, but instead of slowing her down it galvanised her. No one else was going to feel the pain of an Empty Warrior's hand on them. Months of Lyrria trying to distract her while they sparred had paid off. Aimee was able to ignore the roar of dragons and the shouts of guards, the clash of steel as others fought, and focus on killing the warrior right in front of her.

She moved constantly, just as Lyrria had taught her. She sliced and parried, her scimitars scraping his armour or missing him by a hairsbreadth. She kept her eyes on his sword. She couldn't read his next move in his unnatural eyes, so she looked for it in the twist and bend of his wrists. He held his sword two-handed but when their blades clashed, bringing them close, he tried to grab for her with his left hand. The third time he did it, Aimee twisted back, swinging her body to the side. His arm shot past her, exposed, and with a quick slice she severed his hand. It dropped to the ground, fingers still twitching, and molten fire oozed from the stump of his wrist. He didn't scream or make a sound. And he still attacked her again.

Their blades clashed together and apart, Aimee weaving around his blows, her slight stature making her nimble. She could hear the clash of steel behind her and Nathine's huffs of effort. She didn't dare look, didn't risk taking her eyes off the warrior she was fighting. All around the compound she could hear the roar of dragons, the scrape of their talons on armour and the twangs of crossbows from the barricade.

The Empty Warrior was weakening but that only made him as slow as a human. Aimee struggled to find another opening, struggled to get her blades past his armour. She kept her focus on him though, even when she sensed Jess land on the barricade.

'Stay, girl!' she yelled, as she parried a thrust at her knees then swung her chest backwards as the warrior aimed at her heart.

She was afraid Jess would throw herself into the battle and in her weakened state get herself injured or killed.

'I can do this!' she yelled, partly to her dragon and partly to herself.

Lava dripped from the stump of the warrior's wrist, hissing as it hit the flagstones. Aimee was forced to skip backwards as it seethed towards her feet. The Empty Warrior stepped in it as if it wasn't even there. He swung for her head; she ducked and her strike was true, slicing deep into his inner thigh. She pulled her blade free and leapt back as molten fire surged down his legs melting the leather of his boot. He tried to lift his arm to swing but he stumbled.

Aimee stepped back, waiting for him to fall, and bumped right into Nathine. The other girl cursed, swung around and her blade appeared over Aimee's shoulder. She stabbed it right through the Empty Warrior's left eye. He finally fell, and both girls backed away as the fire poured out of him leaving a shrivelled corpse.

'You're welcome,' Nathine gasped, out of breath.

'What? I'd already killed him, he was about to fall,' Aimee protested.

'Really? Because it looks like she's here to save you.' Nathine jabbed a thumb towards Jess.

Aimee's dragon was perched on top of the barricade, claws wrapped around the edge, yellow eyes tracking her Rider. She looked so alert, but her wings had drooped, lying flat along the wooden structure and her head was low as if she could barely keep it up. Aimee sent her a pulse of love and reminded her to stay where she was.

'Ugh, I hate the way they do that,' Nathine said, kicking the Empty Warrior's corpse, being careful to avoid the cooling lava. His blackened bones jangled inside the loose sack of skin, and his clothes and armour all looked too big on him now.

Aimee looked across the compound, adrenaline still rushing through her veins making her heart pound and her fingertips tingle. Sunken corpses littered the flagstones and a miasma of sulphur hung over them. Black tore the head off a pinned warrior, letting his body flop down onto another. He spat the head, trailing molten fire, towards the crushed tunnel. Faradair and Skydance swooped across the compound but the Empty Warriors were all dead.

Nathine draped an arm across Aimee's shoulders and Aimee felt the other girl resting most of her weight on her.

'Are you alright?' she asked, alarmed that Nathine might be injured. She quickly checked her friend's spark but it was still glowing bright in her chest.

'I'm fine,' Nathine said quickly, but continued to lean most of her weight on Aimee. 'I just… my leg hurts,' she admitted, reluctantly. 'I didn't feel it when we were fighting.'

Aimee knew what she meant. The burn in her arm was throbbing now in a way she hadn't noticed earlier.

'Let's find Aranati and get the dressing changed on your leg. And you should put more of her salve on it.'

The fact that Nathine agreed without an argument told Aimee how much she was hurting. But when the scream of pain rang out across the compound, Nathine started running even before Aimee did. She scanned for enemies but the warriors were definitely all dead. Faradair had been standing in the middle of what had been the killing zone and as Jara dismounted, and Faradair moved aside, Aimee saw a Rider on the ground. Another scream pierced the air and the downed Rider kicked her heels frantically against the ground. Aranati was already by her side.

Panic flared in Aimee at the thought that Lyrria, or Dyrenna, or Pelathina might be hurt. She stumbled on an Empty Warrior's corpse, one foot coming down to crack the brittle bones of his arm and her other foot crunching on a crust of lava. She skidded to her knees beside the screaming Rider.

It was Ryka. Relief flushed through Aimee, swiftly followed by guilt. It didn't matter that she'd never spoken to this woman before, she was a Rider and she needed help. There was a burn on her shoulder, right through the thick fabric of her coat and into her flesh. Aimee saw glistening red, the shimmer of white bone, and black at the crusted edges.

Aranati had a hand on Ryka's other shoulder, holding her down as she struggled to pull her medical kit from a saddlebag.

'Here, I can help.'

Aimee reached over and tugged it free. Aranati nodded her thanks and went back to speaking softly to Ryka. Her words were a jumble of their language and Irankish. Ryka whimpered as Aranati liberally poured her salve into the wound. A puff of smoke wafted across them and Aranati waved it away, annoyed but not saying anything. Smaja was curled on the ground beside her Rider's head, yellow eyes carefully watching Aranati.

'Will she live?' asked a soft voice. Aimee heard the click of someone's knees, then Dyrenna was crouching beside her, and Aimee realised she'd directed the question at her, not Aranati.

Aimee automatically looked for the spark in Ryka's chest and had a moment of worry when she saw it was duller than her own. Then she looked again at Ryka's face and realised the other Rider was about twenty years older than her, so of course her spark would be fainter. Aimee still stared at her spark for a few minutes, checking it wasn't growing weaker. Then she nodded and Dyrenna sighed in relief.

'We didn't lose any,' she said quietly.

Aimee knew she meant Riders, and she was glad, but Ryka was badly injured. Aimee looked around and realised the guards hadn't been so lucky. Crossbow bolts littered the ground, some still sticking between the bones of Empty Warriors, but amongst them Aimee could also see dead guards. And behind the barricade a man was screaming, harsh and desperate. So there were wounded too. But the tunnel was closed and they were safe, for now.

CHAPTER 13

PASTRIES AND FRIENDS

Aimee stood up and turned around, almost bumping into Lyrria who'd appeared behind her. Tendrils of hair had escaped her intricate braid and they were stuck to her face with sweat. She wasn't wearing her coat and her shirt, always unbuttoned one button more than was decent, showed a bead of sweat rolling down her freckled chest. Before Aimee could think of something to say Lyrria grabbed her and pulled her into a hug. Shocked, Aimee stood dumb for a moment then hugged her back.

'Thank you,' Lyrria said into her hair.

She didn't mean to, but for a moment, Aimee lost herself in the feel and smell of Lyrria. All the memories of nights spent together came bursting out of the locked box in her mind. And Lyrria was touching her, hugging her, in front of everyone. Before Aimee had a chance to fully process that, Lyrria had pulled back.

'I'm glad to see you're still alive, but then you did have the best teacher.' Lyrria grinned at her then grabbed her wrist, the one with Kyelli's bracelet.

'Jara told us about this. Can you really see people's sparks?'

There was a strand of hair caught on Lyrria's upper lip and Aimee wanted to peel it off. Then kiss those lips. But then it hit her again, the horror of knowing how long a person's life would be and never being able to unknow that. She stared at Lyrria's lips, fighting against the pull of her own eyes, but eventually they slipped down. Lyrria's spark shone brightly in her chest and Aimee breathed a sigh of relief.

'Can you, Aimee?' Lyrria asked again.

Aimee was spared from answering by Jara who appeared with Captain Tenth, from the city guard, on her heels.

'Aranati?' Jara asked, her voice as commanding as always.

'She'll live,' Aranati replied as she wrapped a bandage around Ryka's shoulder. 'But she won't be flying any time soon.'

'She fared better than plenty of my guards,' Captain Tenth said. He had a hooked nose and a thin face that, if he hadn't been a guard, would have made him look shifty. Aimee recognised the concern in his eyes—it was the same as Jara had when she was worrying about her Riders.

'Only a fraction of that army got through the gate, and look what they did,' Captain Tenth continued, waving a long-fingered hand towards the smoking barricade and the row of dead guards. Their friends were laying them out, colourful patchwork cloaks pulled over their faces as shrouds. Aimee had grown so used to seeing sparks that it was weird to see men without anything glowing in their chests. They looked more gone somehow than they would have done if she hadn't seen their sparks glowing brightly only half an hour before.

'But the tunnel's sealed now,' Jara said, sheathing her scimitars. 'And that's bought us some time.'

'Time to do what exactly?' Captain Tenth asked, hands on his hips.

Jara's eyes flicked to Aimee then across the barricade, beyond the guards, to where they'd left Kyelli.

'Time for you to strengthen this barricade. Pull out the timbers that have been burned and replace them. Take down the last of the wagon stores if you need more wood,' Jara told him. 'And get some of your lads to collect all the crossbow bolts that aren't bent or broken and can be fired again.'

'You think they'll break through that rock fall?' Captain Tenth's thin eyebrows shot half way up his forehead.

'I don't know,' Jara admitted. 'But that isn't an army of humans. They can't be reasoned with, or bargained with, or beaten so badly that they give up and go home. They'll keep coming and I'd bet my dragon that even now they've started digging through that rockfall.'

Aimee thought of what Kyelli had told them about the Empty Warriors, about how they were imbued with their master's purpose and would not stop until it had been fulfilled. She reckoned Jara was right and the Empty Warriors were already shifting boulders. She looked up at the sheer cliffs above the tunnel and the snowcapped summit of Norwen Peak. Would they try to climb the mountains too?

'How long do we have?' Captain Tenth asked. A guard had appeared at his shoulder, his young face anxious, but the captain ignored him, focusing instead on Jara.

'Tenth, I don't know, alright.' Jara couldn't keep the exasperation from her voice.

'Well, you could at least fly out and have a look, see what the rest of them are doing.' The captain jabbed a finger in the direction of the army beyond their mountains. 'Since you're the only ones who can leave the city now.' There was a barb in his words and Aimee flinched as she saw Jara's high cheekbones flush.

'I did not want that tunnel collapsed!' Jara rounded on him, her anger flying. 'I've fought for years to make Kierell more open, more connected with the world outside so anyone, whether they have a dragon or not, could travel safely beyond our mountains.'

'Jara, you—' the captain began but Jara cut him off.

'No, we're done.'

She deliberately turned her back on him. Aimee watched, with her shoulders hunched, as the captain swore under his breath and stormed away, the young guard scurrying after him.

'Jara, we need the guards,' Dyrenna said softly, placing a hand on her shoulder.

Jara gave her fingers a squeeze. 'I know, I'll apologise to him later. Or maybe get Myconn to do it for me.'

'I wonder if he's the tenth captain of the guard, or is that his name?' Nathine leaned over and asked Aimee.

It was Lyrria who answered. 'It's his name. Apparently he was his parents' tenth child and they'd run out of names by then. Though that's only a rumour.'

'Lyrria, shut up,' Jara said, though there was no venom in her voice, only weariness. 'Aranati, is Ryka safe to move? Can Smaja take her home?' When Aranati nodded Jara continued. 'Okay, you go with her, make sure she's alright then come back.'

'Where will you be?' Aranati asked.

Jara looked around then pointed towards an inn on Goodsgate Street. 'In The Dragon's Roar.' Then she turned to Aimee. 'You need to tell me everything.' She looked at Nathine. 'You as well. And where's Pelathina?'

Aimee looked around for her and spotted the Rider helping to open up a gap in the barricade so a wounded guard could be carried through. She'd rolled up the sleeves of her shirt and her bronze forearms were streaked with sweat, soot and blood. Skydance was perched on the barricade above them, his long neck stretched down towards his Rider.

'Pelathina!' Jara yelled and, when she looked, beckoned her over. 'Lyrria, take Sal and Fineya and fly out to Lookout Ledge. Do not engage with the army, but check what they're doing and report back.'

Aimee felt Lyrria's gaze on her, looked up and met

the brown-green flecked eyes she'd stared into so many times. There was something unspoken, undecided maybe, in her eyes and Aimee couldn't work it out.

'Lyrria? Is there a problem? Go,' Jara ordered.

Lyrria held Aimee's gaze for a moment longer then turned away, calling across the compound to Sal and Fineya.

'Dyrenna, you come with us,' Jara said. 'Let's go.'

Jara swung herself onto Faradair's back and, without waiting for anyone, urged him into the sky. Aimee scrambled up onto the barricade where Jess was still perched. She climbed into her saddle.

'Sorry girl, just one short flight.'

She pushed Jess's horns very gently and was careful when she squeezed her ribs with her knees. She could tell her dragon was still exhausted but all she felt through their connection was joy from Jess that her Rider was alive and they were reunited. They skimmed the heads of the guards and landed at the far edge of the caravan compound. She jumped down from her saddle and, keeping one reassuring hand on Jess, looked for Kyelli. The older woman sitting on a pile of crates stamped with the name ManPenyn—Nathine's father.

'Explain to me how an old woman who looks like she needs a nap is the mastermind behind all this.' Jara hadn't dismounted and her eyes flicked between Aimee and Kyelli.

'She isn't the Master of Sparks, but she is Kyelli,' Aimee told Jara again.

She hurried over to Kyelli and gently shook her

shoulder. Kyelli looked up and her pale eyes seemed to see something far away before they snapped back into focus.

'I watched you fight them. And the warriors… seeing my brother's face again after three hundred years…' Kyelli shuddered. 'Though of course it's not actually his face.'

'Aimee, what is she talking about?' Jara demanded but it was Kyelli who answered.

She stood up, hands on hips and assessed Jara. 'You must be Jara, current leader of my Riders.'

'I am, and the Sky Riders are mine to protect and command. If you think you can just saunter back in here after a century and take control, you'll be disappointed.'

Aimee flinched at Jara's harsh tone but beside her Kyelli smiled. 'The Riders were never mine to command and I never wanted them to be. You are your own women, and the fact that you've survived the climb, and bonded with a dragon, proves to me that you have all the bravery and skills you need to protect this city. I'll not be stealing your authority, don't worry child.'

Jara bristled at being referred to as a child but she didn't argue further, though Aimee could see she didn't trust Kyelli. Finally Jara dismounted and led them down Goodsgate Street to The Dragon's Roar. The street was empty and they left their dragons outside. There was no one inside either; Dyrenna explained that as a precaution they'd cleared the streets around the caravan compound and built a second barricade between here and the streets of Shine and Barter.

The inn was golden inside as the evening sunlight streamed through the windows, caressing the pale wood of benches and chairs. The floor was slate flagstones and the walls were painted a butter yellow. But without any patrons it seemed sad and lonely rather than welcoming. Dyrenna headed to the small kitchen to make tea while Nathine went in search of food.

'So—' Jara began but Kyelli held up a finger and interrupted her.

'Tea first.'

'I don't have the patience of an immortal,' Jara snapped.

'Well I do, though I am no longer an immortal,' Kyelli admitted. Jara narrowed her eyes at her.

Dyrenna reappeared with a teapot and stack of mugs. Nathine contributed a plate of pastries.

'I think they're from yesterday but they're still good,' she told them, waving a half-eaten pastry.

Aimee could feel Jara's simmering impatience as Dyrenna handed round mugs of steaming tea to everyone except Pelathina. As Dyrenna passed Aimee her mug, the older Rider gave her a quick smile.

'I seem to remember you still owe me a cup of tea. This makes your debt two cups.'

Aimee breathed in the astringent vapours and let her mind relax, just for a moment. Then she looked up and met Jara's eyes—they were hard as emeralds and they seemed to bore right into Aimee as if they could dig out answers from inside her. Everyone else was watching her too, and once that would have set her nerves quivering, but today against a backdrop of dead guards and a bracelet that was sucking the life from her, a few eyes on her unusual face hardly seemed to matter. So she took a deep breath and told Jara what had happened.

She missed out the prowler attack and neglected to mention her own fears, but she told Jara everything else, even admitting that she'd nearly murdered Kyelli's innocent assistant. Jara kept her eyes on Aimee but occasionally they'd flicker to Kyelli. Aimee explained their discovery, that Kyelli was not the Master of Sparks and that in fact she had only one spark left in her chest.

When she reached this part of the story she looked to Kyelli, wondering if she wanted to take over. But the old woman simply shook her head and waved for Aimee to continue. When Aimee explained that the Empty Warriors had been created by Pagrin, Kyelli's brother, Jara turned her attention to Kyelli.

'Are you sure?' she asked, voice firm.

'You don't think I'd recognise my own brother's face?' Kyelli picked up the threads of the story, explaining how she and her father had assumed Pagrin dead and left him behind. 'And he used our tree,' Kyelli added softly.

'What tree?' Jara snapped.

'On the breastplates.' It was Aimee who answered, looking at Kyelli. 'It's the same one that's embossed on your journal and that marked the statues on the map.'

'And was on your cottage door,' Nathine added.

'It's our family emblem. In Vienthon, our old capital city, it was on everything.' Anger flashed in her eyes. 'Pagrin's twisted it. He had no right to brand his warriors with a symbol that meant family and denoted safety.'

'He calls Kierell your city,' Dyrenna joined the conversation. 'On the warriors' breastplates it says "We will not stop until Kyelli's city is in ashes". Knowing what we know now, those words sound bitter, and personal.'

Kyelli sighed so heavily that Aimee felt she could almost see the weight of centuries worth of memories pressing down on her. Jara had pulled her hair free of its ponytail and it hung lank around her face. She ran her fingers through it as if by straightening the strands she could somehow also straighten this mess. Aimee took a pastry and as she bit through the flaky exterior to the meat and vegetables inside, she realised how ravenous she was. She devoured that one and grabbed another.

'So…' Jara began but then trailed off into a desperate half laugh. 'I have no idea what we do now.'

'We find my brother,' Kyelli said, turning to look at Aimee.

Everyone else did the same and she quickly swallowed the half-chewed lump in her mouth, wincing as it went down.

'You have a plan, little one?' Dyrenna asked softly.

'Not really me, it's more Kyelli's plan,' Aimee was quick to point out. 'She thinks that because I can see everyone's sparks, and because I'm bonded with Jess, that I should be able to see other connections. Like I should be able to actually see the link between me and

Jess. And if I can do that then I can see the link between the Empty Warriors and the person who gave them life, and follow that link to find Pagrin.'

Pelathina smiled encouragingly but Jara looked sceptical. Dyrenna was staring down at her scarred hands.

'I didn't explain that very well, did I?' Aimee asked.

'You did fine,' Kyelli reassured her.

'So, can you see these other connections?' Jara asked, one blonde eyebrow raised.

Aimee shook her head. 'I've been trying, but not yet.'

'Perhaps someone else could have a go,' Jara suggested, reaching across the table towards Aimee's wrist.

Aimee quickly pulled back her hands. She'd love to give this responsibility over to Jara but that wasn't possible. She looked at her leader and explained about the bracelet being powered by sparks, and needing the energy of one to be removed.

'Kyelli's sparks!' Jara swore, slapping a palm down on the table. Then she realised what she'd said, and her high cheekbones flushed with colour as she looked at Kyelli.

'Oh don't dare apologise.' Kyelli was grinning. 'I'm actually quite honoured that my name's become a virulent curse.'

'You missed out the part where the bracelet is killing you,' Nathine butted in and Aimee glared at her. She wasn't going to admit that because she didn't want anyone's pity.

No one spoke but everyone stared at Aimee again. So she took a deep breath and told them how the bracelet was draining her life. Before she'd even finished Dyrenna had reached over and taken her hand. Beside her, Pelathina wrapped an arm around her waist. Nathine looked longingly at the last pastry then shoved the plate towards Aimee. Jara pressed her fingertips to her mouth and for a second Aimee thought she saw tears glisten in her eyes.

She was amazed. When her aunt and uncle had died she had no one left in the whole world. And now this group of incredible women cared about her. She had friends and people to comfort her. Aimee had to blink away tears in her own eyes. And it made her more determined to find Pagrin, not just to save the city, but also to save herself. She wanted to stay with these women, for ever.

'I need to learn to use this bracelet,' Aimee said, placing her wrist down on the table, gold cuff clanking on the wood. She turned to Kyelli. 'You need to tell me where I'm going wrong and what I need to do differently.'

Kyelli's lined face was grim, but the determination in her eyes matched Aimee's. 'We're going to need some help.'

CHAPTER 14

TRUST

'WHAT SORT OF help?' Dyrenna asked.
'Aimee needs to learn to use and manipulate life's energy, the way a Quorelle would do. If she can master that then my hope is that she'll be able to see the connections that form between a person's spark and something tied to them, like a dragon or an Empty Warrior they've created.' Kyelli stopped herself before continuing and looked to Jara. 'May I borrow Aimee and two of your other Riders? Just for a little while.'

Jara nodded though she didn't look happy about it.

'I'll help,' Pelathina volunteered.

'I will too,' Dyrenna added.

Jara turned to the older Rider and looked like she wanted to argue but her eyes flicked to Kyelli. Aimee understood. Jara relied on the older Rider for support but she didn't want to seem weak in front of Kyelli.

'Alright then, Nathine you're with me. I need to tell the council that the tunnel is closed.' Jara looked wryly at Kyelli. 'And I need to retell them who the Master of

Sparks is.'

Jara got up from the table and headed for the door.

'Jara,' Kyelli called, stopping her. 'There's a mechanism built into the roof of the tunnel above the outer gate. If activated it'll collapse that end of the tunnel too.'

Aimee watched a hundred questions flit across Jara's face but she settled on only one. 'How do we activate it?'

'I'll be honest, I don't know, my father had it constructed and I ignored it because I never wanted it to be used.'

'The books we found in the library,' Aimee interrupted, waving at herself and Nathine. 'They had drawings of cogs and machines, like the ones we saw by the docks in Vorthens.'

'Callant's already had boxes of those books brought down and he's been pouring through them, along with half of the university scholars,' Jara told them.

Aimee smiled. She could just imagine Callant's delight at reading through all that new knowledge.

'Why did you hide the books?' Nathine demanded, arms folded, staring at Kyelli.

She didn't look guilty, only a little sad. 'Progress was what first tempted the Quorelle to create Empty Warriors. As our cities built machines and factories, we created an expendable workforce for them. I didn't want to see that happen here, so I hid the knowledge.'

'The city states have steam-powered machines, though, don't they? And they don't have monsters working in their factories,' Nathine pointed out.

'I might have been wrong to halt your progress,' Kyelli admitted, 'but for me that knowledge was tied to darkness and I couldn't see a way past that.'

Silence followed her words. Aimee understood Kyelli's desire to protect, but she'd been wrong and her actions had left them vulnerable.

'I'll tell Callant what we're looking for. He could probably do with some focus otherwise I don't think he'll ever leave the library again.' And with that Jara turned for the door.

Nathine hesitated a moment, then hurried round the table and pulled Aimee into a rough hug. Aimee could smell the grass of the tundra in the other girl's hair.

'Don't be an idiot, okay?' Nathine said.

'I won't. It's no fun getting stuff wrong when you're not around to mock me for it.'

Aimee felt Nathine smile against her cheek, then the other girl pulled away and left without a backward look. Aimee swivelled on her seat so she was facing the table again. Kyelli was sitting to her right, Pelathina to her left and Dyrenna opposite her, and they were all looking at her, waiting. She turned her eyes to Kyelli.

'So, what do we do?' Aimee asked.

'The bracelets gave the Quorelle power over life forces,' Kyelli began. 'Both our own, and that of humans, as well as the residual energy that exists in elements. It was that which allowed us to create Empty Warriors. But with thousands of sparks in our blood we already had a greater sense of these forces even before we put on the bracelets. I can remember feeling when my main spark was running low and I had to channel energy from the sparks in my blood to top it up. To me that was a process as natural as sleeping when you're tired.'

Kyelli poured herself more tea, keeping her thoughtful eyes on Aimee. 'When you took Jara's spark, and Petra's, did it feel like the bracelet was doing that or you?'

'The bracelet,' Aimee answered immediately.

'That's where you're going wrong,' Kyelli said. 'You're fighting against the power of the bracelet when you should be embracing it and using it.'

But Aimee didn't want to embrace it. The power was horrible. She could feel it even with the bracelet in neutral. It pressed at her mind and she worried that eventually it would erode away her will. She didn't want to become like the Quorelle, who'd used this power for their own greed. But she didn't tell Kyelli that. Instead she nodded, hoping that there would be a way to master the bracelet without giving in to its power.

'I want you to practice taking and giving sparks,' Kyelli continued.

'What?' Aimee was horrified. She heard a scrabbling sound from above and knew Jess was shifting uncomfortably on the roof.

'The bracelet is a tool and you need to become confident using it.'

Kyelli's eyes flicked to Pelathina and Dyrenna. Aimee's heart felt like it had turned to stone and dropped into her stomach as realisation dawned.

'That's why they're here to help? You want me to steal their sparks?'

'And put them back again.'

'No.' Aimee shook her head.

Then she felt Pelathina's fingers slip into her hand. 'Will it help?'

She asked the question of Kyelli and the old woman nodded. Pelathina shifted on her seat so she was looking directly at Aimee. Astonishingly, she was smiling.

'I trust you.' The words nearly broke Aimee's heart.

'But I don't trust me,' she replied.

'Little one?' Dyrenna's soft voice pulled Aimee's eyes from Pelathina's face. 'Try with my spark first.'

Aimee continued to shake her head. 'No, I owe you two cups of tea, and you owe me your story. And if I kill you neither of us can pay our debt.'

Dyrenna looked down at her hands, mottled by lumpy scar tissue, then back up at Aimee. 'Let me help. Let me... atone.'

'For what? And you do help, all the time,' Aimee insisted. 'You make and fix all our saddles, and you pick Jara up when she falls, and you were the first person ever to be kind to me and see me, and not just my weird face.'

'Beautiful face,' Pelathina whispered beside her.

Everyone was staring at Aimee again and she knew they were right—she had to learn to use this power, even if it made her feel sick. So, resigned, she got up and moved to sit next to Dyrenna, straddling the bench.

Wisps of dark hair had escaped the older Rider's braid and they framed her round face. The little creases at her eyes and mouth softened her further. Looking at her, Aimee was impressed with her inner strength, to sit so calmly, considering what was about to happen.

'Sure?' Aimee asked one more time.

'I trust you, little one.'

'I want you to judge her energy and only take half,' Kyelli ordered from the other side of the table.

So Aimee flicked the dial on the bracelet to *ura* and wrapped her fingers around Dyrenna's wrist. She felt the power of the bracelet immediately, greedily sucking Dyrenna's spark. She looked down and a second spark appeared in her own chest, small but growing as the energy poured from Dyrenna to her. Dyrenna had gasped when Aimee first touched her and now she gripped the edge of the table, knuckles white. Aimee felt awful for causing her pain.

Inside her mind the power of the bracelet pushed against her brain, like the tide on a stormy day, but Aimee threw up a mental wall against it. Instead she concentrated on Dyrenna's spark, and the one growing in her own chest, eyes constantly flicking between the two. The feeling of wrongness swirled through her and she tasted bile at the back of her throat.

When she judged she'd taken half of Dyrenna's energy she pictured slamming a door shut in her mind and yanked her hand off the older Rider. Dyrenna was shaking, but she wasn't dying. Though if Aimee kept her energy, she'd live half as long as she was meant to.

'Alright, now return her spark,' Kyelli ordered.

Aimee flipped the dial and grabbed Dyrenna's wrist again, eager for this part. The bracelet was eager too, but again Aimee ignored its pressure in her mind. She watched the second spark in her chest grow dimmer and the one in Dyrenna's chest brighten again as she gave Dyrenna her life back. She had to concentrate carefully for the point where all Dyrenna's energy was gone from her body and slam shut the connection, before the bracelet started sucking on her own spark and sending it to Dyrenna.

This time she jerked her hand off Dyrenna's wrist so forcefully that she slid backwards on the bench and nearly fell off. Dyrenna reached out to steady her but Aimee shied away from her touch.

'Hang on.' She put the bracelet in neutral. 'Are you okay?'

Dyrenna nodded. 'But that was unpleasant.'

'Now you must do the same with Pelathina,' Kyelli ordered. 'Her spark will have a different amount of energy in it from Dyrenna's but I want you to do the same and take only half, then put it back.'

As Aimee stood up a wave of dizziness washed over her, making the edges of her vision all blurry. Dyrenna grabbed her arm to steady her.

'I'm alright,' Aimee lied.

It felt like her brain was being squeezed and she knew it was the power of the bracelet trying to force its way in, to make a connection with her. Aimee wouldn't let it. Instead she held tight to her bond with Jess and heard her dragon growl on the roof.

'You've been on the go non-stop for three days now with hardly any sleep and no proper meals,' Pelathina pointed out, coming round the table and placing both hands on Aimee's shoulders. 'Maybe you should rest.'

Aimee shook her head at the same time that Kyelli said, 'No.'

Then before Pelathina could argue, Aimee flicked the bracelet to *ura* and gently took both of her hands. The girls were the same height and Aimee found herself staring into Pelathina's dark eyes. She felt the hungry tug of the bracelet pushing against her mind but once again she ignored it. The sickly feeling returned as Pelathina's life force poured into her chest.

This time the bracelet sucked faster and Aimee wondered if that was because she was holding both of Pelathina's hands, making more contact with her skin. The pressure in her brain grew till it felt like fingers were squeezing her skull and Pelathina's face stared to slip out of focus. She almost missed the point where she'd stolen half of Pelathina's life. Aimee scrambled to shut the door in her mind, pulling at her hands in Pelathina's but they wouldn't let go. Closing the door on the bracelet's power felt like shoving a slab of stone.

When she finally managed to release Pelathina's hands, the world swam around her.

Then Aimee collapsed.

Everything disappeared as empty blackness swallowed her mind, pulling her down into its depths. She fell into it, feeling her connections with the world unspool behind her.

Everything was gone, it was just her and the void. She floated there, lost and uncaring.

Then she saw something far above her in the darkness—a tiny flame, flickering, about to go out. She knew it. That was hers, her flame of determination, the one that had never let her give up. And though the darkness pulled her downwards with a force heavier than gravity, Aimee swam towards the flame.

She woke with a scream lodged in her throat and hands all over her. She scrambled back from them, terrified of touching someone. Pelathina and Dyrenna were crouched beside her, concern written deep on their faces. Kyelli sat cross-legged on the floor, leaning back against a table leg.

'How long was I unconscious?' Aimee asked. It felt like she'd been asleep for hours.

'About five minutes. We couldn't wake you.' Pelathina moved closer and Aimee shied back. 'What happened? Are you alright?'

'I don't know.' She looked down at the bracelet on her wrist. 'It felt…' Her words trailed off as her head snapped back up. 'Where are your sparks?'

Three confused faces looked back at her. Panic surged in Aimee like an incoming tide. She looked down at her own chest. She couldn't see her spark, only a crumpled black shirt that really needed a wash. She looked at the others. Nothing. She couldn't see anyone's sparks, their chests were empty. She grabbed the bracelet on her wrist and twisted it. Icy pain shot up her arm and she gasped. It was still on, the spike still inside her drawing her energy.

She scrambled to her feet, boot heels kicking on the floorboards. 'No, no, no,' she moaned.

The others rose up with her. Their faces were confused, frightened. It was Kyelli who stepped forwards, grabbed her shoulders and shook Aimee so hard her head snapped back.

'What is going on?' she demanded.

'I can't see anyone's sparks any more.' She looked up into Kyelli's ancient pale eyes. 'Why? What have I done wrong?'

Kyelli grabbed Aimee's wrist and did as she'd done, twisting the bracelet, trying to remove it. Aimee screamed as the pain shot through her veins again. Vaguely she heard Pelathina yelling for Kyelli to let go. She didn't. She kept pulling the bracelet, the pain growing in intensity until Aimee thought she'd pass out again. Then Kyelli let go and grabbed Aimee's hand. The pain in Aimee's arm instantly vanished and she gasped in relief.

'Take my spark,' Kyelli ordered, squeezing Aimee's hand so hard her knuckles ground together.

With the pain gone Aimee realised with a start that she was touching Kyelli with the bracelet in *ura* and nothing was happening. The insistent pressure in her mind from the bracelet's power was gone. It wasn't sucking Kyelli's spark.

'Come on!' Kyelli yelled, jerking Aimee's arm up and down.

'I can't!' Aimee shouted back.

'You can. Concentrate, focus, embrace the power of the bracelet and let it work.' Kyelli's words were demanding, not encouraging and they stoked the anger and exasperation in Aimee.

'It's not working any more! I can't see anyone's sparks and the stupid bracelet isn't doing anything!'

'You need to try harder. No one else can find Pagrin. You must learn to control the power and see connections.'

'I am trying.' She yanked her hand free of Kyelli's and waved the gold cuff in her face. 'What happened? Tell me what I need to do to get it working again.'

'I don't know!' Kyelli cried. She marched across the room then turned and glared at Aimee, arms crossed.

'But you're supposed to have all the answers!' Aimee yelled at her. 'I have no clue what I'm supposed to be doing but you're six hundred and six years older than me. You have all this knowledge, all the stuff you kept hidden from us, and this is *your* stupid bracelet!' Aimee thrust out her wrist. 'You're supposed to be showing me how it works so I can save everyone.'

'It was never meant for a human.' Kyelli stormed back across the room. 'Maybe you're just too weak to power it.'

'But it's still stuck into me,' Aimee protested.

'So it's likely still drawing on your spark but it's not enough.

'Just enough to kill me.'

'Yes.'

'That's not fair!' Aimee wailed.

Kyelli grabbed her shoulder again. 'Did you embrace the power? Did you welcome it into your mind?'

Aimee glared at her for a long moment, feeling stubborn, then finally shook her head.

'Why not?' Kyelli demanded.

'Because I didn't want to end up like you!' Aimee blurted out.

It wasn't anger that flashed in Kyelli's eyes, but sorrow. 'Then perhaps that's why you are too weak to use it.'

Kyelli stepped away from her and the dismissal hurt. Aimee had never wanted the responsibility of the bracelet but now the thought that it would kill her, when she couldn't even use it to save the city, was even worse. She slumped, surprised when her bum hit the seat of the bench. Pelathina was instantly beside her, wrapping an arm around Aimee's waist. Aimee was too worn out to warn her off from touching her.

Then she realised something horrible and tears filled her eyes. In her desperation and anger at Kyelli she'd forgotten that she had half of Pelathina's spark inside her. She looked down but couldn't see her own or the fainter glow of Pelathina's life force in her chest. She grabbed one of Pelathina's hands, enclosing the other girl's darker fingers in her own white patchy ones. Closing her eyes she willed the bracelet to work. Nothing.

'Hey.' Pelathina's voice was soft and Aimee opened her eyes. The other girl gently cupped her face. 'It's okay.'

'It's not,' Aimee disagreed as her tears began to fall. 'I've stolen half your life and I can't give it back.'

'You've not stolen it, you're just looking after it for me for a little while.' With her thumb Pelathina brushed away Aimee's tears.

She couldn't see it but if she concentrated Aimee could still feel the sickening wrongness of having someone else's spark inside her.

'I will find a way to give it back,' Aimee promised.

'I know you will.'

Pelathina wrapped her in a hug and that only made Aimee cry harder. She didn't understand what she'd done wrong but she'd find a way to get the bracelet working again. She had to. No one else could stop Pagrin, and she needed his sparks to remove the bracelet. Otherwise she'd die and Pelathina would only live half a life.

Footsteps made Aimee pull out of the hug. Kyelli was slipping her arms into her coat as she headed for the door.

'Where are you going?' Aimee asked, jumping up from her seat.

'To find my brother,' Kyelli replied without turning around.

'But, how?'

'I don't know, but since I have six hundred years of knowledge over you all, I'll think of something.'

The door rattled in the frame as she slammed it behind her. Aimee went to run after her but Dyrenna's gentle hand on her arm stopped her.

'Let her go, little one,' Dyrenna said.

Aimee almost argued but she didn't have the energy. Instead she looked around, helpless. 'So, what do we do now?'

CHAPTER 15

SOMETHING NEW

'RIGHT NOW? YOU need to rest,' Pelathina said.

'But…' Aimee waved vaguely in the direction of the door.

'Pelathina is right,' Dyrenna told her. 'The city is safe for now. You can't help anyone if you collapse with exhaustion.'

Aimee wanted to argue but they were right. Being on the go non-stop for three days had made her forget what it was to rest.

'Do you think Jess will be strong enough to fly you back to Anteill?' Pelathina asked.

Aimee nodded. She could feel Jess waiting for her outside and knew from the fuzziness in their connection that her dragon had been dozing.

'I'm not sure I'll be able to sleep,' Aimee admitted. Exhaustion was weighing down her limbs but inside she felt all jittery.

'Well, how about I tell you stories until you grow so fed up of listening to my voice that you fall asleep to get away from me?' Pelathina suggested with a cheeky smile.

Pelathina always had something kind and encouraging to say, and her accent was lovely, so different from Aimee's own. Aimee didn't think that she'd ever grow tired of listening to her voice.

Dyrenna had gathered their coats from the benches and passed them around. As Aimee took hers she noticed the sprig of heather was gone from her buttonhole. She tried not to feel sad. People had died today—she shouldn't waste her emotions on a silly flower, but it was the first birthday present someone outside her family had ever given her. As she pulled on her coat she saw Pelathina grinning at Dyrenna, but when she spoke her words were for Aimee.

'You've never heard the story about how I tried to steal Black, have you?'

'What?' Aimee stared at the other two, thinking she'd misheard.

'Still not forgiven you,' Dyrenna said, but wearing a small smile that crinkled at the edges. She pulled open the door, muttering loud enough for Aimee and Pelathina to hear, 'A dragon thief and a girl who owes me tea but never delivers. What a pair you make.'

Aimee and Pelathina followed Dyrenna outside. Jess had been sleeping on the roof of the inn but she flew down and Aimee mounted up. A moment later all three Riders were in the air above the city. The sky was soft and dark above them, its edges still tinged with blue. As they flew over the caravan compound, lanterns glowed like fireflies where the guards were working to fix and strengthen the barricade.

Aimee was glad it was only a short flight back to Anteill because as she'd climbed into her saddle every muscle in her body ached, worse even than after the toughest of days training. Ahead Black flew so silently, his huge wings like spreading shadows. He disappeared down the vent first, back into the Heart. Pelathina circled on Skydance, letting Aimee go next. She was so tired she hardly felt the spike of adrenaline as Jess dived down through the vent in the rock and swooped into the cavern.

'Hold still, girl,' Aimee told her dragon after she'd dismounted and was trying to unbuckle her saddle. Jess kept trying to get away, eager to find a ledge and sleep. Finally Aimee slid the last strap free of its buckle and she heaved her saddle off Jess's back. Jess head-butted her once then flew over to one of the lower ledges and curled up to sleep.

The saddle was a ton weight in Aimee's arms and she looked around, wondering if she could leave it in a corner here rather than trudging all the way to the store with it.

'Don't dump it,' Dyrenna said as if reading Aimee's thoughts. 'It needs hung up or all the straps will get tangled.'

'I wasn't going to,' Aimee lied, feeling guilty.

'You were.' Dyrenna took Aimee's saddle and heaved it up onto her own shoulder. 'I'll put it away. You go and get some sleep.'

Feeling incredibly grateful Aimee gave the older

Rider a quick hug. She smelled like leather and oil. Dyrenna didn't have an arm free to return the hug so instead she put her chin on the top of Aimee's head.

'Thank you,' Aimee said.

'Go, sleep.'

'Three cups of tea now?'

'Still two, but cake as well.'

Aimee smiled, and turned to find Pelathina waiting for her. She was standing beside one of the poles holding a dragon's breath orb and the flickering yellow glow danced across the bronze skin of her cheeks. Right then she was so beautiful. Pelathina took her hand, leading her into the corridors, towards her room. Exhaustion made Aimee drag her feet and she didn't even realise when they'd reached her bedroom door.

She'd left her room in a mess, but she was too tired to feel embarrassed as Pelathina carefully gathered up discarded clothes from the bed and floor. She folded them neatly, placing the pile on top of the wooden chest at the bottom of Aimee's bed. Aimee hopped on one foot, then the other as she removed her boots. She didn't bother taking anything else off, just collapsed onto her bed. Pelathina pulled her quilted blanket over her, then Aimee felt her weight settle at her feet as the other girl sat down.

Exhaustion wrapped around her body but her mind was buzzing like a fly trapped inside a jar. Worries, fears, and thoughts about everything she'd seen and learned, all flitted through her mind. She couldn't catch any long enough to still them. She turned onto her back and lay gazing up at the purple crystals in the ceiling above her bed.

'Why did you try to steal Black?' she asked, propping her head up on her pillow so she could look at Pelathina.

The other girl had pulled Aimee's blanket over her legs and sat with her back resting against the wall. Then before Pelathina could answer, Aimee's curiosity spilled out. She wanted to know everything about this girl with the beautiful face and endless supply of smiles.

'Where was home? Why did you come to Kierell? Did you and Aranati come together? When?'

The questions poured from Aimee like she'd knocked over a jug of them in her mind. Pelathina snorted a half laugh and Aimee hoped the glow of her one dragon's breath orb would hide the blush on her cheeks.

'Sorry, I'm not good at talking to people,' she explained, 'and when I try it all just bursts out at once. I was always interrupting my uncle when he was telling me stories. He used to say if we had ten presses for every question I asked then we could afford to live in Shine.' Aimee fiddled with a loose thread on her blanket. 'I'm trying to get better at it.'

'I don't think you need to get better at anything. Apart from maybe smiling more.' Pelathina nudged her feet with her knee. 'If keeping quiet, and then bursting out with questions when you want to is your way, then stick with it. You don't need to change.'

Aimee was too tired to think of something good to

say back to that. The idea that she could have her own odd style of conversation, and that be okay, was something she'd never considered.

'So, do I get an answer to my questions?' she asked with a smile.

'You know, I saw you sometimes, back when you were training with Lyrria, and I admired your determination.' Pelathina was resting her head back against the wall but her face was turned towards Aimee. 'I thought maybe once you had your dragon that we could fly down into the city, sit in a little cafe and swap stories. But there hasn't been any time.'

'You wanted to get to know me?' Aimee asked.

'Of course I did. You're beautiful, and strong, and kind, and you don't even realise how amazing you are.'

It was hard to tell in the soft light, and with Pelathina's darker skin, but Aimee thought the other girl might be blushing. Her heart beat faster and under the blanket her toes curled.

'I imagined going flying with you,' Pelathina continued, 'out across the tundra on one of those days where the sky is clear and goes on for ever.'

Aimee wanted to say that they could still do that once this was over, but it would feel like a false promise. Without a way to find Pagrin she couldn't see how they'd ever be safe again.

'I love it out in the sky above the tundra, but I do miss hot days,' Pelathina said with a sigh.

'It gets hot here in the summer,' Aimee said, thinking of earlier when she'd been flying without her coat on.

'It gets a little bit warm here, but never hot, and in the winter it's absolutely freezing.' Pelathina shook her head but she was still smiling. Aimee realised she'd never seen Pelathina, or Aranati, without a coat or a scarf.

'I grew up in Marlidesh, where the winter is as warm as your summers,' Pelathina explained. 'It's so hot in the summer that everything shimmers and people hide in the shade. Sometimes I think I've forgotten what it feels like to be warm.'

'Why did you leave? And where's Marlidesh?'

Pelathina held up one finger. 'What?' Aimee asked.

'I was waiting to see if there were more questions.'

Aimee smiled, embarrassed and delighted at the joke. 'You can start with those,' she said trying to make her voice sound casual, though it came out a bit squeaky.

Suddenly Pelathina's smile dropped and her brow creased into her sister's frown. Aimee panicked, thinking she'd misjudged their banter.

'I…'

'I ran away,' Pelathina spoke over her. She took a deep breath. 'Aranati and I were taken as slaves when our parents were murdered. We escaped. I killed a man to get us out. We ran and made it to Taumerg.' Pelathina's head was bowed as she spoke, as if her memories were pressing down on her. And she was stroking a scar on her wrist. 'I wanted to go back north to Marlidesh. I wanted revenge on the men who'd killed our parents, who'd enslaved us, and who'd stolen all my sister's smiles. But Aranati needed to keep running so I came with her.'

Aimee wanted to reach over and take Pelathina's hand but it would mean getting out from under her blanket, and she worried the movement would break the thread of Pelathina's story.

'We'd heard about a city locked inside a ring of mountains way down at the bottom of the world.' Pelathina looked up and gave Aimee a small smile. 'I thought it sounded awful but Aranati wanted to come. It was as far as we could get from our life as slaves and Aranati needed that.'

'Did you come across the tundra with a caravan?' Aimee asked gently.

Pelathina shook her head. 'This was four years ago and there were even fewer caravans than there are now. We set off alone.'

Aimee thought of the endless miles of grass and heather and tried to imagine walking for days out there alone with no dragons. There would have been Helvethi, and prowlers too.

'Were you scared?'

'Probably,' Pelathina admitted, 'but mostly I was pissed off. I didn't want to be there, I was annoyed at Aranati for dragging us to this desolate place and I wanted to go home.'

'So if you hated it here why did you stay?'

'I couldn't leave my sister, she was the only family I had left. And it turns out Aranati was right, though don't tell her I said that. If we'd never come, I wouldn't have Skydance and when we're up in the sky together I can forget that I was once a slave, kept in a room, locked behind high walls. Here I've got the whole sky.'

Pelathina had tilted her head back and was looking up through the layers of rock above them as if she could see the sky. Aimee understood how an escaped slave would find joy in the complete lack of barriers out on the tundra. And Aimee was amazed at Pelathina's resilience. She must only have been about fifteen when she was enslaved and forced to kill a man to escape, but now she was always smiling, always cheerful.

'How do you do it?' Aimee asked. 'Be so happy, I mean.'

'I choose to be,' Pelathina replied, still looking up at the sky. 'I was holding on to my anger, and my need for revenge, so tightly that I'd forgotten I could feel other things. I was so angry because I'd lost my parents that I'd forgotten I still had my sister. So, I chose to let go of my anger and hold on to happiness instead.'

'I'm not sure I could do that,' Aimee admitted.

Pelathina turned her dark eyes to Aimee and smiled. 'Oh I disagree completely. I've seen the way you set your mind to something and then don't stop until you've achieved it.'

'But that's not me being an amazing person, or anything, that's just what I have to do because of the way I look.' Aimee waved a hand over the colourless half of her face.

Pelathina shook her head. 'Once again, I'd argue that you're wrong. You've chosen to turn your face towards the world and embrace it. You could have hidden away instead.'

Aimee thought of all the years of her childhood where she'd done exactly that and realised Pelathina was right. It was a thought that made her proud.

This time she did get out from under her blanket. She swivelled around so she was sitting beside Pelathina, her back to the wall, and draped her blanket over both their legs. Pelathina's hip was pressed against hers and the contact set butterflies dancing in Aimee's belly. She took a moment, daring herself to do it, then reached across the patchwork squares of the blanket and took Pelathina's hand. Their fingers were so different— Pelathina's bronze but looking darker in the soft light and Aimee's tanned but spotted all over with colourless patches.

Pelathina slowly ran her thumb across Aimee's fingers in the gentlest of caresses. The tingles in Aimee's belly danced lower. She'd always thought Pelathina was pretty but now she really looked at her and saw that she was beautiful. Her bronze skin glowed with an inner light and as she smiled the cute dimples appeared on her cheeks. Aimee had such an urge to kiss them. Her short dark hair was ruffled, sticking up in every direction and Aimee loved that imperfection.

Then she wondered what Pelathina saw when she looked back at her. What made her smile like that? She thought back to when she'd asked Lyrria what she saw when she looked at her freakish face and remembered Lyrria saying she didn't really notice it. Maybe that was the key. Maybe she had to spend enough time with someone so they stopped seeing the freaky side of her and she'd now reached that stage with Pelathina.

'Do you not notice my weird face any more?' Aimee asked, curious.

'Of course I notice it, your face is pretty noticeable.'

Aimee's heart sank and she cursed herself for being an idiot and ruining the moment. But then Pelathina surprised her with her next words.

'I think your face is unconventionally fantastic.'

A small half laugh escaped Aimee's lips. 'Is that a good thing?'

'Definitely. I notice other things too,' Pelathina continued caressing Aimee's hand. 'You have a white patch here on your knuckles that when I tilt my head like this, it looks like a crescent moon. And that's sweet.'

Aimee gaped at her. Never in her life had she thought of her weird skin as a feature that could be sweet. Her heart broke through the worry that clawed at it and beat freely, sending lots of blood up to flush her cheeks. They sat in silence while Aimee's heart hammered so loudly she was sure Pelathina could hear it. She rested her head on Pelathina's shoulder, tentatively at first then, when Pelathina snuggled a little closer, she let her weight slump against the other girl. She wondered if Jess and Skydance were curled up together, her emerald-green tail twisted around his sapphire-blue one. She hoped they were.

'So, why did you steal Black?' Aimee asked, coming back to her original question. Pelathina was warm beside her and she felt sleep tugging at the edges of her mind.

'Well, he was the first dragon I ever saw and I hadn't yet learned about Riders and their bond. I thought I could just borrow him for a little while, fly back to Marlidesh and get him to bite the heads off the men who'd enslaved us.'

'What happened?' Aimee asked sleepily.

'We were out on the tundra, it was when Aranati and I were walking to Kierell, and Dyrenna had just rescued us from some Helvethi. Then, while she was distracted I sneaked over, planning to leap onto Black's saddle and soar off into the sky with him.'

Aimee snorted a laugh at Pelathina's naivety.

'At the time it seemed a perfectly reasonable course of action.' Pelathina laughed too. 'Black disagreed and pinned me to the ground.'

'What?' Aimee roused herself enough to look at Pelathina.

'Look, I've got a scar from where his talon pierced my shoulder.'

Pelathina pulled open the neck of her shirt, sliding it off her shoulder. There was a small puckered scar just below her collarbone but Aimee barely noticed it. Her eyes were drifting lower, across the exposed skin of Pelathina's chest. To her disappointment Pelathina closed her shirt, but she also pulled Aimee's head back down so it was resting on her shoulder again.

'I'm sorry I've stolen your spark,' Aimee said and only half heard her own words. Sleep was wrapping a warm blanket around her mind.

'Shh,' Pelathina said softly. 'I know you'll find a way to give it back. And I promise next year we'll make your birthday a better day.'

As Aimee finally drifted off into sleep, she wasn't sure if she felt Pelathina kissing the top of her head or if she'd only imagined it.

CHAPTER 16

ORDERS

THE DOOR TO Aimee's bedroom swung open and banged against the wall. She jerked up from her sleep, reaching for scimitars that weren't on her back. Pelathina stirred beside her, rising from her own dreams.

'Hey, little hatchling, come on we…'

Aimee rubbed eyes sticky with sleep, opening them fully to see Lyrria framed by light from the corridor. Her eyes flicked from Aimee to Pelathina in bed beside her and back again. Something flashed across her face too quick for Aimee to catch. Was it hurt? Confusion? Feeling guilty, and not sure why, Aimee flung off her blanket and jumped out of bed.

She wanted Lyrria to ask, or to get angry and demand to know what was going on. That would prove that she had at least some point cared for Aimee. Instead she covered whatever she might be feeling with her usual bravado and the voice she'd used when training them.

'Jara's gathering all Riders in the dining cavern, so

get your scrawny selves out of bed and along there sharpish. If you're late I might make you do pushups.' She grinned at them but Aimee noticed the smile didn't reach her eyes.

Then she was gone, leaving the door open and the faint smell of her perfume lingering in the air. Aimee sat on the edge of her bed, pulling on her boots and feeling awkward. She wasn't sure why. It wasn't like she and Pelathina had done anything, and even if they had, she'd broken up with Lyrria; she was free to share her bed with any girl she chose.

As she stood up Pelathina did too and wrapped her in a hug. Aimee resisted for a moment then squeezed the other girl back. Then without a word Pelathina took her hand and led her out into the corridor. They walked through Anteill like that, hand in hand. Aimee wasn't sure what it meant but she decided to take a leaf out of Pelathina's book, enjoy the moment, and shove away all the worries crowding her head.

They heard the anxious buzz from the dining cavern before they entered. Inside the Riders were gathered, sitting on benches and tables, some holding mugs of tea, others with bowls of porridge. And everyone talking, whispering and worrying. Myriad dragon's breath orbs hung from the ceiling, their flickering light painting everyone with a yellowy-orange glow.

Nathine waved to them from her perch on a table near the back of the cavern. If she thought anything about Aimee and Pelathina holding hands she uncharacteristically kept it to herself. Aimee sat on the table next to her, feet up on the bench. Pelathina gave her a quick one-armed hug then wove her way through the cavern to sit with her sister. Nathine had a half-eaten bowl of porridge and she offered it to Aimee, spoon and all. Aimee smiled as she helped herself.

'What's going on?' she asked between mouthfuls.

'Well I've been stuck in the library half the night while Callant, a bunch of other councillors and some know-it-alls from the university searched through those books we found looking for any mention of the mechanism above the outer gate.'

'Did they find it?'

'Yeah, and hey!' Nathine grabbed back the bowl. 'I wasn't giving you all of it.' She snatched the spoon from Aimee's hand and began to polish off the remaining porridge. Aimee grinned to herself, thinking of the days when Nathine would have flown a hundred miles rather than touch a spoon Aimee had used, never mind lick it.

'So, we're going to collapse the tunnel above the outer gate too?' Aimee asked.

'Yeah, though the councillors argued about it for ever. You'd think it wouldn't matter since we've already sealed the inner gate.'

Aimee understood their reluctance. With only one gate destroyed the possibility of re-opening it was easier to hold on to. If the outer tunnel was collapsed too Kierell really would be sealed off, and for how long? She looked down at the bracelet on her wrist and felt frustrated again that it had stopped working. She squeezed her eyes shut and felt inside her mind. She could feel Jess, warm and comforting, but she tried to look past that connection, searching for the power she'd been able to sense before. Nothing. She turned the dial on the bracelet to the different settings, springing her eyes open each time, hoping to see everyone's sparks. Nothing.

'What are you doing?' Nathine asked in a tone that suggested she was being weird.

'The bracelet has stopped working.'

'You broke it?'

'I didn't—' Aimee began, rising to Nathine's bait before cutting herself off. 'Kyelli thinks I'm not strong enough to power it because I'm human and not Quorelle.'

'Can you take it off.'

'Nope, it's still killing me. And I've got half of Pelathina's spark stuck in my chest.'

Nathine raised an eyebrow at her. 'Well, at least your night was more interesting than mine.'

Aimee couldn't help a laugh, swallowing it quickly when several Riders turned to look at her. Nathine stretched up, making herself taller to look around.

'Where's Kyelli?'

'She stormed off because I was so useless.'

'Really, porridge-stealer? You lost track of the world's last immortal? The only person who understands that stupid bracelet.'

Aimee didn't get a chance to respond because Jara stood up on a table and yelled for quiet. She looked just as haggard as she had yesterday, and Aimee wondered if she'd gotten any sleep. Her pale hair was pulled back into a tight ponytail, making her face all harsh angles.

'Firstly, thank you.' Jara's words rang out into the silence. 'I know the last few days have been tough. We lost Lwena, and Ryka won't be lifting a blade or flying any time soon.' Jara's voice cracked as she spoke their names and many Riders bowed their heads in grief. 'But the inner gate is sealed, for now.'

'You think the Empty Warriors will still get through?' Lyrria interrupted.

'The guards in the caravan compound have heard them digging,' Jara replied.

'Kyelli's sparks!' someone swore.

'How long?' someone else asked.

Jara shook her head. 'I don't know. Days, maybe?' Jara held up her hands for silence as voices clamoured at the news. 'I know everyone's tired, and our dragons are weary, but I need to ask you all to keep going. I have no doubt I'm asking some of you to sacrifice more than you have to give but this is what we signed up for. Protecting this city is why we exist.'

Aimee felt pride in her chest and sat a little straighter. She loved that she was being counted in amongst this group of incredibly brave women.

'I've split us into four groups,' Jara continued. 'Lyrria will lead the first with the task of aiding the city guards. The caravan compound barrier needs reinforcing and we need another constructed by the tunnel leading to the harbour. I'll also want scouts from that group to watch the sea. The first hint of a ship heading our way you report to me.' Lyrria gave a mock salute. 'The second group will follow Dyrenna and it's your task to collapse the tunnel above the outer gate. Councillor Callant has the drawings for the mechanism which will let us do this.'

Aimee hoped she was assigned to Dyrenna's group. She wanted to tell Callant everything she'd seen in Vorthens and all that Kyelli had shared with them.

'Why bother collapsing the outer gate if we've sealed the inner one?' someone asked.

'Because when they dig through the rubble blocking the inner gate I'd rather only those Empty Warriors trapped in the tunnel make it through into the city, rather than their entire army.' Jara glared around the room but no one questioned her further. Everyone knew how much it hurt her to block the tunnel 'The group with me will be heading out to Lorsoke,' Jara continued. 'The leaders of the Kahollin and Ovogil tribes are inside the city.'

The mummers grew again till Jara shushed them. 'The line between an alliance and them galloping off into the tundra is as thin as the scratch from a dragon's claw. They may decide this is not their fight.'

Aimee wished she knew the Helvethi better so she could judge what they'd do. Would they decide to leave Kierell to its fate? Would they sacrifice the four Helvethi trapped in the city to prevent more deaths in their tribes?

'The final group will be with Aranati,' Jara told them. 'You are assigned to the Uneven Council, both as protection and as peacekeepers. There's a lot of angry people in the city right now. The smallest pebble can start an avalanche, and we don't need anything that'll turn into a riot.' Jara swept her stern gaze around the room. 'If any team needs reinforcements they'll come from Aranati's group. Does everyone understand?'

Aimee raised her voice in agreement with the others. Jara nodded and jumped down off the table. As the other leaders swept around the cavern, gathering up their teams, Jara headed right for Aimee.

'Come,' she ordered, and Aimee hurried off the table and followed Jara to the shadows in the back curve of the cavern. As Aimee joined her Jara grabbed her wrist, turning it over to look at the bracelet.

'Dyrenna told me,' she said, her voice low so no one would hear. 'It's stopped working.'

Aimee nodded. 'I don't know if I can fix it.'

When she looked up, the desperation in Jara's eyes took her by surprise. She'd sounded so confident issuing orders, but her eyes were wild and panicky. Aimee longed to help her.

'I can take it off and you could give the bracelet to someone else. Maybe they'd be better at using it, and seeing the connections than I am,' Aimee offered.

'I thought you said removing it would kill you?'

'It will, but if it helps save the city.'

Aimee didn't want to die. She didn't want to leave Jess, or never find out what might be with Pelathina, but the bracelet was killing her anyway. Without Pagrin's sparks she'd be dead in a few months. At least this way her death might help. But Jara was shaking her head.

'I'm not going to lose another Rider for no reason.' Jara released her wrist. 'I didn't want to hope, but when you and Kyelli presented your plan to find Pagrin I couldn't help but think maybe there was a way out of this without sacrificing Riders, or guards, or losing anyone from the city.' Jara gave her a sad smile. 'I should have known it was too good to be true. And that's not your fault,' she added as Aimee opened her mouth to speak, 'but if by some magic you do get that bracelet working again, don't wait for orders from me.' Her smile turned rueful. 'Not that you ever do. You just find Pagrin and destroy him.'

'I will,' Aimee promised, with no idea if she'd be able to keep her word.

Jara was about to turn away when she added something else. 'And for now, keep your distance from the council.'

Aimee's brow wrinkled in confusion. 'Why?'

'Just, obey me in this one thing, please.'

'Okay.'

Jara walked away, leaving Aimee with a cloud of worries.

'Aimee.' A soft voice made her look away from Jara's retreating back. 'You're with my group,' Dyrenna told her.

Aimee hurried over and was pleased to see Nathine with Dyrenna too. She looked around for Pelathina, and felt a pang of disappointment when she spotted her in a huddle with Jara's group.

'So, what's going on with you two?' Nathine whispered, her eyes following Aimee's gaze.

Aimee shrugged, not wanting to risk putting into words what she was feeling and hoping.

'She likes you,' Nathine said, sounding smug.

'Maybe. But how can I be sure?'

'You stole half her spark and did she even get mad at you.'

Aimee shook her head and Nathine gave her the *told you so* look she was so good at. Then Aimee had to pay attention because Dyrenna was outlaying their mission. Sal was in their group, biting her lip as she listened, and two others Aimee didn't yet know. According to the books Callant had deciphered there was a mechanism of cogs, like the one inside the Kyelli statue, hidden in the cliffs above the gate. It could only be reached by flying, or up a hidden staircase leading from inside the tunnel.

'Hang on, I've been through the tunnel a few times and never noticed a staircase,' Nathine pointed out.

'Perhaps it's been blocked off,' suggested one of the Riders Aimee didn't know.

'Doesn't matter, we can't access it, even if it's still there,' Dyrenna said, keeping them on track. 'So we fly Callant out to the cliffs above the gate.'

'Above the army?' asked the same Rider.

Dyrenna nodded once and Aimee tried not to let the fear show on her face. Images of Lwena's dragon being pulled down and butchered flitted through her mind. In the cliffs above the gate they'd easily be in range of the

Empty Warriors' weapons.

'Good to go?' Dyrenna looked around at them all. Aimee nodded when the others did, then followed Dyrenna from the cavern. In the corridor she remembered her previous resolution to get to know more of the Riders, so took a deep breath and matched her stride to the two women she didn't know.

'I'm Aimee.'

The Rider nearest her laughed. 'I know. I'm Intilde, and she's Sarthena. You need to tell me everything about Kyelli. I can't believe you've actually met her. What's she like?'

Aimee thought for a moment as they skirted around a stalagmite crusted with pink quartz. 'She's sad. And angry.'

'Why?' Intilde asked. She had long dark hair that she was braiding as they walked. 'Though actually if my brother created an army of monsters and sent them after me I'd be pretty pissed off too. Thankfully my brother's too busy being besotted with his newborn twins to think about anything else.'

Intilde continued to tell Aimee about her nephews but Aimee's mind had wandered, turned onto a path by Intilde's words. The breastplate said the Empty Warriors would not stop until Kyelli's city was in ashes. And from what Kyelli had told them, Pagrin felt betrayed because she and their father had left him for dead. So had he actually sent his army after Kyelli, thinking his sister was still in the city? Could they use Kyelli as bait to find Pagrin?

Aimee didn't get a chance to think on this further because they'd reached the Heart. She'd never seen it so full of Riders. Dragons were flying down from their ledges as their Riders called, filling the air with the leathery snap of wings. Their scales shone in every colour as they swept through the shafts of sunlight. Saddles were being fitted, saddlebags packed, scimitars were buckled onto backs and goggles were pulled down. One after another, dragons and Riders were shooting up the vents and into the sky.

Aimee's eyes found Jess immediately—she always knew exactly where her dragon was in the Heart—and it made her tingle to see Jess sharing a ledge with Sky-dance.

'Come on, girl,' Aimee yelled up to her, not caring who heard.

She felt Jess's eagerness as she glided down, landing beside Aimee and head-butting her so hard that Aimee stumbled backwards. She laughed and ran a hand over Jess's quivering feathers.

'I missed you too.'

Someone had brought all the Riders' saddles to the Heart already and Aimee grabbed hers, fixing it quickly to Jess's back. She felt more confident doing all the buckles now and didn't feel the need to double or triple check each one anymore. She jumped into her saddle, waiting their turn to leave the Heart. Beneath her Jess shuffled with impatience, clicking her talons on the rocky floor.

Aimee watched the other Riders, feeling the same

surge of pride she had at Jara's words. These women with their colourful, powerful dragons were inspiring in the way they confidently shot up into the sky, heading off to protect the people of Kierell. They'd fight if they needed to, risking their dragons and their lives to keep others safe. And Aimee was one of them. Jess twisted her long neck around and licked her right hand.

'Thanks,' Aimee laughed.

Then it was their turn and Jess followed Malgerus up the vent. Aimee still squeezed her eyes shut the whole way up. Outside the sky was soft and pink with morning, the air filled with the tang of the sea. Aimee scanned the sky looking for sapphire-blue wings but Skydance was already gone. Although the wrongness of Pelathina's energy still stirred in her, Aimee guiltily felt glad she had a little part of the other girl with her.

Then she was following Black across the sky, skimming the mountaintops, his huge dark wings rippling like spilled ink. She was terrified of flying above the army again, but excited to see Callant. So like Pelathina would have done, she focused on Callant, imagining the grin in his beard as she told him all she'd seen in Vorthens.

CHAPTER 17

ROCK AND ORBS

They'd found Callant in the library, sitting on the floor surrounded by books like he was a castle and they were his moat. Joy and excitement were coming off him in waves and a huge grin had split his beard when he saw Aimee. He'd waved her over and immediately launched into telling her what he'd discovered, holding up one of the books with their strange non-writing, and pointing to diagrams in it. Aimee longed to grab some tea and sit with him, sharing in his discoveries even if she didn't understand half of what he was saying.

Now they were soaring above the rooftops of Kierell, Callant sharing a saddle with Dyrenna. Black took off with two Riders on his back much more easily than Jess had. Aimee was watching Callant's face and smiling at his amazement. He kept taking a hand off Dyrenna's waist to point at views he'd never seen before and Dyrenna kept reminding him to hold on.

Aimee had learned that Intilde's dragon—his scales

a pale lavender—was called Nojell, and Sarthena's—her scales a vibrant teal—was called Flick. Jess followed Nojell and Flick along the curve of the Ring Mountains. The Griydak Sea glistened to their left, the tops of its waves touched golden by the sun. Dyrenna's plan was to approach the sheer cliffs of Norwen Peak from the south rather than flying over from the caravan compound and arriving right above the army.

Aimee didn't know this stretch of the mountains very well and she held back, following the others. She could sense Jess's delight at being back in the sky. All yesterday's tiredness was gone, and she wanted to speed through the air. They kept close to the rock as they rounded Norwen Peak, close enough that Aimee could see all the spots of colourful lichen and little purple lilybel flowers, their petals waving in the wind. She focused on the beauty knowing what horror awaited them round the cliffs.

Every time she saw the Empty Warriors the fear rose in her. Their eerie silence and the vast number of them gave her shivers. Black hovered in the sky and the others stopped close by. The dragons' backbeats swirled the air and Aimee's short curls blew in her face, tickling her chin. Dyrenna looked so poised on Black's back, her coat buttoned up to her chin and a wide silver band—her Rider's jewellery—glinting on the middle finger of her left hand. She pointed along the cliffs where a horizontal fissure ran through the rock in a dark, jagged line.

'End of that crack there's a natural tunnel through

the rock. Opens out into a cave,' Dyrenna said.

'We think that's where the mechanism is hidden,' Callant added. 'Though I'd just like to point out that my research has been very rushed and I'm only about seventy per cent sure that's where it is. And I'm definitely not certain what will happen when we activate it.'

'Well, let's find out,' Intilde called across the sky. 'And I love flying through the Quartz Teeth. Especially at this time of day.'

Nojell took the lead, zipping towards the cliffs before Aimee had a chance to ask why the tunnel was called the Quartz Teeth. The others followed, Jess at the back. The fissure passed as a dark streak to Aimee's right and then she saw it. The entrance to the tunnel was clustered with crystals, growing from all sides like the opening had teeth all around. It didn't look scary, instead it looked beautiful as all the crystals sparkled in the early morning sunshine.

'Wow. Awesome!' Nathine yelled as they swept through the entrance, their dragons' wings almost brushing the quartz.

Aimee gazed around, amazed and delighted as the crystals continued inside the tunnel, running along the walls in thick rivers of milky white, rose pink and sparkling purple. There were veins of quartz in Anteill but they were tiny, skinny veins compared to these. The sun was at just the right height in the sky that its rays shone directly into the tunnel, following the Riders as they flew between the sparkling walls. Aimee's grin bunched her cheeks up into her goggles as she watched Jess's shadow dance ahead of them through the crystals. The tunnel dog-legged and the dragons all tilted, their wings going vertical as they swept their Riders around the corner.

They plunged into darkness—the sunlight couldn't follow them here and the sparkles were gone. Aimee trusted to Jess's eyes, letting her follow the others. Long minutes passed as they flew through the dark inside of the mountain. Then Aimee saw soft light ahead and a moment later their dragons shot out into a large cave.

When they dismounted Callant had a big coughing fit but waved away any help. As they waited for him to get his breath back, Aimee was glad right now that the bracelet wasn't working. She couldn't see Callant's spark and she didn't ever want to. She worried his constant coughing meant there was something wrong and his spark would be dimming already.

'That was the most amazing thing ever!' Callant grinned at them all when he had his breath back.

Dyrenna held a finger to her lips, shushing him, and pointed to the cave mouth. Callant held up his hands in apology, and cast an anxious look towards the opening. They were too high above the army to see them. Instead the view from the cave was of the expanse of tundra, green mottled with purple heather, and off to the west the glimmer of the Griydak Sea. But the Empty Warriors were right below them, though Aimee couldn't hear a thing. Somehow that was worse. An army of humans would have been shouting, talking, bustling about and doing a hundred small things to get ready for the battle to come. But the Empty Warriors stood still and silent. They were like a monster you could forget was there, that waited till you'd lowered your guard, then pounced.

Dyrenna signalled to Intilde and Sarthena to keep watch. They crept to the cave mouth and lowered themselves to the floor, peering over the edge. Their dragons crouched behind them, wingtips fluttering.

'Where?' Dyrenna asked Callant, gesturing around the cave.

The councillor pulled a book from his coat pocket and Aimee noticed he had little flaps of paper marking different pages. He flipped it open near the middle, scanned the page and then began jogging back and forth staring at the cave floor.

'What are we looking for?' Aimee called.

Callant waved the book at her without stopping his scrutiny of the floor. 'There's a trapdoor somewhere.'

Aimee heard Nathine sigh, loud and dramatic, then both girls joined Callant in searching. Nathine had taken about three steps before she stubbed her toe on a protruding rock and swore loudly. Dyrenna threw her an anxious look and Nathine swallowed any further exclamations. But Aimee spotted something. She scurried over, shoving Nathine out the way.

'Hey,' the other girl protested.

'Callant,' Aimee called in a loud whisper.

He and Dyrenna crowded round and Aimee pointed out the handle on the floor. It had been covered by the rock Nathine had kicked. Excitement shone in Callant's eyes as he grabbed the handle with both hands and pulled. The edges of the trapdoor appeared and all three Riders had to jump back. The door was so cleverly concealed they hadn't realised they were standing on it. Stale, dry air whooshed out.

'What's down there?' Intilde called in a loud whisper from the cave mouth.

Dyrenna pulled a dragon's breath orb from her coat pocket and held it over the dark opening. Aimee saw the metal rungs of a ladder and the edge of a large cog machine. Callant made to climb down but Dyrenna grabbed his arm, stopping him. She pulled free a scimitar.

'I'll go down first. If it looks okay I'll whistle. Then Callant comes down, then Aimee. Nathine, you keep watch here.'

Aimee could feel Callant's impatience, but he stepped back and offered Dyrenna a hand. She smiled ruefully and climbed down without his help. The yellowy glow of her orb spread as she descended, highlighting more cogs and rods of metal.

'Is it safe?' Callant called barely a moment after Dyrenna reached the bottom.

Aimee watched as both the orb's light and Rider vanished out of sight and she wondered how big the space was down there. Then Dyrenna's face appeared below them, looking up and she nodded. Callant had no style or grace as he excitedly swung his legs over and climbed down, boots clanging on each rung. Aimee felt it too, the buzz of discovery just as she had when they'd been following the clues across Kierell. She quickly followed Callant down, jumping off the ladder from three rungs up.

Looking around she found herself in a low-ceilinged cave that sloped downwards in the direction of the outer cliffs. The cave was wide and across its length, just in front of them, was a huge contraption of gears and metal rods as thick as her arm.

'Sparks. What is it?'

Callant flipped the pages of his book to another one he'd marked. There were intricate drawings across the double-spread of pages—drawings of the machine before them. Callant hurried around, climbing over gears and running his thick fingers across a bank of levers as he compared it all to what he could see in the book. Aimee thought again of the knowledge Kyelli had kept from them and felt a fresh surge of anger. If they'd known about this they could have blocked the outer gate days ago and none of the guards in the caravan compound would have died.

'Can you make it work?' Dyrenna asked, eyeing the contraption warily.

'Yes,' Callant replied from behind a row of metal bars that were sunk into the cave floor. 'Maybe.'

'What'll happen when it does?' Dyrenna asked, ignoring the maybe.

'Aimee!'

Nathine's yell from above cut off Callant's answer. Dyrenna reached the ladder before her and Aimee scrambled up after the older Rider. Nathine was standing beside Malgerus, facing a corner at the back of the cave, both scimitars drawn. There was a grinding sound from behind a large boulder that angled towards the cave wall. Malgerus growled, the rumble of it echoing around the cave.

'Sparks,' Dyrenna swore. 'They found the staircase.'

Intilde and Sarthena rose but Dyrenna waved them back. 'No, keep watch there. I'll help Nathine.'

Dyrenna drew her scimitars as she and Black leapt over a ridge of rock on the floor and ran to Nathine. Aimee grabbed the last rung of the ladder, about to pull herself out of the hole but Dyrenna yelled at her without even turning around.

'No, Aimee, stay and help Callant.'

She hesitated. Empty Warriors were going to come pouring into the cave, right at Nathine. So far they'd always fought them together and Aimee didn't want to leave her friend.

'Aimee, I think I need more hands,' Callant called from below.

Jess was standing beside the hole, wingtips fluttering as she felt Aimee's indecision. 'Go and help them,' Aimee ordered, pointing at Dyrenna and Nathine. Jess growled low but she understood and Aimee felt gratitude towards her dragon. If she couldn't support Nathine then at least Jess could. She threw them a last glance. The two women stood facing the shuddering boulder, blades ready, their dragons on either side. Then she ducked back down into the hole, leaving them to face the Empty Warriors.

'What do I do?' Aimee asked, clambering through the machine, between cogs bigger than she was, to where Callant stood. They were on the other side of the machine now, where the cave floor sloped behind them and down to a shallow wall. Callant was staring at three glass circles on the side of a large metal tank. The circles had tiny writing inside and pointy red needles. Callant was chewing his bottom lip, big beard waggling as he looked from the book to the machine and back again, over and over.

From above she heard the final grinding rumble as the Empty Warriors pushed aside the boulder blocking the staircase exit. A moment later the cave filled with the clash of blades.

'Callant!' Aimee yelled.

'Here, it's here!' he cried in triumph. 'Can you get the bottom ones?'

With the book tucked under his arm Callant was unfastening metal catches at the top of the tank. Aimee crouched and found similar ones at the bottom. Up above, the roar of dragons mingled with the ringing of blades. She longed to run back up and help her friends. Jess was tugging at their connection, willing her Rider to be back by her side. Her fingers shook as she flicked open the catches. Then she fell back on her bum as a panel in the tank swung open.

'Oh, wow,' Callant gasped.

Aimee stared at what was inside. Three dragon's breath orbs, each the size of her head, hung suspended inside the tank. Above them was another tank connected to pipes that ran out the top and into the machine.

'Do you remember the cog machine inside the statue?' Callant asked, his voice echoing because he'd stuck his head inside the tank. 'This is the same, only much larger. It's powered by steam and dragon's breath. So…'

He trailed off as he pulled his head back out and studied the book. Long moments passed and the fight continued above. Aimee studied the tank as Callant continued to dither over the book. The dragon's breath orbs were hung on rope, not chains.

'Now, if that connects to there… hmm…' Callant muttered to himself.

They didn't have time for pondering. Aimee pulled a scimitar free and sliced it cleanly through all three ropes. As the orbs fell she kicked the tank door closed. She tried to shove Callant back out of the way but he was so much bigger than her that all she did was smack into him.

'What did you—'

The orbs smashed in the bottom of the tank and the roaring of released dragon's breath swallowed Callant's protests. The metal door of the tank rattled as the flames whooshed up past it. Callant hunched around Aimee, protecting her, but the tank didn't explode. Just like inside the Kyelli statue the sudden intense heat of the dragon's breath wrapped around the smaller tank inside the big one and Aimee heard the gurgle of boiling water. Then there was a hiss and a creak as steam rushed through the pipes above their heads and the cogs began to turn.

'What happens now?' Aimee yelled above the grinding of gears.

'I don't know! I was trying to figure that out!' Callant waved the book at her.

'We should...' Aimee was about to say they should climb back up when she realised the machine was between them and the ladder, and now all the cogs were turning, the pistons pumping. 'Sparks!'

'A normal fire would have taken hours to get that hot, but by using dragon's breath we can activate the machines immediately,' Callant was telling her but right then Aimee didn't care how the machine worked. She was following the flow of pipes with her eyes, trying to work out what was going to happen. How was this going to seal the gate beneath them? And how did they turn it off afterwards?

She stumbled as the floor shook. Callant stared at her, book clutched to his chest, his eyes wide but with fear this time, not excitement. The cave floor rumbled again as if there was a dragon underneath the stone. Aimee had been too busy looking up into the pipes and cogs that she hadn't bothered to look down, below the machine. There was more underneath it and she pointed just as Callant dropped to his knees to examine it.

'Aimee, look.' His voice was wary as he crawled forward.

She crouched beside him. Beneath the machine the turning cogs had opened a compartment and lowered a row of metal spikes. They hung above a series of holes that had been drilled through the rock. Instead of being dark the holes flickered with the yellowy-orange glow of dragon's breath.

'There are orbs down there.' Aimee had to yell as the machine's grinding grew louder.

'And spikes above. Did they use the machine to drill those holes?'

'Does it matter?' Aimee asked.

'Maybe.'

'What's going to happen?'

'I don't know! This is why you do proper research before turning on ancient machines!'

Something rumbled to either side of them and Aimee cast around to find the source. There were two big pipes, each running along either side of the cave floor to where it sloped down, meeting the outer cliffs. She cowered as two huge bangs echoed around the cave. Callant was gripping her arm so tight it hurt but she barely noticed. The machine had shot metal spikes from the end of those pipes, firing them directly into the rock like crossbow bolts. Aimee watched in mounting horror as cracks snaked across the rock from the impacts. Sharp fragments of stone pattered onto the cave floor.

'What's it doing?' she yelled, pointing back at the machine as her brain struggled to put together the pieces of what she was seeing.

Callant was frantically chewing his lip, big beard waggling as his eyes shot everywhere around the cave. Aimee saw them calculating and spotted the moment he figured it out. Excitement flashed across his face only to be chased away by horror. He squeezed her arm harder and this time she felt the pain.

'What?' she yelled again.

'They were fired to weaken the outer wall.' Callant stabbed a finger towards where the bolts were buried in the rock. Behind them the machine's gears spun faster.

'Why?'

Callant was staring around frantically. 'We have to get out of here. Now!'

He pulled Aimee along as he ran back up the slope towards the machine. They skidded to a halt in front of it, searching for a way through the spinning cogs and pumping pistons. Then the ground shook and Aimee wobbled on her feet as a grinding noise rumbled beneath them. It sounded like when the stone sleeve on the Kyelli statue had slid back, only louder. Something had moved inside the cave floor.

Then the metal spikes fell, shattering the glass orbs at the bottom of the holes. Aimee and Callant both screamed and ran back, away from the machine. Suddenly it froze, gears all grinding to an abrupt halt. A horribly expectant silence filled the cave. Then Aimee heard a series of muffled bangs from underneath the stone. They started next to the machine then travelled along the outer walls, underneath the pipes. With each bang the floor juddered.

'There are more dragon's breath orbs underneath us,' Aimee gasped.

'And they're exploding.' Callant stared at her, his eyes wide with fear. 'The whole cave's going to collapse!'

CHAPTER 18

CRASHING DOWN

THE REST OF Callant's words were lost as a series of loud cracks echoed through the cave. Aimee grabbed his hand and tried to pull him.

'Come on!' she yelled.

The machine had stopped. They could get back to the ladder. Callant understood and together they sprinted back up the cave. Two huge, muffled booms followed them and Aimee felt everything in the world around her shake. The floor tilted and she fell, Callant's hand slipping from her grasp. Stone dust engulfed her, catching in her throat, making her cough. Then came a sound like the world ending and it felt like the whole mountain was tumbling down around them. A second later the stone dust was gone, blown away by fresh air as the outer wall of the cave cracked open and tumbled away.

Aimee stared in disbelief as rocks bigger than she was broke free of the cliffs and disappeared over the edge. The explosions had taken out the cave wall and half of the floor with it. Then the floor lurched again and Aimee slid down it, away from the machine, towards the edge.

She scrambled, tearing her fingernails on the rock as she desperately tried to find something to hold onto. It felt like the yawning gap behind her was tugging at her legs. She gasped as she slid over a sharp lip of rock, the edges digging into her stomach. She grabbed it and lifted her head, just missing cracking her chin on the rock. She lay there for a moment, sucking in huge breaths, waiting for the panic to subside. Wind whistled around what was left of the cave, blowing her curls across her face.

Where was Callant? She twisted to the side, too afraid to get up in case the rocks moved again. Half the cave was gone and there was no sign of the councillor.

'Callant!' she yelled.

She thought she heard someone shout her name, but was it just the wind? She twisted to the other side but all she could see were the broken edges where the dragon's breath orbs had exploded and cracked open the rock.

'Aimee!'

The shout was faint but real. She had to get up. She had to find him. Bending her knees, she tried to dig her feet into the rock but her boots found only air. Then she realised her legs were sticking out over the edge. Panic reared up in her but she stamped it down. Callant needed her.

'Kyelli's sparks!' she swore, releasing her fear with the words. She pulled on the lip of rock. Her arms were a lot stronger than when she'd done the climb and she surprised herself by how easily she pulled herself back into the cave. Her feet found purchase and she risked moving up to a crouch.

'Help!'

The cry came again and this time Aimee could pinpoint it as coming from her right. Moving in a crouch she carefully made her way across the broken edges of rock. As she neared the open edge she lowered herself to her belly and crawled the last few feet. Sticking her head over the edge she came face-to-face with Callant.

On this side of the cave the rock beneath the long pipe had fallen away, and the pipe itself was bent, angling down towards the ground below. Callant clutched the end of the pipe with both hands, his body hanging in empty space.

'Sparks!' Aimee swore again, then followed with a few more curses she'd learnt from Nathine.

She could reach Callant, he was barely an arm's length away from her, but there was no way she could pull him back inside the cave. He had to weigh twice as much as she did. She looked down. The mountainside below them was a jumbled mess of boulders. The explosion had caused a rockfall that completely buried the outer gate and entrance to the tunnel. Aimee hoped it had also killed a lot of Empty Warriors. The army had certainly backed off, moving away from the spill of the rockfall.

Callant wouldn't survive the drop, and if by some magic he did, then the Empty Warriors would get him.

She looked back to him and from the look in his eyes he knew his chances too.

'Aimee, leave me. Get the—'

'Don't you dare start being stupid now,' she cut him off. Then she looked to the sky and yelled. 'Jess!'

The explosion had drowned out all sounds of the battle above and she was struggling to hear past the ringing in her ears. At least the cave roof was still above her head so it hadn't collapsed on Nathine's level.

'Aimee, I'm slipping!'

She looked back to Callant and saw his hands were bloody from gripping the broken end of the pipe. She scanned the sky, yelled for her dragon again, then looked back to the rockfall. There was a large flattish boulder below Callant and to his right. She pointed to it.

'Can you jump down to there? Then Jess and I will pick you up.'

Callant looked under his armpit, down at the boulder. 'Marhorn's sparks,' he muttered.

Aimee thought of him ensconced in his office, surrounded by papers and empty teacups. He was a man of books not battles. For a moment she thought he wouldn't do it, but then with a grunt he pushed himself away from the pipe. Aimee held her breath as he fell. A second later he landed on the boulder, crying out in pain.

'Callant!' she yelled, hands squeezing the edge of the cliff.

She watched him try to stand but his left ankle

buckled underneath him and he landed heavily on the rock. He crumpled up as one of his coughing fits engulfed him.

Just then green wings appeared in the sky. Aimee felt the surge in their connection, like a warm wave washing through her brain.

'Good girl!' Aimee yelled as her dragon cut through the sky. She swept past the entrance to the cave, the wind from her wings ruffling Aimee's hair.

Then Aimee realised the flaw in her plan. The broken cave opening wasn't large enough for Jess to land in. Jess flew past again, this time calling to her with a short, sharp roar.

'I know, Jess. I didn't think it through,' she told her dragon.

'Aimee!' Callant yelled from below.

She looked down and saw he'd shuffled on his bum to the far back of the large boulder. And that was because all their shouting had drawn the attention of the Empty Warriors. A group of twelve had detached from the army and headed for the bottom of the rockfall. They'd spread out, scattered amongst the rocks as they each found their own way up. It would only take them a few minutes to climb to where Callant sat, injured and defenceless.

'Jess!' Aimee yelled, 'I need you to hover.'

She created an image in her mind of Jess hovering just below the edge of the cliff and sent it along their connection. Immediately her dragon turned on her wing and flew back in, stopping just below Aimee. But of course she was a wing's breadth from the edge of the cliff. Before her mind could tell her what a stupid idea this was, Aimee crawled back on her belly then stood up. She took three running steps to the edge and jumped.

Pure fear and adrenaline blanketed her brain, and she left her stomach behind in the cave.

She soared through the air, cleared Jess's wing and landed on her saddle. The impact knocked the breath from her in a whoosh as she landed on her front, sprawled over the hard curve of leather. But she made it. She wished Nathine had seen her jump.

Aimee grabbed the pommel with both hands, pulled herself up and swung a leg over. Once settled in the saddle she grabbed Jess's spiralled horns and was about to command her dragon to fly towards Callant but Jess began moving before Aimee sent the instruction. Jess had anticipated what her Rider wanted.

'Good girl!' Aimee called as they swept down towards Callant.

The Empty Warriors were half way up the rockfall. Jess landed on the edge of the large boulder, her talons clacking on the rock. The councillor was huddled at the back of the boulder, still sitting, his big hands clasped around his left calf. Aimee dismounted and ran over, skidding to a halt beside him. Then she saw the shard of white bone poking out of his ankle.

'Snapped it when I landed,' Callant hissed through his beard. 'I said you should have left me.'

Aimee crouched beside him. 'You're a scholar with a

big brain and a hundred brilliant ideas. That means you're not allowed to die a heroic death.'

'I'm not?' Callant asked and Aimee could almost see a smile in his beard.

'No. You get to be rescued.'

Aimee slipped her shoulder underneath his armpit and tried to heave Callant to his feet. Nothing happened. 'I might be rescuing you but you need to help too.'

Callant opened his mouth to reply but Jess's roar cut him off. Aimee's head whipped around and she saw the first Empty Warrior appear on the boulder next to theirs.

'Stay back,' Aimee ordered Callant then ran to Jess, pulling both scimitars free. Another Empty Warrior climbed up beside the first and the others weren't far behind. For a long moment they simply stared across at Aimee. They weren't out of breath from the climb and none of them made a sound. Then came the rasp as they both drew their blades.

It was her and Jess against twelve of these monsters. Aimee felt the fear opening up inside her like a yawning pit in her stomach. It would paralyse her if she let it. Her determination flared and she stamped her foot, imagining she was squashing her fear beneath her boot heel.

'We can take them, Jess, right?'

Beside her Jess growled low and menacing. Her ruff of feathers was sticking straight out. The Empty Warriors were waiting for the others so they could attack together and overwhelm her. She felt a flicker of pride because they considered her enough of a threat to wait for reinforcements. But Aimee had let bullies club together and beat her down all her life. She'd had enough of it.

So she attacked.

With Jess following right behind she leapt across to their boulder. She took the warrior on the left, Jess the one on the right, dragon and Rider working in sync without Aimee needing to issue any commands. She ducked easily underneath the warrior's first swing, his blade whistling above her head. Still crouched, she span on her heels, arms out, blades extended. He dodged her first but her second scimitar sliced clean through his lower leg, severing it just below the knee.

Aimee gagged on the sulphur stench as molten fire spurted from his leg. It hissed as it landed on the rock. Incredibly he didn't topple and instead his sword came stabbing downwards. Aimee sprang up and back. His sword missed her, clanging off the rock. Before he had a chance to raise it again Aimee kicked the blade, knocking it spinning from his fingers. Then she thrust forward with both scimitars, one high and one low, piercing his body above and below his black breastplate. Her blades shrieked against the metal and lava poured from his wounds.

This time the warrior did fall, toppling backwards. Aimee marvelled at how easily she'd despatched him. Was she getting better at fighting Empty Warriors? But that didn't account for how fast she was moving or how strong she felt. Then she remembered the extra spark she was carrying in her chest. Was having Pelathina's energy inside her making her a better Rider? She had no time to ponder the thought—three more Empty Warriors had reached them.

Jess had clawed her first warrior and thrown him off the boulder. Aimee could see his body leaking lava on the rocks below them. She couldn't take to the air on Jess as that would leave Callant exposed. They'd have to fight standing here, side by side. She turned to try and explain this to Jess but her dragon gave her a quick head-butt. She understood.

Then the Empty Warriors were on them.

Aimee dropped into a crouch, blades held out ready. Even though it had no effect, Jess blasted them with a small burst of dragon's breath and the warriors emerged through the flames right at them. Two rushed at Aimee, one heading for Jess trying to get around her. Aimee sprang forward, her blades meeting theirs, the ring of steel bouncing off the rocks.

She delighted at the strength she felt in her muscles, the speed in her limbs. When she'd fought the Empty Warriors before they'd been unnaturally fast but now it was as if they were wielding heavy training swords, their movements sluggish.

Bouncing on the balls of her feet she danced around them, her scimitars lightening quick as she slashed inside the warriors' guard, searching for flesh to pierce. She kept moving, never giving them a target. The footwork she'd always struggled with now seemed easy.

They tried to herd her towards Jess, hoping to tangle Rider and dragon together but even though Aimee had her back turned to her dragon, it was like she could feel exactly where Jess was. As one warrior lunged at her shoulder Aimee jumped back and instinctively crouched. Jess's wing swept over her head and the curved talon on the end slashed across the Empty Warrior's forehead. He didn't make a sound as glowing lava sheeted down his face, but it blinded him to Aimee's next strike. She knocked aside his companion's thrust and with her increased strength took his sword arm off at the shoulder. Her scimitar sliced clean through and a shard of blackened bone protruded from the wound, molten fire pouring out around it.

Then, sensing what her dragon was going to do, Aimee skipped back as Jess's long neck snaked down and she grabbed the dying warrior in her mouth. Aimee heard his breastplate crunch as Jess's teeth pierced the metal. Then she flung the Empty Warrior off the boulder. Aimee barely registered the crash as he landed on the rockfall below—she was already fighting the third one.

His longsword clashed against her scimitars. The judders of the blows still ran up Aimee's arms but it no longer seemed a struggle to meet his one sword with both of hers. The flames swirled in his freakish eyes but Aimee was growing used to them and they no longer unnerved her. He increased the tempo of his strikes, thrusting high then low, feigning left then right. Aimee danced around him, a wisp of black smoke with her blades flashing like silver ribbons.

He'd drawn her away from Jess, across the slab of broken rock, and Aimee had her back to her dragon again. But through their connection she could feel Jess's anger, and her resolve, and knew she was fighting another warrior. Aimee couldn't rely on her help, not yet. She remembered the way Lyrria had taught her to be fast and nimble, her way of fighting a foe bigger than she was. She'd made Aimee practice the same moves, over and over, for hours on end till it felt like her arms would drop off. She was grateful for it now.

There was a crack running through the rock behind the warrior and Aimee pressed forward, striking for his head again and again, hoping to force him backwards. He moved to avoid her blows but when his heel caught on the broken rock he only wobbled briefly then jumped backwards, clearing the crack. Through their connection Aimee felt Jess gathering for the killing blow in her own fight.

Aimee sensed Jess moving behind her and she didn't even need to send her plan along their connection, Jess just knew. Aimee moved and attacked the Empty Warrior's right side, forcing him to block her blades and leave his left side exposed. As their blades clashed together Aimee ducked. She smelled woodsmoke as Jess attacked over her head. There was a satisfying crunch as her jaws clamped around his exposed left side, sinking deep into his thigh.

She slipped back under Jess's wing as her dragon yanked the warrior off his feet and tossed him down the rockfall. He bounced once, his breastplate clanging off the rock before his body smacked into another warrior still climbing up.

'Nice shot!' Aimee whooped, as the pair of warriors tumbled back down to the tundra in a mess of shattered bones and streaming lava.

That was six warriors killed. Half of them. And it felt like she and Jess were truly one, fighting together without even thinking about it. Aimee wondered if this was what the older Riders meant when they talked about no longer needing to give their dragons instructions.

Jess growled low in her throat and Aimee spun, looking up to her left. An Empty Warrior perched on the edge of a jagged cliff. He'd climbed up and around them, taking a different route to the others. He crouched, one hand gripping the edge of the rock, the other squeezing the hilt of his sword. The heat from his cracked, blackened hand had transferred into the blade and it glowed. The wind ruffled his dark hair and he stared at Aimee, flames swirling in his eyes.

Aimee felt the pulse in her connection with Jess, like someone had given her a nudge to the side. She dropped and rolled, moving out of the way as Jess lunged at the warrior. He'd been about to leap down on Aimee and wasn't expecting Jess's attack. Aimee came up from her roll to see him lose his grip on the rock and tumble from the cliff.

He crashed to the ground right beside her. His burning sword clattered along the rock as he landed and Aimee jumped over it. Two steps and she was above him, bringing both blades down. Her scimitars sliced into the exposed skin of his throat, meeting no resistance until they jarred on the bone of his spine. Molten fire began to spurt from the wound and Aimee leapt back. It hissed and sizzled on the rock. Behind her, the warriors they'd killed first had already leaked all their fire and collapsed to sacks of empty skin wrapped around blackened bones.

'That's seven, Jess,' she called up to her dragon, grinning at how well they were fighting together.

Jess called back from the cliff above, her feathers fluttering with pleasure and her emerald-green scales gleaming in the sunlight. Then Aimee noticed something else. There was a faint whiteish-blue line in the air, stretching from her own chest to Jess's. Aimee stared at it. It suddenly winked out of existence, and she wondered if she'd imagined it. But a moment later it reappeared, flickering and insubstantial, but definitely there.

She could see her connection with Jess.

CHAPTER 19

BREAKER OF MOUNTAINS

Aimee stepped to the side and the flickering line that connected her to Jess moved with her. It was spiderweb-thin and glowed as pulses ebbed back and forth along it. She stared down at her chest, blinking furiously. Between one blink and the next two sparks appeared in her chest, pulsing in time with her heartbeat. Then they were gone again.

'It's coming back!' she yelled up to Jess. Her dragon cocked her head to the side as if to ask what Aimee was on about.

Then Jess roared and sprang off her rock. Aimee ducked as Jess's wings skimmed overhead and she heard the crunch as Jess landed on an Empty Warrior. She spun to see her dragon pinning him to the ground, the talons of her front legs hooked right through the metal of his breastplate. The warrior thrust upwards with his sword, aiming for Jess's exposed belly.

The flickering line of connection shrank between them as Aimee ran towards Jess. She had to stretch to her full extent to block his thrust. His blade caught on her scimitar, inches from Jess's belly and with a flick of her wrist Aimee knocked it from his hand. Again, she wondered at the strength she had with two sparks burning in her chest.

Even as she was thinking this she was slicing forward with her other scimitar. Its point slid into his armpit, meeting no resistance as it cut through fire instead of muscles and organs. He scrambled to get up, lava leaking from the wound but Jess held him firm.

'Aimee!'

The shout came from above and she looked up, twisting to peer around Jess's wings. Orange flashed across the sky as Malgerus came swooping down from the higher cliffs. Aimee turned back to the rockfall and swore. Another Empty Warrior gripped the broken edge of a chunk of mountain and was preparing to jump over to the boulder she was on. She slid her blade free of the Empty Warrior Jess had pinned, and the moment her sword tip grated against his breastplate Jess reared back, picking up the still-struggling warrior. With a roar, she flung him at the one about to jump.

Jess's Empty Warrior hit the other one with such force that he was catapulted backwards into the sky. The first crashed to the rocks and Aimee heard the sickening crunch as his brittle, black bones snapped. The second tumbled through the air, away from the rockfall. In a flash of orange scales, Malgerus swooped down and snatched him from the air. Nathine guided her dragon higher and Aimee knew she was going to drop the warrior from high enough up to split him open.

As she watched Nathine she spotted the others in the sky too. Black ghosted down like a huge shadow, Nojell and Flick right behind him. There were three Empty Warriors left, all of them converging on Aimee, but now their faces turned to the new threats above.

Aimee knew the others could handle three warriors, so she turned and ran back to Callant. He was sitting slumped at the back of the boulder. There was a small pool of blood around his broken ankle.

'Hey.'

Aimee crouched down beside him. His face was chalky-white and his hands were shaking with pain. But he looked up at her and he smiled.

'I've never seen a Rider and dragon fight before. You were both incredible.'

Aimee wanted to take the compliment, she really did, but she'd only been so good because she had help—Pelathina's spark giving her a boost of energy and strength.

'But as interesting as it is watching you,' Callant continued, 'I'd really like to be rescued now.'

'Can you stand?' Aimee asked.

'Not sure,' Callant answered through gritted teeth.

Aimee looked down at him, unsure how she could help him to his feet. Could Jess pick him up without hurting him?

'I'll help,' a new voice said from behind.

Aimee turned as Nathine dismounted and hurried over.

'Hey, Beardy,' she said as she slipped her shoulder under Callant's arm. 'Did you have to break the whole mountain?'

It was a sign of Callant's pain that he didn't have a return quip for Nathine. Aimee quickly took his other arm and together she and Nathine hoisted him up. Callant teetered for a moment, almost dragging all three of them back down but they managed to hold him. Aimee remembered the way Nathine had avoided getting too close to Callant before, because he reminded her of her abusive father. But now when he needed her, Nathine hadn't hesitated and Aimee was proud of her friend. They carefully helped Callant hop over to the dragons.

'It's a good thing I appeared when I did,' Nathine said, directing her words around Callant's chest towards Aimee. 'That Empty Warrior was almost on you and Jess. Another minute and you'd have been dead.'

'What?' Aimee spluttered. 'I'd already killed eight before you bothered to show up.'

'Really?'

'Yes! And I was just thinking something nice about you but now I take it back.'

'Oh, what did you—'

'Can you do this when I don't have a bone sticking out of my leg?' Callant cut in, his words squeezed out through gritted teeth.

They reached their dragons. Malgerus was head-butting Jess and she snapped playfully at him. Aimee scanned the cliffs for enemies but thankfully there were none. She looked for Dyrenna and the others, spotting them near the bottom of the rockfall. They weren't close enough for the army to fire at them, but they could stop any others from climbing up while Aimee and Nathine got Callant away.

'I'd be better taking him on Mal,' Nathine said, and her words were soft, not boastful. She was right: Malgerus was bigger and stronger, better able to carry someone as heavy as Callant.

As Nathine gave Malgerus instructions to crouch down so they could ease Callant onto his saddle, Aimee stared hard between Rider and dragon, looking for the line of their connection. Nothing. She couldn't see the one between herself and Jess now either, but she was sure she hadn't imagined it. Why had it only appeared while they were fighting?

Now that she wasn't focused on staying alive she was aware of the power of the bracelet again, pressing against her mind. It was stronger, more insistent, and Aimee realised the mental wall she'd built to keep it out had cracked in places.

With Callant awkwardly perched in the saddle, Nathine climbed up behind him. Aimee doubted he'd enjoy the flight back as much as the one out. He held his leg out, away from Malgerus's body and blood dripped off his boot. Malgerus took off and Aimee jumped into her saddle, Jess following them into the sky.

Black and the others soared up to meet them. Dyrenna assessed the situation in a heartbeat, her face filling with concern.

'Nathine, go. Don't wait for us. Get Callant to the surgeons at the university hospital,' she ordered.

Nathine pulled down her goggles and nodded. Malgerus rose above them, his huge wings eating up the sky as they flew back over the slopes of Norwen Peak.

'Well, it worked, though that was definitely not what I was expecting,' Intilde said, gesturing at the rockfall.

From her vantage in the sky Aimee could finally see the full extent of the destruction the explosion had caused. The explosion she'd set off. The cave with the machine was a shallow, dark hole in the mountainside, the edges of broken pipes jutting from it. Below the mountainside was raw—cracked boulders, a lighter grey than the cliffs around them, had tumbled all the way down to the tundra below. The tunnel entrance and outer gate were gone, buried completely.

'What were the bangs we heard?' Sarthena called over. She and Flick were flying slow circles away from the others, keeping an eye on the army below. Flick's scales shone like polished turquoise as she cut through the sky.

'Dragon's breath orbs exploding,' Aimee shouted back, then lowered her voice. 'Callant wanted to wait, to figure out what the machine did before we started it, but I thought we didn't have time for that. Maybe I should have listened to him.'

'You activated the machine?' Dyrenna asked and Aimee nodded.

'Wow.' Intilde's eyes opened wide and behind the lenses of her goggles they looked huge. 'For a little person you can certainly cause a lot of destruction.'

'I didn't think it would be so...' Aimee struggled for a word, 'so bad.'

'Bad? It's not bad, it's great.' Intilde grinned a lop-sided smile at her. 'And when they write songs of today, you make sure they add you in as Aimee, the Breaker of Mountains.'

Aimee floundered for any sort of reply to that. The idea that anyone would sing a victory song with her in it was too strange an idea for her brain to hold on to. Also, she knew they'd had no choice, but guilt still nipped at her. Everyone without a dragon was trapped inside the mountains now, maybe forever. The city was safe from monsters but it would shrivel. And, thinking of the angry mob in Quorelle Square, maybe turn on itself.

'Did work,' Dyrenna nodded. 'But it's only bought us time.'

'Away and stick your head in a cloud.' Intilde batted the air as if fending off Dyrenna's negative words. 'We've stopped that army from getting inside and trapped the ones in the tunnel. We should take a moment to enjoy being heroes.'

Dyrenna didn't answer, instead she pointed. Aimee followed the line of her finger and spotted them.

'Kyelli's sparks,' she swore softly.

Above the machine cave was the open entrance to the cave that the tunnel led into—the cave where the others had been fighting to give Aimee and Callant time to work the machine. Now the lip of that cave was crowded with Empty Warriors. Their eyes glowed like a row of tiny dragon's breath orbs. Aimee felt all the strength and confidence she'd enjoyed while fighting ebb away. The warriors at the lip of the cave were edging out onto the cliff face, searching for a way up. Aimee traced the sharp lines of Norwen Peak. It was easily four times higher than the cliffs she'd climbed to Anteill and utterly sheer in places. They couldn't climb all the way up there, could they?

She knew they would. They'd find a way. She looked from the cave down the tumbled boulders of the rockfall to the waiting army. She'd made them a staircase. Already the Empty Warriors were gathering at the base of the broken cliffs, splitting into tight groups to begin the climb.

'We're not enough to stop them,' she said, not really meaning to speak the thought aloud.

'No,' Dyrenna agreed.

Four dragons could try and thin them out, pick off the warriors as they climbed, but they'd never get them all. And how long before each of the Riders was shot down?

'What do we do?' Sarthena asked. She'd flown Flick over to join them. There wasn't much point in keeping an eye on the army now.

'Long climb,' Dyrenna said, looking up towards Norwen Peak.

'Yeah, and they might not find a way up. Those cliffs are sheer at the top,' Intilde pointed out.

But despite Intilde's assurances a moment ago, Aimee could see the doubt in her eyes.

'Can't do any good here,' Dyrenna said, quietly and half to herself. Then she turned to Intilde and Sarthena. 'Head back into the city and join Lyrria's group. Make sure those barricades are as strong as we can make them.' She looked up at the snowy peak above them. 'And make sure there's always someone watching Norwen Peak.'

'They won't make it over,' Intilde insisted but it sounded like she was trying to convince herself.

A moment later she and Sarthena were gone, leaving Aimee in the sky with Dyrenna. The older Rider's face was creased with worry and it didn't change when she turned to look at Aimee.

'What now?' Aimee asked, echoing Sarthena's question.

'We find Jara,' Dyrenna told her, nodding towards the open tundra.

Aimee felt torn. She got a buzz of excitement because Pelathina was with Jara, but she wanted to go back into the city. She needed to check Callant was alright. And she wanted to find Kyelli again. Kyelli wanted her to embrace the power of the bracelet, to let it into her mind but Aimee wasn't going to do that. The power was corrupting and she wouldn't let herself become a monster. But the bracelet had started working again while she and Jess fought so maybe there was another way that she, as a human, could use it. She needed to ask Kyelli about it.

'I saw my connection,' she told Dyrenna.

'With Jess?'

Aimee nodded. 'When we were fighting, I saw it between us. And I saw the sparks in my chest, mine and Pelathina's.'

'Now?'

This time Aimee shook her head. 'It's gone again but I don't know why. And I think the only person who understands all this is back in the city.'

'You want to go looking for Kyelli?'

Aimee nodded but Dyrenna shook her head. Before the older Rider could speak Aimee waved the bracelet at her. 'It's the only way I'll be useful again.'

'Useful is the problem,' Dyrenna said so quietly Aimee almost didn't hear her.

'What do you mean?'

For a long moment Dyrenna just watched her, Jess and Black flying slow circles around each other. Then she shook her head.

'Just gotta keep you away from the council for now.'

Jara had said something similar back in the dining cavern after she'd assigned them all their missions.

'Why can't I go near the council? I'm not a danger to them. The bracelet isn't even working right now.'

'It's not that.'

'Then what?'

Dyrenna didn't answer. Instead she turned her face northwards, looking out across the isthmus.

'What?' Aimee yelled this time.

Dyrenna seemed to have made a decision because

when she looked back at Aimee she spoke.

'There's some on the council that want you to use the bracelet.'

'To find Pagrin?' Aimee asked.

'Jara told them what you learned from Kyelli, about how the bracelet can be used to create Empty Warriors.' Dyrenna was shaking her head, disagreeing with her own words even as she spoke them. 'Some, not all but enough, want you to use the bracelet to create warriors for us.'

It took a moment for the meaning of Dyrenna's words to sink in. And when they did Aimee recoiled, accidentally pulling on Jess's horns so her dragon's wings stuttered in the air, unsure what her Rider wanted. Aimee felt again the power of the bracelet pushing against her mind like a headache. She leaned against her mental door, keeping it closed, keeping the power out.

'I can't.' Her words quivered.

'I know. You don't have spare sparks like the Quorelle.'

That was technically true but what Aimee felt more strongly was the wrongness of using life energy to create creatures of war and death.

'Even if I had ten thousand sparks inside me I wouldn't use them to create warriors,' Aimee said firmly.

Dyrenna nodded, her mouth twitching with a smile and Aimee sensed she approved of her words.

'Some on the council don't share your morals,'

Dyrenna told her.

Aimee thought of Beljarn, desperate to always oppose Jara and terrified of the world outside the Ring Mountains. She could easily imagine the ruthless streak in him finding a way for humans to use the bracelet to create Empty Warriors. He'd see it as a way to save his city but what would an Empty Warrior army, given the purpose to protect Kierell, do? Kill Helvethi on the tundra? Kill Riders who opposed the council's plans? Barricade everyone inside the city and never let them leave? Would Kierell become overrun by groups of sparkless monsters with no compassion, no mercy, and no humanity?

With a gentle nod of her head for Aimee to follow, Dyrenna pushed on Black's horns and headed out towards the tundra. Aimee still longed to head back and find Kyelli but she agreed for now to let Dyrenna and Jara protect her and stay clear of the council. She gave Jess's front ribs a squeeze and her dragon flapped after Black. Her thoughts turned to Pelathina who was this way, and that if the bracelet was maybe working again then Aimee could return her spark. And see her enchanting smile.

They stayed high above the army, skimming the underside of clouds until they were over the tundra proper. Then Black led them downwards and they swooped across the land at only the height of a house. Aimee realised she'd never really flown with Dyrenna before and it interested her to see the difference. With Nathine and Pelathina they'd cut through the high sky, with huge views all around and enjoyed the rush of a dive any time they needed to be lower. But Dyrenna kept Black thirty feet above the ground as they flew. It made the view smaller and the horizon closer.

The morning was clear and Aimee could feel Jess's pleasure at being out in the sky again. She sank into the moment, letting her senses merge with Jess's, trying to be so in sync again that she could see their connection. She felt the ripple of Jess's strong muscles beneath her and was aware of the way Jess listened, cocking her head as she flew, hearing hares skip across the grass beneath them. She smiled as Jess stuck out her tongue, tasting the air and rain to come. She loosened her grip on Jess's spiralled horns and tried to guide her more gently.

She slowly peeked down at her chest, wishing, hoping. There was nothing—no sparks and no spiderweb-thin line between her and Jess.

'Argh!' she shouted into the sky, shattering her serene concentration.

Dyrenna looked around at her shout and Aimee shook her head, exasperated. Dyrenna didn't ask and that was fine by Aimee. It felt like she had three hundred things to think about. Why had she only seen their connection when she and Jess were fighting? She hadn't felt any different then to how she did now.

There was another thought in her mind. It had been born during the fight on the rockfall but Aimee had ignored it till now because it made her feel icky. She'd been faster and stronger as she fought because she had extra life energy inside her. Pelathina's spark had made her better. And Aimee had liked the feeling of being more skilled, and less afraid of the Empty Warriors. It made her sick to admit it, but she could finally see the appeal of the power the bracelet granted her. But using that power meant stealing life from other people and that thought kicked and rebelled inside her head like an unruly dragon. She wouldn't do it, no matter how great it felt to be a better Rider.

She could sense the power of the bracelet circling her mind, pushing at her, looking for a way in. She shored up her mental wall. She would not become like the Quorelle.

CHAPTER 20

LIGHTNING AND WINGS

She and Dyrenna flew for a couple of hours into a warm afternoon. But before they reached the Helevthi camp on the shores of Lake Ceil, Aimee spotted Jara and the others in the sky. Dyrenna signalled for her to slow and Aimee pulled gently on Jess's horns. She scanned the sky for sapphire-blue wings and spotted them at the back of the group.

'They're not going to help us!' Jara yelled across the sky.

'What happened?' Dyrenna asked as Jara and the others caught up with them.

'They don't think this is their fight.' Jara kept flying, straight past Aimee and Dyrenna. They both pulled their dragons into quick turns and followed Faradair.

'What about their leaders, trapped in the city?' Dyrenna asked as Black caught Faradair.

Aimee saw Jara shake her head angrily. 'They'd sacrifice them to protect the whole tribe.'

Aimee's stomach clenched. They were on their own.

'What do we do?' she yelled across to Jara.

'All we can do,' Jara replied, without turning in her saddle, 'is defend ourselves for long enough to give you time to find and kill the Master of Sparks.'

'Pagrin,' Aimee whispered.

She wondered for the hundredth time where he was. With his army? Was he watching them scale the mountains with their inhuman strength? Or was he inside the city somewhere? Was he gleefully watching it fall to pieces around him, taking revenge on innocents because his sister left him for dead?

Despite having seen his face thousands of times over in the Empty Warriors, Aimee still struggled to picture Pagrin. His Empty Warriors were everywhere but he was nowhere. It reminded her of the way she'd felt growing up. Bullies, sneers and insults had lurked anywhere she went and the whole city had felt like her enemy. It had been a feeling, a sensation, a nameless thing that scared her. Pagrin felt like that too.

But Aimee was past being intimidated by bullies. This time she'd face up to her enemy, and she would defeat it. Inside her mind she saw the flame of her determination rise higher.

She looked across at Jara. 'I can make the bracelet work again,' she promised.

Jara still didn't turn around, her angry gaze fixed straight again, but she did nod at Aimee's words. The weight of responsibility settled on Aimee's shoulders, but instead of feeling oppressed by it, she embraced it.

When they were back in Kierell, she'd take Nathine

and Pelathina and fly the city street by street if they had to in order to find Kyelli. Then Aimee would make her tell them everything she was still holding back, and in that knowledge Aimee was sure would be the key to getting the bracelet working again.

Aimee let Jess slow and dropped towards the back of the flight of dragons. Here she found Pelathina and they shared a smile. Their dragons' scales shimmered in the bright light of the afternoon. As they soared above the tundra Aimee felt Jess's pleasure at flying in a flight of dragons. Jess was always delighted to be in the sky but Aimee had noticed her joy was always heightened when there were other dragons beside her.

Within a couple of hours the Ring Mountains were looming large and grey ahead of them. And not long after that a summer storm found them. Squally showers swept in off the Griydak Sea, soaking them, and lightning flashed on the horizon above the waves. Aimee looked across at Pelathina who was huddled down, her chin tucked into her scarf and her coat collar pulled up. She looked miserable and Aimee tried to think of something funny to say to make her smile.

She didn't get a chance because Dyrenna called out a warning to Jara. Aimee scanned the sky, spotting purple wings that looked almost black underneath the dark clouds. It was Lyrria and Midnight. Worry scrunched up Aimee's brow. Lyrria been tasked to lead the group strengthening the city's defences. Why was she out beyond the mountains?

'Jara!' Lyrria yelled across the sky.

Faradair put on a burst of speed, the other dragons all following him. Lyrria guided Midnight around, dragon and Rider slicing through the sky till they were facing back the way they'd come.

'Those freakish bastards have come in boats! They appeared this afternoon, rowing from the beaches at the edge of the Ardnalich Forest. We thought they'd take till tomorrow to arrive.'

'The barricade at the harbour?' Jara called back, shouting above the wind and rain.

'It's only half finished!'

'Might not know where our harbour is,' Dyrenna joined in, bringing Black closer to Midnight.

'Oh they know.' Lyrria gestured wildly, cutting through the rain. 'Their first boat landed there half an hour ago. The others will reach it within the hour. Those monsters row fast!'

'Did you close the gates?' Jara asked, her voice high and panicky.

'Of course we closed the bloody gates!' Lyrria shot back.

Fear gripped Aimee's insides with an icy hand. The gates that sealed each side of the short tunnel through the mountains to the harbour were flimsy compared to the ones at the main tunnel. The Empty Warriors would break through them both tonight. Then the army would be inside the city.

Jara didn't bother issuing orders. Everyone knew what they had to do. She simply looked around at them, her blonde hair plastered to her head, and yelled.

'Fly!'

Jess practically leapt in the air as Aimee pushed her horns and flooded their connection with her need for speed. The sound of wingbeats almost drowned out the rush of wind. The dragons' wings batted aside the rain, sending droplets flying in every direction. Within moments Aimee was even more soaked than she'd been before. They were heading into the storm and the wind blasted rain at her face, stinging her cheeks like a slap.

At least she could still see. The rain ran straight off her goggles, barely disrupting her vision. She remembered Lyrria explaining once how the lenses were coated with something that made them water repellent. She hadn't really been listening at the time because she was thinking to herself that if it was raining that heavily then she hoped she wouldn't be out flying.

They followed the eastern curve of the Ring Mountains as the evening deepened and the storm worsened. Forked lightning lit up the sky and Aimee saw dragons in the air ahead.

'Lyrria!' Aimee heard Jara yelling above the wind. 'Go and grab anyone who can be spared from building the barricade. Now!'

Midnight peeled off, one wingtip pointing downwards, the other upwards, as Lyrria turned her in the air. Aimee watched as she disappeared into the rainclouds above the city. The others kept flying onwards and a moment later they were past the mountains and above the roiling sea. The storm whipped up the waves, giving them life and sending them crashing into the cliffs of the mountains. The noise was intense.

Lightning snaked across the sky again and Aimee saw the boats. They were the same longboats she'd seen the army arrive in. The wooden boats curved upwards at bow and stern, their bellies filled with rowing benches, and each had a single mast in the middle, their sails all furled. So far only one had made it into the calmer waters of the small harbour. The others were being tossed around by the waves but the Empty Warriors were strong and they'd keep rowing till they made it or drowned.

Aimee tried to count them but she kept losing sight of the boats as the lightning came and went. There must have been fifty of them, each boat holding thirty Empty Warriors. And eight Riders to stop them.

Thunder rumbled across the sky above them like the world's largest dragon. They were right in the eye of the storm now. Aimee's gloves were sodden and her hands were freezing as she gripped Jess's horns. She hadn't put her scarf on and the rain ran right down her neck and inside her coat.

Faradair let out a roar and a burst of dragon's breath. 'Don't let them get to the harbour!' Jara shouted as she pulled free one scimitar. 'Companion formations and swooping falcon attacks.'

Aimee waited a moment for more orders, but that was it. She looked around, unsure what to do because she hadn't been taught about companion formations or swooping falcon attacks. The darkness, the rain and Riders' goggles meant she couldn't see any of the other women's faces. Were they as scared and usure as she was?

Blue filled the corner of her vision as Skydance swept past Jess. 'Stick with me!' Pelathina called over.

Aimee pulled a scimitar free and gripped it tight. She felt the vibrations as Jess growled, the sound lost in a crash of lightning. Skydance dived and Aimee pushed Jess's horns. Her dragon tucked in her wings and shot after him. Her stomach lurched and the wind blasted her face, but her veins pulsed with adrenaline. She was diving at top speed and only holding on with one hand. It was terrifying and exhilarating.

The churning sea came rushing towards them and Aimee spotted the boat that was Pelathina's target. She barely had to adjust Jess's course as her dragon understood and tucked in behind Skydance, following him exactly. Skydance levelled off from his dive with a whoosh of wings. Jess mirrored him, and Aimee revelled in the strength of her dragon.

The Empty Warriors were rowing, their blackened hands concealed inside chainmail gloves as they gripped the oars. None had weapons out and none were ready for the dragons. As the dragons swept towards the prow of the boat Pelathina switched hands on Skydance's horns and leaned over, her blade in her left hand. Aimee did the same, her heart hammering as she took a deep breath before switching hands on Jess's horns, letting go for a split second. Jess seemed to understand what she needed and stopped flapping just for a moment, keeping her body as still as she could.

'Good girl,' Aimee said, her words torn away by the wind.

She leaned down to the right just as Jess swept over the raised prow. Ahead Skydance raked his talons along the heads of the warriors, Pelathina slashing down at any body part she could reach. They were low enough that the Empty Warriors could have easily grabbed Skydance but they were unprepared for the attack and he was too fast.

Jess followed right on his tail. Aimee felt the juddering impacts as Jess's talons sliced through the warriors' flesh, grating on bone. She flicked with her tail too, knocking Empty Warriors into the roiling waves. Aimee attacked as well, feeling an increased strength in her arm as her blade cut cleanly through raised arms and faces. She was leaning right out of her saddle but her left hand held firm to Jess's spiralled horn.

Even through the rain Aimee smelled the stench of sulphur as lava poured from the wounds she inflicted. Her eyes flicked up, seeing something at the edge of her vision. It was the ship's mast. Jess caught her thought the moment it sprang to life in her brain and she gave a powerful flap of her wings, tilted them to the side and grabbed the mast with the talons of her lower legs. Aimee used the moment to stab straight down, once, twice, again and again, piercing Empty Warriors before they could let go of their oars and draw their blades.

Then the moment Aimee thought they should move, they did. With a powerful push of her legs Jess launched them back into the sky. Every muscle, fibre and nerve in Aimee thrilled at how strong she was. And she loved the way it felt as she and Jess moved like they were one being.

They cut through the air, rain still battering against them and Aimee looked down at the boat. Lightning forked across the sky above the mountains, illuminating the scene with white brilliance. In that moment Aimee saw that she and Pelathina had killed more than half the warriors on the boat in one pass. The ones still alive kept rowing, their purpose driving them towards the harbour. Fires flickered to life amongst the wooden benches, where lava poured from injured warriors, but the rain quickly doused them. The lava kept eating through the wood, though, and as Aimee watched the bow of the boat began to sink.

The Empty Warriors didn't scream or thrash as they drowned. They simply kept rowing as the waves washed over them, dragging their bodies down. Aimee felt relief as the boat disappeared—thirty less warriors to harm people in Kierell. But there were still hundreds more.

Skydance was already flying towards the next boat, the colourful ribbons tied to his saddle whipping around in the storm. Jess sensed Aimee's desire and flapped after him. Riders cut through the sheeting rain around them, their dragons' wings dark one moment then shimmering brightly as lightning forked across the sky.

'You good?' Pelathina yelled, half turning in her saddle.

'Good!' Aimee replied and it was true. She felt as she had fighting the Empty Warriors to protect Callant—

strong, skilled and in tune with her dragon.

Skydance tucked his wings and nosedived, Pelathina a small dark shape on his back. Aimee sheathed her scimitar, pushed both of Jess's horns and squeezed with her thighs. Jess dived. Her wings pressed against Aimee's shoulders, and the wind pushed the rain droplets from Jess's scales. They streamed off her in glistening ribbons.

Aimee didn't worry about pulling up at the right moment, or what would happen if she didn't, she simply trusted her dragon.

Skydance pulled out of his dive and skimmed the length of the boat, blasting the warriors with dragon's breath. They were impervious to the flames but their boat wasn't. Skydance's breath danced and crackled down the keel, along the hull and shot up the mast. Dragon's breath burned hotter than normal fire and it burned for a few long moments, eating into the wood, before the sheeting rain dampened the flames.

There was no jolt as Jess pulled out of her dive. She flared her wings and they swept along the boat. Aimee pushed gently on her right horn, guiding her towards the blackened mast. Jess's talons crunched into the fire-damaged wood as she grabbed the mast with her fore and back legs, pressing her belly against it. Aimee held tight to Jess's horns to stop herself sliding backwards off her saddle and down into the boat below.

An arrow thunked into the wood of the mast beside them and Aimee swallowed a scream. This time the Empty Warriors were ready for them.

'Push, Jess!' she yelled above the roaring wind.

The boat rocked wildly in the waves and Aimee was grateful because it threw the Empty Warriors off balance. Their arrows cut the air around her and Jess, but all of them dropped harmlessly into the seething waves.

Aimee pressed her weight against Jess's, trying to help her dragon. She'd seen the way Skydance's breath had burned the mast and assumed it would be weakened enough that she and Jess could snap it, but it wasn't budging. Just as she was about to give up and head for the sky a judder ran down the wood. Looking up she saw Skydance clinging to the mast, same as Jess, but near the top. His additional weight was enough to do it and the mast snapped.

The crack of wood was lost in a rumble of thunder and Aimee felt suddenly weightless as she and Jess tumbled forward. She straightened and pulled on Jess's horns, pressing her lower ribs with her heels instead of squeezing with her thighs. It was the command to lift off but she hardly needed it because Jess was already rising, her wingbeats swirling the rain. The mast continued to fall as they rose above it and Aimee watched as it smashed through the stern of the boat, shooting splinters of wood into the sky.

'That was awesome!' Pelathina called across the sky at her.

Aimee beamed at the praise then blinked. She guided Jess close to Skydance and stared at Pelathina's chest. Slowly, as if it was emerging from inside her, Pelathina's spark began to glow. Aimee looked down at her own chest and saw two sparks there, her own bright one and the fainter energy that she'd stolen from Pelathina.

'They're back!' she yelled.

'Who's back?'

'Our sparks. I can see them again!'

Aimee turned Jess, looking at the battle around them. Others had joined them from the city and Riders flew through the air in pairs, attacking the ships in quick swooping dives. Even in the dark and the rain Aimee could see the positions of everyone because once again she could see their sparks. Greenish-white balls of light danced through the sky, each one pulsing faintly in time with its owner's heartbeat.

She turned back to Pelathina and gasped. There was a faint line, spiderweb thin and glowing blue, reaching from Pelathina's heart to Skydance's. She looked to the other Riders but they were too far away for her to see their connections. She could see her own though. And as if sensing that she'd just spotted it, Jess snorted a small puff of smoke that seemed to be saying that she knew it was there all along.

'Aimee! Pelathina!' a voice called from behind.

Aimee turned Jess, her dragon gliding smoothly through the air, to see a Rider speeding towards them. Lightning forked across the sky, striking the jagged mountains behind the Rider. Her dragon's scales shimmered a blazing orange and her spark shone bright like a sun in her chest.

'Nathine!' Aimee yelled. 'Is Callant—'

'Beardy's fine but the harbour isn't.' Nathine cut her

off. 'Come on!'

Malgerus swept underneath Skydance and Jess, roaring a quick greeting to his dragon friends before he and Nathine turned back towards the mountains.

Jess and Skydance followed, and Aimee glanced around, seeing other Riders converging on the harbour. Half the longboats were gone, their crews sank beneath the waves without a sound or trace, but two were rounding the jutting curve of rock that protected Kierell's harbour. With the one boat that had already landed, that meant there were close to one hundred Empty Warriors about to break through into the city.

Aimee pushed Jess for more speed.

CHAPTER 21

THE WORST PLAN

THE STORM WAS moving across the city, taking the rain with it. As Aimee and the other Riders sped towards the harbour it turned to a drizzle that pattered on their dragons' wings. Aimee hardly noticed. She could feel Jess's strength underneath her and sensed her own determination reflected back at her. Kierell was Jess's home too and she'd fight to protect it.

'Arrow-tip formation.'

The order came from somewhere to Aimee's right and she recognised Jara's voice. She'd never flown in formation with so many Riders but Jess seemed to know what to do. She timed her wingbeats to match those of Skydance and Malgerus, the two dragons closest to her, and the three slotted into a line with Malgerus at the rear. The Riders flew in a V-shape like migrating geese. Aimee heard the rasp as blades were drawn and pulled hers free too.

Now she was close to them, Aimee could see the connections between each woman and her dragon. They glowed a soft blue and pulsed every time a command or emotion was shared through their bonds.

The Riders rushed towards the mountains, skimming above the sea, spray from the heaving waves coating the dragons' bellies and their Rider's boots. An arm of rock curved out from the base of the cliffs making a natural harbour, inside which Kierell's small fleet of fishing boats was safely tucked away from the storm. As they neared, the second of the Empty Warriors' longboats disappeared inside the harbour.

'Left side, last boat. Right side, first boat.' Jara called back the orders from her place at their formation's point. 'Arrow tip, we'll take the gate.'

Aimee was flying in the right side of the V-shape which meant she'd be attacking the first boat. She squeezed the hilt of her scimitar.

The Riders swooped up and over the rocky arm of the harbour in a sinuous wave. Flying second from the back, Aimee was one of the last to enter the harbour and she missed the moment the weapon was fired.

The Empty Warriors from the very first boat had occupied the wide rocky ledge at the back of the harbour and the base of the cliffs. Behind them was the locked gate that led into the tunnel. Around them were piles of crates and lobster pots. They'd shifted them together to make a defensive wall, and on top of it they'd mounted one of their bolt-firing weapons.

The bolt shot through the air and straight into the Rider beside Jara. Its deadly tip tore through her dragon's neck and pierced her body. She screamed as she fell from her saddle, tumbling through the sky. Aimee saw her spark flare bright before extinguishing.

'Fineya!' Pelathina cried.

Fineya's dragon Burnish collapsed in on himself, wings, neck and legs all curling up as he died in the air. Aimee watched with horror as the line of his connection with Fineya blinked out of existence. He dropped from the air, knocking Fineya's body as they both fell into the sea, disappearing beneath the dark water. The whole thing had happened in a matter of seconds.

'Another one!' someone yelled.

Aimee heard the grind and clink of gears as the Empty Warriors fired another bolt. The Riders scattered, their formation torn to shreds as they all pulled their dragons up, down, out, and away, desperate to avoid the same fate as Fineya. Aimee and Jess shot high above the harbour. She twisted around frantically, searching the sky for Nathine and Pelathina. Fear clawed at her heart when she couldn't find them. Dragons littered the sky, scattered above the harbour all seeking safety, their attack abandoned.

The weapon fired again. Aimee hated that these monsters were taking the sky from her. Up here on their dragons was supposed to be where they were safe. The bolts were on ropes so as they fired one, warriors were winding in the previous. It meant they could fire almost continuously. And the machine rested on cogs, which meant the warriors could swivel it to fire anywhere in the harbour.

The lightning had moved across the city and as it

forked the sky it lit up the harbour just enough for Aimee to see a flash of blue and orange behind her. Jess circled in the air and Aimee spotted her friends landing on the jagged rocks of the arm of the harbour. Relief at seeing them safe let her heart beat again and she flew Jess over to join them. On the rocks they were out of range of the bolts and Aimee had a chance to take in the scene. The lightning had dragged the storm clouds after it like they were a soggy bundle of baggage, and above them the sky was clear. A full moon painted the harbour in silvery light.

The other Riders were following them, dodging the bolts and flying to the safety of the rocks. High above Faradair roared and Aimee heard Jara's scream of anguish at losing another Rider. The shimmering line of her connection with Faradair vibrated with emotions. The waters inside the harbour were calmer than the sea beyond but there was no sign of Fineya and Burnish. They were gone.

Blood-red wings cut the sky as Jara flew down to join them. Under the cover of their bolt-firing weapon the other two boats rowed easily up to the shallow cliffs of the harbour. Aimee watched, feeling angry and useless. There were rings in the wall for boats to tie up and steps cut into the rock leading up to the ledge.

'Kyelli's sparks!' someone swore as the Empty Warriors began filing up to the harbour.

Beyond the barricade of crates and lobster pots, behind the bolt weapon, the Empty Warriors were hammering at the gate with a makeshift ram. The gate was wood, unlike the ones at the main tunnel, and Aimee could hear the resounding thumps every time the ram hit.

'If we rush them all at once they might not have time to fire,' a voice further along the rocks suggested, though she didn't sound certain.

'Can't. If we bunch together, and they fire, it'll rip right through us,' Dyrenna replied.

'What about flying away from the harbour, up into the mountains behind them, and then attacking down the cliffs onto their heads?' This suggestion came from Pelathina.

'Won't work,' someone else called. 'They'll just swivel that machine and fire up at us.'

'Sparks!' Jara yelled in frustration.

As the Riders threw more and more desperate suggestions into the mix Aimee studied the bolt machine. The cogs meant it could swivel, so no matter what direction the Riders flew at the warriors, they'd be shot from the sky. But what if they didn't attack from the air?

An idea took shape in Aimee's mind. When the bolts had been flying Aimee had desperately wanted to hide—it was what she'd always done after all. But what if hiding was the way to win here. Not hiding and running like she'd done all her life, but hiding and attacking.

The machine was positioned so the metal tube that fired the bolt was sticking out over the edge of the harbour cliff. If they could mount a sudden attack from underneath, then they could knock the machine off and into the sea before the warriors could manoeuvre and fire. Aimee turned to Nathine.

'Can dragons swim?' she asked.

'What?' Nathine looked at her like she'd lost her mind. 'I dunno. Why?'

'They can,' Pelathina said from Aimee's other side.

'Do they need to learn or do they just know how?' Aimee asked, turning to Pelathina.

Even with her googles on and her face wet from the rain, Aimee could see how skeptical Pelatina looked.

'Skydance dives for fish sometimes when I let him and he always seems quite happy in the water,' Pelathina replied.

That was good enough for Aimee.

'If you wanted to swim you should have bonded a whale instead of a dragon,' Nathine muttered on her other side. Aimee ignored Nathine and outlined her plan.

'Seriously?' Pelathina looked horrified. She glanced down at the rippling dark water of the harbour and shivered. 'I'm freezing just thinking about it.'

'You're insane,' Nathine told her. 'If we were to build a monument to the worst plans ever, this one would be the crowning glory.'

This time Aimee ignored them both. Her plan was good. It was the only way they could take out the weapon.

'Jara!' Aimee yelled, getting their leader's attention. 'I have a plan.'

'Of course you do!' Jara called back. 'What do you need?'

Aimee explained her idea again. 'So, once the weapon's gone everyone else can swoop in and attack. But it would be good if you did it the moment we destroy the weapon so they aren't ready.'

Aimee winced at her own words. Jara would have given proper orders and probably given a name to the attack and the formation the Riders would use. But Aimee's clumsy words didn't matter because Jara nodded.

'Go,' she said.

'I'll take Nathine and Pelathina with me,' Aimee stated.

'Wait, hang on, we didn't agree to that. You didn't even ask us!' Nathine protested.

'Oh Aimee, you owe me a cake so big I could hide behind it,' Pelathina said as she tucked her soggy scarf further into her coat and closed another button.

'I hate you.' Nathine glared at her.

Aimee reached over and gave Nathine's arm a patronising pat. What they were about to do would be incredibly awful, but nowhere near as bad as being shot from the sky. Aimee had seen two Riders killed by those bolt machines now and she vowed to herself they wouldn't get anyone else.

'Ready?'

She looked right and left at the Riders on either side of her. Both nodded. Beneath her Jess quivered as she sensed her Rider's anxiety. Then, with hardly a push on her horns, Jess unfurled her wings and stepped off the rocks into the sky. Aimee immediately heard the clicking of gears as the bolt machine swivelled to track them. She glanced back, glad to see that despite their misgivings Nathine and Pelathina had followed her. All along the rocks, Jara and the other Riders readied themselves, their dragons stretching out their necks and fluttering their wings, eager to take off again.

Aimee pushed Jess for more height and they climbed into the sky above the harbour. The wind buffeted them from behind, pushing her towards the Empty Warriors. She heard the grinding as they readied the weapon to fire.

'Dive!' Aimee yelled.

She pushed hard on Jess's spiralled horns. Her dragon turned her snout to the sea and tucked in her wings, diving just like they did when heading back down through the vents and into the Heart. Beside her Malgerus and Skydance did the same. The dark sea came rushing towards them. Jess's head entered the water and Aimee had a split second to regret her decision before sucking in a huge breath.

She was already soaked from the rain, and shivering in her wet clothes, but the cold of the sea was on a whole other level. It gripped her like a vice and she almost released her breath with the shock of it. It was like her skin had tightened and was now too small for her body. Her extremities prickled painfully with the cold and it felt like a boulder was crushing her chest. Her mind screamed silent swear words.

Jess glided through the water with ease, her powerful back legs kicking and her tail flicking to propel them forward. With her goggles on Aimee had an underwater view, not that there was much to see. The silvery moonlight hardly penetrated the dark water and she tried not to think about the black depths beneath them.

Her fingers, feet and face had gone completely numb. Her chest felt like the cold was cracking it open and she was desperate for breath. Then she saw the underside of the two longboats and knew they were close. She couldn't feel if her fingers were working when she tried to guide Jess but thankfully her dragon knew what to do. The cliff of the harbour filled their vision, slimy with seaweed, the long fronds waving in the current. Jess gave one last powerful kick and pushed upwards.

Rider and dragon burst from the sea in a spray of water that sheeted off Jess's wings as she unfurled them with a snap. From the lapping waves to the rocky ledge of the harbour was only the length of a dragon, so the Empty Warriors had no time to react as Jess and Aimee shot up from underneath their position.

They'd emerged slightly to the left of where the bolt machine was placed. Jess's outstretched wing tipped the metal tube of the machine, knocking it off-kilter but not breaking it. That was why Aimee had brought her friends with her. She'd known it would be hard to judge underwater the exact spot to emerge. So, as Jess grabbed an Empty Warrior in her jaws and cracked his bones, Skydance and Malgerus burst from the sea as well.

Skydance was too far right and missed the weapon completely, but he grabbed two warriors in his talons and flung them off the cliff. With their armour on they immediately sank into the cold sea. Malgerus and Nathine emerged, shooting seawater right up the cliffs. Malgerus roared as he flapped once, his huge wings bright in the moonlight, and he crashed straight into the bolt machine.

The machine burst apart, bolts and springs shooting off in every direction. Malgerus wrapped his long neck around the firing tube and twisted it free with a screech of tortured metal. The body of the machine tumbled off the cliff, dragging three Empty Warriors with it. The dark water accepted the bounty of monsters and metal, pulling them down into the depths.

'Yes!' Nathine cried in triumph. 'I win!'

'Jara, now!' Aimee called across the sea to the waiting Riders, waving her arm wildly.

Jess swept across the harbour, grabbing an Empty Warrior in her talons. Aimee nudged her towards Malgerus and they skimmed underneath the orange dragon as he rose into the air.

'It wasn't a competition!' Aimee yelled up at Nathine.

'Of course it was. You're just a sore loser!'

Nathine's words grew louder as Malgerus dived back down, his talons spread, eager to join the fight. Aimee could see her friend was grinning wildly, spurred on by their victory against the bolt machine. Aimee felt it too, the fizz of adrenaline in her veins, the thudding of blood in her head. After the freezing sea the night air felt warm in comparison and Aimee was surprised to find she wasn't shivering. She felt the swelling of pride in her chest, created by knowing they were fighting and winning. She could see it too in the way that the glowing line connecting Nathine and Malgerus pulsed with blue light.

And then there were wings all around her as Jara and the others joined the battle. The greenish-white glow of the Riders' sparks darted through the air like fireflies and their connections with their dragons shimmered like spiderweb strands in the sun.

The Empty Warriors had no time to muster and the dragons tore through them. They didn't scatter or hide like humans would have, instead each stood his ground and tried to fend off this attack from the air. Black and Skydance swooped in together, flying wingtip-to-wingtip and smashed through the barricade of crates and lobster pots. Aimee saw the splinters from one crate pierce an Empty Warrior's throat, and lava poured down his breastplate.

She and Jess hovered on the edge of the battle as Aimee watched the others in amazement. She'd never seen so many dragons attacking together and they swarmed through the air cutting above and below one another, brushing each other with the wind from their wings. They were like a colourful and deadly murmuration of starlings. Nathine had already thrown herself into the battle, not knowing the correct formations but trusting her dragon. So Aimee did the same.

Jess shot forward and everything disappeared from Aimee's mind except this moment. Her ears were full of the rustling of wings and the deep-throated roars as dragons breathed flames. Her nostrils sucked in the stench of sulphur from injured Empty Warriors, mingled with the salty tang of the sea. And her eyes darted everywhere like a bat flitting between the trees. She picked a target and didn't need to tell Jess which warrior it was, her dragon knew and dived straight for him.

The Empty Warrior thrust upwards with his straight sword, aiming for Jess's exposed belly, but at the last second Jess tilted her wings and swooped past out of reach. Aimee sliced downwards as they passed, her scimitar ringing against his sword and her momentum knocking the blade from his fingers. She heard it clatter across the rock then felt the impact as Jess's thrashing tail smacked into him. The barbs on the end of her tail crunched through his breastplate, impaling him. Jess dragged him across the harbour and then with a flick of her tail tossed him into the sea.

With two powerful wingbeats Jess lifted them back into the air above the battle and Aimee thrilled with the strength she felt.

'Target the ones at the gate!' Jara's yelled order cut through the noise and Aimee obeyed, steering Jess towards the gate in the harbour.

The Empty Warriors had severed the mast from one of their longboats and had been using that as a battering ram. But now, as dragons swooped from the air picking them off, they'd abandoned their ram and a group of them pressed their hands against the wood of the gate. Aimee thought of their blackened palms with open cracks running across them, exposing the fiery lava inside. The planks of the gate were thick, and wet from the rain, but under the warriors' hands they were already smouldering.

The Empty Warriors' hands sank into the blackened wood as it burned. They were burning through in a line, right across the middle of the gate where they'd already weakened it with the ram. Faradair was first to reach them, talons extended, but at the last second he banked to the right and swooped cleanly past the gate. Jara screamed in frustration. Aimee, following on Skydance's tail, saw the problem. There was a lip of rock above the gate, like a natural porch, and it sheltered the warriors.

'We'll need to land!' Lyrria yelled.

But before Jara could reply the weakened gate collapsed with a crash of splintered wood, embers shooting into the sky. And the Empty Warriors ran into the tunnel and through to the city.

CHAPTER 22

ONE SINGLE MOMENT

Aimee found herself in the sky, surrounded by dragons, and feeling helpless. She looked for red wings and saw Jara rise above them before swooping back down.

'Orders?' Dyrenna called to her.

Every Empty Warrior still alive at the harbour had disappeared into the tunnel. There were only about twenty, but that was still enough to break through the inner gate and take the lives of the guards waiting on the other side.

'Arrows!' someone yelled, and the dragons scattered.

Aimee and Jess swept left, alongside Skydance, and she heard the whir as arrows cut the air behind them. A dragon roared and Aimee glanced back to see Midnight had been shot. She pulled the barbed arrow from the membrane of her wing with her teeth while Lyrria yelled curses down at the warriors. Another longboat rounded the curved rocky arm of the harbour and this one was prepared—half the warriors were still rowing but the other half fired another volley of arrows. Jess followed Skydance higher into the cloudy sky.

Faradair cut through the middle of the flight of dragons before swooping back down and along the curve of the harbour arm. The archers on the boat turned towards him but he was already climbing back up into the sky, swirling wisps of cloud with his powerful wings. Aimee could see in Faradair's movements his Rider's panic. She felt it too, but still she watched Jara, hoping for orders.

'There's another boat coming!' someone cried just as Aimee spotted it, oars dipping as it rounded into the harbour. Even though the dragons were out of range it shot a warning volley. The air filled with voices as Riders called out desperate suggestions.

'We need to attack those boats, stop them coming!'

'We'll be torn from the sky by their arrows!'

'What else can we do?'

'I don't know!'

Clouds had scudded across the moon and Aimee couldn't see who was arguing but she could hear the panic in the way their voices rose higher. The first of the new longboats was pulling up beside the harbour cliff. Aimee didn't know what Jara would order, didn't know what the right choice here was. It felt like defending the city had suddenly become impossible and the Riders were frozen in place, not making any decisions because whatever Jara chose, people would die.

A dark shadow passed in front of Aimee as Black circled the Riders, seeking out Faradair. Aimee missed

Dyrenna's words but she saw Jara straighten in her saddle.

'Back inside the city. Go! We defend the inner gate.' Jara called the order as she turned Faradair towards the mountains.

Aimee and the others followed, abandoning the harbour to the Empty Warriors. Jess flapped steadily, Skydance beside her, following a dragon as pink as a new dawn. As they rose into the heights above the Ring Mountains, Aimee felt like she'd left her adrenaline behind and she began to shiver with cold.

'*Hu-karjee*, this is awful.'

Aimee heard Pelathina's complaint as Skydance drew closer, his wingbeats matching Jess's.

She looked at Pelathina, her darker face lit by the soft glow of her weakened spark, and Aimee saw how pale her lips were. Then she noticed Pelathina was shivering too and Aimee felt really guilty. Pelathina found the nights cold anyway, but now she was soaked through with freezing seawater, and all for nothing— they'd lost the harbour. And Aimee still had half of Pelathina's spark in her chest.

'I'm sorry,' Aimee apologised.

'Don't be, it was a good plan. I'd just really like to be able to feel my toes again.'

Pelathina was shivering so much that her teeth were chattering. In a counterbalance to Aimee feeling stronger, was Pelathina struggling to find her strength because she was missing half her life force? Was she even colder because Aimee had stolen half her energy? She felt a twinge in her heart almost as painful as if one of the arrows had pierced her.

The dragons soared over the spine of a jagged ridge and across a plateau of scree. There was a narrow gully ahead and as the dragons approached it Aimee risked another glance at Pelathina. Then, feeling like an idiot, Aimee realised that if she could see sparks again then the bracelet might be working. She could try giving Pelathina back the life she'd stolen.

She was about to call over to Pelathina when Jess, following the others through and out of the gully, tipped into a dive. Unprepared Aimee gasped and squeezed Jess's horns. The wind rushed past her, pressing her wet clothes against her body and she practically bounced in her saddle she was shivering so much. The Riders glided down the inside cliffs of the Ring Mountains, the glow of their sparks softly lighting the colourful scales of their dragons.

With a snap of her wings Jess levelled off above the rooftops and the chaos below. There was no clear space around this gate as there was at the caravan compound. The warehouses and workshops crowded right up against the cliffs here, or at least they had, until Riders and guards had begun dismantling them to build a barricade as best as they could. Aimee saw a line of guards, arms linked across Fiskhavn Street, keeping back an angry mob. People were scared of the Empty Warriors but few in the city had actually seen them, and right then Aimee could understand that they'd be more afraid of losing their livelihoods.

Skydance settled on the peaked roof of an intact warehouse and Aimee guided Jess in beside him. She pulled off a glove and reached over, taking Pelathina's hand. Her own fingers were so cold she could hardly feel Pelathina's but the other girl's hand quivered in hers with the force of her shivers. Aimee wished she could fly Pelathina back to her room in Anteill, strip off her wet clothes, bundle her in a blanket and hug her till she was warm. Even if that took forever.

'I think the bracelet's working again,' Aimee said. 'I can try giving you your spark back. It might help keep you warm.'

'Proper summers would help keep me warm,' Pelathina replied with a laugh that morphed into a sigh.

'Can I—' Aimee began but her words were engulfed in the roaring whoosh as the gate in the cliffs that led to the harbour ignited from the inside. There was no time to try the bracelet now.

'Riders, dismount!' Jara yelled and the order was repeated across the rooftops where dragons had landed.

Aimee swung out of her saddle and ordered Jess to stay. She could feel her dragon's urge to join the fight but she obeyed, crouching down with her wings half furled. Pelathina took her hand again. The other girl's fingers were cold and clammy but they still gave Aimee a tingle.

'Look after my spark for just a little while longer and I'll get it back from you after this,' Pelathina told her. 'With the way you've been fighting we'll have the Empty Warriors beaten before breakfast. Then you can take me out for pancakes.'

Aimee felt the guilt wriggling inside her again. She was only fighting so well because she was borrowing extra strength from Pelathina.

'As soon as this fight's over,' Aimee promised.

'I know,' Pelathina smiled.

Then she kissed her.

Aimee was so shocked she almost stumbled backwards off the roof but Pelathina caught her, wrapping an arm around her waist, pulling her close, and laughing softly against her lips. Aimee kissed her back fiercely, tasting the salt on the other girl's lips. Then it was over, too soon, and Aimee wanted more. But there wasn't time. Pelathina's smile as she pulled back though was full of such promise that Aimee almost grabbed her and carried her back to Anteill right then.

Letting go of her, Pelathina slid down the slate tiles of the roof. Aimee followed after, grabbing hold of the gutter at the edge with her numb fingers, and lowering herself enough so she could drop to the street below. As she landed her wet boots squelched with cold seawater.

She had a brief moment to marvel at the spiderweb-thin line that stretched from her chest all the way back up the roof to Jess, before turning and sprinting after Pelathina. Fiskhavn Street was wide enough for two wagons to pass but not wide enough for dragons to fight in. Aimee found herself amongst Riders from Lyrria and Aranati's groups as they ran towards the collapsing gate. Thin blue lines that only Aimee could see stretched from each Rider up to her dragon, all pulsing as emotions were shared along their bonds.

'I need to see Arri, but I'll be back.' Pelathina gave her hand a quick squeeze before splitting off and running towards her sister.

Aimee scanned the Riders looking for Nathine and finally spotted her high ponytail bobbing as she climbed the hastily erected barricade to peer over at the burning gate. Aimee clambered up beside her. Ahead the gate crackled and burned like a bonfire, smoke blowing in their faces. Through the flames Aimee glimpsed rows of Empty Warriors waiting for their moment to break into the city. Fear clutched Aimee's insides, colder than the seawater in her boots.

'No, we can't lose the harbour. Just give me more time.'

Aimee heard a voice raised in anger and looked over her shoulder to see Jara, hands on hips, facing Captain Tenth of the city guards.

'Those monsters will be through that gate any second. We need to clear this area, collapse the bridges and stop them spreading further into the city,' Tenth insisted.

'And leave a gaping hole in our mountains for them to pour through?' Jara's voice was shrill and she spat her words into Tenth's face.

'If we try to fight them here they'll kill us and march through anyway!' Tenth held his ground, his hawkish nose quivering with his anger. 'Across the river we can hold them.' Tenth pointed back towards where the River Toig cut through the city, separating the harbour district from the eastern curve of Barter.

'These are the council's orders,' Tenth continued.

'There has to be another way,' Jara said, her voice lowering.

'Alright then, what?' Tenth demanded.

'I don't know!' Jara shot back, her voice rising again, but her eyes flickered sideways, alighting on Aimee.

Aimee felt again the heavy coat of responsibility she'd put on. She needed to find Kyelli and learn how to work the bracelet properly, especially now she could see sparks again, but she couldn't leave the fight. They were hugely outnumbered and every Rider and dragon was a precious asset in this battle. Jara held her eye for a moment but didn't order Aimee to leave.

The barricade shook as Jara climbed up it too. All the Riders were on it now and Aimee could feel how flimsy it was. It blocked the street ten paces from where the gate burned, stretching between the brick walls of two warehouses—warehouses that were missing their doors, window frames and anything from inside that could be dragged out and added to the barricade. The street behind them was empty as the city guards forcefully shoved people back, herding them out of the harbour district. Other guards patrolled the small side streets, gathering up anyone they found and evicting them.

'The plan is this,' Jara began, her voice raised above the crackling flames and the yells from the streets behind them. 'We hold here for as long as we can to give Tenth and his men time to evacuate this area. No heroics.' She looked left and right along the barricade, her fine hair plastered to her face from the storm, her expression grim. 'I will not lose another Rider for this harbour.'

Jara's voice wavered and Aimee felt emotion well up in her own chest—fear at the fight to come and grief as she remembered the horrible way both Lwena and Fineya had been shot from the sky.

'When Tenth gives the signal we grab our dragons and fall back,' Jara continued, her voice still cracking at the edges. 'His guards will collapse the bridge and we'll patrol the edge of this district from the air. Not a single Empty Warrior will get further into the city than that.'

The unspoken *then what* hovered in the air. Aimee braced herself against the barricade with her knees, pulled free both scimitars and made her own plan. She'd fight here, giving Tenth and his guards the time they needed to get people to safety, then once that was done she'd go find Kyelli.

Beside her Nathine was nervously rubbing the blue topaz on the pommel of her scimitars and staring intently at the burning gate. If fierce looks could stop monsters, the Empty Warriors would never make it past Nathine. Aimee knew now wasn't the time, but still she elbowed her friend and leaned in close to whisper.

'Pelathina kissed me.'

Nathine snorted. 'Great. I've just spent the last five minutes conjuring the perfect image in my head so I can die thinking of that, but now I'm going to end up dying whilst thinking about your love life.'

'It was a really good kiss,' Aimee insisted.

'Well, whoopee for you.'

'What was your perfect image?'

'I'm flying through the sky on a beautiful day and inside every cloud is a mug of tea. I can just fly through them, grab some tea and fly on to the next one.'

It was Aimee's turn to snort with laughter. 'Well, save it for next time because you're not going to die today.'

Then the last burning timbers of the gate collapsed inwards and the Empty Warriors burst through. Aimee expected them to come cautiously as they had at the caravan compound, wary of an ambush, but they didn't. Instead they charged at the barricade, all of them, pouring from the tunnel in a silent stream of armour, swords and burning eyes. They smashed into the flimsy wooden structure at the far end and Aimee heard the crack of breaking timbers, the screams of Riders and the roars of their dragons.

They'd hit the barricade right where Pelathina was.

Riders rushed across the street to reinforce the breach and Aimee ran with them, Nathine beside her. Above, dragons clawed at their perches, talons scraping on the roof tiles, and they called down to their Riders. Aimee skidded on the wet cobbles, only stopped from falling by Nathine grabbing her arm, hoisting her upright.

Only a door, placed lengthways, separated the Riders from the warriors. But as Aimee arrived it was smashed to pieces, splinters flying, and the Empty

Warriors broke through. The breach was four strides wide and three Riders held it, their blades glinting with reflected firelight as they fought the warriors. The clash of metal joined the roaring of dragons and the crackle of flames.

The press of Riders was tight and Aimee wasn't tall enough to see over them. She didn't know who was fighting at the front. And as she shoved herself in amongst them the glow from so many sparks half blinded her. Lines of light snaked through the air above them too, stretching from Riders to dragons, making a tangled web that was hard for Aimee to see through.

Sal was on top of the barricade, firing arrows down into the press of warriors. Riders waited behind the three holding the breach, ready to step in if any of them fell. Jara shouted orders but Aimee couldn't hear her over the din. Nathine bounced on the balls of her feet looking for someone to fight.

The quiet street had become a nightmare. Aimee watched feeling helpless. One of the Riders in the breach screamed and the anguished sound tore at Aimee's heart. The press moved forward as another Rider stepped in to take her place. Feet shuffled as the wounded Rider was pulled towards Aimee and Nathine.

It was Pelathina.

Aimee's heart skipped a beat then rushed in double-time to make up for it. Aranati held her sister under her arms and dragged her free of the fight, placing her on the cobbles beyond.

'No, no, no,' Aimee whimpered as she ran over,

skidding and falling this time. She smacked her hip and her elbow but the pain hardly registered.

She crawled to Pelathina. Aranati had pulled up her sister's shirt and Aimee saw the sword cut in her belly, welling dark blood that coated her smooth bronze skin. Aranati pulled off her scarf and pressed it against the wound, whispering to her sister in Irankish. Aimee's hands hovered uselessly above Pelathina, unsure what to do, tears streaming down her face. Pelathina's eyes fluttered open, dark and full of pain. They alighted on Aimee and a smile twitched the corner of her lips. Seeing it broke Aimee's heart. Even now Pelathina could smile.

'Not you, please not you,' Aimee whispered.

Aimee heard the whoosh of wings and the clack of talons as Skydance landed on the cobbles beside them. He pressed his belly to the ground and gently nudged Pelathina's head with his snout.

'You can heal her, yes?' Aimee looked desperately at Aranati. 'With stitches and bandages and dragon's saliva.'

'*Nahin-mat*. I need to get her back to Anteill. This is bad but she has a strong spark.' Aranati had taken off her belt and was wrapping it around Pelathina, using it to hold in place her balled-up scarf.

A fresh wave of horror washed over Aimee. Pelathina only had half of her spark burning in her chest. If her body used that up trying to heal her wound then she'd die. By stealing her spark Aimee had halved her chances at survival.

Aranati slid her arms gently under her sister, preparing to lift her.

'Wait!'

Aimee grabbed Pelathina's wrist. With her other hand she shoved back the sleeve of her coat to reveal Kyelli's bracelet. Even though it hadn't been working she'd been wearing it in neutral, just in case. She turned it over to reach the dial and flick it to *zurl*, so she could give Pelathina back her spark. As her fingertips touched it a shout rang out behind them.

'There!'

Aimee heard thudding footsteps then arms grabbed her from behind, pulling her up and away from Pelathina.

CHAPTER 23

A LINE UNCROSSED

'NO! I NEED to put her spark back!' Aimee yelled as two city guards pinned her arms behind her. 'Let me go!'

She tried to twist in their grip but they were too strong. They'd lifted her up off the ground and her legs kicked in the air trying to find a shin or a knee. She was panicking about Pelathina too much to even wonder why two city guards had grabbed her. She just needed to get free of them and save Pelathina. But she'd dropped her scimitars when she fell running towards Pelathina and without them she was just a young woman, held by two grown men.

Aranati was staring up at her, bloodied hands pressed against Pelathina's belly. Nathine was there too, and she had her scimitars. But she stood awkwardly, casting anxious glances from Aimee back to the fight at the barricade, her face twisted with indecision. Pelathina's eyes fluttered closed, all traces of her smile vanished. Her weakened spark pulsed erratically in her chest and her connection with Skydance wavered.

Aimee thrashed, crying out to be let go. The guards had pulled her arms behind her, pinning her hands into the small of her back, and her shoulder sockets screamed in pain. They'd been too clever to wrap a hand around her front where she could bite them.

Swirling air rushed over them, pushing the guards back a step, dragging Aimee with them.

'No! Stay, girl!' Aimee yelled as Jess landed on the street.

Her wings were outstretched, tips brushing the bricks of the warehouses on one side, as she made herself as big and threatening as she could. Her head whipped forward on her long neck and she snapped her teeth, her rumbling growl sounding even over the din of the fight. Aimee felt the guards tense, but they didn't let go.

'Don't,' Aimee whispered, sending the command along their connection. She actually saw it go, a pulse of blue energy shooting along the shimmering strand between them.

More than anything she wanted Jess to rescue her, but if a dragon attacked a citizen of Kierell that was a line that could never be uncrossed.

'Bring her.'

The commanding voice came from behind.

'Beljarn! What the blazing sparks are you doing?'

Jara came marching from where her Riders were only just holding back the Empty Warriors. Had anyone else been hurt? Killed? How long could the Riders keep them out? The questions skittered through Aimee's mind but she was pulled away from any answers as the guards dragged her around, facing down the street towards the bridge.

Jara's boot heels clicked as she stormed past Aimee and grabbed the lapels of Councillor Beljarn's fancy coat.

'The Council can't have her! This isn't the way, Beljarn.' Jara was nose to nose with him, spitting the words in his face.

Beljarn calmly wiped Jara's spittle from his glasses and moved to step around her. But Jara held onto his coat and shoved him back away from Aimee. Beljarn stumbled, righted himself, then his right arm whipped around and he slapped Jara across the face. She reeled from the blow.

A roar split the air as Faradair landed, wings outstretched and curved protectively around his Rider. Beljarn winced as Faradair roared again, his long teeth cutting through the air as he swung his head back. Flames were crackling along the barricade now and in their light Aimee saw the sly look on Beljarn's face as he turned his eyes to Jara.

'Go on, give me an excuse,' he said.

Jara glared at him for a long moment before placing a hand on Faradair's scales, calming him. He pulled his neck back in and furled his wings. Jara knew, same as Aimee did, that if a dragon attacked a councillor it would be as good as signing a death warrant for all dragons.

'Bring her,' Beljarn repeated, waving a hand at

Aimee.

She felt the guards start to move and began kicking and screaming again. If Jess couldn't free her, she'd need to free herself. The guards struggled as she wriggled and she felt the grip loosening on her left arm. She yanked it free and reached out for the other guard, fingers searching for his eyes, his nose, anything she could grab and hurt to make him let go. But a third guard stepped out of the darkness by the warehouse wall and punched her in the face.

Pain blasted through her skull. Her teeth clattered together and she tasted blood as she bit her tongue.

'Sparkless bastard!'

Jara's shout was muffled by the ringing in Aimee's ears. She'd gone limp and the guard grabbed her arm again, twisting harder than he needed to as he pinned it against her back. She heard the flutter of wings and saw Jess crouched low to the ground, cowering and scared, not understanding why Aimee was pushing against her.

The guards were dragging her backwards and Aimee could see what she was being pulled away from. Her friends fought desperately to keep the Empty Warriors out of their city, while Pelathina lay bleeding in her sister's arms. Aimee couldn't move her arms, and her head was still fuzzy from the punch, but she kept struggling, kept trying to get free. She had to give Pelathina back her spark. Then the guards could take her anywhere they liked.

'Please!' Aimee begged.

She wouldn't let that one kiss be all she ever had

with Pelathina. It wasn't fair. Jara stood helpless, glaring at Beljarn's back as he hurried away, back towards the bridge and the safety of Barter.

'It won't work, Beljarn!' Jara called after him. 'The council can't use the bracelet. This isn't the way to save our city!'

Aimee went rigid in the guards' arms, digging her heels into a gutter running across the street. It barely slowed them and her wet feet slipped free of her boots. They flopped to the ground, left behind. Aimee screamed, no words, just pure frustration. Still huddled to the ground Jess roared, but her sound was mournful not fierce.

'Would you just stop,' one of the guards grunted, getting frustrated with her struggles.

Aimee flung her head back, hoping she'd hit something. Pain flared through her skull as she smacked a guard's chin. He grunted and his grip slackened, just for a moment. Aimee threw herself forward but the other guard still had her arm and all she did was drag him to his knees. Her arm sprang free of his grip and she felt a glorious moment of freedom.

'Dull sparks! You stupid girl, I'm—'

The guard's words disappeared in a flash of pain as he punched her on the side of her head. She fell, her forehead smacking the cobbles, and darkness took her.

She slipped down into unconsciousness and everything floated away. Her worries and fear dissipated. Even Jess was gone. And the insistent pressure of the bracelet on her mind eased off.

She floated through the peaceful dark until the first tendril of pain wiggled its way back in. A full flare of pain followed and it jolted her back to consciousness.

Aimee woke still struggling, still feeling like the guards were holding her and dragging her away from Jess and Pelathina. She thrashed, felt hands on her and scrambled backwards.

'Be careful. Calm down.'

A women's voice. Aimee struggled to place it. Her brain felt like it was twice its normal size and trying to burst free of her skull.

'Jess,' she mumbled and did a panicked sweep of her mind. She ran down corridors of thoughts and memories, searching for her connection. Finally she felt it but it was small and very faint as if the door between them was closed, their bond linked only though the tiny crack of space at the bottom. She breathed a sigh of relief. Jess was still alive but she must be far away. Aimee sent a pulse of love along their connection but had no idea if Jess received it or not.

'Can you sit up?'

The women's voice again. Aimee realised now that she was lying on a cold, stone floor, her eyes still closed. She felt hands on her knees and kicked them away before rolling onto all fours. The movement sent a wave of nausea through her and her stomach heaved. Bile burned the back of her throat as she was sick, but she'd hardly eaten yesterday and only a tiny dribble of vomit splatted on the ground between her hands.

After a few deep breaths which did nothing to lessen

the pounding in her skull, she pushed herself back to kneeling and tried to open her eyes. Her right one opened a crack but the left was crusted shut.

'Here, hold still.'

Hands cupped her face and she felt a wet cloth being wiped over her left eye. The woman was a dark blur as her right eye struggled to focus, but Aimee was too tired to care who she was and let the woman clean the blood from her face and caked eyelashes. She winced as the woman pressed the cloth to her forehead and knew she must have a cut there.

Finally she could open both eyes. The world was blurry, like she was looking through clouded glass, and she had to blink several times before things wobbled back into focus. She looked around and saw the bare stone walls and floor of a cell. A door of iron bars led out to a dark corridor lit by a single torch at the far end. High on the opposite wall was a small window, no glass, just more iron bars. It was too high up for Aimee to reach and too small to even fit her head through.

The woman still held her face and Aimee gasped with recognition.

'Kyelli!'

The old woman released Aimee and sat back, wincing as her knees clicked. Questions buzzed in her mind like a swarm of angry bees, but for once Aimee didn't know which to ask first. Everything in her body seemed to hurt and suddenly she felt too tired for answers. Then her recent memories came flooding to the front of her sore brain and she heaved again, head down between her knees.

Tears stung her eyes as she remembered Pelathina and the blood on her belly. Was she still alive? Had Aranati saved her? Or had she died of her wound because Aimee had stolen half her life?

All the stresses, worries and fears from the last few days that she'd been able to shove into a box at the back of her mind now escaped and rampaged through her brain. She saw Lwena and Fineya and the horrible way they'd been killed. She saw the guards dying in the caravan compound as fiery hands burned their flesh. She saw the Empty Warriors breaking through from the harbour and the terrified faces of the people the guards herded back.

Her thoughts engulfed her, and it felt like they were the cold waves of the sea and she was sinking beneath them.

Her ribs began to ache from the force of her sobs and as she tried to suck in enough breath to cry harder she choked on snot. Kyelli took her shoulders, trying to gently pull her into a hug but Aimee shoved her away. She didn't want comfort from her. Too much of all this was Kyelli's fault. Instead she pushed herself back against the cold stone wall, hugging her knees to her chest and not caring a damn what the immortal thought of one of her Riders crying like a small child.

The guards had taken her from Jess. They'd taken her from her fellow Riders, from her friends, from the girl she was beginning to love and who she might have killed. They'd taken her from where she belonged and she hadn't been able to do a thing to stop them.

Finally, she was too exhausted to cry any more and her sobs retreated, her tears slowing to a trickle. She moved to wipe her face and something around her neck rattled. It was her flying goggles, the glass in both lenses cracked.

Kyelli said nothing, no words of comfort or encouragement but Aimee didn't really expect her to after the last time they'd spoken and the way they'd argued.

'Where have you been?' Aimee asked, her voice croaky from all her crying.

'That doesn't matter,' Kyelli's voice snapped out, quick and sharp.

'But I needed—'

'Listen to me and please don't ask any questions,' Kyelli cut her off.

The young woman she'd been a few months ago would have meekly shut up, but not this Aimee, not the Saviour of a Caravan, Finder of the Bracelet and Breaker of Mountains.

'I'll ask all the bloody questions I want to because we,' Aimee waved her arm around to encompass the whole city, 'are in this mess because of you! The Quorelle had all these powers and centuries of knowledge but you kept it from us!'

'I was protecting you!' Kyelli argued back.

'Oh and look how well that worked out!' Aimee borrowed a little of Nathine's sarcasm. 'I want answers and you need to give them to me, now!'

Aimee waved the bracelet in Kyelli's face and as she

did so she noticed something—she couldn't see the glow of a spark in Kyelli's chest. She looked down searching for her own, and for the half she'd taken from Pelathina. They were invisible too.

'Damn it! Stupid, worthless, idiot bracelet! Why does it keep not working?'

'Because you keep refusing to embrace the power of it,' Kyelli snapped back.

Aimee's thumping headache had retreated enough to let her once again feel the questing fingers of the bracelet's power, pushing against her brain, seeking a way in. It had been there ever since the bracelet snapped closed on her wrist, sometimes fading into the background, other times battering at her mind like rain on a windowpane. Aimee held herself firmly against it.

'I won't become like you,' she said resolutely.

Kyelli grabbed both of Aimee's arms and gave her a shake. 'That bracelet is killing you, child. If you don't learn to accept its power and use it, then thousands of people in Kierell will die alongside you.'

'I know that! But I can't...' Aimee's words trailed off as she noticed something.

Kyelli was gripping her upper arm, firmly, squeezing right where the Empty Warrior had burned her. But it didn't hurt. And as she thought about it she realised she hadn't felt the pain in her arm for hours. The burn hadn't hurt while she fought the Empty Warriors on the rockfall or when she attacked them above the harbour.

She pulled herself out of Kyelli's grip and began stripping off her still damp clothes. Her coat and shirt fell to the floor and she stared at her arm. There was nothing. No burned handprint, not even a scar. She prodded her arm so hard it hurt but her wound had completely vanished.

'How am I healed?' She looked up at Kyelli, eyes wide, demanding answers.

'You were wounded?' Kyelli had stepped back and crossed her arms.

Aimee nodded. 'Four days ago, the first Empty Warrior I fought grabbed me and burned a handprint into my arm. Aranati put dragon's saliva on it, but still it couldn't have healed so quickly.

'You're sure?'

'I didn't imagine getting wounded!'

Kyelli's wrinkles deepened as she furrowed her brow. 'It doesn't make sense. The reason Quorelle are near immortal is because we have extra sparks inside us. We can burn their energy to heal ourselves if we get sick or wounded, and to keep us youthful. But you don't have extra sparks.'

Realisation crashed down on Aimee as heavy as the rockfall that had buried the tunnel. 'Oh no.'

'What?' Kyelli demanded.

'I've got half of Pelathina's spark inside me. Does that mean I've been using *her* energy to heal myself?'

The look on Kyelli's face answered her question. Aimee's stomach rolled and she felt sick again. She grabbed the bracelet on her wrist and tugged it, trying desperately to get it off. Icy pain shot up her arm and she screamed in frustration. Her legs buckled and she collapsed to the floor.

'I don't want it. Please.'

She held her arm up to Kyelli, begging her to take the bracelet. Right then Aimee didn't care if removing it killed her. She couldn't live with stealing someone else's life energy to prolong her own. It was wrong. She didn't want to be that person.

She heard the click of joints as Kyelli crouched down beside her. The older woman gently lifted Aimee's chin.

'You've been unconsciously using the bracelet and its power. If you accept it and master it, you'll be able to control it,' Kyelli told her.

Aimee thought about the way she'd been able to see sparks and Riders' connections when she'd been fighting. In those moments all her focus had been on the next sword thrust, when to attack, when to defend, and she'd let her guard against the bracelet's power drop. While she'd fought, the bracelet had been using Pelathina's spark to make her stronger, faster, and to heal her arm.

Aimee gingerly touched the power she could feel pressing against her mind and flinched back. What if she let it in and it overwhelmed her? What if she wasn't strong enough to control it? She wasn't one of the Quorelle, she was just an eighteen-year-old who right now didn't even have her dragon.

'I'm scared,' she admitted, her voice a whisper.

'I don't know why. You're one of the bravest young women I've ever met. And I've known six centuries' worth of women,' Kyelli told her softly.

Aimee felt like she'd been backed into a corner. She didn't want the power of the bracelet, but she desperately wanted to use it to give Pelathina back her spark. She didn't want to become like the Quorelle, holding the power of life and death over others, but she longed to find Pagrin. She wanted to stop him and his army of monsters, to kill him and take his sparks so she could take off the damn bracelet and save herself.

That feeling, of having no choice, no way out, and being surrounded by forces who felt so much stronger than she did, churned up all the memories from her childhood. Memories of being taunted, and backed into corners by those who bullied her.

'But I'm not that girl anymore,' Aimee said aloud, ignoring the puzzled look on Kyelli's face. 'And if I can stand up to them, I can face down some stupid bracelet and its stupid power.'

She straightened and looked directly at Kyelli.

'Teach me how to use the bracelet fully.'

'Excellent, that's exactly what we need,' a new voice cut in before Kyelli could reply.

Aimee and Kyelli spun in their cell. Councillor Beljarn stood on the other side of the iron bars, an eager grin on his face.

CHAPTER 24

MONSTERS AND BLOOD

Beljarn was accompanied by two other councillors. Aimee recognised Cyella but didn't know the younger man's name. Cyella's face was crinkled round the edges with worry, but the younger man looked as eager as Beljarn did. A city guard stood at the edge of the stone corridor, just behind the councillors, and Aimee recognised him. It took her a moment to place his face, before she remembered he'd been at the caravan compound when they collapsed the gate. He'd also been with the caravan when they'd travelled beyond the mountains and he'd rebuffed her when Aimee had tried to speak to him, dismissing her because of her face. At the time he'd made her cry but right now, she couldn't have cared less what he thought of her.

'Why am I in here?' Aimee demanded, throwing her question right at Beljarn. 'Where's Jess?'

'Your dragon?' Beljarn waved a dismissive hand. 'We didn't touch her. She'll be around the city somewhere. That's not important. We don't need you as a Rider, we need you because of that.'

He pointed at the bracelet on her wrist. Aimee moved to hide it behind her back but stopped herself and instead straightened her spine, pulling her shoulders back.

'I know what you want,' she told him.

'Oh you know, do you?' Beljarn asked, his tone mocking.

'You want me to use the bracelet to create Empty Warriors, but I won't do it.' Aimee's voice was firm. 'That won't save our city.'

Beljarn took a step closer to the iron bars of her cell. 'What does a scrawny girl like you know about what it takes to keep this city safe.' He pushed his glasses up his nose and ran his eyes up and down her.

Aimee was still damp from her dunking in the sea and stood in her socks, her boots lost from when she fought the guards who took her, and her coat and shirt lay crumpled on the floor. She wore only her trousers and the tatty old vest she'd made the climb in, the one she couldn't bear to throw away. She still had her goggles around her neck but they were broken and useless. Without her dragon, her scimitars, or her coat and boots, she'd been stripped of the outward things that marked her as a Rider. But inside she still had her strength, and her determination, and that made her a Rider.

'I am the reason the entire council wasn't slaughtered out on the tundra,' Aimee told him. 'It's because of me that you even have a chance to fight off the

Empty Warriors. *I* found the bracelet. *I* found her.' She jabbed a finger towards Kyelli. 'It was me who triggered the machine that blocked the outer gate. I've watched two Riders die, killed by those monsters. And with the help of my dragon, and a rockfall, I've killed *hundreds* of Empty Warriors.'

She might have been exaggerating that number but it had to be pretty close and she'd damn sure killed more than Beljarn had. She felt Kyelli's hand rest on her shoulder and knew she had her backing.

'Very impressive, I'm sure,' Beljarn drawled, sounding almost bored, 'but the Empty Warriors are inside the mountains. They broke through at the harbour, despite you and your amazing dragons.' He made air quotes when he said the word *amazing*. 'And I'd give them till tomorrow before they've dug their way through the rocks blocking the other tunnel.'

'That wasn't our fault!' Aimee yelled, defending herself and the Riders.

'But aren't you our guardians? Isn't your sole purpose to protect Kierell? That's why we allow you to bond with dangerous creatures, isn't it?'

'My Riders have done—' Kyelli began but Beljarn cut her off.

'Shut up! You've already proved less than useless.'

At his words something clicked in Aimee's mind. She'd been too wrapped up in her own pain to wonder why Kyelli was in a cell with her but now she understood. Beljarn and his little cohort had kidnapped her, thinking Kyelli could be a weapon for them against the

Empty Warriors. But when they'd discovered that without her bracelet, and only one spark in her chest, Kyelli couldn't help them, they'd snatched Aimee instead.

'This isn't your city anymore,' Beljarn continued, directing his words at Kyelli. 'We should have listened to your father and stayed inside the mountains. You think your influence on the city has been for good but it's because of you that we ventured beyond the mountains. And the consequences? We drew the attention of an army of monsters.'

'They were coming anyway!' Aimee spluttered. 'Pagrin sent his army to destroy us. That's their purpose. They didn't come because we bumped into them and they thought *oh look, here's some people to attack*!' Aimee channelled some more of Nathine's sarcasm.

'You have no proof this Pagrin person even exists,' Cyella said, joining the argument.

'He's her brother!' Aimee pointed at Kyelli and jabbed her in the shoulder. 'She didn't imagine having a brother.'

'A brother who was killed over three hundred years ago.' Cyella looked pointedly at Kyelli, one perfectly groomed eyebrow raised. 'A tale you yourself told us.'

'I said we believed he'd been killed and we left him.' There was a crack in Kyelli's voice as her centuries-old grief butted up against her fresh grief over her brother.

'Enough!' Beljarn snapped. He slowly pushed his glasses up his nose with one finger and looked directly at Aimee. 'The council have decided and either—'

'Only three of you have decided,' Aimee shouted over him. 'You're the Uneven Council, you're supposed to vote on things, all eleven of you.'

Beljarn swatted her words away. 'Myconn has had his way with the council for too long. He places far too much trust in his sister.'

'That's because—'

'You,' Beljarn continued as if Aimee hadn't spoken, 'will either work with us to create a counter army of Empty Warriors, one bound to the will of the council, or we'll take that bracelet from you and give it to someone more deserving of its power.'

The younger councillor stepped forward, an eager light shining in his brown eyes.

'You don't understand, the bracelet will kill him.' Aimee could hear the frustration in her own voice, making it rough at the edges.

'Seth knows the risks, and I think even the more reluctant of our members would agree that ancient power would be better held in the hands of a councillor than some scrawny freak-faced girl.'

Aimee opened her mouth to argue but Beljarn continued, his voice infuriatingly calm and assured.

'Either you take off the bracelet or we'll take it off for you.'

Beljarn flicked his fingers and the guard who'd waited quietly further down the corridor appeared at his side. Aimee didn't understand what difference the guard would make until she saw the knife he carried. It was so long it was almost a short sword. Realisation hollowed out her stomach. She could use up the energy in Pelathina's spark and most of her own to remove the bracelet. But that would half the span of both her life and Pelathina's, if the other girl was still alive. Or the guard could sever her wrist and take the bracelet that way. She'd survive but with only one hand she'd never fly again.

There was a torch flickering on the wall just outside her cell and its flames were reflected in the lenses of Beljarn's glasses. It made him look scarily like an Empty Warrior. But Aimee didn't need to see his eyes to know he'd do it. He'd take off her hand, crippling her, to get the power of the bracelet. And all for nothing.

'You don't understand,' Aimee said and this time her voice quivered on the edge of tears. 'I can't make Empty Warriors, neither can Kyelli, and neither can Seth. You need sparks and an element to create them, and we don't have enough sparks. Only the Quorelle could do it because they had thousands of sparks in their blood.'

Beljarn waved away her argument. 'You can use the bracelet to take people's sparks, yes? So we take them from prisoners, there are plenty here in the city gaol. And at the university hospital there are people who're dying. I'm sure they'd give what's left of their spark to save the city. There might even be fully healthy people who'll donate their spark to the cause.'

Aimee recoiled, stepping back from the bars, retreating into the cell as if she could get away from the councillors and their monstrous plans. The idea of taking sparks from prisoners and those too sick to be healed horrified her. And where would it stop? If Seth, wearing the bracelet, had come across her a year ago would he have pulled her spark from her chest? Would he have looked at her odd face and decided she was weak, or infectious, and taken her life?

Only Cyella looked uncomfortable, twisting the shiny rings round and round on her fingers, but she didn't disagree with Beljarn. The guard stood quiet and impassive. Aimee remembered again the way he'd shunned her because of her face. He'd have no problem taking the bracelet from her and giving it to someone more 'worthy'.

Aimee felt Kyelli wrap an arm around her shoulders but it gave her no comfort. Kyelli couldn't protect her. And Jess wasn't here—Aimee couldn't even sense her dragon anymore. She was alone, and she was helpless, and Beljarn was reaching to the guard for the keys. He passed them to the councillor with the hand not holding the knife. The knife that would soon be used to cut off her hand while she kicked and screamed and begged.

Without realising she was doing it Aimee pulled away from Kyelli and backed into the corner of the cell. Her shoulder blades bumped up against the cold stone and she huddled there. Beljarn slid the keys into the lock and the mechanism grated as it turned.

Aimee's eyes darted around the cell looking for anything she could use as a weapon but the room was bare. Her gaze flew up to the tiny window but it was far too high and way too small. Panic clawed up her chest, tearing at her throat, trapping her breath till it felt like she'd pass out from pure fear.

Beljarn and Seth entered the cell, the guard and his knife a step behind them. Cyella stayed outside and turned her face away, but she said nothing to stop the men. Kyelli stepped in front of Aimee, blocking her with her body.

'Embrace the power,' Kyelli said, so quietly only Aimee heard her. 'If you do, the bracelet will work again and you can stop them.'

Aimee knew what Kyelli meant by stopping them. If the bracelet was working she'd have a chance to grab the guard and steal his spark, killing him before he could maim her. She could steal Beljarn and Seth's sparks too, halting them and their horrific plans.

Aimee closed her eyes and felt the power of the bracelet wrapped around her mind, testing the defences she'd thrown up against it, searching for a way in. All she had to do was let it.

'Do it!' Kyelli begged. 'It's your only chance to save yourself, and your friends, and the young woman you love. Only a Rider can see all the connections, between dragons and people, between Empty Warriors and their master.'

Kyelli was right, Aimee knew she was. She was the only person who could use the bracelet to find Pagrin. Seth wasn't bonded with a dragon, he wouldn't be able to see those shimmering blue lines that connected Riders to their dragons. He wouldn't be able to see the lines of power leading from the Empty Warriors to the man who'd created them.

If Aimee lost the bracelet they'd all be doomed. But if she used it to kill Beljarn and the others she'd be no better than them. She'd be a monster too.

The bracelet's power pressed itself against her mind as Beljarn stepped closer.

'Move,' he commanded Kyelli, and when she didn't he backhanded her across the face. The force of his blow knocked Kyelli to her knees and a line of blood trickled from her nose.

'Embrace the power, Aimee!' Kyelli yelled, struggling to get to her feet as Seth grabbed her and shoved her back to the floor.

Aimee's eyes cast around the room, still desperately looking for a way out that didn't involve murdering three people.

'Do it.' Beljarn signalled to the guard.

'Jess!' Aimee screamed even though she knew her dragon couldn't save her this time.

'Seth, we'll need—'

Beljarn's words were cut short by a grunt. Aimee was staring right at him as his eyes bulged, his face a mask of confusion. Then he coughed hot blood that coated his lips and splattered Aimee's face. She flinched, smacking her head off the wall behind her. Beljarn gurgled, blood pouring down his chin as he toppled forwards. His glasses slipped off his nose and broke on the floor. Aimee's eyes followed them down but her sight caught on the long knife protruding from between Beljarn's ribs, its hilt held firmly in the guard's grip.

Slowly the guard pulled the knife out and Beljarn dropped to the floor as if the blade had been all that was holding him upright. The cell filled with the coppery stench of blood as it pooled under Beljarn's corpse, seeping towards Aimee's sock-clad feet. It dripped from the end of the guard's blade and for a long moment it seemed like the blood was the only thing in the cell that moved.

Then before Aimee could react the guard sprang over Beljarn's body, grabbed Seth and cut the younger man's throat. On the floor, Kyelli scrambled back as Seth's lifeless body crashed down beside her.

Aimee's fingers twitched, reaching for the hilts of scimitars she'd left lying in the street. Her legs tensed as the urge to leap at the guard swept up them. But she was weaponless and shock at what was happening froze her to the spot.

Without wiping his blade the guard turned and strode towards the cell's door. Beljarn and Seth's blood dripped from his knife leaving a trail along the floor. Cyella, standing with her beringed fingers clasped to her chest, saw him coming and screamed. She turned to flee but in three long strides the guard was on her.

'No!' Aimee cried.

The blade slid into her back, its bloody point emerging from her chest. She plucked helplessly at it, slicing her fingers till the guard pulled it free with a sickening, sucking sound. She collapsed, blood as red as the silk of her dress pooling around her.

Kyelli had climbed unsteadily to her feet and Aimee

rushed to her side, letting the older woman lean on her.

The guard turned from Cyella's body to face them. Half his face was splattered with gore but what made it more horrific was how entirely relaxed he was. He moved with the confidence of a man who knew he was the biggest threat in the room. Aimee gripped Kyelli as her mind rushed to work out what was going on.

'Why did you do that?' she yelled at the guard.

He ignored her, instead lifting up the hem of his patchwork cloak and using it to clean his blade.

'These ridiculous cloaks were father's idea, weren't they?' the guard said. His focus was still on his long knife and Aimee wasn't sure if the comment was directed at her.

'What?' Kyelli gasped beside her. 'No.'

Aimee could feel the older woman beginning to shake, her whole body shivering. The guard strode back into the cell, not caring that he splashed through the blood on the floor. Kyelli was clinging to Aimee, hyperventilating beside her. He stopped before them, the long knife held by his side. His hand was coated in Cyella's blood, and drips from his fingers tip-tapped on the stone floor. Aimee was frantically trying to work out how to protect Kyelli and get them both away from him. Without her boots she couldn't even kick him with any force.

The guard calmly reached out and stroked Kyelli's face, leaving a smudge of blood on her cheek. Kyelli whimpered.

'I'm sorry,' she whispered.

'It's three hundred years too late for sorry,' the guard replied.

'Pagrin.'

The name from Kyelli's lips was softer than a whisper, but it drifted out into the room with the force of a thundercloud.

Aimee looked from Kyelli to the murderous guard. He wasn't Pagrin, he was just a city guard. He was older, his face grizzled, and he looked nothing like the Empty Warriors. Kyelli had said the warriors looked like the person who created them because they were made from his sparks.

'I was amazed when you didn't see it earlier,' the guard continued, directing his words at Kyelli, ignoring Aimee, 'but then I should have known you'd still be too self-involved to see me, hiding here in plain sight.'

Aimee watched mesmerised as the guard changed. The wrinkles on his face filled in and smoothed out. His grey stubble receded into his chin. The hair on his head began to grow, the strands coming in thick and dark. In the space of half a minute he'd turned the clock back twenty years, and there, behind the grizzled disguise was a man Aimee recognised. The guard stood before them wearing the same face as the thousands of Empty Warriors.

He was Pagrin.

CHAPTER 25

POWER

Pagrin spread his arms in a gesture that suggested he knew his own capabilities and they were far above Aimee's. She saw the flash of a gold cuff on his wrist and realised he was wearing a bracelet too. His face made Aimee shudder and her fingers twitched again, longing for the grips of her blades. His eyes were hazel, not fiery, but other than that he was identical to the Empty Warriors. Aimee knew this face had belonged to Pagrin first, but she couldn't help thinking he was the one now wearing the features of the monsters she'd been fighting.

'How?' she breathed the question.

It was Kyelli who answered without taking her eyes from her brother. 'The Quorelle use their sparks to stay youthful, burning the energy of the thousands of them in our blood. Pagrin obviously let himself age, then used spark energy to restore his youth.'

'It's the perfect disguise when you think about it.' Pagrin continued. 'When the councillors brought you here and I first realised who you were, I thought you'd done the same. Until it became clear you'd squandered yours.'

'Kyelli gave up her sparks to protect us!' Aimee yelled.

The whirlwind of emotions she'd felt since Pagrin stabbed Beljarn had settled, leaving behind just her anger. This arrogant bastard was the reason Kierell was under attack. He was responsible for the deaths of Lwena and Fineya. Aimee wished Jess was here so she could bite his head off.

Finally Pagrin turned to look at her and the deep disgust in his eyes made Aimee flinch.

'This is the sum of all your achievements?' He pointed at Aimee but turned back to face Kyelli. 'Three hundred years to build a new world, to take the fresh start I planned for us and make something better. And what have you got? A backward, insular city that doesn't even have gas lighting. And your failures are summed up perfectly by this sickly-looking freak of a girl who's wearing *your* bracelet. A bracelet she can't even work because she's too weak to understand its power.'

'The Pagrin I knew would never have said something so cruel.' Kyelli reached out a hand towards her brother but didn't dare touch him. 'My little brother. You were kind. It was your plan we followed to save our people. You were the one desperate not to leave anyone behind.'

A moment of silence followed Kyelli's words. And then, his movements unnaturally fast, Pagrin grabbed

Kyelli by the throat and yanked her from Aimee's grip.

'You left me.' He spat in Kyelli's face.

His anger kindled Kyelli's and she shouted her words back at him. 'Kierellatta was overrun by Doralleni's army. Everything was destroyed. And you didn't come back. We had to go. I thought you were dead.'

'I killed Doralleni!' Pagrin yelled. 'I kept to my part of the plan but when I got back to Vienthon, you and father were gone.'

'We didn't—' Kyelli began but Pagrin shouted over her.

'I was trapped! I couldn't get to you! Your Empty Warriors were still there, still protecting Vienthon, keeping anyone from entering the city. You and father sailed away, leaving me with no way back to my home.'

'Pagrin, I hoped—' Kyelli tried again.

Pagrin shook Kyelli, his hand still around her throat, choking off her words. 'Over three centuries we'd spent by each other's side, and I waited for my sister to come back for me. I never for one second believed you'd abandon me.'

He pushed and released Kyelli, and she fell to the floor. Pagrin towered over her. 'I waited on that island of death, surrounded by the ruins of our world. I didn't know where you'd gone but you knew where I was. Surely you'd come back for me, so I stayed. For almost a century I waited. No one for company except the warriors wearing the faces of my sister and father.'

He crouched down, holding the hilt of his long knife in both hands, its tip resting on the stone floor between his feet. 'Finally I left. And then I learned you'd founded a city without me. Built the new life for our people that was my idea. And that father was dead. Did you kill him? Was that your plan? To get rid of us both and rule like a queen with this city as your own dollhouse to play with.'

'No! Father ran out of sparks. He'd used so many to create warriors,' Kyelli argued back. 'And I left this city to protect it.'

Aimee had taken a step away from the two Quorelle. As they argued, she realised that she didn't care; she was sorry for all Kyelli and Pagrin had lost on Kierellatta, but it had happened three hundred years ago. Their lives, their pasts, they were gone even if the ripples of them had reached Aimee's world. But Aimee didn't give a single dull spark for who was to blame for things that happened so long ago. What mattered were the people fighting to stay alive right now. What Aimee did care about were her friends.

As the two Quorelle continued to shout, Aimee very carefully touched the bracelet's power with her mind. It responded immediately, like a cat who'd been sleeping poked awake. Pagrin was an example of what using the power could do. Driven by his grief at being abandoned and anger at his sister, he'd embraced the power of his bracelet and created monsters in his image.

Aimee hesitated, feeling like she was in a mental staring contest with the power. Would she be strong enough to control it if she let it in? Or would it gobble up the energy in Pelathina's spark and hunger for more?

Would she succumb to the temptation and wind up thinking Beljarn and Seth's plan had merit?

The Quorelles' argument had ebbed and now they glared at each other, Kyelli still on the floor and Pagrin crouched over her. As Aimee watched she saw the way Kyelli shifted her feet, getting them underneath herself, and spotted her bracing her palms against the floor. She was readying herself to spring at Pagrin.

Aimee knew what Kyelli was doing. All she had to do was distract Pagrin's full attention for just a moment and that would give Aimee a chance to grab him. She could pull all his sparks from him, killing him and his army of monsters. But she could only do that if the bracelet was working. Kyelli was giving her no choice but to embrace the power. If she didn't, Pagrin would kill Kyelli a moment after she sprang at him.

Aimee took a deep breath and glanced down at the bracelet, flicking the dial to *ura*. The power pressed urgently against her mind, perhaps sensing what she was about to do. She wished Jess was here beside her.

Pagrin leaned closer to Kyelli. 'I'd planned to let you watch the destruction of this city you built without me, but actually...' his words trailed off and he shrugged.

Moving so fast his arm became a blur, Pagrin stabbed Kyelli through the heart.

'No!' Aimee screamed.

Without meaning to Aimee opened her mind and let the power pour into her. It rushed through her brain like water released from a dam and it felt just as relentless. A smell came with the power, fresh and green, like new leaves in spring but a thousand times stronger. The smell of life, all life, and energy flowing everywhere around her. The power surged into every corner of her mind, coating every emotion, every memory, each thought Aimee had ever had. She went from being one person to suddenly feeling like she was connected to every living thing.

It was overwhelming and she dropped, gasping, to her knees.

It felt like her mind was being ripped from her head and pulled outwards in a hundred different directions. She squeezed her eyes shut but even through her lids she could see the wavering white-green light of sparks and lines of every colour, the glowing connections between the energy in all living things. It was like the walls of the cell were gone, and not just the cell but the gaol too and every other wall in Kierell. The glow of sparks and energy shone through them all, blinding her through closed eyes.

The ancient power of the bracelet continued to rampage through her brain, trying to control her, to change her. It was trying to bully her out of the way.

'No,' Aimee said through gritted teeth.

Her legs wobbled but she pushed herself back to her feet. A year ago she'd have given half her spark to be a different person but not now. She *would not* let a stupid bracelet try to change her, regardless of how old and important its power felt. This was her mind and she was in control of it. Gritting her teeth so hard that her jaw ached, Aimee pulled her senses back from the world, bringing them inside her own head where they belonged.

The power sensed what she was doing and rose to meet her. She imagined herself fully dressed as a Rider, with her scimitars in both hands and Jess beside her.

'No one bullies me.'

She wasn't sure if she said the words out loud or only in her head but it didn't matter. In her mental image she and Jess sprang forward together and grabbed the power, wrestling it under control. Aimee felt it pulling back from the corners of her mind like it was winding in hundreds of tentacles. The smell of spring leaves went from being overpowering to floating subtly around her. And she could feel Jess again in her mind, their connection strong and the door between them fully open. Aimee knew her dragon had added her strength to hers.

'Thanks, girl,' she whispered.

Slowly, she opened her eyes to see Pagrin's knife still buried to the hilt in Kyelli's chest. Before Aimee could speak he whipped it out, the blood spatter painting an arc on the stone wall. Aimee's fight with the power in her mind had taken barely a few seconds. But in that short time everything had changed.

She watched, unable to do anything, as the little energy remaining in Kyelli's spark tried and failed to heal her. Aimee could see it clearer than ever before. She saw Kyelli's spark pulsing, and the pulses growing slower as her heart failed. Tendrils of white-green energy leaked from the wound in Kyelli's chest, dissipating in the air, her energy returning to the world.

Then her spark winked out and Kyelli was gone.

Pagrin stood over her, blood dripping from his knife onto Kyelli's trousers, and he glowed. Aimee could clearly see the spark in his chest glowing as bright as a child's, its energy barely used, but she could also see the ones in his blood. They shone through like fireflies trapped underneath his skin, and they moved, carried around his body as his blood flowed. It would have been beautiful if Aimee didn't know the horrific potential of each one of those glowing pinpricks of light. Pagrin could take every one of those sparks and turn them into Empty Warriors.

As he turned towards her, Aimee clearly saw his connection to his Empty Warriors. Just like the shimmering blue line that connected her and Jess, Pagrin had lines of energy stretching from his chest. He had two stretching off in opposite directions, one towards the army outside the mountains and one towards the warriors who'd broken through at the harbour. Just like hers, Pagrin's lines were spiderweb-thin but where Aimee's glowed a soft blue, Pagrin's were a black so dark they seemed to suck in the light. His were a corruption of the bond that connected Riders and their dragons.

He turned his eyes from his dead sister and fixed them on Aimee. She in turn was staring at his connections, her eyes flicking back and forth along them. Pagrin caught her gaze and anger clouded his regal-looking face. Now that Aimee saw the Empty Warrior's face animated with human emotion she could see the similarities between him and Kyelli—the almond-shaped eyes, high forehead and pointed chin.

'What did you do?' he hissed, sensing the change in her.

'I embraced the power,' Aimee replied, holding her chin up in defiance, eyes now scanning the room for a way out.

'You? A freak of a human.' He took a step towards her. 'That wasn't meant for you.' He pointed to her bracelet with his blade, Kyelli's blood still dripping off its tip. 'That bracelet will suck out every morsel of life from your spark, and the spark you're carrying with you. Whose spark did you take? She must be someone important if you haven't used her energy to fix that disgusting face of yours.'

'Fix my face?' Aimee didn't understand.

Pagrin took another step towards her. He was within striking distance now. One small lunge and he could bury his blade in Aimee's insides.

He waved a bloody hand towards her head. 'The energy from a spare spark can be used to heal you, leaving your own untouched.' He cocked his head to the side, the movement almost like a dragon. 'Yet you haven't fixed your skin, haven't used that girl's energy to put colour into your face and hair.'

It took a second for the full meaning of Pagrin's words to sink in but when they did a wild hope flooded through her. She could have a normal face. All she had to do was use some of Pelathina's spark to heal her skin, the same way Pagrin had used energy to reverse the ageing on his face. The bracelet's power stirred inside the cage in her mind, eager to be used.

This was her chance to be normal, to look out at the world from a face no one thought was freaky. To never again be sneered at, bullied or excluded because of the way she looked. To look in the mirror every morning and see a pretty young woman staring back at her. To never need to fear that her girlfriend might shun her in public.

The power rattled the bars of its cage, a beast hungry for freedom. All she had to do was open the cage, just a crack, enough to let a sliver of the power out into her mind. And in a few moments she'd have a normal face.

She mentally slammed a hand down and stopped those thoughts in their tracks.

Would the Aimee of last year have done it?

The Aimee of now would not.

She left the power right where it was, locked up and tamed, and pulled on her best sneer, directing it at Pagrin.

'You're the one who's broken if you think there's anything wrong with my face.'

She injected her words with a little of Jara's authority and a sprinkling of Nathine's sass. And she pictured Pelathina smiling at her as she spoke, dimples curling in her cheeks.

Pagrin stared down at her, his face twisted with contempt. Kyelli said her brother had been kind, that it had been his plan to save their people. But whoever that noble Quorelle had been, he was gone. Three hundred years alone with nothing but the corrupting power of the bracelet and his own grief for company had driven him mad. If he'd simply been a broken shell of a person Aimee would have felt sympathy for him, but he'd let himself become a monster. And now, because of one Quorelle, thousands of people and all the Riders were facing their deaths.

Aimee's hatred was hot in her chest, and the bracelet sensed her desire to end Pagrin. But Aimee kept her mind clamped down around it, not letting even a tendril of that power seep into her brain. When she killed Pagrin she needed it to be her own choice, her own actions. She could not let the bracelet's power control her.

Pagrin was watching her. 'I can see you wrestling with it. This power was never meant for one as weak as you. It'll tear through your mind, ripping your consciousness to tatters.'

Aimee flinched as he raised the knife but all he did was caress her cheek with its tip. She felt the wetness of Kyelli's blood, left in a streak down her face. Below Pagrin's line of sight Aimee's fingers slid around the engraved gold of the bracelet till she felt the dial, checking it was set to *ura*. All she had to do was grab him.

She swirled her tongue around her mouth, gathering saliva, then spat in his face. Pagrin wasn't expecting it and flinched, taking a step backward. That was Aimee's moment.

She shot out her left arm, reaching across her body for his hand. Her fingertips brushed his wrist but that was as close as they got. Moving fast, faster even than the Empty Warriors, Pagrin slapped aside her arm. Before Aimee had even registered what had happened, Pagrin dropped his knife. She heard it clatter to the stone floor, and he grabbed her around the throat with both hands.

Aimee gasped then choked as he squeezed her windpipe. Pagrin lifted her off her feet with ease and slammed her against the back wall of the cell. In a split second he'd shifted his grip, taking one hand from her throat and using it to pin her left arm against the wall. She heard the clang as the gold of the bracelet struck the stone. It was useless to her now—with her arm pinned against the wall she couldn't grab Pagrin, couldn't suck out his sparks. Aimee kicked, feeling her sock-clad feet connect with his thighs but Pagrin hardly seemed to notice the blows.

'Your spark's going to burn through all its energy trying to make your lungs work, but without air every flicker of that energy will be wasted. Yours and the energy of the girl whose spark you carry.'

Pagrin leaned in till his face was inches from Aimee's. His eyes might have been hazel brown and normal, but they were even more terrifying than the swirling flames in those of the Empty Warriors'. Theirs were unnatural and that was creepy, but his brimmed with self-righteous hate and that was terrifying.

'I'm even tempted to give you one of my spare

sparks, just so you can burn through that as well,' Pagrin continued. 'Give you a little boost of energy so it'll take you even longer to die and I can watch your suffering go on and on.'

Panic fired every nerve in Aimee's body. She kicked and struggled and clawed at him with her fingernails but Pagrin held on. The pain around her throat was unbearable. It felt like his fingers were biting through the soft tissue, squeezing against her spine. Black stars danced at the edge of her vision. Aimee's kicks grew weaker but she fought it, fought with every shred of determination she could muster.

'Freak,' Pagrin spat the word in her face.

Voices floated through the pain gripping her mind. She thought she heard her friends—Nathine was shouting, Jess was roaring, Lyrria arguing about something—but they were phantoms in her mind. She was alone and about to die.

CHAPTER 26

LIFE AND SPARKS

Pagrin's hateful face leaned closer to her, his intense eyes drinking in each moment of her suffering. Aimee's vision darkened. The voices of her friends floated through her mind as if come to say goodbye. She struggled to hold on to her connection with Jess but it was slipping away into the darkness.

'Move you idiots!'

This time, Nathine's voice sounded like it was coming from right behind the wall Aimee was pressed against.

'What if it doesn't—'

A second voice was cut off by a crash that rocked the gaol. The cell wall six feet along from Aimee was blasted to rubble. Bricks flew through the cell, smacking into the councillors' bodies and splashing in the pools of their blood. The vibrations of the explosion spread through the cell in a rushing wave, knocking Aimee and Pagrin to the floor. As they landed hard on the stones, Aimee was thrown free of his hands and she skidded along the floor.

She sucked in a huge gulp of air. Then coughed, pain ripping up her throat. The cell was full of brick dust and Aimee's body spasmed as she breathed in much-needed air at the same time as coughs racked her lungs. It felt like her chest and throat had been scraped raw and tears squeezed from her eyes with the pain of it. Pagrin's hand was gone from her neck but she felt like it was still there, like he'd crushed her throat and now it wouldn't open properly.

Pushing herself up onto her elbows she gaped at the ruin of the cell. The explosion had ripped open the outer wall and morning sunlight streamed in, coating the destruction in soft yellow light. Bricks and rubble littered the floor, half covering the bodies still lying there. The force of the blast had blown the door of the cell off its hinges and flung it down the hallway.

Two figures stepped carefully through the gap in the wall. Aimee winced in the sunshine and tried to blink away the swirling dust. The figures were dark shadows as they stepped closer. And they weren't making any sound—no talking, no shouting. Fear clawed its way up Aimee's chest. The Empty Warriors had broken through the barricades at the harbour and made it into the city.

She scrambled back on her bum, fingers searching for a weapon. Her hand curled around a chunk of brick and she grabbed it.

The figures loomed over her, dark shapes backlit by the sunshine, their freakish eyes hidden by shadow. There was no sound in the cell as Aimee readied herself.

The one in front knelt down and the movement took it out of the blinding sunlight.

Aimee gasped in relief and the brick tumbled from her fingers. Nathine crouched, grinning, before her. Her lips moved but Aimee couldn't hear her words. She looked up, only now recognising the shape of Dyrenna. Was she speaking too? Why couldn't she hear? Then she realised the ringing in her ears wasn't just the rush of blood she'd felt when Pagrin released his grip, it was from the boom of the explosion.

'I can't hear you!' Aimee shouted.

Nathine rolled her eyes and reached out to grab Aimee under her arms. She hoisted her to her feet, not very gently, and looked her up and down as if to comment on what a state she was in.

'Pagrin!' Aimee yelled, spinning from Nathine's grip and casting her eyes across the ruin of the cell. She couldn't let him attack the others. And if he was wounded, maybe knocked out, she could kill him now and end this.

But she couldn't see him. He'd been flung to the floor just beside her but his body wasn't there. Aimee hopped over the scattered bricks, yelping as splinters of rock stabbed through her socks. Cyella's body still lay out in the hallway, crushed now by the cell's door. Beljarn and Seth were bloody heaps inside the cell, their slack faces coated with a fine layer of brick dust. And then there was Kyelli. But Pagrin was gone.

Aimee crouched beside Kyelli's body and gently closed the old woman's eyes. Sadness swirled through

Aimee. Six hundred years of life and Kyelli was murdered in a prison cell by her brother. A man who'd once loved her, until he succumbed to the temptation of the bracelet's power. It didn't seem fair that her life had ended here, like this.

Nathine and Dyrenna crouched on the other side of Kyelli's body. Aimee could see their lips moving but their words were still muffled by the ringing in her ears.

Now the sunlight wasn't blinding her Aimee could clearly see the other Riders' sparks, glowing with bright white-green light in their chests. And stretching behind them were the pulsing blue lines that connected them to their dragons. Now that Aimee had embraced the bracelet's power, and tamed it, their connections were so easy to see. And not just see: she could feel them too, sense the way they hummed with life. She watched a pulse push back along Nathine's connection and knew her friend had just sent a command to Malgerus to wait. Dyrenna's connection gently pulsed with a constant back and forth, and Aimee could feel the love she and Black were sharing.

By using the bracelet as the Quorelle had, Aimee could not only see sparks and connections, she could understand them too. She could read them. Nathine's spark wasn't just a light glowing in her chest, Aimee could see in it now the decades it would give Nathine and the tiny trickle of energy that constantly flowed from it into Nathine's blood, giving her energy, powering her life. It was beautiful.

Nathine reached across Kyelli's body and grabbed

Aimee's arm with one hand, pointing through the gap in the wall with her other.

'Wait! I need to check something!' Aimee yelled, forgetting that the others could hear her fine.

She closed her eyes as Nathine gave her an exasperated look. Gently she tapped the power of the bracelet without letting it out of its cage. Instantly she felt the life all around her again, the energy and connections that linked everything living. That smell of fresh green grass filled her nostrils. When she'd first felt the full breadth of what the bracelet could show her it had been overwhelming, but this time she was prepared. She ignored the pull of the lives right next to her—of Nathine and Dyrenna's sparks—and glossed over the void where Kyelli's life had been, and sent her mind wider.

Even with her eyes closed she could see thousands of sparks, one for each person in Kierell, and they sparkled in the darkness like fireflies. She resisted the urge to go looking for Pelathina, to check that her spark still burned. If it didn't, that wasn't a truth she could handle right now. Instead she searched for Pagrin.

She could sense the Empty Warriors, their unnatural existence a black swarm that drew closer to the city from both sides. Aimee probed the swarm closest to her, the ones gathering in the harbour district, still held back by the city guards and Riders. She flinched and almost yanked her mind back. Their hatred, channelled into them by Pagrin, was vicious and all-consuming. She could feel their absolute need to fulfil their purpose—to destroy Kyelli's city—and the way it controlled them. There was nothing else inside them, no sparks, no humanity.

Aimee shivered and tried to follow the warped lines that connected them to Pagrin. They were a deeper black against the darkness of her closed eyes and they pulsed, not with love or a shared life, but with anger. The lines led across Kierell, towards where she crouched in the city gaol, but then it was as if they entered a bank of mist. Aimee couldn't see where they led, where Pagrin had run to.

'He's blocking me somehow,' Aimee whispered, talking to herself. Frustration bubbled inside her, and mixed with it was a feeling of deep regret that Kyelli was gone. Aimee had done as the Quorelle had advised but now she had no one to explain what she was meant to do with this new power.

Nathine tugged her arm again and Aimee's eyes flew open, her mind reeling back into her brain.

'Aimee, we need to go.' Nathine's voice was muffled like she was underwater but at least Aimee heard her words this time. 'The guards are going to be really pissed that I blew a hole in their wall.'

Nathine didn't look ashamed of the destruction she'd caused, instead she looked super pleased with herself. Aimee allowed herself to be pulled to her feet but her eyes lingered on Kyelli's body. Dyrenna's lips moved, but her soft words didn't make it past the ringing in Aimee's ears. The older Rider crouched and carefully lifted Kyelli's body. Aimee smiled her thanks, glad that Dyrenna too didn't think it right to leave her here.

Aimee tugged her coat free of the rubble and slipped her bare arms inside. Then Nathine was dragging her from the cell. She'd barely stepped out into the sunshine when Jess barrelled into her. Aimee laughed and wrapped her arms around her dragon's neck, pressing her forehead against Jess's cool scales. Her ruff of feathers fluttered in delight, catching on Aimee's curls.

'I love you too, girl,' Aimee whispered. Jess's mind was overflowing with the sense that things were right now—she was back with her Rider, their clutch was once again complete. A growl rumbled in her throat, the vibrations soft, almost like a purr. Aimee could have stayed there for a long time, wrapped safe in her dragon's love.

The hole Nathine had blasted in the wall was only large enough for a person, not a dragon, and so Jess had waited outside. Another Rider had waited too, and as Aimee finally pulled back from hugging Jess a set of arms grabbed her, wrapping her in a new hug. Aimee smelled Lyrria's familiar scent and felt the soft tickle of her hair on her face.

Before Aimee could speak Lyrria leaned back, took Aimee's face in her hands and kissed her. Aimee tasted apples as Lyrria's tongue brushed her lips and desire bloomed in her. The kiss was sweet but hungry and Aimee could tell Lyrria wanted more. Right then she did too.

Lyrria ended the kiss and caressed the colourless half

of Aimee's face. She gave Aimee a smile and a wink before pulling away. It took Aimee a moment to get her mind back in gear, the unexpected kiss having pushed away all thoughts of Pagrin and death. She was distracted too by the realisation that Lyrria had just kissed her in front of Nathine and Dyrenna, and she hadn't been ashamed to do so.

Aimee pulled her eyes from Lyrria's pretty face and turned to take in all three Riders and their dragons. They'd come to rescue her. The comfort of that thought was like being wrapped in a blanket which had been warming by the fire.

'Thank you,' she told them.

'Was Nathine's plan,' Dyrenna said as she gently laid Kyelli's body beside Black.

'Yeah, and aren't you impressed?' Nathine demanded, waving at the hole in the gaol. 'I told you that when it was my turn to think up a plan it would be the best.'

Aimee was impressed, because finally Nathine had been the one to take the initiative. And her smile was so smug Aimee couldn't help but laugh. 'How did you do it?'

'Well obviously, since it was the council and guards holding you, we couldn't swoop in with our dragons, kill everyone and rescue you.'

Aimee breathed a sigh of relief that Nathine hadn't attempted that.

'But, and this is where my genius really comes to the fore,' Nathine continued, 'the rules about dragons not endangering citizens don't say anything about destroying property.' Her self-congratulatory grin grew even wider.

'They might write some new rules now,' Dyrenna added with a small wry smile.

Aimee looked at the rubble scattered around the hole in the gaol's outer wall and spotted curved shards of glass.

'You used dragon's breath orbs,' she said to Nathine.

'Yup, just like you did when you blew up the whole mountain.'

'It wasn't the whole mountain,' Aimee objected but Nathine only shrugged.

Aimee closed her eyes, tapping into the power of the bracelet, and tried once again to locate Pagrin. Perhaps now she was outside it would be easier. She quickly found the thousands of dark connections, twisted together into a thick strand, snaking across the city from the harbour district. They were leading now towards the centre of the city but still they disappeared into a cloud of murky grey fog. Aimee imagined reaching into the fog, seeing her hand sink into its shadows, but it resisted her, actively pushing against her.

As she watched, the cloud of fog grew, blooming outwards to cover Quorelle Square, most of Shine and half of the eastern curve of Barter. Pagrin could sense her looking for him and was obscuring his trail. Frustration gnawed at Aimee, along with the unfairness that she was trying to fight someone with power she'd had for ten minutes whereas he'd had centuries to master it.

She had to find a way.

Aimee opened her eyes to find Nathine staring at her.

'Are you okay?' her friend asked. 'You look kinda weird.'

'Don't tell me, I made the constipated dragon face?'

'Exactly what I was going to say.'

'I embraced the power of the bracelet,' Aimee admitted.

'Like Kyelli told you to do?'

Both girls turned their eyes to the body at Black's feet.

'What does that mean?' Lyrria asked, arms outspread.

'Means Aimee's a super, half-Quorelle, spark-manipulating, magical person now,' Nathine said with a casual shrug, as if she'd known all along the power Aimee was going to have.

'I always knew you were my best student,' Lyrria said with a grin and a look that suggested she was suitably impressed. Despite nearly dying a short while ago Aimee felt the pleasant flutter of butterflies in her belly. Dyrenna was still looking down at Kyelli's body.

'What happened, little one?' she asked softly.

Aimee wanted to tell them everything, and she would, but right then there was something else she needed to do first. She stepped over and took Dyrenna's hand, trusting only the older Rider to give her awful news gently.

'Is Pelathina still alive?'

Aimee held her breath.

'For now.' Dyrenna nodded and Aimee nearly collapsed with relief. 'But I don't know if even Aranati's healing skills can save her.'

'I can,' Aimee told them. 'Where is she?'

'Aranati took her back to Anteill,' Dyrenna replied.

'Okay, we'll go there first.'

No one questioned her decision or authority, they simply mounted up. As she swung a leg over Jess's saddle Aimee caught Lyrria's gaze and thought she saw a flash of hurt on the woman's face. It was gone so quickly though that she couldn't be sure.

'Aimee, wait,' Nathine called as she rummaged in her saddlebag. Pulling something out she ran over to Jess and presented it to Aimee. 'I brought your boots.'

Aimee reached down and took them. They'd been crushed in Nathine's bag and were still soggy with seawater.

'You couldn't have brought me a dry pair?' Aimee asked.

The pleased look on Nathine's face morphed into one of outrage. 'Hey, I could have left those on the street for the Empty Warriors to burn, then you'd be spending the rest of your life wandering around in your smelly socks.'

Aimee thought of the spare pair of boots she owned, sitting by her bed back in Anteill all nice and dry, but chose not to mention that.

'Thank you,' she managed, around the wince as she slipped her feet into the cold, soggy leather.

'I should think so,' Nathine said in a haughty voice but also threw Aimee a smile before running back over to Malgerus.

The four dragons took off in a whoosh of wings. Black had picked up Kyelli's body with his talons and he carried her back to Anteill with them.

'What happened at the harbour?' Aimee called across the sky as their dragons skimmed the rooftops of Barter. She'd twisted in her saddle now they were in the air and worry clenched her stomach when she saw plumes of black smoke rising from the streets and warehouses. She knew the Empty Warriors were still there—she could sense them.

'We lost the whole harbour district,' Lyrria replied, 'everything across the River Toig. The bastards have set it alight. They didn't ransack or loot anything. We watched them from the air go street by street, pressing their horrible hands against anything wooden and letting it burn.'

'But the Toig is too deep there for them to wade across without drowning,' Nathine picked up the telling. 'The city guards destroyed all the bridges and now there are rows of Empty Warriors waiting on the river's banks. They're just stood there, silent like statues and it's creepy.'

'What are they waiting for?' Aimee asked but no one had an answer for her.

They flew over Quorelle Square and Aimee scanned the streets of the city centre even though she knew it was wasted effort. Pagrin wouldn't be standing waving a flag waiting for her. The warehouses at the western edge of Barter passed beneath their dragon's bellies, then they were catching the updrafts and soaring into the mountains. Aimee felt a surge of longing as the familiar peaks and stone pillars around Anteill came into view. Not long ago she didn't think she'd ever make it back here.

She and Jess were first to dive down into the Heart, and she hoped desperately all the way down that she wasn't too late to save Pelathina.

CHAPTER 27

BREACHED

Anteill was eerily quiet as Aimee, Nathine, Lyrria and Dyrenna ran through the empty corridors. Every Rider who could fight was out in the city. There had only been three lonely dragons in the Heart—Skydance, Harmony and Smaja.

They'd left their dragons saddled and in the middle of the cavern. None had flown up to their ledges, and in fact the three already there had flown down. As Aimee and the others had run from the Heart the seven dragons were huddled together in the light from the dragon's breath orbs, seeking comfort in each other.

Aimee took a sharp left, skidded in her haste, smacked her hip off a stalagmite of pink quartz and kept running. She was heading for the little infirmary where Aranati treated injured Riders. The shimmering blue lines of three Rider-dragon connections led her on, telling her where to go. One line was much fainter than the others and Aimee knew that was Pelathina's. Her bond with Skydance was failing as she died.

The door to the cave housing the infirmary was open and Aimee dashed inside. The cave was long and thin, illuminated at the far end by sunlight from a vent in the rock, the same as the ones in the Heart only smaller. Shelves lined the wall to the right, and beds stood against the one to the left. Aranati kept the infirmary nice, with vases and jugs of wildflowers sitting on any ledge large enough to hold them. Perhaps she was trying to persuade injured Riders to stay and rest, but none ever wanted to—they always longed to fly again as soon as they could.

Ryka, injured at the fight in the caravan compound, was sitting up in the first bed, but Aimee barely registered her as she ran over to the second bed. Pelathina lay on top of a blanket crusted with her own blood. Aranati sat beside her, holding her sister's hand, her face shiny with tears. Her head jerked up as Aimee appeared and the despair in her dark eyes told Aimee everything she needed to know. She couldn't save her sister. But Aimee could.

'I've cleaned and closed her wound,' Aranati said as Aimee sat on the bed, 'so it should heal but she's got a fever and I don't think she can fight it off.'

Pelathina's spark pulsed faintly in time with her slowed heart rate. Aimee gently took Pelathina's other hand and gave it a squeeze. Her normally lovely bronze skin was ashen and the circles under her eyes were so dark they looked painted on. The Rider's eyes fluttered open and found Aimee's face. Pelathina smiled and Aimee's heart nearly broke in two.

'Hey, you're safe,' Pelathina said, her voice a whisper.

'Shh,' Aimee told her, as she confidently flicked the dial on the bracelet to *zurl*.

Immediately Pelathina's energy began flowing from Aimee and back into its rightful place. For the first time when doing this Aimee felt in control. She watched as the spark in Pelathina's chest grew brighter and brighter.

She felt the moment that the last of Pelathina's energy left her, but Aimee didn't cut the flow there. Remembering what Kyelli had told her, that she'd unintentionally used some of Pelathina's life energy to heal the burn on her arm, Aimee gave a little of her own spark to the other young woman in recompense. Pelathina would never know but Aimee thought it was only fair.

This time she didn't have to fight to stop the flow of energy—now that she'd embraced the power of the bracelet she was in complete control and simply stopped, like flicking a switch in her mind. She kept hold of Pelathina's hand but turned the bracelet's dial back to neutral. Already Pelathina's skin looked less grey and her eyes were more alert. Her hand was still clammy with the fever but she would have the strength now to fight it off and heal.

'Pellie?' Aranati brushed her sister's sweaty hair off her forehead, smiling at her through her tears.

Pelathina cupped her sister's face and gave her a small nod before turning to look at Aimee. 'See, I knew you'd find a way to give me it back.'

There were tears in Aimee's eyes too but she gave a half laugh at how trusting and upbeat Pelathina was. Aimee clung to the other Rider's hand, her patchy fingers locked together with Pelathina's bronze-coloured ones. The shimmering blue line connecting Pelathina with Skydance was pulsing and Aimee could tell that Pelathina was reassuring him that she was alright, and he was sending her thoughts of soaring free through the sky again soon.

Aimee felt someone move behind her and then Nathine's face was by her ear.

'Kiss her already,' Nathine ordered in a whisper loud enough that Aimee was sure everyone in the infirmary heard her.

She felt the familiar flush in her cheeks and was suddenly very aware that the last woman she'd kissed was the one leaning against the wall beside Ryka's bed, chatting to the injured Rider and throwing apparently casual glances towards Pelathina's bed.

In that moment Aimee felt the conflicting desires inside her heart raise their heads and weave around each other like snakes fighting. Pelathina was sweet, and kind, and supportive, and Aimee longed for the time to get to know her better. But Lyrria was the first woman who'd ever liked her and she still felt a tug of loyalty towards her because of that.

'What's the plan, little one?' Dyrenna asked and Aimee was grateful to her for switching everyone's focus.

Aimee opened her lips to reply but the words died in her throat. Something was wrong. She felt it the exact same moment everyone else did but only Aimee saw the warnings come flaring along the Riders' bonds. The lines connecting everyone in the infirmary with their dragons in the Heart flashed bright blue all at once. In her mind Aimee sensed Jess was suddenly on high alert. Something inside Anteill had spooked their dragons.

'I'll go,' Dyrenna offered, already walking towards the infirmary door.

'Wait,' Aimee called.

The older Rider stopped, turned on her heel and raised an eyebrow at Aimee. All her questions were in that simple gesture but Aimee ignored them for now. Instead she closed her eyes and reached out with her mind. She pushed past the vibrant life energy she felt from the Riders around her and searched for what had alarmed their dragons.

Her mind flew along the corridors, following the pulsing blue lines, back towards the Heart. The walls of the cavern didn't matter, Aimee could sense life through them. There was a bright pulsing well of energy off to her right and she knew that was the city, but there was something else, right above the Heart. Aimee reached up towards it with her mind. Anger and hate flooded through her and she felt the warped lines of connection that stretched back into the city towards Pagrin.

Her eyes flew open. Everyone was staring at her, their faces a mix of confusion and awe.

'There are Empty Warriors in Anteill. We need to get out now!'

The Riders sprang into action at Aimee's words,

obeying her, trusting her, without question. Ryka climbed out of bed, her arm in a sling and her shoulder bandaged, and almost stumbled but Lyrria caught her. Aranati struggled to help Pelathina up and Nathine ran over to help. Dyrenna pulled free a scimitar. Aimee instinctively reached over her shoulder for her own blades before she remembered that she'd left them on the streets of the harbour district. She felt a pang at losing the blades she'd been gifted, the ones crafted bespoke for her.

'Aimee,' Dyrenna called and tossed her other scimitar towards her. Aimee snatched it from the air and wished there was more time for her to thank Dyrenna for trusting her with one of her blades.

'Where are they?' Dyrenna asked as the others helped the two injured Riders towards the door.

'There are some above the Heart but I can sense more in the tunnels near the entrance,' Aimee replied.

'You alright taking point if I bring up the rear?' Dyrenna asked.

Aimee nodded and moved out into the corridor. She heard the footsteps of the others behind her and threw a glance back, checking everyone was there. Ryka could walk by herself but she was grimacing in pain from the burn on her shoulder. Lyrria stayed close to her, one hand hovering by Ryka's elbow, the other holding a blade. Behind, Aranati and Nathine half carried Pelathina between them. Aimee could tell Pelathina had put on a brave face but it was a thin mask and her pain shone through. Aimee's heart squeezed in sympathy.

Dyrenna brought up the rear, guarding their backs.

With the injured Riders they couldn't run and Aimee had to force herself to keep her pace steady. They just needed ten minutes to get everyone to the Heart and away.

She listened carefully and checked every corner before leading the others around. She couldn't sense or see the Empty Warriors themselves—they had no sparks—so all Aimee could feel was their connection with Pagrin and that made it hard to pinpoint exactly where they were.

No one spoke as they crept through the tunnels of their own home. Pelathina's breath was ragged and Aimee winced at the way the sound clawed through the silence.

She stepped softly, her weight only on the balls of her feet, ready to fight if she had to. They passed the dining cavern. The myriad dragon's breath orbs shone down on empty tables and a horrible thought flitted through Aimee's mind—what if no one ever sat eating and laughing in there again?

They were only three turns away from the Heart now. Jess was tugging at her, urging her to hurry. Emotions flicked along the glowing blue line of their connection. Aimee approached a wide junction where three tunnels met around a cluster of glittering stalactites. The tunnel to her right led to their bedrooms, the one to her left would take them towards the armoury. Straight ahead led to the Heart. All three tunnels were empty.

Aimee crossed the intersection, ducking under the lowest of the stalactites, and waited for the others. Ryka and Lyrria crossed, Aranati, Nathine and Pelathina right behind them. Pelathina's face was shiny with sweat.

Aimee heard the scuff of a footstep at the same moment as she sensed the dark, twisted connections of the Empty Warriors. Three of them sprang from the bedroom tunnel, blades unsheathed, flaming eyes glowing.

'Keep going!' Aimee yelled at the others, pointing towards the Heart.

As she slipped past them she grabbed the hilt of one of Nathine's scimitars, unsheathing the blade.

'Don't lose it!' Nathine yelled without turning around.

'I won't,' Aimee promised.

'You lost my pencil,' Nathine retorted.

Aimee thought it would feel weird, having the hilts of two different scimitars in her hands, neither of them her own, but actually it felt good, like she had a little of Dyrenna and Nathine's strength. It wasn't like when she'd been using Pelathina's spark to make herself stronger, this was more like having her friends' support rather than stealing their skills.

Dyrenna was already fighting and Aimee threw herself into the fray. Dyrenna's blade skidded off a warrior's breastplate and she ducked as his sword cut through the air. Another warrior sprang from behind him, his blade swinging at Aimee's chest. She caught it with her own, deflecting the blow. His sword tip scored a groove in the wall by Aimee's head. In the split second he took to adjust his grip and attack again, Aimee had stepped back and crouched.

His sword fell in a blow that would have split her skull but she crossed her blades above her head. Metal screeched on metal as their swords crashed together. The flames in his eyes swirled, furious as an inferno, as he glared down at her. He added his other hand to the hilt of his sword and pushed downwards. Without the added energy of Pelathina's spark Aimee wasn't strong enough to stop his blade inching closer to her face. Her wrists quivered with the effort of holding him back.

She let her eyes slip from his, down to his breastplate of black metal. The silver tree engraved there was level with her face. It was beautiful, intricate and had belonged to Kyelli. But Pagrin had turned it into a symbol of evil. Right then Aimee swore she would claim it back, along with her city.

Instead of pushing against the warrior Aimee released her blade and rolled. He hadn't been expecting the sudden lack of resistance and stumbled over her. Aimee sprang up from her roll in time to see the warrior's head collide with the lowest stalactite. The glittering purple quartz was harder than rock and his head cracked open. Aimee gagged on the rotten egg stench of sulphur as molten fire burst across the crystal.

The Empty Warrior collapsed to the floor, his forehead split open down to his nose, lava gushing across his face. It dripped from the stalactite too, hissing as it landed on his chest. His legs twitched, and his fingers still gripped the hilt of his sword but he didn't get up.

Aimee spun around to find Dyrenna pulling her blade from a warrior's neck, lava sheeting down his breastplate. Another lay on the ground, both arms missing, molten fire pouring from the wounds as his legs kicked trying to propel him back to his feet. Dyrenna's second warrior collapsed on top of the first and a spray of lava shot towards the older Rider.

'Sparks!' she hissed as the droplets of molten fire landed on her hand. She scrapped them off with her coat sleeve but the fire had already burned through her skin.

'Dyrenna!' Aimee called, rushing over.

'I'm fine,' Dyrenna waved away her concern but the edges of her mouth were tight with pain.

The three Empty Warriors at their feet had stopped twitching and already their bodies were sagging, turning into blackened skeletons wrapped in skin. A door crashed further down the corridor, around the bend and out of sight. An image of her little bedroom flashed into Aimee's mind and she pictured Empty Warriors kicking down the door, placing their fiery hands on her patchwork blanket, setting her bed alight, burning the home she'd found for herself.

Her determination flared like a firework.

'We need to go.' She grabbed Dyrenna's arm, tugging the older Rider. But Dyrenna's grey-blue eyes were fixed on the bedroom corridor. There was another crash and this time footsteps echoed towards them.

'Get the others to safety,' Dyrenna said firmly, gripping her scimitar hilt and gritting her teeth against the burning pain in her hand.

'No!' Aimee yelled, stamping her foot. Her boot heel crunched down on an Empty Warrior's hand, crushing his bones to splinters.

Dyrenna didn't look at her as she spoke. 'I never told you my story, little one, why I became a Rider.' Her eyes were fixed down the corridor, or perhaps at a past Aimee couldn't see. 'But I have things to atone for. Let me stay. It'll give you the time to get the others out.'

Aimee looked at her, this older woman who'd been the first person to see her and not her unusual face. This incredibly strong Rider who'd been kind and generous and a friend when others still bullied her. Aimee's eyes flicked down to Dyrenna's scarred hands, her missing fingernails and she remembered many months ago overhearing Jara suggest that Dyrenna was responsible for someone else's death.

'No, no, no!' Aimee screamed again. 'You're not allowed to make a stupid noble sacrifice. I won't let you.' She tugged again on Dyrenna's arm. 'You need to live so you can tell me your story and I can repay you those cups of tea I owe.'

'You don't understand, little one,' Dyrenna said, finally turning to look at Aimee.

'I do.' Aimee wanted her voice to be soft but she couldn't stop shouting. 'You're letting the past ruin your future. And that's exactly what Kyelli and Pagrin did! Look at all the pain and death doing that causes! I'm tired of fighting against people who hoard secrets and let stuff that happened years ago put my friends in danger.' Aimee waved a scimitar, the one she'd borrowed from Dyrenna, in the direction of the city. 'Don't be a Quorelle! Don't be a selfish monster! Be a Rider and help me save people!'

Aimee heard a whoosh of flames from down the corridor and gave Dyrenna's arm another yank. This time the older Rider yielded and turned with Aimee. Together they ran across the intersection and down the corridor towards the Heart. Aimee heard the thud of running footsteps behind them and knew they were being chased.

'Selfish monster?' Dyrenna asked.

'Nathine's rubbing off on me.'

The tunnel sloped down and as they got close to the Heart Aimee saw Jess and Black crammed together in the opening. Both dragons were trying to get through a space that was too small for even one dragon to fit.

'Black, move!' Dyrenna yelled as they sprinted down the tunnel. The blue line of her connection flashed as she sent the command.

Black untangled himself from Jess and pulled back into the Heart. Jess took the opportunity to thrust herself further into the tunnel's opening, blocking it completely. She roared when she saw Aimee.

'Get out of the way!' Aimee yelled, waving frantically at Jess.

Her dragon had managed to squeeze half a wing into the tunnel and it flapped frantically against the cave wall. The shimmering line of their connection reeled in as Aimee drew closer.

'It's okay girl, I'm safe but we need to go.'

Jess was still trying to squeeze through to her Rider when Aimee barrelled into her. The familiar smell of woodsmoke replaced the sulphur stench in her nostrils as she shoved against her dragon. 'Move, Jess!'

Finally understanding, Jess backed into the cavern, letting Aimee and Dyrenna rush through. Aimee caught the flash of purple as Midnight's tail disappeared up one of the vents in the roof. Smaja was circling the cavern, Ryka gripping tight with one hand, the other strapped to her chest. She shouldn't be flying with her injuries but it was the only way out. Aimee baulked at the idea of shooting up through the vents whilst only holding on with one hand. Smaja's pale green scales shimmered as he gathered speed and shot up a vent. Aimee's whole body clenched as she waited for the sickening sound of a crash, or the thud as Ryka fell from her saddle. Thankfully neither came.

Jess followed her, head-butting her shoulder, as Aimee ran to the centre of the Heart. Aranati and Nathine had lifted Pelathina into her saddle. She clung to Skydance's horns and looked like she was about to throw up. She was too weak, she shouldn't be flying and fear for Pelathina settled over Aimee's heart like a heavy, wet blanket. Ryka and Smaja had made it safely into the sky but it felt too risky to trust to luck a second time.

Harmony and Malgerus flapped anxiously around Skydance as Aimee and Jess ran over. Aimee's mind whirred through ideas. Was there another way out? Was

Jess strong enough to make it up through the vents with two Riders on her back.

'Go!' Dyrenna yelled.

Aimee turned to see what had put such panic in her voice and saw Empty Warriors crowding the entrance to the Heart.

CHAPTER 28

BROKEN HEART

AIMEE HEARD A rumble and watched, frozen in disbelief, as the Empty Warriors hefted two dragon's breath orbs, each larger than a person's head. They released the orbs, throwing them towards the Riders at the centre of the Heart.

The air of the cavern swirled around Aimee as Skydance flapped furiously and erratically. He was trying to get airborne, to take his Rider to safety, but Pelathina was yelling at him to wait, wanting to stay, to help her sister and her friends.

The first dragon's breath orb smashed into one of the shepherd's crook poles, the other one hitting a moment later. The glass shattered and flames burst free. Aimee screamed, throwing herself backwards as Jess leapt between her Rider and the fire. Hot air from the exploding orbs washed over Aimee but Jess was crouched above her, wings spread wide, protecting her from the fire.

'Aimee! Arri!'

She heard the shout from above and rolled over to look up. Skydance was circling the cavern.

'Go!' Aimee and Aranati both yelled at the same time.

Aimee held her breath as she watched Skydance disappear up a vent.

'Don't fall, please don't fall,' she whispered to herself. She reached out with her new senses till she could see Pelathina's spark through the rock. She watched its light shoot upwards then slow and hover as Pelathina made it into the sky.

Jess crouched over her and nudged her face, her long tongue rasping across her cheek.

'I'm okay, girl, thank you,' Aimee said, resting a hand on Jess's cool scales even as she kept her eyes on the ceiling.

As Aimee pushed herself to her feet she heard another sharp crack.

'Move!' someone yelled as a third dragon's breath orb exploded against a pole.

This time Aimee pressed herself against Jess's chest as her dragon wrapped her wings around her, protecting her from the flames. She hated that the Empty Warriors had taken something that was theirs—the dragon's breath orbs—and turned it against them. Behind her she heard Nathine yelling above the leathery flap of wings.

'Come on, get mounted up, you idiots!' Nathine shouted from Malgerus's back.

'Get flying, you idiot!' Aimee shot back as she reluctantly left the safety of Jess's wings and grabbed her own saddle.

Malgerus took off, his huge orange wings swirling the air as they sped around the cavern, gathering enough speed for the dive up the vent. The click of multiple crossbows echoed around the Heart. A dozen Empty Warriors had crowded the cavern's entrance and half of them knelt, crossbows tracking Malgerus through the air.

'Nathine!' Aimee yelled.

'You'd better follow me, mushroom head!'

The words of Nathine's familiar tease echoed down from the vent she and Malgerus shot up—just as a flight of crossbow bolts shot through the air after them. The bolts clattered harmlessly off the ceiling, but by then the Empty Warriors were cranking their next and aiming for the three Riders still in the middle of the Heart.

Aranati and Dyrenna were already in their saddles and Aimee grabbed hers, boosting herself up. Another dragon's breath orb flew into the Heart but the warrior's aim was off this time and it shot past the Riders, crashing into the back of the cavern. Flames flashed up the wall, licking the edges of the stone ledges where dragons normally rested.

Jess was already pumping her wings, desperate to get her Rider away from the danger. The line of their connection ran right from Aimee's heart to Jess's, and was glowing an intense shimmering blue. Aimee felt the familiar lurch in her stomach as they left the ground.

Then a scream cut through the air, the piercing sound full of pain and anger.

Aranati and Harmony were still on the ground and Aranati was hunched over in her saddle. As Aimee guided Jess towards them Aranati slowly rose, both hands pressed to her belly. A crossbow bolt protruded from between her fingers.

'No!' Aimee yelled. She refused to watch another Rider die.

Jess's talons skittered on the rock as Aimee pushed her into a hurried landing beside Harmony. Aranati was panting with pain, her face grey at the edges, and her forehead creased into an even deeper frown than usual.

'Can you fly?' Aimee called over.

Aranati shook her head, dark hair swishing. And it was then that Aimee saw the second crossbow bolt sticking from the muscle of her thigh. Aranati's spark was pulsing frantically and Aimee could actually see its energy flowing through her body towards her wounds. Her spark was trying to heal her, to keep her alive, even as her blood poured out, draining her life.

'Go, Aimee,' Aranati ordered, her voice cracking at the edges.

'No! We're not doing desperate last stands. Everyone is going to make it out,' Aimee argued. She hadn't left Dyrenna and she wasn't going to leave Aranati either.

Another orb exploded against the wall behind them. Aimee pushed on Jess's horns to get her closer to Harmony. If she could take Aranati on Jess then Harmony could follow them and they'd all be safe. But Harmony growled and snapped at Jess, her long teeth just missing Jess's snout. Jess jerked back and roared. Harmony met her displeasure with a roar of her own and swung her head around. Aimee heard the crack of their skulls as Harmony head-butted Jess. Jess cowered from the other dragon's anger, tucking in her neck and wings.

Aimee heard a rumble and twisted to look behind. Black swept through the air in front of the Empty Warriors, blasting them with dragon's breath. They were impervious to the flames but it obscured their view and kept them from firing on Aimee and Aranati. It bought them time.

Aimee tried again to get close to Harmony but the other dragon was ready for a fight. The golden-coloured ruff of feathers around her neck was flared, her wings open wide as her head snaked from side to side, watching Jess.

'Aranati, don't do this,' Aimee begged. She couldn't rescue her if she was telling her dragon to keep Aimee away. The anguish felt like a vice clamping around Aimee's ribs. Those two crossbow bolts were taking away all that Aranati was—her skills at healing, the delicious spicy soups she made, her endearing frown, her love for her sister and the way she'd believed in Aimee.

With a gasp of pain that tore at Aimee's heart, Aranati reached up and slid free both her scimitars. Her eyes met Aimee's.

'Promise me you'll look after Pellie.'

Aimee shook her head. 'No last stands,' she repeated.

'Promise.' Aranati grated out the word between teeth clenched against the pain. Aimee nodded and Aranati gave her a small, sad smile. 'Good. She loves you.'

Then Aranati released her control over Harmony. Aimee saw the bright blue flash travel along their connection as it happened. Untethered by her Rider's control, and feeling Aranati's pain and sorrow, Harmony roared, the sound rumbling around the cavern like thunder. Aranati gripped Harmony's horns as her dragon flew at the Empty Warriors in a flash of golden scales, wings and teeth.

'No!' Aimee yelled.

Harmony blasted them with fire then burst through the flames, slashing and biting. Shock washed through Aimee as she watched the frenzy of an out of control dragon. Harmony tore apart three warriors in a matter of moments. Lava spurted and hissed against the cave walls and Aimee gagged on the stench of sulphur. Aranati fought from her saddle, slashing down at the warriors, screaming at them in Irankish.

'Aimee! Fly!'

The shout came from above and as Aimee tilted her head back tears ran down her cheeks. Black's shadow passed over her as he and Dyrenna swept around the cavern. A single crossbow bolt pinged off a shepherd's crook pole right beside her and Aimee flinched. Most of the Empty Warriors were locked in battle with Aranati and Harmony but all it would take was a single well-aimed shot. Aimee gripped the hard spirals of Jess's horns as they took off. Her wings swirled the hot air of the cavern, stirring up embers from the fires raging across the Heart and Aimee felt the heat pressing on her skin.

As they rose through the air Aimee kept her eyes fixed on the fight. Maybe Harmony could kill enough Empty Warriors to allow Aimee to swoop in and rescue Aranati. Even as she had the thought, two warriors got past Harmony's talons and their swords sank deep into her belly. Harmony and Aranati screamed together.

Before Aimee had even thought the command, Jess turned, skimming above the shepherd crook poles towards Harmony.

'Don't!' Dyrenna ordered from somewhere behind her.

Harmony's roaring filled the cavern. A scattering of crossbow bolts shot through the air and Jess swerved to avoid them, taking them up and past the fight. Aimee twisted in her saddle, looking back and down, desperate to keep her eyes on Aranati, longing to see the moment when she could swoop in and rescue her.

But instead she saw the scimitars drop from Aranati's grip. Her spark was a faint flicker in her chest, like a candle about to go out. The burning hands of the Empty Warriors grabbed her, pulling Aranati from her saddle. As her Rider hit the floor, Harmony went berserk. She kicked and thrashed, with two swords still lodged in her belly. Viscous dragon's blood sprayed across the Empty Warriors.

'Aimee!' Dyrenna yelled again and Aimee felt like

she had to physically pull herself away from Aranati and Harmony. Every fibre of her baulked at leaving a Rider behind. But she'd seen Aranati's spark flicker and die. Seen the blue line of her connection with Harmony vanish.

With tears making everything blurry Aimee and Jess followed Black up through a vent and into the sky. The others were waiting for them, their dragons flying circles above the peaks. Aimee's eyes instantly went to Pelathina. She was hunched in her saddle, and as Aimee flew closer she saw Pelathina's face was beaded with sweat. But her spark was still bright. Pelathina's dark eyes met Aimee's then slipped past her to the vents, waiting to see her sister appear.

'Pelathina, I'm so sorry. Aranati—'

'No, don't say it!' Pelathina cut her off.

She turned back to Aimee, and she obviously saw the truth in Aimee's face because her own crumpled. Tears mixed with the sweat on Pelathina's cheeks and she looked so anguished that it broke Aimee's heart. Rapid pulses fired along her connection with Skydance as Pelathina's grief took hold and she struggled to keep it from her dragon. Skydance's long tail flicked in the air and he swung his head from side to side, looking for the enemy that had upset his Rider.

Pelathina coughed and wheezed as grief mixed with her fever, both of them squeezing her chest. Aimee flew Jess as close as she could to Skydance. She longed to pull Pelathina into a hug and protect her from grief and pain and monsters.

Black appeared in the sky beside Jess just as Pelathina urged Skydance into action, commanding him with an anguished shout to fly back towards the vents. He pulled up short, snapping at the air as Black blocked his path. Gasping through her tears Pelathina pulled on Skydance's horns, turning him so they could swoop around Black and Jess and get to the vents. But Midnight, Malgerus and Smaja boxed him in.

'Move!' Pelathina yelled. '*Mujje kee hai*!'

'You can't go back down there,' Dyrenna told her and Aimee was amazed at how steady her voice was.

'Arri!' Pelathina called towards the vents.

Skydance dived, cutting underneath the other dragons. Jess acted on Aimee's will a split second later, swooping down after the sapphire-blue dragon. Aimee didn't even register how close they came to smacking into the side of a jagged cliff as they cut in front of Skydance, blocking his way. He tried to climb into the sky and go over Jess, but again she swept through the air in front of him, cutting off his path. Again and again he tried but Jess matched him move for move and kept him from the vents.

Pelathina's cries echoed back from the stony cliffs and each one tore another little piece off Aimee's heart.

'Dyrenna!' she called as Skydance thrashed and snapped in the air.

'I'm here,' the older Rider replied as Black swooped into Aimee's vision.

Pelathina was losing herself to her grief and her control over Skydance was slipping. His ruff of feathers was up, every one of them twitching. He didn't know what to do.

'Everyone, help me guide him down there,' Dyrenna called to them all and pointed to a rocky ledge in the cliffs just to the north of them.

Black, Jess, Midnight and Malgerus closed in around Skydance and guided him down towards the ledge. Without instructions from his Rider, Skydance was lost and so he followed the other dragons of his clutch. Smaja and Ryka brought up the rear, and Aimee could see the injured Rider was struggling to stay in her saddle, gripping Smaja's horn with her one good hand.

As soon as they landed on the rocky ledge, Skydance hunkered down and Pelathina slipped from her saddle like she had no bones in her body. Jess was next to land, and Aimee the first to dismount and hurry over to Pelathina. She didn't notice how cold or hard the ground was as she sat beside Pelathina and pulled her tight into a hug. The other girl's whole body was shaking with the force of her sobs and Aimee wished there was something, anything she could do to ease her pain.

The others dismounted and everyone's dragon hunched down as they sensed the grief permeating the group of Riders. Aimee's neck was sticky with Pelathina's tears, snot and sweat but she didn't care and pulled her closer. Skydance had curled his long neck around Pelathina's hip and rested his head in her lap.

'What do we do?' Nathine asked.

Aimee looked up. The others were standing around

her and Pelathina like sentinels. She turned her face towards Anteill and closed her eyes. Reaching out with her senses she could see, deep within the rock, the corrupted black lines of the Empty Warriors. They'd taken the Heart and infested Anteill. Aimee felt a hot flash of anger in her chest. They'd taken the home she'd fought so hard to find and forced her out. But unlike when the Guild had kicked her out of her home after her aunt and uncle died, this time Aimee would fight. Opening her eyes she looked back at the others, resolute.

'We find Pagrin and we kill him,' Aimee said.

'Simple as that?' Lyrria looked sceptical.

'How?' Nathine demanded. She had her hands clenched in fists, ready for a fight.

Aimee closed her eyes again, tapped the power of the bracelet and let her senses unspool across the city. She followed the lines of connection from the Empty Warriors in Anteill. An ocean of life swirled around her, thousands and thousands of sparks twinkling in the darkness of her closed eyes but Aimee kept her focus. The black lines led towards the harbour district where they disappeared into the bank of mist Pagrin was using to hide himself. But that gave them somewhere to start.

Still hugging Pelathina, Aimee explained to the others what she could sense.

'Alright, little one, but the harbour district is lost,' Dyrenna said.

The ledge they were on gave them a view across the city and Aimee saw the plumes of smoke rising from the buildings across the River Toig.

'Yeah, it's full of Empty Warriors and half of its on fire,' Lyrria added. 'And I know you're amazing now with your magical powers, but how can six Riders fight our way through that?'

Even now, hearing Lyrria say she was amazing gave Aimee a warm glow, but it was soured by the other Rider's scepticism. She needed support, not doubt in her abilities.

Nathine snorted. 'I don't think even an army could stop Aimee when she has her determined face on.'

Aimee smiled at her friend, grateful as always for Nathine's brusque support. 'We'll manage, and actually we're only four Riders, not six.'

Aimee turned to Ryka, the only other Rider to have sat down. She was leaning back against Smaja, her face tight as she fought not to show her pain.

'Can you stay with her?' Aimee asked, nodding to Pelathina, who was still curled up in her arms.

Aimee watched the relief on Ryka's face and knew it was caused not by getting to avoid flying into danger, but by being given a task, a way she could still help.

'Of course.' Ryka struggled to her feet and came to sit beside Aimee and Pelathina.

Pelathina's wailing had subsided to hiccupping sobs. She was still clutching Aimee as if she was drowning and only Aimee could keep her afloat.

'I need to leave you for a while,' Aimee whispered, her lips against Pelathina's face, 'but you stay here and cry all the tears you need to. And if you've still got more when I come back, that's okay. I'll hold you till they stop.'

Aimee wasn't sure if her words made it through Pelathina's grief. She kissed the top of the other girl's head, breathing in the soft scent of her, then peeled Pelathina's arms from around her waist. Pelathina was unresponsive as Aimee gently pushed her towards Ryka. As she slumped into Ryka's arms, Aimee stood up. It felt like she'd left a piece of her heart behind as she walked away.

Nathine, Dyrenna and Lyrria joined her at the edge of the ledge, all of them staring out across the city. Even from this distance Aimee could make out colourful dots in the air above the harbour district. She knew Jara would be there, directing the defence, keeping the Empty Warriors from breaking through into the rest of Kierell. But how long could the Riders and guards hold them back?

'Aimee!' Nathine grabbed her sleeve and pointed at the cliffs just south of them.

A horde of dark figures were climbing down the mountains. The Empty Warriors had found their way out of Anteill and were heading for the city. The route up the cliffs that had led Aimee to safety and a new life was now crawling with monsters bringing pain and death to the city.

'Do you think they ransacked Anteill?' Lyrria asked.

All four Riders were staring back towards the tunnels and caves where they lived. Aimee thought of her bedroom and Nathine's, of the weapons store where

Lyrria kept all the blades she used to teach recruits, and of the little workshop where Dyrenna made their saddles. Aimee wasn't the only one who'd had her home violated today.

She clenched her jaw as she boosted herself up into Jess's saddle. It was time to put a stop to this. With one last look at Pelathina still huddled in Ryka's arms, Aimee and Jess took off, the others following.

CHAPTER 29

INTO A TRAP

THE RUSH OF air against her face was welcome as Jess dived off the ledge. Aimee felt like it cleared her mind, blowing aside the horror of Empty Warriors inside Anteill and the pain of watching Aranati die. It gave her space in her brain to focus on what she needed to do.

At the nadir of her dive Jess opened her wings with a snap, Malgerus, Black and Midnight doing the same. The sound echoed back from the cliffs like four cracks of thunder. As Jess skimmed the outer warehouses of Barter, Aimee heard the sounds of a city falling apart.

Shouting was being carried on the wind from the caravan compound as guards and citizens there struggled to build a barrier high enough to stop the Empty Warriors when they poured through the tunnel. And they would break through again, Aimee didn't doubt that. Black pulled ahead and Jess followed him along Marhorn Street. The trading stalls were either still closed or half-open and abandoned. Wooden shutters were firmly closed on houses as people hid.

As the Riders swept past the Council Chamber Aimee stared at the crowd gathered in the square. Previously it had been a mob, held together with anger; now people huddled together seeking comfort in each other. If the Empty Warriors broke through into the city proper all they'd need to do was surround Quorelle Square and they could kill thousands.

'If they reach here, it'll be a massacre.' Dyrenna's words were quiet, as if she feared saying them aloud would make it happen.

'We'll stop them,' Aimee assured her.

She pushed Jess's horns for more speed and her dragon eagerly obeyed, keen to get away from the tumultuous emotions swirling around the square. It seemed to take ages to cross the eastern curve of Barter but finally the plumes of smoke were just ahead.

The River Toig glistened in the morning sun, unaware of its part in keeping death from Kierell. Dragons patrolled its length, and Aimee spotted Faradair's blood-red scales. The bridges had all been deliberately destroyed, the wooden struts of their supports protruding from the water like broken sticks. Where the streets on both sides met the river, fighters gathered—guards on one side, Empty Warriors on the other. And the difference between them was stark.

Aimee heard shouts from the Barter side of the river as guards, more used to patrolling peaceful streets for pickpockets, did their best to co-ordinate a defence. Crossbow bolts shot across the river and Aimee heard the pings as they bounced off Empty Warrior breastplates.

They'd built barricades across the streets which led to the bridges and Aimee could hear the swearing and banging as they constructed backup barricades further into Barter. She heard cries in a language she didn't understand and looked back to see four Helvethi, their front hooves up on the barricade, firing recurve bows across the river. Their shots were more accurate and she saw arrows pierce Empty Warriors in the neck, lava streaming down their breastplates.

It gave Aimee hope to see them—the leaders of the Kahollin and Ovogil tribes who'd come to the city to talk peace. Their tribes may have chosen not to aid Kierell when Jara asked, to stay out of this battle, but these four Helvethi trapped inside the city were fighting. It meant the future Jara and others had worked for might not be lost. But only if Aimee could save Kierell.

On the harbour side of the river the Empty Warriors stood at the edge of the streets in silent rows. They made not a single sound.

'What are they waiting for?' Aimee asked no one in particular.

She got her answer a moment later as the four dragons crossed the Toig and they saw into the guts of a burned-out warehouse. Inside it, working efficiently and silently, the Empty Warriors were constructing a makeshift bridge. Aimee had no doubt that with their freakish unnatural strength they'd be able to manoeuvre it into place, hold it against attack, and cross into the city.

'Kyelli's sparks!' Lyrria swore as they flew over the impromptu workshop.

Aimee wondered at the validity of that curse now that Kyelli was gone and had no sparks, but the thought was a fleeting one.

The wide streets below them were full of Empty Warriors—silent rows stood waiting for their chance to destroy Kierell. More longboats must have berthed at the harbour disgorging hundreds of warriors. In the hours since she'd been here Aimee could see they'd almost destroyed the harbour district. The acrid stench of burning buildings caught in her throat and made her eyes water. She wished her flying goggles weren't lying broken in a gaol cell. Doors and windows had been smashed and flames licked at the roofs of warehouses and homes. Aimee could feel Jess's disgust as she flew through the haze of smoke.

'Aimee, where do we go?' Nathine called over.

Aimee closed her eyes, letting Jess follow the other dragons, and tapped the bracelet's power. Instantly she felt the overwhelming surge of the Empty Warriors' anger, of Pagrin's hatred of his sister's city. She flinched at its violence. In her mind's eye she saw the corrupted black lines of connection unspooling through the rumble-strewn streets of the harbour district. They all disappeared into a bank of grey mist near the tunnel that led to the harbour.

Aimee was about to open her eyes and give the others directions when suddenly the mist vanished. She hadn't done anything different, it simply disappeared. Without it obscuring the buildings Aimee could see the way all the Empty Warriors' lines converged on a single warehouse. Pagrin had dropped the mist he was using to hide and was showing her where he was.

'I can see him,' Aimee announced flicking her eyes open. 'He's this way.'

She pushed Jess's horns, steering her dragon around a thick plume of smoke from a high warehouse roof. She swore the smoke smelled like dried fish.

'Wait, Aimee, how do you know?' Lyrria brought Midnight in beside Jess, matching her wingbeats.

'Because he's showing me where he is. The connections all lead to a warehouse over near the cliffs,' Aimee replied.

'Aimee, can he sense you the way you can sense him?' Dyrenna asked, Black appeared on Aimee's other side.

Aimee shrugged. 'I don't know. Maybe. The bracelet probably gives away where I am.'

'That's bad, isn't it? He'll know we're coming,' Lyrria called across as Midnight swooped around a tall chimney flickering with flames.

'Does that matter?' Aimee countered. 'We don't have a choice.'

No one had a reply to that. Aimee blinked smoke from her eyes and looked around at the others. Dyrenna and Nathine looked resolute, but Lyrria's expression was unconvinced. Suddenly Aimee was tired of trying to win Lyrria's approval. Sensing her thoughts, Jess twisted in the sky and snapped at Midnight.

'Lyrria, either stop questioning me and come with us, or fly back across the Toig and help Jara,' Aimee ordered. 'I don't care what you chose.'

Shock washed over Lyrria's face which she tried to hide with an awkward smile that didn't reach her eyes. 'Hey, I'm just trying to protect you from doing something stupid.'

'I didn't ask for your protection and I don't need it,' Aimee shot back.

She wanted Lyrria to put aside the jokey way she treated her and admit she was wrong to still be doubting her. She wanted Lyrria to prove she trusted and respected her. She wanted Lyrria by her side. But instead annoyance twisted up Lyrria's face.

'Fine.' Without another word she turned Midnight in the air and they flew back towards the river. Aimee watched her disappear into the haze of smoke, Midnight's tail flicking in annoyance.

Nathine and Dyrenna said nothing as Aimee pushed Jess's horns for more speed. They followed her through the thinning smoke until they reached Fiskhavn Street where the guards had abducted Aimee earlier. The barricade Pelathina had almost given her life to defend was nothing but kindling scattered across the street. To their left, behind a warehouse with smoke roiling from its shattered windows, was a building untouched by fire. Aimee steered Jess towards it.

The buildings all around were broken and burning but this one—a two-storey workshop close to the cliffs—was untouched. It stood out like an oasis amidst a sea of flames and rubble. Aimee tapped the bracelet's power and lines sprang to life, leading right into that building.

She circled it, keeping Jess high above its peaked roof. Malgerus and Black joined them, the three dragons flying around and around.

'In there?' Dyrenna asked, pointing down at the workshop.

Aimee nodded as she looked for the best way in.

Nathine looked at the destruction around them, then back to the single untouched building. 'You do know this is a trap, right?'

'Yup, it's definitely a trap,' Aimee agreed, 'but we're running out of time.' Pagrin had shown her where he was, knowing she'd come after him, but what choice did she have? But the others… they had a choice. Images of Aranati flashed through her mind. She couldn't face watching another friend's spark go out.

'You don't have to come in with me,' she told them.

Even above the flapping of wings and the crackle of flames she heard Nathine's snort. 'As if I'd abandon you now.'

Aimee looked at Dyrenna and the older Rider simply nodded. Aimee felt a warm flush of gratefulness for them both. They landed on the workshop's peaked roof, their dragons' talons scraping the slate tiles. The building was tall and narrow. Pagrin had chosen well because it wasn't a space they could squeeze their dragons into. They'd have to leave them behind.

There was a skylight, its glass dusty with cobwebs. Nathine hopped down from Malgerus and stamped on the glass with her boot heel. It cracked and the pieces tinkled down into the workshop.

'He'll have heard that,' Aimee pointed out.

Nathine shrugged. 'You said he knows we're here anyway.'

But Nathine did pause before the skylight, listening for movement in the room below before carefully lowering herself through it. Aimee went next, cautious of the jagged shards of glass still locked in the frame, and Dyrenna followed.

They were on the upper floor of the workshop—a set of rooms where the owner lived. With a scimitar in each hand Aimee crept through the rooms, wincing each time a floorboard creaked beneath her.

'They're empty,' Nathine said, coming back into the living room from the bedroom.

There was a set of wooden stairs in one corner. As Aimee walked towards them her eyes caught on a scene of domestic bliss. There was an old green armchair in the corner by the window, its cushions saggy and squishy. On a small table beside it someone had left a half-drunk cup of tea and an open journal, the pages filled with neat lines of writing. Was the person who'd curled up in that chair with their tea and journal still alive?

At the top of the staircase Aimee could hear nothing from below. She led the way, Nathine and Dyrenna following close behind. They stepped quietly but the stairs creaked in the silence of the workshop. On the ground floor the shutters were all closed, creating a twilight within the open space.

Half way down Aimee stopped and crouched, making herself a smaller target in case there were Empty Warriors in the workshop. She wouldn't have heard them if they were silently waiting for her. Fishing nets hung from the ceiling rafters like sheets of laundry. Some were waiting to be repaired, others were new and only half woven, but together they obscured Aimee's view of the workshop. She tried to peer through them, her eyes searching for any movement, her ears straining for any sound.

'I don't understand mortals. You're always so willing to risk your lives.'

Pagrin's voice came from the far end of the workshop and Aimee froze two steps from the bottom of the staircase. She motioned for the others to still as well. Nathine made a stabbing gesture with one blade towards Pagrin but Aimee held up a hand, telling her to wait. Nathine rolled her eyes.

'You have a single spark, and you all know this, it's not a secret. And yet you throw yourselves into danger.'

'To protect others.'

It was Dyrenna who sent the reply across the workshop towards Pagrin.

'That isn't your place,' Pagrin growled, his words rumbling with the anger that infused him. 'We, the Quorelle, are the ones who protected you. We built up Kierellatta for you. Beautiful cities, strong trade networks, industries you could grow wealthy from.'

'And Empty Warriors to kill everyone!' Nathine's shout interrupted him.

'I didn't!'

Pagrin shot back. Aimee couldn't see him through the nets. She quietly stepped off the staircase into the workshop proper, the other two following her, their footsteps soft.

'Back on Kierellatta I never used a single one of my sparks to create a worker or an Empty Warrior. My father did. Kyelli did. They don't look like such glorious saviours now, do they?'

Aimee lifted up the edge of a fishing net with one scimitar but all she saw beyond it was another net hanging from the next rafter along.

'Out of them all, only I was innocent of the destruction they caused, and she left me!' Pagrin continued, his voice twisted with the anger he'd nurtured for three centuries. 'This city, the new home she and father found with its mountains and dragons, it should have been mine.'

Aimee slipped around the net and stalked towards the next one. Parallel to her, across the workshop floor, Nathine and Dyrenna were doing the same.

'I thought it would be fitting to make Kyelli watch as I destroyed the city she'd built without me, but when I saw her I realised I didn't want her in my head any more. I wanted her gone.'

Pagrin's words slipped through the hanging nets carrying with them anger and grief. Aimee could understand those emotions—if her family had left her for dead she'd probably feel the same. But what made all the hairs on her arms stand on end was the absolute confidence in everything Pagrin said. He believed what he was doing was right.

For a moment Aimee wondered, if she hadn't risked the climb and found a home with the Sky Riders, if she'd spent her days alone, an outcast, would she have turned bitter like Pagrin? Would her loneliness have made her twisted like an old tree stood alone out on the tundra?

A whispered 'psst' from Nathine broke into Aimee's thoughts and for a brief second a smile flitted across her face. She wasn't alone. She had friends, other women who'd fight for her.

Nathine was waving her scimitar towards the front of the workshop, through the nets and shrugging each time she moved the blade. She was asking Aimee where Pagrin was. Aimee tapped the power of the bracelet and watched the dark lines of connection appear around her. They stretched towards the far right corner, closest to where Dyrenna was, and Aimee pointed that way. The others nodded, stepping softly and lightly between the nets.

'I can feel you using it,' Pagrin's voice was filled with disgust. 'The bracelets were meant only for the Quorelle, not someone like you.'

'Why not me?' Aimee called back. 'Because I don't think I'm entitled and better than everyone? Or because I can see that no one, ever, should have power like this?'

Nathine and Dyrenna had reached the far wall of the workshop. Aimee could see their sparks glowing a bright greenish-white in stark contrast to the black lines leading to Pagrin. Aimee ducked around another net, making her way quietly towards them as Pagrin's next words filled the workshop.

'Kill them all!'

Aimee heard the clomp of boots on floorboards a second before a sword sliced through the net hanging beside her. It parted and three Empty Warriors poured through. Aimee instinctively leapt back, her blades crossed in front of her face to block the warrior's blow. The air in the workshop vibrated with the clash of swords. Aimee slashed and parried, deflecting the Empty Warrior's attack. But another slipped around her side and she was forced to duck and roll to avoid his blade.

'Nathine! Dyrenna!' she yelled.

'Over by the wall!' Dyrenna replied her voice strained as they too fought off the warriors.

'Do something awesome, Aimee!' Nathine added, then followed it up with a string of swearing.

'Like what?' Aimee yelled back.

She bounced up onto her feet and attacked the two Empty Warriors who'd been closing in on her. As her limbs moved automatically, her mind whirred, trying to think of some way to use the bracelet to save her friends and get to Pagrin. But the Empty Warriors didn't have sparks. She couldn't steal their lives.

She ducked under a sword thrust and her own blade scored a line along her attacker's breastplate. She feinted left then dashed right, trying to get past him and over to Nathine and Dyrenna. Together the three of them would stand a better chance. But the Empty Warrior saw through her ploy and the hilt of his sword cracked along her jaw.

The force of the blow knocked Aimee backwards and she fell.

'No, no, no!' She goaded herself back to her feet. It wasn't going to end here, not like this, not with failure.

'Wait!' Pagrin ordered.

And the Empty Warriors froze, turning back into eerie statues, completely still except for the flames swirling in their eyes.

'It isn't enough that you simply die, girl. You dared to think you were as good as one of us by putting on that bracelet so you could take my sister's place. Instead of her, it'll be you watching as your city burns.' Pagrin's words were cold, his voice devoid of humanity. 'Bring her to me. And kill the other two.'

Aimee saw the dark lines of connection from Pagrin to the Empty Warriors pulse as he sent the command. He was controlling them the same way Riders sent commands to their dragons.

CHAPTER 30

SCIMITARS AND TOAST

'No!' Aimee yelled as the Empty Warriors, acting on Pagrin's direct command, sprang back to life. Three surrounded her, their swords held across their bodies, blocking her in. She attacked. Using every trick, every technique Lyrria had taught her, but the warriors held her in place. Her blade sliced through the leg of one, lava pouring down his boot and sizzling on the wooden floor, but he didn't fall. Another of her slashes cut across the face of a warrior, slicing open his cheek. A flap of skin hung down to his chin, molten fire dripping from it, showing his black skull underneath.

But she couldn't get past them, couldn't reach Nathine and Dyrenna. The warriors were taller than her and she couldn't see over them, couldn't see if her friends were still alive. She screamed as she increased her attack but it was like battering against a wall. More Empty Warriors crowded around her, holding her in place, deflecting her blows and taking the injuries she dealt, all without a sound.

Her mind scrambled for a way out. She was still reeling from the revelation that Pagrin was issuing controls to his Empty Warriors in the same way she did with Jess. She could see it now, the way the dark connections linking each warrior to him pulsed just as the shimmering blue line between her and Jess did.

Up on the roof she heard the dragons roaring. All three were desperately trying to get to their Riders. She heard an anguished roar and felt Jess's pain. She knew her dragon had tried to squeeze through the skylight and cut herself on the glass. Black's roar shook the whole workshop and Aimee heard Dyrenna screaming with him. She couldn't hear any swearing. Was Nathine dead already? The thought tore at her heart, making it hard to breathe. What made it worse was that she still held one of Dyrenna's scimitars and one of Nathine's. Her friends were fighting for their lives with only one blade each.

Aimee crouched and spun on her heels. Whipping both scimitars out in a deadly whir of blades, aiming for the warriors' shins. She felt her blade bite once but the others jumped back, widening the circle while still keeping her enclosed. Everywhere she looked her vision was full of Empty Warriors. More waited behind the hanging nets, their fiery eyes glowing.

Her desperation started in her toes and dragged up through her body, hollowing her out until it burst from her lips in a wordless scream.

She heard a cry of pain from the far side of the

workshop and in her mind she saw Aranati again. Saw the brave Rider tumble from her saddle as her spark winked out. The thought of losing Nathine and Dyrenna too was like dragon's claws scraping out her insides.

The little flame of determination that she'd protected and nurtured all through her training, and on the quest to find Kyelli, flared inside her. She would not lose the first two friends she'd ever had. She would not let herself be taken away from the group of women who'd become her home.

Her despair and determination crashed together and fused inside her head. Without meaning to Aimee freed the bracelet's power. Panic made her body jerk as the bracelet tried to swamp her mind. The eager tentacles of its power reached inside her thoughts, pushing through her memories. Horror choked her as she felt herself succumbing to its will.

In desperation she reached out, searching for help. And she found it. She saw her connection to Jess and the power in it—the strength, trust and love that made it so strong. But she also saw the same in Nathine's connection with Malgerus, and in Dyrenna's with Black. Aimee was surrounded by power, not the corrupting power of the bracelet and the Quorelle, but the raw strength of women working together, fighting to protect what they loved.

Aimee tapped into the power of Nathine and Dyrenna's connections with their dragons. She didn't steal it the way she'd done with sparks, she simply joined it with her own, boosting her strength with theirs. She clamped her mind around the bracelet's power, as if closing her fist on a burning ember. And then, bolstered by the strength from her friends, Aimee opened her mind, reaching out.

She felt the bracelet's power stretching out into the world but still tethered in her brain. It was like when she'd bonded with Jess at the nesting site, casting out from her mind, searching for the connection with her dragon. Coated now in her will, and the Riders' combined strength, the bracelet's power seized the connections of the Empty Warriors surrounding her.

She felt it, the moment she yanked control of the Empty Warriors from Pagrin. And she saw it, the way the dark connections pinged away from the far corner of the workshop and now ran into her chest, right beside her spark. She was so shocked she'd done it that she almost released her hold, but caught herself in time.

'Get out of my way!' she yelled at the Empty Warriors circling her.

To her astonishment they lifted their swords and stepped aside. She was controlling them just like Pagrin had. She ran past them, shoving aside fishing nets.

'Stop killing my friends!' she yelled, and saw the black lines from her chest pulse with the command.

Over by the workshop's far wall she saw Nathine and Dyrenna. They'd been forced back against a window and were surrounded by warriors. Nathine's teeth and lips were smeared with blood, and Dyrenna clutched bloodied fingers to her upper arm. Both stared warily at the warriors who'd been trying to kill them a moment before as they stepped back, sheathing their swords.

'Bitch!' Pagrin's cry was followed by the sound of running footsteps.

Aimee felt him tug at the Empty Warriors' connections, trying to pull them back. In the sudden assault Aimee almost let them slip from her mental grasp.

'What did you..? How did you..?' Nathine was gaping at her. 'Actually, never mind. Just keep being awesome.'

'Dyrenna, are—'

'Fine,' the older Rider interrupted her.

She wasn't fine, deep red blood was seeping between her fingers where they gripped her upper arm. Their dragons were still roaring on the roof, the sound even louder now the clash of blades had stopped. Aimee clutched the Empty Warriors' connections as she felt Pagrin tugging them again.

With the warriors frozen, this was their chance.

'If we attack Pagrin now—' Aimee began but Nathine cut her off.

'Sparks, yes! Let's do it.'

Aimee spun as the fishing net in front of them was pulled down, revealing Pagrin behind it. He still wore the guard uniform he'd disguised himself in and his eyes now brimmed with anger. They were even more terrifying and malicious than the fiery eyes of his warriors.

Nathine didn't hesitate. She attacked Pagrin, swinging from her shoulders, cutting and lunging. But Pagrin had a guard's longsword and he swatted aside her attack. Nathine's six months of training were almost worthless against Pagrin's centuries' worth of knowledge and skills. He knocked aside her scimitar, stepped inside her guard and backhanded her across the face.

Nathine's already split lip burst again and she was flung against the wall by the force of his blow. Dyrenna caught her before she hit the ground, gasping at the pain in her arm.

Glass shattered, spraying across them all, as Black swiped the window beside them with his barbed tail. Aimee caught a flash of green and orange behind him— Jess and Malgerus were there too.

In the moment that she was distracted—filled with concern for Nathine, and joy at seeing Jess—Pagrin wrenched back control of the Empty Warriors.

Aimee fell to her knees gasping. It was like having parts of her brain pulled from her head. The connections she'd made with Nathine and Dyrenna were ripped to tatters. Through eyes blurry with tears she saw the dark connections snap away from her chest and shoot back towards Pagrin. She tasted copper and realised her nose was bleeding. Heat blasted her face and she looked up in time to see Black fire a blast of dragon's breath at Pagrin. The fishing nets all whooshed with flames, the dragon's breath eating up them and into the rafters.

She knew she needed to get up, to move. Pagrin would command the Empty Warriors to capture or kill her any moment. But Aimee felt drained, her limbs too heavy to lift.

Then arms were grabbing her, hauling her upwards. Her feet dragged along the floor. She was too exhausted to even walk. The crackle of flames filled her ears as the workshop burned. But she couldn't find the energy to care. Her eyelids drooped and she struggled to open them again.

She felt someone lift her up and pass her out the window. Their hands were gentle and she knew it was Dyrenna. Her trousers caught on shards of glass and tore. Another someone grabbed her roughly, carrying her away from the building before dumping her on the street. By the curses she knew this someone was Nathine.

Cool scales wrapped around her and Aimee leaned into Jess. She could feel her dragon's concern but she was too tired to give Jess any reassurance. She wanted to reach up and stroke Jess's feathers but her arm felt like it was made of stone and it wouldn't move. Urgent whispers raced above her head.

'What if she's dead?'

She tried to speak, tried to tell Nathine that she was alright, but the effort was too much. She slumped against Jess.

Finally she forced her eyes open. Through the crack of her lids she saw flames eating the workshop. The rotten egg stench of sulphur coated the back of her throat as the Empty Warriors melted inside. Was Pagrin still in there? Had the flames got him too?

Was it over?

Aimee felt a pulse of energy in her mind and flinched, thinking it was the bracelet, trying to exert control while she was weak. But then the pulse came again and Aimee's mind filled with warm love and the joy of freedom, with companionship and a longing for the sky. Jess was drip feeding her strength. With every pulse Jess sent along their connection Aimee felt a little stronger.

It felt like she sat there for days, with her dragon wrapped around her. But when she fully opened her eyes, Dyrenna and Nathine were still arguing about what to do, the workshop a roaring inferno behind them.

'Thank you, girl,' Aimee whispered to Jess. She pressed her forehead to Jess's, enjoying the feel of her cool scales against her skin. Then she stood up.

Nathine jumped in surprise but Dyrenna just cocked an eyebrow at her.

'Just needed a nap, did you?' Nathine said sarcastically. Then grabbed her in a rough hug.

Dyrenna simply looked at her, a question in her single raised brow. Aimee nodded. 'I'm okay.'

'What did you do in there?' Nathine punched her on the shoulder to get Aimee's attention. 'You controlled the Empty Warriors! How is that possible?'

'Pagrin is controlling them, sending them commands, the same way we do with our dragons,' Aimee explained.

'Pagrin is? Not Pagrin was? He's still alive?' Dyrenna

asked, turning to look back at the workshop. The roof rafters collapsed, sending a whoosh of flames into the sky, embers dancing down around them.

Aimee thought about what she'd realised unconsciously—she could still see all the Empty Warriors' connections and they were leading to somewhere north of the workshop. Pagrin had escaped. She nodded at Dyrenna.

'But the Empty Warriors are Pagrin's because he created them using his sparks. So how did you control them?'

'Did you feel it?' Aimee asked, thinking back to the moment she'd tapped Nathine's connection with Malgerus.

'Feel what?'

Aimee tried to explain what she'd done but Nathine's eyes grew wide with horror. She looked down at her chest then her eyes flicked to Aimee, accusatory.

'I didn't take any of your spark. I promise.'

'Good, because if you did I'd get Mal to sit on you until you gave it back.'

As if to underline the threat Malgerus, crouched on the street behind Nathine, gave a low growl.

'I…' Aimee faltered. 'I'm not sure what I did, or how I can do it.'

'You're unique, little one,' Dyrenna said softly. She had a hastily tied bandage around her upper arm that was already red as her blood seeped through. 'None of the Quorelle have ever been a Rider, so you're the first person to see the immortal connections between Empty

Warriors and their masters, as well as those between Riders and their dragons.'

Aimee thought about Dyrenna's words. She'd stood up, and Jess rested her head on her shoulder. Aimee stroked her dragon's snout as she considered what this meant. She could see both types of connections so that meant she could control them both. But a Quorelle had a near endless supply of energy in their blood from all their sparks. Pagrin's strength would always be a thousand times greater than hers.

'Ugh, they're going to write songs about how amazing you are,' Nathine was saying. 'I'll need to make sure there's a verse about how smelly your feet are to balance it out.'

'And another about how she never makes the tea,' Dyrenna added, wincing as she tested moving her arm.

'Yes,' Nathine agreed, crossing her arms and glaring at Aimee. But the corners of her mouth twitched in a smile.

Aimee looked down at her empty hands and then back up at Dyrenna and Nathine.

'I lost your scimitars,' she admitted. 'I think I dropped them somewhere in there.' She pointed to the still-burning workshop.

Dyrenna counted on her fingers. 'That's two cups of tea, one slice of cake and a scimitar that you owe me now.'

'And you owe me one scimitar, a pencil and a whole pile of toast,' Nathine added.

'What's the toast for?' Aimee asked, trying to remember if she'd lost something else of Nathine's.

'I dunno, but I'll think of something because I could eat a whole loaf of toast right now.'

As Aimee looked at her friends, she realised what she had to do. Pagrin might have more strength than she did, but he was alone. She was not. The thought of what she was planning terrified her and her mind shied away from it, but she forced herself to look at it from all angles. It was the only way to save everyone. However, it would mean sacrificing herself.

CHAPTER 31

SACRIFICE

With her course of action fixed firmly in her mind, Aimee and Jess took to the air just as the walls of the burning workshop collapsed. Jess growled as embers chased them into the sky. Black and Malgerus followed on Jess's tail. From above the rooftops Aimee saw more Empty Warriors, pouring through the streets from the harbour to join the battle at the river.

They were running out of time.

Jess didn't bother gaining height—as soon as they were above the rooftops she shot westwards, back towards the River Toig. Aimee hadn't told the others her plan, they'd simply followed her, but now in the air Nathine shouted questions at her.

'Where's Pagrin? Are we following him?'

'No!' Aimee yelled back as Jess swerved around a chimney stack.

'Why not?' Nathine shouted but Aimee ignored her.

There wasn't time for explanations. And she didn't want to tell Nathine her full plan because she knew her friend would try to talk her out of it.

She'd spent the last few days searching and finding nothing. She'd followed the clues across the city, hunting for Kyelli only to find her bracelet. Then she'd journeyed all the way to Vorthens, seeking the Master of Sparks and a way to stop the battle before it began. But she'd been tricked again and the Quorelle she'd found was the wrong one. Then she'd risked her life, her mind and her dragon to control the bracelet's power and find Pagrin. But he'd escaped.

She'd had enough. No more quests. No more searching.

They reached the river and Aimee swore. The Empty Warriors had completed their makeshift bridge and had already pushed it half way across the water. On the other side guards were still firing, the clank and ping of their crossbows echoing off the walls of buildings.

Dragons shot along the river and blasted the makeshift bridge with flames. But Aimee heard the dreaded clunk of gears and three bolts shot into the air. The dragons swerved away from the bridge, abandoning their attack.

Arrows flew across the river, shot by warriors with unnatural strength and it seemed like every one found its mark. Guards cried out as the barbed tips tore into their bodies. Some toppled into the Toig, others were pulled back by their friends, into the streets where they lay wounded and screaming.

Behind them flames crackled and roared as the harbour district was destroyed. Homes, warehouse and lives were all gone. A plume of smoke drifted across the river, obscuring Aimee's view. With powerful beats of her wings Jess took them up and out of the haze, snapping in annoyance at the smoke. Aimee coughed as she breathed it in.

'Aimee!'

She twisted in her saddle to see Nathine pointing across the city. Dark clouds of smoke, tinged orange with flames, billowed into the sky. The Empty Warriors had broken through the tunnel again. They were inside the city. How long till they reached the crowd in Quorelle Square? An hour? Two?

Aimee turned her eyes back to the river and spotted blood-red scales. Faradair was perched on the struts of a broken bridge as Jara yelled orders to Riders and guards alike. Jess tucked into a dive, Aimee gripping her spiralled horns so hard it was painful. Jara saw them coming, and with a flick of his huge wings Faradair rose into the sky. Aimee had barely registered the need to pull out of their dive early when Jess performed the manoeuvre. Aimee's stomach flip-flopped as Jess's wings spread and caught the air.

Faradair flew level with Jess and Aimee could see Jara was about to shout over so she got in first. There wasn't time for explanations.

'I need all the Riders. Everyone,' Aimee told her, raising her voice above the battle below.

'Why? Three of you should be enough to hunt one man. And I can't spare anyone!'

Faradair and Jess were circling each other, Malgerus

and Black hovering above them. Their wings swirled the air and Aimee had to keep swatting away smoke and embers.

'I'm done searching for the Master of Sparks!' Aimee called.

She saw the anger flash across Jara's face, saw her high cheekbones flush with it. 'You're giving up now?'

Faradair's tail slashed at the air, the barbs on the end only just missing Jess as she circled past him.

'Don't think I won't take that bracelet from you and use it myself. Even if that kills you! It's the only way to stop this!'

Aimee knew Jara's words were true. She would take the bracelet from her, draining Aimee's spark and killing her. And Jara would put it on, even though she knew it would kill her too, if it gave her a way to save the city. Aimee didn't feel hurt, or insulted. Instead she was glad that Jara was still full of conviction, that she'd do anything to protect her Riders. It was that strength that Aimee planned to use.

'I'm not giving up!' she yelled back.

Ever since she'd first read the name engraved on the Empty Warriors' breastplates, the Master of Sparks had been a shadowy figure lurking in Aimee's mind. They'd been a faceless evil, hidden but threatening everything she loved. She'd been afraid of them, but she'd forced herself to go searching for them. She'd always run and hid from her bullies but she'd gone out to find this one, to stop them.

But she'd done it all wrong.

She'd been hunting, always on the back foot, running to catch up with someone who'd had three centuries to plan his destruction of her home. Pagrin was always one step ahead. But now she was going to stop. Now she was going to stand her ground, with her friends around her, and make him come to her.

But she couldn't do it alone. And she couldn't do it here.

A crash thundered through the air and Aimee glanced down to see the makeshift bridge had thudded onto the far bank. Empty Warriors were already marching across it. From behind the hastily made barricade city guards fired at them. Many warriors toppled off into the river, trailing streams of molten fire. But the guards couldn't kill them fast enough.

'Jara! Call all the Riders and follow me,' Aimee ordered. She saw the indecision on Jara's face, saw it tearing her in two. 'Please, trust me!'

Aimee expected Jara to look to Dyrenna as she always did when she needed help and support, but instead her emerald-green eyes locked onto Aimee's. Aimee didn't flinch from that hard stare and didn't need to make herself sit straighter in her saddle to appear more confident. She believed in herself and her plan.

'I can do this!' she promised Jara. 'But I need your help. I need everyone's help.'

'Alright!' Jara yelled as Faradair broke free of the circle they'd been flying and swooped back down to the river.

Jess, Malgerus and Black followed. Jara yelled orders, screaming above the clash of the battle and Riders began to fly towards them. Aimee urged Jess for more speed and she led the way. The dragons fell into line behind her like the colourful strands of a broken rainbow knitting back together. There were Riders fighting at the caravan compound too but Aimee didn't have time to gather them as well. She wished Pelathina was with them but perhaps it was a good thing she wasn't. If Aimee saw her pretty face then her will, to do what needed to be done, might crumble.

Aimee needed a specific place for what she planned. She needed somewhere quiet so she could concentrate, and a spot beyond the buildings so their dragons could all land. She wanted to be far from the crowds of people in case anything went wrong—she didn't want to endanger them. And she needed somewhere empty she could draw the army towards. On the brief flight to the river she'd thought of the perfect spot.

She led the dragons up the Toig River to where the Fall of Dragon's Tears tumbled down the cliffs. Fields and orchards stretched along the river's west bank, and if Aimee looked only at them she could almost convince herself the city wasn't burning behind her. At the foot of the waterfall white froth tumbled over the rocks sending spray across a wildflower meadow on the eastern bank. Aimee and Jess landed there.

The others set down around her, their dragons' colourful scales making them look like overgrown flowers. She hadn't managed to gather all the Riders, but close to thirty were now staring at her, wondering what was going on. She hoped that would be enough.

'You're going to do the thing, aren't you? But with all of us,' Nathine called over from Malgerus's back. Aimee nodded at her friend. 'Will it work?'

Aimee didn't answer that one, because she knew it would work, but it was going to cost her everything. And she didn't want Nathine knowing that. Instead she dismounted and walked over to Jara, Jess following behind her. Jara had stayed mounted and Aimee had to tilt her head to look up at her.

'I hope you know what you're doing,' Jara said. Her eyes flicked from Aimee back towards the city. Smoke rose from both the east and west as it burned. Aimee's own eyes were drawn to the mountains, thinking of the Empty Warriors rampaging through Anteill, setting fire to the Heart.

Aimee ignored Jara's comment. She did know what she was doing, but she was terrified to do it, and if she wavered for just one moment she might change her mind. All around the meadow Riders waited, their anxious dragons shifting from foot to foot. The was filled with the sound of fluttering wingtips. Aimee felt all their eyes on her but the familiar flush to her cheeks didn't come. She turned to face them and raised her voice.

'Pagrin is controlling the Empty Warriors through his connections to them,' she began. 'He gives them instructions just like we do with our dragons. I'm sure you all know by now that I'm wearing Kyelli's bracelet.' Aimee held up her arm. She'd rolled her shirt sleeves to the elbow and the wide gold cuff glinted in the sun. 'With it on I can see people's sparks and I can see the connections between you and your dragons.'

Aimee saw them all now. Each spark was like a mini sun, glowing in the chest of each of the women around her. Some were more full of energy than others, but every single one was bright. For the past few days Aimee had hated seeing them, hated the knowledge it gave her about how long a person would live, and detested the power the bracelet gave her to steal those sparks. But now Aimee was glad she could see them. They were beautiful and strong, just like their owners. And each spark, each Rider, was connected to her dragon with a shimmering blue line, thin as a spiderweb but a thousand times stronger.

'When we found Pagrin,' Aimee gestured to Nathine and Dyrenna, 'and his warriors attacked us, I managed to steal them off him.'

'What do you mean?' It was Lyrria who called out the question.

'I took his connections to the Empty Warriors and for a short while they obeyed me. I made them stop attacking us.' Aimee saw shock on some faces, but no disbelief.

'How?' This time the question came from Jara.

'Because I borrowed strength from my friends.'

Aimee turned to smile at Nathine and Dyrenna, but she looked back just in time to see the flash of fear on Jara's face. Jara's was the first spark Aimee had stolen and she'd nearly killed her.

'I didn't take anyone's spark,' Aimee quickly yelled. She was sure by now everyone had heard how she almost drained Jara's life and how she stole half of Pelathina's spark. 'We've all got strong sparks. Every one of us made the climb and survived. And we're even stronger because of the bond we have with our dragons, and the love they give us.'

Jess nudged Aimee gently with her head, her spiralled horns plucking at Aimee's hair. All around her Riders stroked their dragon's feathers or smiled as their dragons nudged them with a wing or a tail. The Riders were arrayed across the meadow, wildflowers brushing the underside of their dragons' bellies. Some at the back were perched on the tumbled down rocks at the base of the cliffs. And every one of them was looking at Aimee. Every eye was watching her intently, every person was waiting for her to speak.

And for the first time in her life Aimee felt no urge to hide.

'But it's not just our dragons that make us strong,' Aimee continued. 'On my own I'm still just one girl with her dragon. I couldn't have found this bracelet, or gone in search of Kyelli, or stolen Pagrin's warriors from him if I was doing those things alone.'

Aimee felt a catch in her voice as what she was saying, what she'd realised in that burning workshop, stirred up her emotions. If she lived, she'd never be alone ever again. But she wasn't going to survive this.

'We're stronger together!' She shouted. 'That's what makes us Riders. It's what makes us amazing!'

'Yeah!' Nathine was the first to yell but a moment later all across the meadow women were shouting their agreement. Then Aimee's tears of happiness did come and she quickly brushed them aside.

'So you'll help me?' Aimee cried out above the noise.

The Riders' voices rose in agreement and their dragons roared, the sound echoing back from the towering cliffs above them. Jess had wrapped her long neck around Aimee's shoulders and Aimee's bittersweet tears dripped off her chin and beaded on Jess's shimmering scales.

As the cheering died down, Jara dismounted and came to stand beside Aimee.

'What do you need us to do?'

'Nothing, just be here with me,' Aimee told her. 'I'm going to steal as many of the Empty Warriors as I can and order them to march here. I'll pull them away from the city. Pagrin will follow them.'

'How do you know he'll come?'

'Because he wants to kill me. He set a trap for me and I willingly fell into it.'

'But this time you're the bait. How is that better?'

'Because I'll be the one in control,' Aimee replied.

'You promised no last stands,' Dyrenna called over.

'And this won't be one,' Aimee lied.

Jara looked around at her Riders. 'And if we're not strong enough, if we can't give you enough power and Pagrin takes back control of the Empty Warriors? What happens then?'

'We'll be surrounded and killed,' Aimee admitted.

'But I can do this. No, *we* can do this.'

'Once you've stolen his warriors, and Pagrin follows them here, and if he doesn't wrench them back from you, then what? We just kill him?'

'Yes and no.' Aimee took a deep breath.

Jara's green eyes narrowed to slits. 'I'm not going to like this part of your plan, am I?'

Aimee lowered her voice so only Jara would hear her words. There was no one else she could rely on to fulfil the last part of her plan, not because she didn't trust the others, but because they would try to stop her. The fact that she had people in her life who'd fight to protect her, even from herself, sent a fresh wave of bittersweet tears down her cheeks. But Jara was fierce and ruthless—she'd forced Aimee, Nathine and Hayetta to become Riders before they were ready, she'd fought for ten years to make a peace with the Helvethi, she'd kept Kyelli's secret and tried to kill Aimee when she put on the bracelet. Aimee could trust Jara to do what needed to be done.

'To kill all the Empty Warriors we need to sever their connections to their master. They don't have sparks so those connections are the only thing keeping them alive.'

'And to destroy their connections?' Jara was keeping her voice low too and she asked the question, but Aimee could tell by the hard glint in her eyes that she already knew the answer.

'You need to kill their master, the one controlling them.' Aimee forced the words out quickly, trying not to let their full meaning register in her brain.

'You'll be controlling them.'

Aimee nodded and tightened her grip on Jess. 'You'll need to kill me.'

Someone else would have argued with her, told her to come up with another plan. But Jara didn't and that was another reason Aimee had chosen her for this task. Jara didn't flinch from hard choices. Instead she pulled Aimee into a hug. Jara's shirt was sweaty and smelly, and her hair was greasy where it brushed Aimee's face, but Aimee still hugged her back tightly. And besides, she doubted she was any more presentable right now. Then Jara pulled back and slid free one scimitar.

Aimee tried not to think how it would feel when that blade pierced her heart.

'And Pagrin?' Jara asked.

'You'll need to kill him as well,' Aimee told her. 'He still has hundreds of sparks in his blood. He could make more warriors and this would start all over again.'

She motioned for Jara to step back and the Rider obeyed. Aimee didn't need the space but she wanted to speak to Jess and she didn't want Jara to hear her words.

'Remember what I told you back in that meadow above Vorthens?' Aimee asked, pressing her forehead against the cool scales of Jess's neck. 'When I learned the bracelet was killing me, I told you that when the time came you had to fly away.' A growl rumbled in Jess's throat and her feathers quivered. 'It's time to do that, Jess. Not right now, but soon. I can't survive this, but you will. So promise me you'll fly far away and hide.

Find somewhere you can live and be free.'

The wave of love that flowed into Aimee's mind almost undid her. It wrapped around her core and infused her limbs with warmth and strength.

'Promise, girl,' Aimee whispered.

Jess licked the side of Aimee's face, her rough tongue leaving a long trail of saliva. Aimee laughed quietly between her tears.

'I'll take that as your agreement.'

Then, with her arm still wrapped around Jess's neck, she turned to face the burning city. Closing her eyes, she tapped the bracelet's power and reached out with her mind. The life all around her instantly crowded her senses but she was getting used to that assault now and pushed it to one side. Instead she reached out for Pagrin, searching the streets of the harbour district for the feel of his malice.

'Come on, you bastard,' she whispered.

CHAPTER 32

MEMORIES AND GRIEF

Back in the workshop, when Aimee had harnessed Nathine and Dyrenna's energy, she'd done it in a panic without actually knowing what she was doing, or how she'd done it. Now she had to do it deliberately and with more Riders. Jess was solid and calming, both beside her and inside her mind. Aimee took a deep breath, slowing her heart and trying to expel the adrenaline that seemed to have taken up permanent residence in her veins.

Sharing the Riders' power, harnessing their strength, meant opening herself up to them completely. It meant letting people see all of her. Her mind baulked at the idea, her old habits of hiding resurfacing for a moment, until she remembered she wasn't that fearful, bullied girl any more.

She could feel the Riders and their dragons around her, see their glowing sparks and shimmering connections, even with her eyes closed. All the connections were one-to-one. They stretched from Riders to dragons and no further. But life and energy flowed through everything, so all she had to do was pull the connections into a circle. Then she could harness their collective power and be the conduit for it.

Tethering herself to Jess, she reached out with her mind to Jara, the Rider closest to her. It was like stretching out and taking her hand. Aimee felt her and Jess's energy click together with the connection that flowed between Jara and Faradair. Then she reached out again, towards Dyrenna this time. She added her and Black's energy into the loop. Nathine and Malgerus were next.

Aimee continued her way around all the Riders, pulling their connections from one-way lines into a shimmering circle of blue energy. She wished the others could see how beautiful it was. She could feel them all—their lives, hopes and fears, and the love they shared with their dragons. She sensed their dragons too, each one like a flower blooming on the energy from their Rider.

Once they were all connected Aimee was vibrating with power. But it wasn't like the corrupting power of the bracelet that wanted to take, this was a power that wanted to protect. She had the strength of the Riders and their dragons behind her. She was one of many, and she belonged with these women.

Pagrin was alone. He had thousands of Empty Warriors but they were exactly that, empty. All that Pagrin had was his hate. Facing the city, but with her eyes still closed, Aimee went in search of that hate. It didn't take her long to find it. The threads of life spooled all around her and Pagrin was like a twisted knot in the middle. He hadn't bothered concealing his location from her. Maybe because he wanted to ensnare her again, or perhaps because he felt there was no point, he was close to his victory now.

Last time she'd grabbed the Empty Warriors in a panic and fought to hold onto them. This time, thanks to the Riders, she simply reached out and took them. She plucked at the pulsing black strands of their connection to Pagrin and watched as they pinged to her chest instead.

Pagrin's fury was instantaneous. She felt him scrabbling against her, trying to take back his warriors but Aimee swatted him away. One lonely Quorelle couldn't stop the combined power of the Riders and their dragons.

The more Empty Warriors Aimee took, the easier it became. She'd started with the ones in the harbour district because she had to stop the killing as soon as she could. The lines pulsed as she sent the command to stop fighting and march towards the Toig waterfall.

Pagrin was like an angry bee buzzing against a windowpane as he desperately tried to pull his warriors back from her grip. His anger seemed to push through the world like a heartbeat and Aimee could feel it in the connections she stole. His warriors were full of it too, his twisted grief and hate swirling with the flames inside them. Without the Riders Aimee would have been crushed by it, but their strength kept it from breaking her.

All the Empty Warriors in the harbour district were now connected to Aimee and marching towards her. With her eyes still closed she turned towards the western curve of the mountains. Dark lines gathered there as the warriors attacked the caravan compound. Aimee reached out and started plucking their connections, pulling them towards her, adding them to the others tethered to her chest.

She heard a shout behind her and opened her eyes to see lines of Empty Warriors marching towards the meadow. Flames swirled in their unnatural eyes and their swords were bared. Some were splattered with blood. Aimee heard the rasp as scimitars were drawn behind her. Dragons growled, low and rumbling.

'You're controlling them, right?' Lyrria called.

'I am,' Aimee replied.

Fear still prickled her palms, though. It was unnerving, watching thousands of monsters march towards them. Beside her Jess growled too. If she lost control, if Pagrin managed to wrench back the connections, the Empty Warriors would attack in a heartbeat.

At her command the Empty Warriors began to line up in the fields, like rows of statues. They trampled all the crops and for a moment Aimee felt bad for whichever farmer owned that field.

She continued to pluck connections, feeling the warriors from the caravan compound respond to her commands. She didn't order these ones to march towards her—that order would look like an invasion of the city. Instead she told them to simply stop fighting and stand still. Hopefully the guards and Riders at the compound would take advantage of that and kill them.

'Tell me when,' Jara whispered behind her.

Jara's scimitar wasn't touching her, but Aimee could feel the cold breath of steel on the back of her neck.

'Not yet, I haven't got them all,' she replied and was amazed at how steady her voice was.

Still with an arm around Jess, Aimee reached upwards with her mind. The Empty Warriors who'd invaded Anteill were still in the mountains. She could sense them climbing down the cliffs. Aimee felt her own bubble of anger for these ones—they'd attacked her home and killed Aranati. Aimee sent them a command. She told them to stop climbing and let go. She couldn't see them fall from the cliffs but she felt a whole bunch of connections wink from existence as they died.

The rumble of dragons around her grew louder. Aimee turned her eyes back towards the statue-like Empty Warriors in the field. Pagrin was running through their ranks. His face was exactly the same as the thousands around him, but whereas theirs were stoic, Pagrin's was red with rage. He was still wearing the guard's uniform but he'd lost the cloak.

Dark lines of connection still pooled from Pagrin's chest towards the warriors across the city, but Aimee plucked at them, watching them ping from his chest to hers. In his mind Pagrin threw all of his strength at her. It hit Aimee like a wave of cold water, but she gritted her teeth and held on. The life energy of the Riders and their dragons flowed through her, bolstering her against his attack.

Pagrin burst from the ranks of warriors and stopped before them. He faced Aimee and the Riders with his army arrayed behind him. Except that it was Aimee's army now.

His regal face, the one he shared with his warriors, was twisted with hate, his mouth a snarl. One sleeve of his guard's uniform was torn to the elbow, and his trousers were smeared with ash. Strands of hair, greasy with sweat, hung down over his forehead. Aimee knew she looked a mess as well, in her dirty, bloodied trousers and shirt, and her boots that were still soggy with sea water. She didn't have her Rider's coat, her goggles were broken, and she'd lost not only her own scimitars but one of Dyrenna and Nathine's too. But with Jess beside her and a flight of dragons behind her, Aimee didn't give a damn how she looked.

As Aimee looked at Pagrin, raging before her, the terrifying shadowy figure of the Master of Sparks that she'd carried in her mind shrank until it became this lone man, angry and surrounded. She tasted pity at the back of her throat, bitter and unwelcome. She swallowed it down. Kierell's future belonged to the Riders and all the people of the city. It no longer belonged to the Quorelle. Kyelli and Marhorn might have saved them once, but the city was strong enough now to stand on its own.

'Our future belongs to hope,' Aimee told Jess and felt her dragon's rumbly growl of agreement.

Pagrin was screaming at the Empty Warriors, all his smug confidence gone.

'Now?' Jara whispered behind her.

Aimee shook her head just as Pagrin rallied for another attack and shoved against her mind. Aimee gasped, bent over, clutching her knees.

'Aimee!' The call came from Nathine.

Aimee squeezed her eyes shut so tightly that patterns of red danced across her eyelids. Pagrin's mental attack was pounding against her, like waves crashing into the cliffs around Kierell. But like those cliffs Aimee held firm, keeping him out. It took every ounce of effort she had. Sweat rolled down her face, dripping from her chin, and she'd clenched her teeth so hard she worried one of them would crack.

There were still Empty Warriors in the city answering to Pagrin's commands. Aimee uncurled and stood upright, reaching for those last warriors. She could feel Jara waiting right behind her, the tip of her scimitar so close Aimee imagined she could feel it piercing her already.

'You think they make you stronger?' Pagrin's voice snarled out across the meadow.

Aimee opened her eyes. He stood ten paces from her, his hazel eyes fixed on her face, his lips twisted with the sneer of disgust she'd seen all her life.

'These women,' he waved an arm to encompass the Riders, 'are nothing but a crutch you're leaning on. What happens if I kick it away?'

A dagger appeared in the hand he'd been waving

and before Aimee could react he'd thrown it. With the strength of hundreds of sparks in his blood, the dagger flew true and hit its mark. Aimee could only follow it with her eyes.

'No!'

The cry was torn from her as Pagrin's dagger pierced Nathine's chest. The force of it knocked her from Malgerus's saddle.

Memories and grief overwhelmed Aimee. As Nathine landed in a heap on the grass, Malgerus crouched over her roaring, Aimee remembered seeing other Riders injured and killed, shot from the sky or burned by fiery hands. But because she was connected to all the Riders in the meadow, she felt their anguish as well. And there was so much of it. Every woman there had lost a friend, had a piece torn out of their close-knit community.

Aimee felt Nathine's energy ripped from the circle, leaving a hole. It was what Pagrin had planned. Aimee felt the angry-hot energy of his power strike out towards her. Still reeling from his attack on Nathine, Aimee couldn't stop him. Pagrin began pulling back connections.

Aimee didn't remember falling to the ground and only realised she was there when panic made her fingers scrabble in the grass and dirt. Her plan was falling apart like a quilt ripped at the seams, the stuffing all pouring out.

Connections flew from Aimee's chest and back to Pagrin. The front row of Empty Warriors raised their swords and charged silently at the Riders. Jara's orders to take off overlaid Dyrenna's shouts to attack. Connections continued to ping from Aimee's chest and back to Pagrin. Dragons roared and Riders yelled. The air filled with the leathery flap of wings. The movement stirred up the scent of wildflowers, so out of place in a battle.

'Nathine!' Aimee cried, shoving herself back to her feet. Jess was ahead of her, already skimming back across the meadow to where Malgerus crouched over his prone Rider. Malgerus whipped his long neck around and snapped at Jess, forcing her to back off. Then before Aimee reached them, Malgerus gathered Nathine in his talons and took off. Aimee had no idea if her friend was alive or not.

A blast of dragon's breath shot over Aimee's head, right into a group of Empty Warriors running towards her. It did nothing. They burst through the flames and kept coming. All around her, Riders and dragons were attacking from the sky. Blades clashed and talons screeched on breastplates.

Aimee didn't know what to do, until a hand grabbed her arm, boney fingers painfully squeezing her muscles.

'Get into the sky and get back control,' Jara ordered, her green eyes glinting hard as emeralds.

She didn't ask if Aimee could, and that belief was all Aimee needed to spur her back into action. She jumped up into her saddle and Jess flapped so hard she hit Aimee with her wings. A moment later they were in the sky.

Riders and Empty Warriors fought in the meadow. Aimee could see bright pools of glowing lava where warriors had been killed but even as she watched, Pagrin pulled more connections from her chest. He'd taken over fifty now and within a few moments he'd have hundreds back under his control.

It felt impossible to ignore everything around her— her friends fighting for their lives, Nathine somewhere dead or dying, guards still battling inside the city—but Aimee took a deep breath and dismissed it all. Just like when she'd been training with Lyrria all those months ago and she'd learned to ignore the discomfort in her quivering muscles, to ignore the cold wind nipping at her ears, to ignore Nathine's taunts about not being good enough. Aimee called up those skills and focused.

The Riders and their dragons were scattered across the meadow and sky. Their emotions were a tangled mess of fear and tiny tendrils of hope and Aimee could still sense them all. They were still connected—their energies flowing between Riders and dragons but also in a circle through Aimee. There was a ragged hole though where Nathine had been torn away. Aimee reached out with her mind, grabbed the frayed ends and tied them back together.

Pagrin felt it, and somewhere below them he screamed in frustration. He still had almost one hundred Empty Warriors though, enough to kill thirty Riders or force them to retreat.

'Jara!' Aimee called across the sky.

Fardair was beside them in four quick wingbeats, his

scales rippling like spilled blood.

'Follow me!' Aimee yelled.

She pushed hard on Jess's horns and her dragon tucked her wings and dived. Pagrin was a nexus at the edge of the army, easy to spot. Dark lines of connection shot from him into the battle, and behind him the rows of Empty Warriors stood still and silent as statues. He looked up just in time to see Jess before she barrelled into him. Her talons scored deep gashes in his shoulders and the whip of her tail knocked him to the ground.

Aimee leapt from her saddle before Jess had landed. She hit the grass, fell, rolled and sprang up again. Then she dived on top of Pagrin. She grabbed him, flinging all her weight onto him, pinning his body down before he had a chance to react.

It was time for her secret plan. The one she hadn't told Jara about. The one she hadn't even shared with Jess. It was the plan where she had no idea if it would work. Only a desperate hope that it would.

She grabbed Pagrin's wrist and released her hold over the bracelet's power, letting it steal his sparks. He kneed her in the stomach and Aimee's insides spasmed with pain. With a kick he flipped her off him and she rolled on the grass, but still kept hold of his wrist, still kept sucking at his sparks.

Jess growled and Aimee heard Pagrin grunt in pain as her dragon pressed a clawed foot down on his chest, pinning him to the ground.

'Good girl,' Aimee wheezed.

She watched a light grow in her chest beside her

own spark as she stole energy from Pagrin. The familiar nausea hit her, the wrongness of having someone else's life inside her but she kept going. Another spark appeared in her chest, a pinprick of light at first but growing fast. Pagrin swore and thrashed beside her and Jess kept him pinned, holding him down with a physical strength Aimee didn't have.

As a third spark began to glow in her chest the sounds of battle intensified. The tortured screech of a dragon in pain tore across the meadow.

'Aimee?' Jara's voice was low, questioning and panicky.

She was standing above Aimee, Faradair behind her, his wings outstretched so they almost looked like they belonged to Jara.

In his desperation to seize back control Pagrin assaulted her mind again, pushing against her with three centuries of twisted hatred. Aimee felt her circle of connection with the Riders wavering. She couldn't hold on much longer. Three extra sparks in her chest would need to be enough.

'Jara, now!' Aimee yelled. 'And kill Pagrin too!'

Jara didn't hesitate, not for a single moment. She did what needed to be done to save her Riders. Aimee saw the tip of her scimitar catch the sun before it stabbed down into her chest.

CHAPTER 33

THREE SPARKS

In the split second before the hot pain became all-consuming, Aimee imagined wrapping her hands around her own spark, protecting it.

Then agony tore through her body. Jara's blade seemed to slide free of her chest in slow motion, making a sucking sound as it did. Aimee watched, blinking heavily, as droplets of her own blood appeared to hang suspended in the air before splatting down on her face. Jara had missed her heart but she'd still bleed out in a matter of moments.

She knew her chest was soaked in blood but she couldn't feel it. Beside her Jess was roaring as she shared her Rider's pain but Aimee couldn't hear her. All that existed was the sharp agony inside her. Dark clouds crowded the edge of her vision. She knew she only had a few short moments to act.

Tapping the power of the bracelet she began to use the energy from the three sparks she'd stolen from Pagrin to heal herself. One spark would never have been enough. With a wound like the one Jara gave her, Aimee's own spark would have burned through all its energy trying and failing to heal her. But Aimee had spares.

Through eyes blurred with tears she watched first one, then a second of her stolen sparks dim as her body used their energy to heal. She burned through the full energy from two of them before she could breathe again without pain spearing her lungs. She kept going, letting the power of the bracelet use up all the energy in the third spark as well. The pain faded from her chest, becoming a dull ache.

She felt the moment the third spark winked out, all its energy drained, and she shoved the bracelet's power back into its cage. Jess had curled her body around Aimee's as if she could protect her from everything. Her heavy tail was pinning Aimee's legs and her wings formed a canopy above her head. Aimee sat up in a rush, pushing against Jess, trying to peer around her wings.

'Come on, girl, move. I need to see if it worked.'

Jess shifted aside and Aimee felt an almost sulky pang from her dragon. As soon as she was free of tails and wings, she shot to her feet.

One by one, the Empty Warriors were collapsing. They didn't cry out, they didn't try to run away, they simply shrivelled like all the fire inside them had extinguished and they fell to the ground in a clatter of bones. The dark connections leading from Aimee's chest to the warriors had winked out. The pulsing lines leading away towards the caravan compound had vanished too and Aimee pictured the warriors there deflating and dropping dead.

Faradair's roar of triumph pulled Aimee's eyes back from the dying warriors. On the grass, right beside her, lay Pagrin's corpse. Jara's scimitar, the same one she'd stabbed Aimee with, protruded from his chest. With his thousands of sparks he could have healed himself from a wound like that. But the neck of his shirt held nothing but a ragged stump. Faradair roared again, the sound coming from the sides of his mouth as his long teeth at the front held Pagrin's severed head. Blood gushed from the torn stump of his neck and Aimee saw it sparkle with hundreds of sparks.

She watched for a moment, mesmerised as Pagrin's blood soaked into the grass. His Quorelle sparks vanished as their energy was absorbed by the earth. Across the meadow the Empty Warriors who'd been attacking the Riders had deflated and collapsed. The hundreds of pulsing connections that had streamed from Pagrin's chest had vanished as he died.

Then Jess nudged her, hard and insistent.

'Yes, I know,' Aimee told her, snapping her attention back.

Her plan had worked. She'd saved the Riders, protected the city, but she was still dying. She dropped to her knees, squelching in grass wet with Pagrin's sparkly blood. She held out her left hand, the wide cuff of Kyelli's gold bracelet gleaming under the blood splatter. It was still locked on her wrist, still draining her own spark. If she didn't remove it, the bracelet would kill her. And only energy from a spark could open the catch and release her wrist.

For one last time Aimee tapped the bracelet's power and as she did so she grabbed Pagrin's dying body. He was a mess of energy as sparks burned and flared trying to heal his impossible wounds, and others poured out of him, giving their energy to the land. Aimee only needed one. With ease she sucked a single spark from his bloody corpse into her chest. She let it glow there for a moment as she stood up.

She needed to check though, before she gave up the bracelet and its power, that it really was over. Jara was staring at her, eyes wide, high cheekbones flushed. Beside her Faradair spat out Pagrin's head. It flew through the air trailing sparkling blood drops and landed with a thud at Black's feet. Aimee's eyes traveled up to see Dyrenna in her saddle, face creased at the edges with pain, but alive. And behind her other Riders were coming in to land, safe now the army of Empty Warriors was nothing but shrivelled corpses.

Aimee cast her mind out across the city, searching for any hint of Pagrin's malice, any Empty Warriors that still lived. She sensed nothing. Only the pulse of life—wonderful, normal, ordinary life.

She looked back down at the bracelet on her wrist and doubt reared its head. What if it didn't come off? Sensing her worries Jess crouched behind her and rested her head on Aimee's shoulder. Her scales were pleasantly cool against Aimee's neck.

She took a deep breath, wrapped her fingers around

the bracelet, and pulled. Icy pain shot up her arm but Aimee gritted her teeth against it.

'Come on, please,' she begged.

What if it didn't work because she'd taken a spark from Pagrin after Faradair had killed him? She was staring at her chest, watching her own spark pulse faintly in time with her heart. The last spark from Pagrin glowed stubbornly beside her own. Then it was like a lock mechanism clicking into place. The spark from Pagrin vanished in a burst of light, its energy consumed by the bracelet. Aimee retched as she felt the metal spike in her arm retract into the bracelet. With a click, the gold cuff sprung open and fell from her wrist. It landed with a splat on the bloody grass. Aimee jumped back, away from it, as if it might suddenly leapt back onto her wrist and trap her again.

Relief made her legs wobbly and she collapsed backwards into Jess. It was like the elation she'd felt at surviving the climb, only a thousand times stronger. Then hands were grabbing her and for a moment she wondered why Jess wasn't protecting her until she heard the babble of Riders' voices. Jara's sharp tones cut through them all as she pulled back from giving Aimee a bone-squeezing hug.

'Sparks! Why am I hugging you and not picking up your corpse? I killed you!'

All around Aimee was a sea of faces, Riders grinning, staring at her in delighted disbelief. And sticking up above them were their dragon's heads, scales of every colour shimmering in the sun. More arms grabbed her, pulling her into hugs. She felt Dyrenna land a gentle kiss on the top of her head and smelled Lyrria's familiar sent as she wrapped an arm around her waist. Everyone wanted to touch her, hug her, be part of her victory. It was incredible, and combined with the relief of no longer wearing the bracelet Aimee felt like she'd downed a cask of cloudberry liqueur.

'Aimee!' Jara grabbed her again, still staring at her like she couldn't believe she was alive.

'If you'd stabbed before we attacked Pagrin then I would have died,' Aimee explained. Her words came out in bursts as she felt breathless from the attention. 'My spark would have used up all its energy trying and failing to heal me. But I stole three of Pagrin's sparks and used their energy to fix my wound. Mostly.'

'Mostly?' Worry flashed across Jara's face.

Aimee pulled open her shirt, not feeling the slightest bit self-conscious, and stared at the hole Jara's blade had sliced in her vest. Beneath it, right between her breasts and in the middle of a patch of colourless skin, a shallow cut still wept blood.

'Sparks,' someone swore.

'How did you know that would work?' Lyrria asked. She'd stepped right up close to Aimee and linked her little finger around Aimee's as if not quite sure about taking her hand proper.

'I didn't,' Aimee admitted. 'I wasn't sure if I could keep the energy in my own spark or if it would get used up too. I thought if I could hide it, then I could protect it.'

Aimee thought about what she'd just said, and the way she used to always hide from her bullies, and a wry smile touched her lips.

'What?' Lyrria nudged her, seeing her smile.

Aimee shrugged. 'Sometimes hiding does work, but only if you do it with friends.' Lyrria's face crumpled in confusion. 'I think the combined strength from all of you, and your dragons, is what gave me enough power to protect my own spark.'

Jara pulled her into another fierce hug. 'I was all ready to carry the guilt of your death.'

'I know. But you're strong enough, you could have handled it. You carried the secret of the bracelet all those years,' Aimee said.

'Yeah, but I'm still bloody glad I don't have to. You owe me.'

Aimee laughed, a genuine, delighted, glad-to-be-alive laugh. 'I need to bake the world's biggest cake and give everyone a piece.'

'Damn right you do,' Dyrenna added with a smile.

Aimee's own smile dropped as a flash of panic exploded inside her like a firework.

'Nathine!' she cried.

She shoved through the Riders, ignoring their yells and sprinted across the meadow. She had to jump over piles of corpses—the Empty Warriors lay in deflated heaps, sunken skin wrapping their blackened bones, empty of the fire and hate that had given them purpose. There were no dragons in the meadow, no Riders except the group behind her. She spun around desperately, searching for her friend. Jess nudged her with her horns and growled, pointing to the cliffs with her snout.

Malgerus crouched a short way up on a ledge beside the tumbling waterfall. Aimee grabbed her saddle and was about to fly up to him when Jess called out. Malgerus gave an answering roar before opening his wings with a snap and gliding down. He was carrying a limp body in his talons.

'No, no, no,' Aimee mumbled as she ran to meet him.

It wasn't fair. She couldn't have saved everyone but lost the girl she'd turned from a bully into her best friend. Malgerus laid Nathine's body gently on the grass. Aimee collapsed to her knees beside them, crushing wildflowers. Malgerous growled at her as she grabbed Nathine.

'Ow!' Nathine complained. 'You can't just go manhandling a girl when she's injured.'

Aimee sank back on her heels as relief once again washed through her, sweeping out the dregs of adrenaline. Suddenly she was exhausted. The city was safe, Pagrin was dead and Nathine was as alive and as annoying as ever. Aimee wanted to sleep for a month, curled up with Jess wrapped around her.

With a hiss of pain, Nathine sat up and leaned back against her dragon for support. Malgerus wrapped his neck around her, laying his head in her lap. A dark patch of blood stuck Nathine's shirt to her shoulder. Aimee could see she'd balled up a dressing and shoved it into the wound.

'I got Mal to pull the dagger out with his teeth,' Nathine said, wincing as she prodded the wound just below her collarbone. 'And he gave it a good lick as well, but still, ow.'

'That's nothing, Jara stabbed me right through the chest,' Aimee said with a casual shrug and a smile.

Nathine stared at her in disbelief for a moment before ragged laughter exploded out of her. 'Did you piss her off?'

'I asked her to.'

'Don't tell me, it was part of your plan?'

'Yup.'

Nathine shook her head, high ponytail swinging. 'That's your worst plan yet, Aimee.'

And Aimee grinned because Nathine was grinning. Then a spasm of pain twitched across Nathine's face.

'I don't suppose you could lend me an extra spark?' she said, half joking.

'Sorry, I used them all to heal the mortal wound in my chest,' Aimee replied.

Nathine shook her head as she shuffled closer to Malgerus, trying to get comfy. 'You're so selfish.'

This time it was Aimee's turn to laugh. Nathine's brusque jokes were exactly what she needed. The amazement and awe on the faces of the other Riders had been wonderful, but overwhelming. Having Nathine play down Aimee's role as the hero of the day felt like she was back on familiar ground.

But then a niggle of worry wormed its way into her brain, growing larger as it pushed all other thoughts aside. Aimee remembered the way Pagrin had sneered at her, back in the gaol cell, that she hadn't used the bracelet to 'heal' her unusual face. But she'd just burned through three sparks healing her body. Had she accidentally 'healed' her face as well?

A year ago she'd have given anything for a way to fix her face but now the thought horrified her. It was *her* face. The colourless half, with her one set of white eyelashes and white eyebrow, the twists of white hair at her temple, they were part of who she was. Without her unusual face she'd never have pushed herself to achieve everything that she had done.

She stared down at her hands, searching for the white patches of colourless skin that marred her knuckles. But her hands were covered in blood, her own and Pagrin's. She scrubbed them, smearing the blood and not making them any cleaner. She tried rubbing them on the grass, desperate to see her skin properly.

'Hey, Aimee, what are you doing now?' Nathine sounded bemused.

Aimee's head snapped up and she stared at the other girl. 'Is my face still mine?' she blurted out.

Nathine's eyebrows twisted with her confusion. 'Yeah. Why wouldn't it be?'

Aimee only just managed to stop herself from grabbing Nathine and pulling her into a hug. The bracelets had given the Quorelle power above humans and changed them, warped them, but Aimee had held that same power and let it go, and she'd done it without losing any of herself.

'What are you looking so smug about?'

Aimee didn't get a chance to think of a good retort as Faradair landed beside them. Jara swung down from her saddle and cast a critical eye over Nathine before turning to Aimee.

'I'm flying to the council to let them know what happened here,' Jara announced.

Aimee nodded, wondering why Jara was telling her. Jara raked her fingers through her greasy hair and continued.

'It should really be you who goes. You should be the one to tell them that it's over since it was you who saved us all.'

A few months ago the thought of standing up in front of the council with an announcement like that would have terrified Aimee. And more recently she'd have wanted to make herself do it to prove that she could. Now she smiled as she realised that actually, she was happy to leave it to Jara.

Aimee shook her head gently. 'No, I want to stay here with my friends.'

Jara nodded, and then as if the mention of others had tugged at her she raised her eyes from Aimee and looked around. Slowly Aimee stood and followed her gaze. Near the heaps of deflated Empty Warriors there were two colourful mounds. One was the sunshine yellow of a dragon Aimee didn't recognise and the other was the pine-needle green of Whisper.

'Sal,' Aimee breathed the name.

'And Theaga,' Jara added. 'We should be grateful

that we only lost two Riders, but...'

Her words trailed off and Aimee knew why. She felt it as well, that even losing two—added to the deaths of Lwena, Fineya and Aranati—was too many.

'We'll give them all a proper Rider's funeral this evening,' Jara promised, taking hold of Faradair's saddle. 'Aimee, one more thing.'

She held out her hand, and resting in her palm was a wide gold cuff. Kyelli's bracelet.

'If I take this to the council, you know what they'll suggest,' Jara said.

Aimee did know. The Uneven Council would argue and debate, but eventually they'd decide to keep the bracelet, just in case. They'd lock it away, of course, but how long till the urge to use it pushed someone to snap it closed around their wrist? She remembered how justified and sure councillors Beljarn and Seth had sounded with their plan to take sparks from those they'd decided could be sacrificed.

Though it made her skin crawl to touch it again, Aimee reached out and took the bracelet from Jara.

'It was lost in the battle,' she said.

Jara nodded. 'It's a shame.'

Then she and Faradair were gone, blood-red wings soaring back towards the city. Aimee lowered her eyes slowly, looking around the meadow. Riders sat or stood in clusters, tending wounds, comforting each other, hugging their dragons with relief that they were still alive. Aimee flopped back down to the grass. Jess lowered herself more gracefully and curled around her

Rider. Aimee stroked her ruff of feathers.

'We did it, girl,' she whispered.

Grief was a tight ball in her chest. Her eyes snagged on the scales of Sal and Theaga's dragons, dead but still curled protectively around their Riders. And her mind turned to Pelathina, heartbroken at losing her sister. Then she felt Nathine tugging her wrist and turned to see her friend had lain down on the grass, Malgerus pressed up against her side. Aimee slid down so she was lying against Nathine's other side, Jess curled at her feet, head resting on Aimee's thighs.

For a long moment they just lay like that and Aimee watched the clouds drifting overhead. A hundred million thoughts and emotions clambered to get inside her mind but Aimee shoved them away. They could wait, right now she just wanted to rest.

'I've got a plan,' Nathine whispered, nudging Aimee in the ribs.

Aimee turned to see Nathine grinning at her. 'Does it involve brushing your teeth, because your breath is revolting.'

'*Mine's* bad? When did you last brush yours?' Nathine sounded outraged and Aimee laughed.

Grief could wait too, just for a little while.

CHAPTER 34

GOODBYE

THE SUNSET WAS dragging colours across the sky as Aimee and Jess took off from the mountain ledge. Jess lazily flapped her wings. For the first time in days there was no need to rush. Aimee enjoyed all the small sensations of flying—the wind tugging back her curls, the shift of Jess's muscles underneath her, the openness of the sky all around them.

After a few minutes she pushed Jess's horns and her dragon tucked her wings, gliding downwards before levelling off above the caravan compound. Hours had passed since she'd stolen and destroyed Pagrin's army, but Aimee had missed most of them. She'd fallen asleep in the grass of the meadow, lying beside Nathine, and with Jess curled around her feet. Dyrenna said no one had the heart to waken her.

Jess flew over the caravan compound and Aimee gaped at the destruction. Not a single building still stood upright—all the workshops and stores were gone, turned into twisted piles of broken timbers and shattered bricks. Some still smouldered from the fires that had gutted their insides.

Faces turned to look up as Jess's shadow passed over them. Aimee heard a few whoops and cheers. Did they know who she was? Or were they just cheering any dragon? Nathine had teased her about being famous now and the thought made Aimee nervous, but also a little bit excited.

Empty Warrior corpses littered the caravan compound and more poured from where they'd broken out of the tunnel. Guards and workmen, and anyone who wanted to help, were busy piling up the bodies. Aimee shuddered as she thought of the horrible way they'd all deflated, leaving nothing but skeletons wrapped in skin. She was glad she didn't have to touch them, and admired the people below getting on with the unpleasant task.

She made herself look at the other collection of bodies, the ones laid out in respectfully neat rows. Many were covered with the patchwork cloaks of the guards. They were the people who'd died fighting, the ones she hadn't been quick enough to save.

Jess's belly skimmed the rooftops as they left the caravan compound behind and passed over the edge of Barter. The fires had spread into these streets too. Aimee spotted The Dragon's Roar where she'd sat with Kyelli only two days ago. Half its roof was gone, burnt rafters sticking up like the blackened bones in the Empty Warriors' corpses.

The acrid tang of smoke chased her across the city.

They passed over Quorelle Square, the wide space empty now of people, the crowd dispersed to help start to put their city back together. Aimee and Jess continued, into the eastern curve of Barter where the fighting had been fiercest. Here fires still burned and people, darkened with soot, struggled to put them out. She passed rows of homes with their doors broken in, their windows smashed.

There were no neat rows of bodies here: they were still disentangling them from the heaps of Empty Warriors, or pulling them from the smoking buildings.

Across the River Toig the entire harbour district was gone, destroyed. Aimee didn't know the area, she'd rarely walked its streets, yet tears still gathered in her eyes. All those warehouses, all the homes nestled above shops, all those lives that would take years to rebuild.

She pulled on Jess's horns, guiding her with her knees, the movements automatic now. She heard the rumble of a building collapsing as Jess took them up into the mountains. Jagged peaks and slopes of scree passed below them unseen as Aimee stared out across the Griydak Sea. Longboats still crowded the harbour, empty now of warriors, as Jess and Aimee glided silently above them.

Free of the city, Aimee pushed Jess for more speed and her dragon eagerly obeyed. A cold wind off the sea blasted her face and Aimee blinked behind her borrowed goggles. She could see a summer storm, far out to the east, dark clouds dragging rain behind them.

For half an hour Aimee thought about nothing but

flying. She sucked in deep breaths of fresh, salty air and let go of the fear that had gathered in her bones over the last few days. When the Ring Mountains were only a jagged spot on the horizon behind them, Aimee pulled Jess to a halt. Dark grey waves heaved beneath them, pushed against each other by the fringes of the storm.

Aimee slipped a hand into her coat pocket and pulled out Kyelli's bracelet. She thought she might feel sad when she reached this point. She was holding the last little piece of Kyelli. Instead, as she tipped her hand, letting the gold cuff fall, all she felt was relief. Both she and Jess watched the bracelet tumble down and disappear into the sea without even a splash. Jess gave a rumbly growl of approval.

Aimee laughed. 'Well said, girl.'

The relief was intoxicating. It flushed through her veins, more buzzy than adrenaline, more fizzy than lust. She turned back towards Kierell and pushed Jess for all the speed she could give. Her dragon was delighted and they shot through the sky, flying faster than Aimee had ever dared before. Her grin was huge, and the wind made her teeth ache with the cold, but she didn't care. Jess felt like a whirlwind of power beneath her and Aimee revelled in it.

This was what she hadn't yet had since becoming a Rider—flying simply for the pure joy of it.

This time she and Jess followed the curve of the Ring Mountains rather than flying across the city. The soft oranges and pinks of the sunset were gracefully bowing out to the silky navy of early night. Jess had swooped down to be amongst the peaks and Aimee let her choose their course. They skimmed around jagged cliffs, and swooped over slopes of shale, Jess's wings setting the tiny stones dancing. They tilted almost vertical to squeeze between two pillars of rock and Aimee clung tight to Jess's spiralled horns. The joy of flying pulsed in time with her heartbeat and Aimee savoured every second of it, knowing soon she'd need to set it aside.

Riders had gathered on a wide ledge which ran along the northern side of Norwen Peak in the north-west curve of the mountains and Aimee was last to arrive. Jess landed softly, her talons clicking on the rock and Aimee dismounted. In the centre of the ledge was a large stone slab, held up by two crouching dragons. They were so skilfully carved that they looked like real hatchlings that had been turned to stone. Aimee had been here once before, when they'd said goodbye to Hayetta.

This time there were five bodies on the slab—Aranati, Lwena Sal, Theaga, and Kyelli. The Riders' dragons were curled around them, all except Lwena's. Glaris had been pulled down into the Empty Warriors' army and no one could find her body afterwards. Fineya and Burnish had been lost to the sea but although their bodies weren't here, they were still in the Riders' thoughts. Kyelli wasn't properly a Rider but everyone had agreed to honour her with a Rider's funeral.

Jara's face looked like it had been carved from stone as she and Faradair stepped up to the slab. Lyrria and Midnight stood on the other side.

Aimee felt a hand slip into hers. Nathine was beside her, squeezing Aimee's knuckles and wearing her angry face. Footsteps sounded on her other side and Dyrenna appeared, an arm around Pelathina, holding the young woman up. Aimee forgot Nathine at the sight of the raw anguish on Pelathina's face. She slumped, like her bones had turned to water, and Dyrenna gently lowered her to the ground. Aimee fell to her knees beside her and gently wrapped her arms around Pelathina, pulling her into a soft hug.

'It's not fair,' Pelathina mumbled, her words muffled by Aimee's shoulder.

'No,' Aimee agreed. 'It's not.'

Dyrenna crouched on Pelathina's other side and took her hand, enclosing Pelathina's brown fingers in her own scarred ones. Nathine stood beside them like a sentry. Behind them Skydance had his belly pressed to the rock, his wings tucked in, making himself smaller. Aimee watched with a sad smile as Jess crouched and draped a wing over him, nuzzling him. Their spiralled horns clacked gently together.

'Riders,' Jara's voice echoed back from the cliffs above them. 'Thank you. We all knew this life was dangerous when we made the climb. But it has always been worth it.' Faradair turned and blew a small puff of smoke towards Jara. She smiled as she waved it away, but her smile vanished as swiftly as the smoke. 'I'll be honest, there have been times over the last few days when I almost regretted making the climb. And standing here now, looking at the broken bodies of four of my friends, I still feel that tug of regret. This,' she waved her arm to encompass the funeral pyre and their damaged city, 'has been shit!'

Jara yelled the last word and Aimee felt the ripple of shock in the gathered Riders. Jara's stoney face had crumbled, revealing the vulnerable woman she'd always kept hidden beneath. But Aimee saw something else too, something she recognised all too well. That glint in Jara's emerald eyes was one of determination and it warmed Aimee to see it. Their leader had come through the trials of the last few days stronger, and that gave Aimee hope for the future, for rebuilding the city, and the Riders.

'I got through these horrific days because I believed in us, and I still do.' As Jara continued her eyes locked onto Aimee. 'We always knew it in our hearts, but I think Aimee really showed us, and the world, just how strong we are together. Every single Sky Rider lost something in our battle with Pagrin and his Empty Warriors. Some gave their lives to protect our city, some were injured and will face a long road back to flying, and all of us lost friends.' Her eyes flicked to Pelathina. 'And family.

'I fought for years to forge a peace with the Helvethi and that is a dream I'm still holding on to. The future doesn't look the way it did a few months ago. Our city needs to be rebuilt and we need to open up the tunnels again. The Helvethi left us to fight this battle alone, so we need to convince them that we are friends worth having. And the city's leadership is depleted because three councillors are dead.'

Aimee felt the weight of Jara's words settling on the ledge around them. They'd saved the city but there was still a ton of work to do to rescue their future.

'But we can do this!' Jara yelled the words of encouragement that Aimee had whispered to herself so many times over the last few months. 'Kierell's future is one that is no longer dictated by the past. For three hundred years we looked backwards, revering Kyelli and Marhorn for saving us, and giving us this home. We were grateful to have these mountains to hide behind. But the future is out there.'

Jara stabbed a finger in the direction of the tundra stretching out beyond the ledge, its grasses painted orange and pink by the fading sunset.

'Kierell will be a city open to the world, not hidden away, not afraid of what's beyond our mountains,' Jara continued. 'Riders will travel with caravans all the way to Taumerg and Nallein. We'll be emissaries and diplomats for Kierell. Messengers and peacekeepers.'

Jara's words conjured images of that future in Aimee's mind and for the first time since that fateful caravan trip to Lorsoke, she felt optimistic. She imagined herself and Jess, carrying messages from Kierell to the city states. Maybe they'd get to explore while they were there. For the first time ever, her future seemed full of possibilities.

'But this future is only possible because of the sacrifice we've all made.' Jara stepped with Faradair towards the slab. On the other side Lyrria and Midnight also closed the gap. 'We will carry their memories in our hearts.'

Aimee felt Pelathina's whole body tense like a pulled bowstring and she held her closer, as if she could absorb some of the other girl's grief into herself. At a nod from Jara, Faradair and Midnight breathed fire and set the funeral pyre alight. Aimee felt the vibrations of Pelathina's scream as it left her chest.

The faces of the Riders around them were shiny with tears and Aimee let her own fall and drip from her chin. She watched the smoke from the funeral pyre drift up into the evening sky. The Riders and their dragons were gone, but their essence would be forever flying through the sky. And they took Kyelli with them. She'd forever be their founder, and an inspiration to many girls to make the climb, but her story was over. The Sky Riders would forge their own future.

Pelathina howled and screamed till she was hoarse. Then her normally smiley face went slack, as if even the effort of wearing an expression was too much for her. Aimee held her the whole time. As the fire died down, Riders began to drift away, many with comforting arms around each other.

'Aimee, I'm going to take her back inside,' Dyrenna spoke over Pelathina's drooped head.

Together they gently lifted Pelathina to her feet. She seemed empty, as if her sister's death had scooped out part of her and it too had turned to smoke and drifted away. Aimee's heart was full of cracks as she cupped Pelathina's face and gently wiped away the other girl's snot and tears. For the first time since she'd taken it off, Aimee wished for the bracelet's power, just for a moment, so she could see Pelathina's spark and reassure herself that it was still bright.

She was about to tuck herself under Pelathina's arm and help her walk inside when fingers brushed hers. Aimee turned to see Lyrria, with Midnight behind her.

'Aimee, can I talk to you?' Lyrria asked and from the way Midnight crouched, her feathers quivering faintly, Aimee could tell Lyrria was nervous. And that wasn't like her.

'I've got her,' Nathine said, elbowing Aimee aside and hoisting Pelathina's arm around her shoulders.

Aimee felt an absence at her side as Nathine and Dyrenna guided Pelathina back inside and she felt torn in two. She longed to follow and wrap her arms around Pelathina again, holding her until the hurt stopped. But being alone with Lyrria stirred up the feelings of longing she'd tried to smother. Jess nudged her hand and Aimee stroked the cool scales of her dragon's head.

'Well, looks like you're the hero of the hour now,' Lyrria grinned at her, but Aimee could see her eyes were still wary and unsure. 'In hundreds of years I'll bet teachers like me will be telling the new recruits stories about you.'

'If they do, I hope they tell about how I only got the strength to defeat Pagrin from all the Riders together,' Aimee said. The praise still made her feel uncomfortable. It wasn't her victory, it belonged to all the Riders.

'Yeah, but you're still awesome,' Lyrria said and

took a step closer.

Aimee could smell her perfume, and the scent underneath that was distinctly Lyrria. She could almost taste the apple tang in her mouth from Lyrria's kisses. Lyrria took another step, the space between them now less than a handsbreadth. Memories danced through her mind, and she remembered the way Lyrria's touches had made her feel. Lyrria leaned in, her face inches from Aimee's. Her brown-green eyes sparkled with mischief and Aimee felt tingles in her belly.

'Do you want to?' Lyrria's words caressed Aimee's lips.

And part of Aimee really did. She wanted to close her eyes and lose herself in Lyrria. She wanted to kiss her freckled skin and taste her sweetness.

But Lyrria had still never apologised for dismissing Aimee in front of her brother. And when Nathine and Pelathina had given Aimee their support, Lyrria had always questioned her. She was the first woman who'd returned Aimee's love, and her hair shone with copper and her crooked smile tugged at Aimee's heart. But someone else had taken up space in her heart now and Aimee's thoughts turned to Pelathina. What if she was too broken by the loss of her sister to ever smile or feel love again? Aimee had spent the last six months building bridges and she was afraid to start burning any.

'Aimee?' Her name was a whispered promise on Lyrria's lips.

Aimee reached up, cupped Lyrria's face and gave her a quick, soft kiss on the lips. Then she stepped back.

Lyrria was popular, beautiful and confident, but Aimee didn't need to be validated by her anymore.

'No,' Aimee said softly.

Hurt washed through Lyrria's eyes and Aimee almost buckled, almost pulled her into a deeper kiss. But she made herself take two steps back.

'Really?' Lyrria tried to smile but her lips wobbled at the edges.

'Do you only want to be with me now because I'm the hero of the hour?' Aimee asked.

'Of course not.'

But Lyrria's answer came too quick and felt too forced to be true. Aimee smiled sadly and shook her head.

'I'm sorry,' Lyrria tried instead.

'I know,' Aimee told her.

Then with Jess at her side she turned and walked away. And she was pleased with herself because her heart wasn't breaking. She grabbed Jess's saddle and boosted herself up. Lyrria watched her go, but there were no tears in the other woman's eyes. Aimee's stomach did its familiar lurch as Jess took off, and with every flap of her wings Aimee's smile grew wider. As they rose into a sky deepening with night, stars just beginning to sparkle above, Aimee felt like she knew herself. This is who she was—the Sky Rider who'd saved Kierell.

Jess roared and Aimee whooped, their mingling shouts of joy spreading out into the freedom of the sky.

EPILOGUE

IT HAD BEEN a week since Aimee defeated Pagrin and she was in the university hospital visiting Callant. Jess was perched on the roof, despite Callant's insistence that Aimee bring her inside. Aimee had been to visit him most days and each time he asked to see Jess—apparently he wanted to thank her too for rescuing him from the Empty Warriors on the rockfall. Instead of squeezing Jess in through one of the windows, Aimee had promised to take Callant for a ride once his broken ankle had healed.

'Can you put that one on the "ship mechanics" pile?' Callant asked, passing her a green-covered book. 'Oh and this one on the "factories" pile.' He shoved another at her before Aimee had a chance to put down the first.

She laughed and added the books to the carefully catalogued piles surrounding Callant's bed like a mini mountain range. Since he was stuck till his ankle healed, Callant had demanded that boxes of the books Aimee had found hidden in the library be brought to him.

He'd then spent his days reading and categorising them.

'They're printed,' he announced as Aimee settled herself at the foot of his bed. She gave him a quizzical look and he continued. 'All these books with the strange writing in them. It's not writing, they've been printed on a printing press. It's really quite ingenious. Here, look'

He rummaged among the bed's blankets till he found the book he was searching for and passed it to Aimee, open to a page near the middle. There was a sketch on the page of a complicated looking machine. Aimee nodded and smiled.

She hadn't seen Callant when the bracelet was working so had never discovered if he had a weak spark. They'd never know if his coughing was draining his spark. And for that Aimee was grateful. She couldn't stand the thought of anything discouraging Callant from his enthusiastic study. She could tell he was going to be an important player in the city's future. And maybe Aimee would insist he stay inside in the winter and drink more thyme tea, just in case.

'You're not listening,' Callant's accusation cut into her thoughts.

'I am. Metal plates and magic words and ta-da, you've got printed books.'

Aimee grinned at him as Callant shook his head, brushing his chest with his beard. Callant laughed and sank back against his pillows.

'Help yourself to the biscuits,' Callant gestured to a tin beside his bed. 'My mother brought them, but between you and me, she'd a dreadful baker and they're not very good.'

'I'll pass,' Aimee said, feeling a small pang for her Aunt Naura's wonderful cakes.

'I—' Callant began but a new voice interrupted him.

'Still lounging in bed, Beardy?'

Nathine strode across the infirmary, high ponytail swinging. She stopped at the foot of Callant's bed, hands on hips and a wide grin on her face. Callant opened his mouth to retort but Aimee got in first.

'Biscuit?' she grabbed the tin and offered it to Nathine.

As expected Nathine helped herself to two, immediately shoving the first in her mouth. Aimee and Callant waited, giggles suppressed as Nathine chewed, her mouth twisting downwards in displeasure.

'Ugh, that's as dry as eating one of Aimee's old socks,' Nathine commented after she swallowed. But then still took a bite out of the second biscuit. Aimee gave her an incredulous look but Nathine just shrugged. 'I'm not going to pass up a free biscuit. And don't give me that look or I won't give you this mysterious message.'

'What message?' Aimee demanded.

Nathine brushed crumbs from her fingers before passing Aimee a folded sheet of paper. She opened it to reveal a single handwritten line.

Meet me in the bathing caves. P.

Aimee's heart fluttered. Every night for the last week Aimee had gone to Pelathina's room. For the first few nights after Aranati's funeral she'd simply held the other girl till she cried herself to sleep. Then last night they'd sat up together all night, cosy under one of Pelathina's blankets. Pelathina had talked almost non-stop and Aimee listened without interrupting. Pelathina had told stories about Aranati, sharing with Aimee their lives back in Marlidesh and anecdotes about learning to fly together once they became Riders.

In the morning Pelathina had finally fallen asleep, half way through a story about how she'd once been so annoyed with Aranati that she'd tipped a bowl of porridge over her head. Aimee had covered Pelathina with the blanket and slipped quietly from the room.

Now Pelathina wanted to meet her somewhere private and Aimee tried not to get her hopes up about what that might mean.

'Why are you still sitting here? Go,' Nathine's voice intruded on her thoughts.

Aimee looked round to see her friend peering over her shoulder, reading the note.

'Hey,' Aimee objected, crumping the paper to her chest. Nathine just gave her a knowing smirk and helped herself to another biscuit. Callant gave them both a *what's going on* raise of his eyebrows but Aimee was too excited to stay and explain.

'I'll come back tomorrow, I promise, and you can tell me more about those printing thingies,' Aimee said as she leapt up off the bed, throwing a wave over her shoulder. Nathine would have no doubt given Callant the juicy details before Aimee had even left the hospital. Not that there were any juicy details but Nathine would likely invent some.

Jess was waiting for her in the courtyard, sensing her Rider's anticipation. Aimee couldn't see their connection any more but she could still feel it. They were airborne in moments, the peaked roofs of the university buildings falling away below them. Aimee barely saw the city as Jess soared above it—her eyes were fixed on the mountains, to where Pelathina was waiting for her.

By the time they reached the vents above the Heart Aimee felt like a whole rabble of butterflies had taken flight in her belly. Jess zipped down one of the vents so fast Aimee barely had time to squeeze her eyes shut. As they landed, she jumped from Jess and unbuckled her saddle so quickly it fell to the floor before she could catch it. She thought for the briefest of moments about putting it away properly but then decided she'd deal with Dyrenna's quiet reprimand later. She already owed her a whole tea party any way.

Jess gave her a nudge, but, caught up in Aimee's excitement, she shoved her Rider so hard that Aimee stumbled and almost fell.

'Alright, girl, I'm going,' Aimee laughed.

Most of the shepherd's crook poles had been broken when the Empty Warriors ransacked Anteill and without their dragon's breath orbs the Heart was darker than usual. Aimee almost tripped on the channels in the rock three times as she jogged across the cavern.

The corridors bore wounds from the warriors too. Doors had been shattered and twisted off their hinges. Some were burnt to nothing but charred splinters. Many of the crystal stalagmites had been chipped and broken, and the cave walls were scarred by swords.

The bathing caves were in the lowest level of Anteill. Aimee grabbed a small dragon's breath orb, the size of an apple, from a ledge at the entrance to the tunnel leading down. With the flickering light leading her, Aimee jogged down the switchbacking tunnel. There were three bathing caves, each containing pools filled with naturally warm mineral water. Somehow Aimee knew Pelathina would be in the smallest one. She ran to it, ignoring the entrance to the other two and dashed inside.

It was empty. The small cavern had two pools and the water in both was perfectly still. Pelathina wasn't here. Disappointment sucked at Aimee's chest. She ran back to the second carven. Empty. Finally she stopped before the entrance to the first, and largest, of the caverns. She took a deep breath and tried unsuccessfully to calm her jittery heart.

Then she stepped inside.

'Hello.' Pelathina smiled at her from the middle of the largest of the cavern's five pools.

Aimee had assumed, because of Pelathina's lingering grief, that she'd be secluded in the smallest of the caverns, wrapped in its soft darkness. The largest bathing cave had vents in the ceiling, like the Heart, and Aimee watched mesmerised as Pelathina swam across the pool, through shafts of sunlight that danced on her bronze skin. Standing awkwardly in the doorway, the dragon's breath orb held down by her side, Aimee didn't know what to do so she explained that she'd first looked for Pelathina in the other caves.

Pelathina reached the edge of the pool and rested her elbows up on the wet rock.

'You know, that's where I went first. I stood in the entrance of the littlest cave and I realised that if I went in there I'd be choosing my grief.' She smiled a sad little smile. 'I will ache for Aranati every day of my life, and without her, there will always be a little piece of me missing. But she would frown at me so sternly if I let that grief rule my life.'

'Feel it, let it go, and choose to be happy.' Aimee repeated Pelathina's words, the ones she'd shared out on the tundra.

'Here, I have something for you.'

Pelathina pushed herself up on the edge of the pool and reached across the rock. And that's when Aimee realised she was naked in the water. Her eyes swept hungrily across Pelathina's chest and skin dappled with water droplets. Pelathina pulled a small green velvet pouch towards herself and smiled up at Aimee. This was a proper Pelathina smile, one that made her cute dimples appear and her dark eyes sparkle.

'What is it?' Aimee asked, pointing at the small bag.

Pelathina bit her bottom lip. 'I'll only give you this present if you get in the water with me.'

Aimee did not hesitate, not for a single moment.

Placing the orb on the floor she unbuttoned her shirt and let it slide off her shoulders. Next she pulled off her vest, letting it fall to the floor as well. She smiled at the way Pelathina's eyes travelled over her naked skin. As Aimee kicked off her boots and slid free of her trousers, she felt not the slightest bit of shame as she revealed her patchwork body. She might have odd patches of colourless skin all over her, but her body was strong, it could fly a dragon, and fight off monsters. It was hers, and right then she wanted to share it with Pelathina.

The water in the pool was blood warm and crystal clear. In the sunlight from the vents above, it sparkled a light turquoise colour. Aimee sat on the edge and slipped into the water. Her feet found a rocky ledge and she stood, warm water lapping at her waist. Pelathina swam closer then stepped up onto the ledge beside Aimee, her top half rising out of the water, dripping and tempting.

Pelathina held up the velvet pouch. 'Most of the shops in the city are still closed, but I managed to find one jeweller with exactly what I was looking for, and convinced him to open up just so he could sell me this.'

'You've been down in the city?' Aimee asked. Pelathina hadn't left her room for a week.

'Yes, I had to get this for you.' She passed Aimee the pouch.

'What is it?'

'It's your Rider's jewellery.'

A lump appeared in Aimee's throat and tears threatened in her eyes.

'Are you okay?' Concern creased Pelathina's forehead.

Aimee smiled to reassure her. 'Yes, it's just…' her words trailed off and she had to take a deep breath before continuing. 'I thought that Kyelli's bracelet was my Rider's jewellery and that I'd die wearing it. I didn't think I'd get my own.'

'Before I went down into the city, I asked around the other Riders.'

'Asked them what?'

'If we should continue the tradition of Rider's jewellery, now that we know it originated from a bracelet with the power to kill.' Pelathina ran her fingers over her own Rider's jewellery—a fine gold chain, the bottom third strung with colourful beads. 'But everyone I spoke to said the same thing, that we'd made the tradition our own. It wasn't something Kyelli, or any Quorelle, told us to do. It's a way for us to honour each other and we should keep that.'

Aimee looked down at the small pouch in her hands. It was the same colour as Jess's scales. She pulled open the drawcord and slipped her fingers inside. The gold chain she pulled out was so pretty that she forgot all about the pouch and dropped it into the water. Pelathina laughed as she fished it out, dumping it on the side. Aimee held up the fine chain and admired the little gold pendant hanging from it.

'It's a lilybel flower,' Pelathina explained. 'They are small, and beautiful, but very resilient because they only grow up here in the mountaintops. They're just like you.'

Now Aimee's tears did fall, but they were happy ones. She handed the chain to Pelathina and let her fasten it around her neck. The lilybel pendant hung just above her breasts. Pelathina's fingers, so beautifully dark against Aimee's pale skin, stroked the pendant before drifting lower.

In the warm water Aimee stepped forward, her hands finding the small of Pelathina's back and her lips pressing against Pelathina's. She tasted like love, and belonging, and endless possibilities. She tasted perfect.

Acknowledgements

I can't quite believe I am writing the acknowledgements for my third book! What a journey it has been! And like all the best fantasy quests I've had a band of amazing companions keeping me company. Alone, I'd have never got this far.

Again a huge thanks to my beta readers—Colin Sandie and Penny van Millingen. Your thoughts, feedback and ideas (yes, even the daft ones!) really have helped me shape Aimee's story. This book is better because of you both.

My editor, Rheanna-Marie Hall, once again did an amazing job on this book. I'm really grateful for the time you've dedicated to Aimee's story. And I'm sorry I can't spell lightning!

The cover of this book was created by the wonderful team at Damonza. And I love it! Isn't it awesome?

Thank you to my mum and dad who have always supported me, in this project and everything I've ever done in life.

One of the most lovely things I've discovered on my self-publishing journey has been you lot—my readers. I've been absolutely blown away by the way you've embraced Aimee's story and I love that you've all been rooting for her. Thank you for letting this wonderful freak of a girl, and her dragon, into your hearts.

Thank you for all the brilliant reviews (keep them coming!) and for the shares and likes on social media. I've loved sharing the world of the Sky Riders with you. I'd give you all dragons if I could. What colour would you like?

About the Author

Kerry Law grew up reading Tolkien and David Eddings, and has never looked back. A love of the past took her to the University of St Andrews where she did an MA in Medieval History. During her degree she learnt all about castles, but her imagination had to fill in the dragons.

The Immortal Rider is her third novel and is book 3 in the *Sparks* series.

Kerry enjoys exploring uniqueness in her books and takes inspiration from her own interesting skin condition—vitiligo. She's also inspired by the incredible magical-looking landscapes of her home in Scotland.

Kerry lives with her husband and cat in a small town in the Scottish Borders where there are more trees than people.

Contact Kerry:
kerrylawbooks.com
facebook.com/kerrylawbooks
instagram.com/kerrylawbooks

Also by Kerry Law

Sparks Series
The Sky Riders
The Rider's Quest
The Immortal Rider

Printed in Great Britain
by Amazon